'To Ann,
a fellow PEO —

LIPEO!
BEST WISHES!

Margaret Garrison

PREZ

A Story of Love

MARGARET GARRISON

abbott press

This is a work of fiction. All of the characters, names, incidents, organizations, and dialogue in this novel are either the products of the author's imagination or are used fictitiously.

Jacket design by RLR Associates, Inc., Indianapolis

Abbott Press books may be ordered through booksellers or by contacting:

Abbott Press
1663 Liberty Drive
Bloomington, IN 47403
www.abbottpress.com
Phone: 1-866-697-5310

Because of the dynamic nature of the Internet, any web addresses or links contained in this book may have changed since publication and may no longer be valid. The views expressed in this work are solely those of the author and do not necessarily reflect the views of the publisher, and the publisher hereby disclaims any responsibility for them.

Any people depicted in stock imagery provided by Thinkstock are models, and such images are being used for illustrative purposes only.
Certain stock imagery © Thinkstock.

ISBN: 978-1-4582-1662-5 (sc)
ISBN: 978-1-4582-1663-2 (hc)
ISBN: 978-1-4582-1661-8 (e)

Library of Congress Control Number: 2014910976

Printed in the United States of America.

Abbott Press rev. date: 7/10/2014

To the memory of my parents,
both of whom knew well
the power of story
and the joy of words.

If I can stop one heart from breaking,
I shall not live in vain;
If I can ease one life the aching,
Or cool one pain,
Or help one fainting robin
Unto his nest again,
I shall not live in vain.

—Emily Dickinson (1830–1886)
Manuscript c. 1865

Table of Contents

Part I   LIFE

             Prologue   xi

Part II   DEATH   365

Part III   LIFE AFTER DEATH

             Epilogue   385

A Final Word   395

Acknowledgments   397

PART I

LIFE

Prologue

Mine has been a good life, if lives are measured by decency and prosperity and the number of mourners you expect to sign your funeral book. If gauged by other standards, such as the intensity of love both given and received, mine has been magnificent.

When people praise me for my achievements, asking how I accomplish those things that I do, I surprise them. I deny the title of a great educator but tell them, rather, that I am a small human being, as weak and malleable as they. I look at shining bridges that span chasms, at tall buildings that soar, at rockets that scrape the sky. These, I think, are great achievements. No less are those of electricians who string wires after a storm, or plumbers who know which wrench to turn.

I am a teacher, yes, and a manager, a strategist, a writer, and a thinker. I am a daughter of a wise mother and a troubled father, a granddaughter of Scandinavian flint and English steel, a sister once to five, a neighbor, a friend, a lover, a sinner, a confidante. I am a child of God and a child of grace.

I am dying, I've been told, or words to that effect. My doctors no longer look into my eyes when they speak. They gaze at the slats of the aluminum blinds behind me, or study their hands as if pondering a hangnail. We have grown close these past five months, my physicians and I. We are bound not only by disease but by common ties of education and professional stature. Perhaps my eyes have become a window into their souls, and they fear to see the flicker of their personal pain.

They need not speak so gingerly. I no longer fear death. I fear only the pain of detachment from my loved ones, not that of body and certainly not of soul. My soul, I now know, is anchored in a good place.

But all was not always well with my soul. Like fabled Ulysses, I have heard the Sirens. I was captured by their singing and writhed in their embrace. But unlike Ulysses, who was fettered to a stake, I found myself tossed ashore, quivering on the sand. For one black night I feared I had touched the last vestiges of my faith.

Now I am whole again, despite this slippery hold on my earthly life. And before my brain is too dimmed by physical pain, I feel charged to unspool my tale. It's an old-fashioned love story of the richest kind, unique in all the world. I know no other woman who has borne such joy and grief *and joy* in secret. Yet surely there are many, reluctant to undress in front of strangers.

That's why, in whatever time remains, I am recording my remarkable story. I actually began months ago, inspired at the time by the glow of new love as Paul entered my life. Now, as the leer of death dims my future, I continue to write. I am typing out memories in words known only to me and, when the time is right, will give them to Paul to preserve. He can keep them to himself, or share them, or hide them away. I trust Paul to know how to care for them. Perhaps, in time, our spiritual journey can help "one fainting robin" find solace or peace.

Let mine be the voice of the bold.

Chapter 1
SEPTEMBER

It rained the day we buried Benny—not a heavy drizzle, gray and stricken like our souls, but a furious spate that fell with the rush and rip of surging water. Thunder boomed overhead as the hearse pulled in front of St. John's concrete steps. I could scarcely see the garnet-painted arched doors as I peered up through the blurry car window. The stormy heavens swept me back to a moment two months earlier, when a crashing organ chord had jolted our somber Good Friday service. The sound had been so raucous that we had all jumped in our pews—even though the moment had been forewarned in the printed bulletin as the *strepitus,* the instant when Christ drew his last breath on the cross and died.

That awful day at the funeral, we clung together. My older sisters, Marianna and Sarah, flanked our mother as we stumbled down the aisle behind the child-sized casket. I, the middle sister, followed, gripping the hands of Emily, who was nine, and Jane, seven. Behind us came Daddy, his bearded chin jutting out and his back as straight as a galvanized steel pipe—walking alone.

For years after Benny's death, our broken family was fodder for Arden's town chatter. One story came from my childhood friend, Sally Gordon, who overheard someone in the Wednesday Canasta Club say in a hushed tone, "I will never, *ever* forget the look on Harold Embright's face as he followed that casket down that aisle. To lose that boy after all those daughters! No wonder he's gone plumb crazy."

Eight years after Benny died, our family drove again to St. John's in that same gray hearse from Marley's Funeral Home—this time to lay Daddy to rest. By now we had seen the insidious effects of grief. The cancer had come fast, without warning, searing Daddy's body and mind and piercing our family anew.

Especially me.

I tried to avoid thinking about our sad family history, but I was remembering it not quite a year ago while driving in Virginia—the September afternoon when my car broke down. It was Labor Day, the Monday of a three-day weekend. Classes at Wickfield University where I was chancellor were cancelled. My office was officially closed.

Instead of enjoying a holiday, however, I found myself dragged into a two-day board of trustees meeting—a make-up for one cancelled earlier—at Arden College in Virginia. I had never planned to serve on Arden's board. "It's all I can do to manage my *own* board of trustees," I had protested when Arden's president asked me to join his board. Arden was a small liberal arts college, less than half the size of my Wickfield and even smaller in reputation. I should have turned the offer down cold and fast. I could have pointed out that, in addition to my chancellor duties, I served on an elite national board that already overtaxed my time.

But it was hard to say no to Arden College. Daddy had been Arden's dean of students for nearly thirty years.

The car mishap occurred Monday as I was returning to Wickfield to savor what was left of the frayed holiday. In that instant when my big Ford began to falter, I felt a momentary flash of anger. "So betrayed!" was how I put it to Alex over the phone that night, recounting those surreal moments when I realized the car was struggling to stay alive. But I had responded deftly, spotting an open span of shoulder between two long curves of the hilly highway. I edged the sputtering Crown Victoria into a refuge of soft dirt and scraggly yellow grass.

"Great!" I announced too loudly as I turned off the ignition. The sound of my own voice steadied me. My stockinged foot fumbled for a missing shoe, and I checked myself in the rearview mirror. A white car sped past, then an RV. I watched in dismay as they vanished into the curve ahead.

Cautiously, I slid out on the driver's side, having only seconds to close the heavy door before another car swept past. The front left tire looked fine. I stepped gingerly to the rear. There were no dripping fluids. I realized how ridiculous I must have appeared as I stooped and peered in my high heels. The late-summer sun hammered my chalk-lined navy suit.

With sweat slipping down my cheeks, I minced around the back of the car to the passenger side. It was difficult to keep my balance on the sloping ground. The shoulder angled downward into a shallow ravine lined with trees, their massive tops looming to the level of my knees. I stared dismally below into a plumage of leafy hardwoods and thick-needled pines.

But the hood release was on the driver's side, and in the end I sprawled across the front seat, feet flailing as I fumbled for the mechanism. I felt indignant tears, salty and harsh as they stung my eyes. When I heard the distinctive pop I slid out hastily, mopping my hot face with my hands.

"Darn!" I held onto the car's frame as I maneuvered back to the front. I grappled with the hood while fiddling around for the metal support rod. I pried it out of its groove and into the metal slot that held it in place. Below, my eyes scanned a tangled nest of tubing.

I was still bending over the open hood when the stranger appeared. I did not hear his sports car pull up; he seemed to materialize from out of nowhere. Suddenly he was at my side, and I straightened up to look into a set of steel-blue eyes.

"Need help, lady?" the man asked casually. I merely stared, as startled as if he had dropped from the sky.

He tried again. "Where are your keys? I'll give it a crank."

A truck sailed by, horn wailing. I hesitated before surrendering my keys. "The engine suddenly quit, and I had to coast to the shoulder. I had it checked before I left home." I wouldn't try to explain that a university crew kept my car in tiptop shape.

The stranger slipped behind the wheel and inserted the rubber-headed ignition key. I tried to guess his age. Forty-five? Fifty? He was attractive enough, in a casual sort of way. He was not particularly tall, but he was fit and tanned and had a pleasant voice. His polo shirt bore the logo of a Pinehurst golf resort.

The engine tried valiantly to turn over, making earnest scratchy sounds. I held my breath. "Sure sounds dead," the man said agreeably, joining me under the hood. He tugged at belts and poked into mysterious vats of fluid. I watched silently, aware of confident hands and clean fingernails. Fine black wrist hairs curled around the band of his classy gold watch.

Finally he straightened up and reached for the handkerchief in his rear pocket. "Ma'am," he said politely, wiping his hands and looking directly into my eyes, "when was the last time you filled up with gas?"

ARDEN

That evening, stretched out on the chaise longue on my backyard deck, I sorted through the events that had marred the day. It was frustrating to lose this precious holiday to work, not to mention the stress of dealing with a disabled car. True, I had enjoyed the Appalachian countryside on the familiar drive between Arden and Wickfield, but today I had also been acutely tired. Too often these days I felt the coldness of bone-deep fatigue.

"Battle wounds," I would tell myself whenever my academic whirlwind dropped me on top of my four-poster at night. More than once I had awakened at 2:00 a.m., lights blazing, my bedroom television sputtering out the crisp dialogue of a CNN reporter. The bedspread would still be pulled over pillows that Lennie, my faithful housekeeper, had plumped up that morning.

Now, as I enjoyed the balmy evening on my deck, my thoughts shifted wistfully to Alex, far away in Chicago. I wondered what he was doing tonight. Dear, *dear* Alex. He was not only my best friend but my confidant, the ear that let me vent about my job. Recently I had complained about the visibility of my 1989 license tag—WCKFLD1. The Wickfield University alumni board had presented it in a charming ceremony, first getting permission from the North Carolina Department of Motor Vehicles to supplant the required government plates. In truth, the tag diluted my privacy. No matter where I went—dentist, church, hairdresser—the event was duly noted. To my utmost dismay, the residents of Hurley, North Carolina, relished every detail of my personal business.

"I feel like a nursery rhyme," I told Alex during one of his treasured weekend visits.

"Humpty Dumpty?" Alex asked, setting a bottle of Riesling inside the refrigerator. We were putting away groceries on a Saturday afternoon, a job performed by Lennie during the week. But this time I had felt a domestic surge, so Alex had willingly wielded a grocery cart at the local Food Lion.

"No, 'Mary Had A Little Lamb.' Only it's 'everywhere that Katherine went, the town was sure to know.'"

Alex had chuckled and leaned over for a quick kiss. Yes, Alex was special, but I had no regrets about refusing his nudges toward marriage. Wickfield was too important right now. The capital campaign was scarcely halfway along, and the new arts school would be announced soon. There was much yet to do. As for Alex, his active medical practice kept him rooted in Chicago. A commuter marriage was possible—quite the modern thing these days—but those thousand-mile treks would surely be daunting.

Not to mention how an absentee husband would raise eyebrows among my conservative colleagues at Arden College.

I had known and loved that century-old college since childhood. As faculty children, my sisters and I, perfect stair-steps in age and sometimes in height, had explored every Arden building during our heady summers. From the Norbert Hall turret we played pirate games, letting whoever was the littlest sister be the kidnapped princess. At five, each of us began piano lessons from Professor Shoup, a lavender-scented spinster who taught music in the Little Conservatory by the rule of a metronome. When older, we snooped out the lairs of campus lovers, throwing pebbles through *ligustrum* hedges before exploding in giggles into the night.

For each of us eager Embright daughters, a highlight of our teen years occurred when we were high-school seniors. Under the scrutiny of our parents, who served as chaperones, each of us was "allowed," as our mother put it, to attend the elegant spring formal at the college. For my debut, my hair was swept into a convincing French twist by Marianna, who dabbed Faberge's Aphrodisia on the back of my neck.

"It smells dreamy, Kat," she breathed in sisterly conspiracy.

And the evening had proved triumphant. I danced twice with my father and once with a wavy-haired freshman. Later, a tall junior in an NROTC uniform glided me around the floor with assurance, his arm confidently on my waist and his chin skewered between my left earlobe and neck.

But for reasons never made clear by my parents, I—unlike Marianna and Sarah ahead of me—was never encouraged to attend Arden. I spent two years at Hollins College, lapping up Emily Dickinson poetry like Perrier before transferring to the University of North Carolina in Chapel Hill. Carolina was my parents' clear preference, and it was a good choice. I fell completely in love with the beautiful campus, redolent with history as the nation's first public university. "Carolina is clearly the right school for you, Kat," my father said somberly when I earned a Phi Beta Kappa key. That was all he ever said on the subject.

That rite of passage in Chapel Hill shaped me fully, making me an English professor by profession and a progressive liberal by passion. As the years clipped by, I felt myself outgrowing Arden's stodgy culture. The school was decidedly divergent from the regional state college in coastal Maryland where I taught in my fledgling years as a young married professional. It was an even farther cry from Chicago's Keck College, an affluent liberal arts college where I later worked my way up to dean and vice president. Now that I was appointed to Arden's board of trustees, I had secret hopes of "unstifling" some of its religious rigor. The mere fact that Arden had requested the board to meet over a holiday seemed absurd.

Arden's beautiful setting always calmed my soul, however, and this evening, continuing my reveries on my deck at home, I recalled the stunning scenery surrounding Virginia's mountains. In spite of today's Labor Day traffic, I had reveled in the drive through the sometimes steep terrain. I had slipped a cassette into the dash, and my spirits had soared when the precise tempo of a Rachmaninoff piano prelude spilled into the car. Early September was one of my favorite times of year. Crimson geraniums and lacy dusty miller dominated the roadside yards. Golden sassafras framed the highway, and bronzed dogwoods blinked through the verdant woods.

In fact, there was nothing during the ride to warn me that a car breakdown was imminent. When I finally glanced at my watch, the small valley city of Pickney lay just ahead—the perfect place to grab a sandwich and fill up with gas.

As I continued driving, my thoughts wandered back to the close of Arden's meeting. As usual, it had ended with a prayer. I remembered peeking through half-lidded eyes at fellow trustees, heads uniformly bowed around the antique oak conference table, and marveling anew at Arden's careful rituals. Students were immersed in them. Between freshman convocation and their ultimate commencement, Arden students would attend more than a hundred weekly chapel programs. The carillon—a cherished donation of forty-seven French-made bells—chimed hymns as students moved between classes. They marched, almost, in four-four time, like Christian soldiers headed into battle.

The wording of the prayer had almost annoyed me: *"And as thou hast promised through thy well-beloved Son that when two or three are gathered together in His name thou wilt be in the midst of them: Fulfill now, O Lord, the desires of thy servants . . . "*

Servants? I was both the Wickfield University chancellor and an Arden College trustee. I hardly considered myself servile.

". . . granting us in this world knowledge of thy truth, and in the world to come life everlasting. Amen."

Amen. That word, at least, I was comfortable with. *Life everlasting. Amen.* These words delivered a brief image of Benny, white and innocent in his small brass casket, his hands crossed over the little gray suit that we, his grieving sisters, had chosen from his closet. Even after all these years, the memory riddled me with pain.

It was in that precise moment of memory that my Ford Victoria lost its power and limped to the side of the road. I thought again about the mysterious stranger who had driven me into Pickney to find gas. Greg. Gregory Archer. *Doctor* Archer. Nice man. I vowed to remember his name.

Now, from my position on the deck, I could see that the sun was dipping behind the Wellstone Hall turret that towered over campus. It was nearly seven o'clock—nearly six in Chicago.

I reached for the phone on the patio table beside me. It was time to call Alex.

Chapter 3
CARRINGTON HALL

Dressing for work the next day, I wondered for the hundredth time why I held weekly cabinet meetings on Monday mornings. In this case it was a Tuesday, following yesterday's holiday, but even after a day off, it was hard to face such structure.

The Monday meetings had not been my idea. My cabinet members had met on Mondays under my predecessor. From the beginning they'd told me how they hated the constrictions of a Monday regimen, but I decided to continue the practice. It made sense at the time to signal that I would be a no-nonsense leader.

"It ensures a disciplined routine," I once explained to Alex, who objected testily during our over-ambitious commuter days when we were trying to see each other on alternate weekends.

"It would be nice if you could occasionally fly back to Wickfield on Monday mornings," he noted. "Meet your staff every Wednesday. Fly to your next alumni event from O'Hare rather than Charlotte."

"But we're not a normal couple with normal schedules," I protested. Besides, I told him pointedly, Alex had the option of returning to Chicago on Mondays when he visited *me*.

"You know my schedule," he said with a shrug. Alex was a general surgeon. His first scrub of the day was often before 7:00 a.m.

So we had deadlocked, and I maintained a vigorous series of Monday-morning staff meetings. Today's would be interesting, I decided, adjusting a cranberry silk scarf at the throat of my suit. I knew in advance how each member would respond concerning yesterday's highway incident.

Bob Atterbury, vice president for Development, would listen to my little tale while pulling thoughtfully on his pipe, tapping it frequently to dislodge the packed tobacco and relighting it with cupped hands while offering little comment.

Marilyn Lyons, vice president for Finance, would first be startled, then highly concerned for my safety. In the end she might admonish me for riding with a stranger to search for gas.

Jake Mooney, vice president for Student Life, would laugh in delight and retell the story a half-dozen times by noon.

Theodore "Pud" Padgett, athletic director, would make an inappropriate comment such as "A doctor? Really? Got a fixation with surgeons, Kat?"

But it was Dan Jones's opinion that I cared most about. Vice president for Academic Affairs, Dan had an instinctive ability to capture the big picture, to think through situations maturely and make prudent decisions. I trusted Dan explicitly. He was the one I turned to, over and over. Dan would immediately understand my predicament on the highway and applaud the course I had taken.

"And then he introduced himself," I told my quintet an hour later as they sat spellbound around the conference table, coffee mugs in hand. "He went for his wallet and pulled out a business card. 'Gregory Archer, M.D. General Surgery. Surgery of the Breast, Abdomen, Chest, and Thyroid.'"

I was reading from a cream-colored card extracted from my vinyl folder. "'Offices at 1201 Vine Avenue, Suite 321, Pinckney, Virginia.' I couldn't believe my good luck, actually. My gas tank was empty, he offered to drive me six miles into town, he was obviously safe, and I had to make a quick decision. So off we rode in his little Triumph." I chuckled, delighted with the solution that had fallen into place.

The group was silent, musing. "How long did it take? To get back with gas and get on your way?" It was Marilyn who asked the question.

"About thirty minutes, I guess. They all knew him at the gas station. The owner gave him a gas can and told him it was on the house, but I insisted on paying cash. My Victoria was still there when we returned, although looking a bit forlorn in the weeds." I smiled at the group around the table, eager to move on to pertinent business. Tucking the card into the file, I pulled out my typed copy of the day's agenda.

Dan, as though on cue, moved with me. "And so we welcome back our fair chancellor from her hour of distress," he said gallantly. "All is well. We are grateful to Dr. Archer for her rescue and unfettered return." Dan held an endowed chair as a professor of European history and was nationally renowned in medieval studies. His elegant words flowed naturally.

"Was he married?" Pud asked the question with a sly grin, but I stared back coldly.

"His wife is the mayor of Pinckney."

Our discussions proceeded, as did the day. I moved in and out of meetings with what I hoped was grace and speed. I enjoyed the rhythms of my academic routine. To my surprise, but not to my sisters', I had established a reputation as a decision-maker early in my career. At the Maryland campus, I was identified as a logical thinker with good presentation skills. I was appointed to countless committees, many of them nameless and faceless and exorbitant wasters of my time. But they gave me an identity, and I was elected to the faculty senate upon my first nomination.

As a senate member, I earned a reputation as a voice well respected by the president's office. My reputation as a faculty negotiator soared—perhaps undeservedly, but it pushed me quickly up the academic ladder. Divorced by now from my husband, Tim, I snagged the coveted position at Keck College, where my salary increased handsomely. There I again taught English, sat again through too many committee meetings, and soon enough became associate dean of arts and sciences. By the time a national search firm called me for the Wickfield position, I had advanced to vice president for academic affairs.

There were snarls on my road to advancement. Most were personnel problems. Even when things were running smoothly, I dealt with complicated hires. At Keck I was plagued by a fine arts dean whose tantrums led an entire queue of secretaries to quit—five within four months. I called him my Maalox Plus problem.

And here, at Wickfield, there was Carrington Hall.

"He sounds like a dormitory," I had joked to Marianna before my first interview for the Wickfield job. His name had been listed in my letter as chairman of the board of trustees. I quickly found he was not a joke. He stared at me through rimless glasses atop his beaked nose and demanded to know why I thought myself worthy of the Wickfield chancellorship.

"Our young women have been coming to Wickfield for over a century," he intoned, skirting reference to the fact that the school had been coeducational for a decade. "They have, through the years, received the very finest of instruction. They have educated countless children in North Carolina classrooms. They are from the finest families of the South and marry the finest men." He savored his words, in spite of their monotony, enunciating with precision. He warned about the dangers of the "new day" while I studied his face, fascinated by jowls that flapped as he spoke.

I was quick to respond. I was familiar with Wickfield's history and reputation, I asserted, especially the legendary stories about "the girls of Wickfield" and their protected lives through decades behind the legendary wrought-iron fence. Now, a century later, that fence still surrounded the heart of Wickfield's campus.

"Today, of course, the school has changed dramatically. It's now a university of nearly five thousand young women *and men*," I reminded Carrington, "and they face challenges on a global level. I would consider it an honor to help raise Wickfield to its *next* level and make this the most splendid era in the school's history."

I won the battle and also the job, but sometimes I wondered whether my perpetual war with Carrington would ever abate. When he had an issue with me, he called in advance for an appointment. He would arrive dressed immaculately in business suit, buttoned vest, and silk tie. He would seat himself in the burgundy upholstered armchair, facing me on the slip-covered settee of green-and-mauve florals. He would clear his throat, sometimes several times in a row, and begin.

"Sometimes I think he's just lonely," I sighed once to Alex, exasperated. "He's pushing eighty, his wife is half-deaf, and he loves the sound of his voice. He wants to score points. I'm a game to him."

But my greatest contention with Carrington involved—the fence.

When built in the late 1800s, Wickfield's original six buildings had been laid out in a rectangle, enclosed by a wrought-iron fence whose sturdy posts sank six feet into the ground. Wellstone, the main administration building, faced a dirt road that led into the village of Grove a mile to the north.

Now the historic cluster was surrounded by more than forty buildings that sprawled over rambling acres. The community had grown into the thriving textile-manufacturing town of Hurley. The old dirt road had become Grove Boulevard, a north-south conduit that carried traffic from the interstate to the upscale Grove Hills shopping mall. Thousands of cars drove directly past our campus every week.

To my utmost dismay, however, passersby missed much of the beauty of the campus. The front lawn was overgrown with towering oaks. Some had grown impregnable through the decades, their heavy branches hanging low to the soil.

"The campus needs to be open and inviting," I told Carrington in an early discussion. "We're missing a huge marketing opportunity by sheltering these gorgeous historic buildings from the public eye. Think how many potential parents and students drive by and see only a snippet of what we have to offer." My idea was to take down the aged fence, trim back the boxwoods, and selectively remove a few oaks. "The results will be spectacular! Trust me, Carrington."

"Rubbish!" he snorted. "The fence is central to Wickfield's history and privacy. If the campus looks like a sanctuary, that's because it was always intended to be one. Leave your *Better Homes and Gardens* ideas to the magazine folks. You're a university chancellor, Katherine, and don't you forget it!"

Now, late on this Tuesday afternoon, eager to head home after my lost holiday, I was startled to hear Carrington's voice in my outer office. I heard Jackie, my secretary, greet him. Then she loomed in my doorway, sending strong eye signals as she said clearly, "Chancellor Embright, Carrington Hall is here to see you."

I nodded, silent. A feeling of foreboding engulfed me; I had mere seconds to collect myself.

Carrington was inside instantly, twitching in front of my desk. "Katherine, I must have a word with you."

"Why, Carrington, what a pleasant surprise." I kept my voice measured as I gestured toward the armchair. "Please sit down." Jackie gently closed the door behind us.

And so we sat. I listened in silence while Carrington thundered through his outrage at the "humiliating story" he had heard from not one but "a deluge" of people that very afternoon about my highly improper behavior with a strange man during my out-of-town trip. I let him spout his relentless mixture of fact and fiction, marveling to myself at the speed at which news travels in a Southern town—not to mention the diffusion of its accuracy.

He finally paused for breath.

"Carrington, Carrington," I sighed, almost in admonition. "Obviously this story has taken several turns along the way. I do so wish you had called when you first heard this to avoid such gross miscommunication." I continued with my version of the story, refuting Carrington's belief that I had been whisked away against my will and that the stranger, who by now had assumed truly sinister proportions, had "improper designs."

But Carrington would not be placated. I had never seen him so distraught. He vacillated between distrust of the interloper and a deep disappointment in what he deemed to be indiscreet judgment on my part.

"This can't happen again, Katherine," he said severely. "We can't have our chancellor running around the countryside and being vulnerable to all the elements of society. You could have been harmed—or worse. This school's reputation is unblemished, and it must remain so. The chancellor must keep strong control, Katherine! Your careless behavior has given me great pause." And, true to his words, he paused.

Uneasy now, I spoke quickly. "It won't happen again, Carrington, I assure you. That gas tank has my full attention now." I smiled gamely, thinking fast. "You know that the motor pool takes wonderful care of that car, don't you? There's no possible way I could have a mechanical breakdown, and I truly foresee no future problems on the road. I do appreciate your concern, though. Not every university chancellor has the good fortune to have someone as thoughtful and—*worried*—as you for an advisor." I had started to say "involved" but thought better of it.

"A good motor pool is not enough, Katherine." He drawled out my name in three syllables, as if warming up to what would follow. "From now on, whenever you go on your out-of-town trips, you must have someone who represents the college drive you there."

"That's ridiculous." The sharp words slipped out before I could catch myself. "No way, Carrington! No one needs to drive me anywhere. I can handle myself on the road quite nicely, thank you. As I've already pointed out, there will be no more incidents."

"This will be for all trips over fifty miles from Wickfield." He continued as though I had not spoken. "I've already spoken to Chief Sutton, and he's assigning a security officer for the times you need to travel. You can ride in the officer's car, or he can drive your car. You choose. This is only for official school business, of course."

The little aside was an unexpected jab. I had spent a long-ago conversation convincing Carrington that my Arden trusteeship was the result of my

Wickfield position, thereby making my Virginia trips "official business." My anger was mounting by the second. What audacity! What *arrogance!*

"To begin with, Carrington, Chief Sutton can't spare an officer to drive me *anywhere.*" I was sputtering, my words tumbling fast. "We're short on staff for campus security as it is. Secondly, it's entirely unnecessary. I've been an independent female professional for years and have managed myself quite capably, thank you very much. Third, there are obviously other options, if you're really so worried about my safety. I could get a two-way radio. Or I could have one of those nice new car phones installed. A couple of my colleagues have them, and they work just fine. They're installed between the front seats and are anchored to the floor—"

"But they are limited, Katherine. They have poor reception outside a certain range, and they don't take the place of a man's physical presence. You need someone who can drive you to the front door of your meeting and escort you wherever you need to go."

"*Escort* me? Good God!" By now I was enraged. "I don't need a bodyguard, Carrington! This is 1989, for heaven's sake, not the Civil War!" I lowered my voice slightly to control its tremor. "I'm not some Southern darling in hoop skirts. I don't need someone to escort me. I don't need a companion. I don't need a limo. I don't need a chauffeur. This is the craziest idea I ever heard of. You're way out of line, Carrington! I won't stand for this!"

"It's all settled, Katherine," Carrington said, wetting his lips with finality, "and will begin immediately. This will be just between us and Security; no one else needs to know. Chief Sutton will call tomorrow and discuss arrangements."

Sam Sutton doesn't know beans about what I need, I thought fiercely. The aging chief of security had been an ongoing problem for years. He was too hidebound to know what Wickfield needed for its growing population but too much of a fixture to be forced from his position. He reeked disgustingly of cigarettes, and I would bet a week's groceries that booze was stashed in his bottom desk drawers.

Suddenly I was much too weary for combat. "Good evening, Carrington," I said, rising to my feet. My tone was icy. I stared, unflinching, waiting for him to stand as well. At that moment I wanted nothing more than to retire to my sun porch with a bulbous glass of red wine and figure out how to fight this insane plan.

Chapter 4
CABINET

When it had been announced in the spring of 1987 that I was coming to Wickfield as chancellor, the press gave a lot of attention to my age—or, rather, to my "youth." Wickfield's public relations director at that time—a young man named Carl—called shortly before I left Keck College to ask if my new role would make me the youngest woman college president in the United States.

The question caught me off guard. "The office I'm accepting is that of chancellor," I replied rather pointedly. Carl already knew that, of course. The North Carolina university system referred to the heads of its sixteen campuses as chancellors. Only Charles Pettigrew, who presided over the entire campus system, bore the title of president.

Still, the idea of "youngest" was so startling that I was unprepared to comment on it. I suggested he contact the American Council on Education in Washington for this information.

The outcome was that I was touted at age forty-seven as the "nation's youngest woman to head a public college campus." State and national press picked up on it instantly. The *Charlotte Observer* featured me in a Carolina Living spread, photographing me in one of Wickfield's picturesque garden nooks. The *Raleigh News & Observer* ran a Sunday feature about my rapid career advancement.

For my inauguration, nearly a thousand people jammed Wellstone Auditorium. Charlie Pettigrew came from Chapel Hill to install me. Seated in front-row reserved seats were three of my four sisters and their husbands and children—all but my youngest sister, Jane, who was expecting her fourth child momentarily. She was crushed to miss the event and the family reunion. "We're so proud of you, Kat!" she said when she called from San

Diego to convey her disappointment. "And if this new baby is a girl, we're naming her after you!"

In those early months as chancellor, I debated on how best to staff my cabinet—a curious process in higher education. Most new executives absorbed the staff of their predecessors, without question. Others accepted them on probation, agreeing to keep or fire them within six months. One Midwest president whose path I crossed at ACE meetings—I particularly remembered his over-arching disdain of women professors—assembled the cabinet on his first day in office and fired them all in a single swoop of a sentence. "You have one month to find another job or convince me you are worthy of being rehired," he told them. Two of those staffers, I recalled, decided to leave immediately. Both were women.

In my case, I was fortunate. In inheriting Dan Jones as vice president for Academic Affairs, I had acquired a superb strategist and a creative thinker. His career path was carved from a deep commitment to scholarship, and his slingshot mind popped out new ideas with a snap. The faculty respected him, which meant he would advocate my academic agenda with success. Dan's wife, Mimi, convinced me that keeping up with these two Joneses would be a delightful challenge.

"We all think you're insane to come here," Mimi had said, greeting me at a reception soon after my arrival. She didn't crack a smile, but her eyes twinkled wickedly behind her oversized glasses. "But we're mighty glad you did. Welcome to Wickfield!"

Jake Mooney, the highly energetic vice-president for student affairs, first caught my attention at a backyard party hosted by the search committee. "I'm Jake," he said, stretching out his hand, "and I'm in charge of student affairs. And since Wickfield is now coed, that keeps me, well, pretty busy." He chuckled meaningfully at his joke. I smiled back coolly.

Like Dan Jones, Jake was slight and of medium height, but where Dan was charmingly cerebral, Jake seemed fixated on people. He laughed heartily at everything. He seemed to spring from one location to another like a leaping lizard—probably a handy trait, since numerous campus departments reported to him. His wife, Alma Earle, plump and gregarious, taught first graders—a fact that alarmed me when I overheard her say, "We growed a ton of tomatoes last summer." But what she lacked in grammar she made up for in friendliness. People gravitated toward her.

Pud Padgett, the athletic director, had played basketball for the Wickfield Red Devils as a student. When quoting him in the newspaper—and he was quoted frequently, considering the comings and goings of various coaches—reporters now referred to him as Theodore R. "Pud" Padgett. The "Pud" had evolved from his childhood, a moniker from a younger brother who had mixed up "Ted" and "Padgett."

The quirky name had stuck. Everyone called him Pud, including me. And I decided early that Pud would need some careful watching. I didn't fault him for being divorced—I, too, was divorced, and I well understood the variants that could dissolve a marriage. But he was good-looking and flirty in a much-too-flamboyant way. Susceptible women found him charming. "Here comes royalty!" he crowed grandly the first time he encountered me in the gymnasium. I hoped he would avoid the temptation to date women students.

That left me with two positions to fill: vice president for Advancement and vice president for Finance. For both I had to utilize a campus search committee, an annoying structure within public institutions that slowed hiring to a crawl. The advancement slot—it covered fund raising, public relations, and alumni relations—was so important to me that I considered engaging a professional search firm. However, our *Chronicle of Higher Education* ad produced an impressive stack of responses, and, after phone interviews, the committee scheduled three applicants for campus visits.

Bob Atterbury, the final candidate, fit my expectations so perfectly that I would have hired him on the spot had there been no committee. As a Virginian, I understood the prestige of his Woodberry Forest prep-school background, and his Angier B. Duke scholarship at Duke University put him among the nation's most distinguished college graduates. His MBA came from Wharton, which was fast becoming one of the nation's most elite business schools. His first job after Wharton had been raising funds for a private Georgia college.

Fortunately, Bob won over the search committee as well. His dignity came from upper-class breeding; his athletic build came from prep-school sports. Although he was conservative to the point of blandness, he articulated such a beautiful vision for Wickfield that we all felt certain he could woo a check from the most stubborn of potential donors.

Best of all, Bob was married to Susan.

It was impossible not to notice Susan Atterbury. She had a grace that lit a room the moment she entered it. Part of it was her height—she was tall and leggy, maybe even more so than I—and part came from her chiseled cheekbones. But Susan had a presence about her that transcended physical beauty. Like Bob, she was intelligent and well spoken—"a veteran of seventeen years of Catholic schools," she liked to say, "including kindergarten." Her sentence structure was as precise as my own—four years of high-school Latin, I was betting. My only concern was that Hurley might seem small to the Atterburys after their years near Philadelphia and Atlanta.

It turned out that Bob accepted the job happily, and Susan proclaimed Hurley to be the ideal small city in which to raise their three young sons. They were well-mannered boys, aged ten to fourteen. It was rare these days to find a sharp stay-at-home mom among administration wives; many pursued careers of their own. "This town is going to love you," I promised, envisioning her as a leader among volunteers.

My one controversial hire was Marilyn Lyon, a career accountant who'd applied for vice president of Finance. Her resume was impressive. In short order she had zipped from high-school math teacher to commercial bookkeeper to certified accountant. My expectations were high the day of her first interview.

But when Marilyn walked into my office, my heart sank. I saw a mid-fifties belly pouch, triple chins, and tiny rimless glasses that disappeared into her heavy facial folds. Her mint-green pants suit was polyester from the seventies and hung shapelessly on her body. Her posterior wobbled as she moved. The tight brown coils of her permed hair threatened to reverberate if touched. She smelled nicely of scented bath lotion and showed a faint flair for makeup, but the overall first impression was foreboding, if not forbidding. I wondered how anyone who looked so alarming could bear the lovely name of Marilyn.

Of even more concern was the fact that Marilyn had never worked in higher education. Her background showed no understanding of our tuition-driven budgeting nor our reliance on endowed funds. On the positive side, her auditing skills had caught the attention of Charlotte's Big Eight firm of Touche and Ross. Marilyn's ascent through the firm's hierarchy was nothing short of phenomenal.

The search committee, however, was not as enthusiastic. They voiced "concern" about her willingness to grant seed money for projects, but I sensed that Marilyn's appearance was the real problem.

"We don't know how well Marilyn will be willing to listen to us," noted a math professor on the committee. "I had to wait two years to get funding for the tutoring lab." I inwardly winced. I was convinced Marilyn had the skills to be the perfect vanguard of our treasury, an able executor to keep us in grace with state auditors. I fought hard for her. In the end, the committee relented.

Now, beginning my third year as Wickfield's chancellor, I realized I had grown incredibly fond of my cabinet. Overall, they were loyal and quick to follow my lead. Or so I had thought.

After this wildest of all my confrontations with Carrington, I realized that fidelity had its limits. My "loyal five" had not been discreet about yesterday's adventure on the interstate. If Carrington were to be believed, my story had made the rounds and been garnished to the pleasure of countless narrators. Not that I could blame any one of them. How many women executives would run out of gas among Virginia's winding hills— much less take a ride with an utter stranger?

By now I was totally dismayed at my carelessness. My ego had led me to tell what I had thought was a humorous story. Tonight I was stuck with Carrington's idiotic plan and saddled with a police escort for distant trips.

"So much for independence," I thought dismally.

I suddenly missed Alex. He alone would be able to lift me out of the doldrums. Even though we had talked only last evening, I placed another call to Chicago.

Chapter 5
FIRST RIDE

On the phone that night, Alex surprised me by defending Carrington.

"It's not such a bad idea, Kat," he said after hearing my spiel of indignation. "Frankly, I rather like the idea of someone being on hand. To keep an eye on things. You really could use someone to look after you, you know." This was an old line he had used when trying to cajole me into marriage.

His attitude annoyed me. "It's a ridiculous idea, and I don't need someone to look after me," I sputtered. "And I certainly don't have time to make small talk with some half-brained policeman." I had fully expected Alex to commiserate, perhaps even offer a solution.

"Look at the bright side," he said reasonably. "You won't have to make small talk. You can practice your speeches while riding, or write, or get caught up on your reading. You can't do that while driving." He knew I was a voracious reader who kept three or four books stacked beside my bed. I even kept a bestseller on the front seat of my car in the event of a traffic jam.

"I hate to read in a moving car," I retorted. "I get headaches."

"Well, you may just find this officer to be bright and well trained. The forensic sciences are vigorous. Who is the lucky guy, anyway?"

"I don't know," I replied tiredly. "It's probably that new fellow we hired last year—Paul Stafford. He's the only one I can figure who would be suitable. He has no business gallivanting around with me when I can manage things by myself. We'll probably have to hire a couple of part-timers to cover while he's gone, and they won't know the ropes for months." I sighed. "It shouldn't have to be this big a deal." I sounded so dejected that Alex laughed.

"Come on, Kat, it's not the end of the world. You may actually enjoy the company. I certainly hope this guy is married. Right?" Alex's voice was teasing.

"You know better than that. If it *is* Paul, I think I met his wife at the staff picnic last fall. She's a pretty little thing. Can't remember her name. I think I met their kids, too—teenagers, a boy and a girl."

"Well, be nice to him. He may come in handy. You can handle this, Kat. You have always risen to crises in your life and made the most of them. This is no different. There are career women everywhere who would be grateful for someone to help free up some time."

Suddenly I was weary—weary of problems, weary of admonitions. "What time do you get here Saturday?" I asked, changing the subject. Alex would be visiting me in Hurley this weekend. We had pinpointed this time several weeks earlier, juggling our two busy calendars to find a mutually free weekend.

"Wheels down at Douglas at 11:32."

"Safe trip, Alex. Love you."

"Love you, too."

Alex was right, I thought reluctantly as I turned out the bedside light. I was beginning to realize that there were both positives and negatives to this turn of events. I never seemed to have enough time to get things done, and one side of my mind was already ticking on how to massage these extra hours. I could spread out my notes in the back seat and mentally rehearse the openings of my speeches—the part I did without script. Better yet, I could work through my famous task menus, the ones the cabinet pretended to groan about. I loved to strategize, to plan, to make lengthy lists and prioritize each item. This new time in the car would be ideal.

Even so, I craved periods when I could be alone, especially while driving. I liked the openness of the highway and the comfort I found behind the wheel. Driving allowed me to sort through private thoughts. There was something about the hum of soft rubber and the vibes of the steering wheel that balanced both freedom and control.

Being alone and being lonely were two distinctly different things. I had surmised this long ago and had clung to the discovery jealously, as though this special revelation was known only to me. Since my Wickfield calendar was full of speeches and dinners and visitors, there was little time for loneliness. I fell into bed at night exhausted, almost immune to the missing parts of my life.

The difference was that I *enjoyed* being alone. And to find time to be intentionally alone—that, now, took meticulous planning.

Until now, my long drives had been the antidote—especially those three-hour drives through the lovely mountains to Arden. Tonight, reflecting on the last few hours of my strange day, I deeply resented the thought of sharing this berth of freedom with another human being.

It would be imperative, I decided, staring at my darkened ceiling, for me to lay down rules. This Paul Stafford needed to know from the outset—our very first trip—that I required personal quiet time. His physical presence should under no circumstances interfere with that.

Eased by that thought, I finally fell asleep.

The following day, Chief Sutton made his obligatory phone call and reported that Paul Stafford was indeed my assigned driver. I promptly pronounced the plan absurd.

"Now, Miss Katherine, Officer Stafford has a pretty good idea how you must feel about all of this," intoned the police chief. I could picture him shifting his portly body in his swivel chair, stretching across his cluttered desk for a messy ash tray. "Judge Hall told me you wouldn't like this, and I can see you're not happy one little bit. And I can tell you I don't like one little bit giving up my top officer, either, even if it's only here and there a couple times a month. I suggest we all try to make the best of the situation."

This was the second time in twelve hours that someone had advised me to make the best of the situation.

"Send him to my house tomorrow morning, 9:30 sharp," I replied briskly. "I'm speaking to a group of women in Charlotte. It's a noon meeting, and we must be there by 11:30 so I can mingle beforehand. We'll need the full two hours to get there. Traffic is terrible on I-85. We'll take my car, of course. He can leave his car in my driveway, or he can walk over from his office. If he drives, tell him to park at the back and come in through the kitchen. Lennie will let him in."

"Yes, ma'am. Yes, Miss Katherine, I'll have him there, 9:30 sharp."

The rest of the day flew. I pulled notes from an earlier speech and fine-tuned them to suit Thursday's audience. I would be addressing professional women, some notably advanced in their careers as well as those aspiring to reposition themselves. They met monthly to discuss such topics as the disparities of a workforce dominated by men: unequal opportunities, unequal promotions, unequal salaries. This was a subject I loved to speak on, and my passion for the topic had made me a popular mentor among women's groups.

Thursday morning I dressed carefully and made the five-minute walk to my office well before eight o'clock. I dictated two memos for Jackie before dropping in on Dan Jones. Dan introduced me briefly to his new secretary, a statuesque brunette named Lana Underwood who looked as though she had just emerged from a tanning booth. I was startled at her height and extremely slender build, both of which contrasted abruptly with her ample chest. She was taller even than I. Her skirt hit high above her knees, a throwback to the miniskirt of the seventies.

"She looks like a Playboy bunny," I suddenly thought, starting back to my house to meet Paul. I had seen photos of bunnies, mostly from the stack of girlie magazines collected by my former husband, Tim. Tim had been an aspiring television journalist at the time he read *Playboy*, open-minded and adventuresome, but this Lana created a curious image for Dan. He was one of the more conservative souls on my staff. I made a mental note to ask him more about her.

I loved this brief walk between my house and my office in Wellstone. I often wished the college's forefathers could see how beautifully the campus had blossomed into its current setting. In the warmer months, Wickfield looked like a well-tended park, a Southern paradise of azaleas, ferns, and blooming perennials. Photographers from garden magazines sought us out to shoot a well-placed bench edged by coral bells and an aged oak, or twisted wisteria vines netted against weathered stone.

Like any proper noun, the Chancellor's House was always capitalized in campus literature. As its sole resident, I was acutely aware of the propriety it commanded. The grand two-story house faced Grove Boulevard, but I always entered the grounds from the rear, driving nearly a block behind the house before looping around to approach the back driveway. The layout afforded me privacy. The deeply wooded grounds were decently removed from the traffic of dorms and classrooms. Most convenient of all was the house's close proximity to Wellstone Hall. It was my custom to walk to my office each morning, returning for my car if needed later in the day.

Now, as I entered my driveway to prepare for the Queens trip, a police car loomed behind me. I stepped gingerly to the right as the car slowed. The driver leaned across the front seat to lower the passenger window, and I found myself gazing upon the face of Paul Stafford.

"Good morning," he said pleasantly, his motor idling.

"You're early," I said tartly. "I told Chief Sutton 9:30."

"It's 9:10," he said, still pleasantly, "and I came early to find out where we're going, exactly. Charlotte's a big city. Sure hate to get us lost on my first day." He grinned.

I was taken aback.

"The meeting is at Queens College, in the Claudia Belk dining room. Didn't Chief Sutton tell you? I know exactly where it is. It's in the Myers Park neighborhood. I can direct you." My tone was almost prim.

"Sounds good, President Embright. Want a lift?" We were less than a hundred feet from the back door. Was he joking? And why had he called me "president"?

"No. Thank you. I'll be ready in a few minutes." Paul gave a little wave and moved his squad car up the drive. He parked beside the massive rhododendron hedge.

I swished past the Swedish ivy baskets on the breezeway and disappeared upstairs, busying myself with last-minute grooming. Minutes later, I heard deep chesty laughter downstairs, followed by high-pitched titters. *Goodness, was that Lennie?* I had known dear Lennie since the first day I moved into the Chancellor's House, but I could not remember *ever* hearing her burst into spontaneous giggles.

I checked myself once more in the long mirror, pulling the cuffs of my long-sleeved blouse to cover my wrists. The magenta color contrasted boldly against my lightweight gray plaid suit. I looked professional. I should pass muster with the women instantly. Yet, for whatever reason, I felt sort of fluttery, like walking on an icy sidewalk without rubber-soled boots. It was a new sensation. Keeping my balance had never been a problem.

"Stop it!" I scolded my image in the mirror. I headed downstairs to face a beaming Lennie, who was holding a thermos bottle and a sack, and Paul, who was considerably taller than I remembered.

"Here's coffee for the road, Miz Katherine. Now y'all be careful. What time you be back?"

I shot Lennie a sharp sideways stare. She made me feel like a teenage daughter. "Officer Stafford will drop me off at Wellstone about 3:30," I said coldly. "I'll walk home around six. Don't forget the flower arrangement for tomorrow night."

Why the reminder? That was unfair of me. The flowers were for a private dinner with a wealthy out-of-state donor and his wife. Lennie and I had been discussing the décor for several days. I had never before "ordered" her to do anything in such a demanding tone.

"Shall we go?" I said, turning to Paul and finally eyeing him directly. He was wearing a dark navy-blue suit and brightly printed red tie with sprinkles of tiny dots. I wondered if he always wore a suit and tie to work or whether he wore a police uniform, as Sam Sutton did. I had seen Paul in passing several times before, but no details had stuck.

At the car, he stepped ahead to open the front passenger door.

"No, I'll sit in the back, thank you. I have work to do." I held up my briefcase.

"Busy lady," Paul said in mock surprise and then shot me that grin again. He opened the back door, and I slid in, tugging my skirt over my knees as I swung my legs inside. Paul walked around to the driver's side, buckling up as he settled in.

"Queens College, you say?" He turned halfway to speak over his shoulder, like a taxi driver.

"You exit off the interstate at Freedom Drive, which takes you right into Morehead. Then you go past some businesses to the college. I'll know the streets when I see them."

Paul was silent, mulling that over. "Goodness, lady, you must like downtown driving," he said. "Morehead puts you close to the heart of the city. Traffic is busy there. Have you ever taken Billy Graham Parkway?"

I frowned. "That seems out of the way. Besides, Billy Graham puts you into the thick of airport traffic."

"It's actually not so thick," he said. "Yes, it's more southern, but it's a pretty drive, and it takes you along Woodlawn and up Selwyn past all those beautiful old homes."

I hated to admit I knew only one way to Queens College. I had gotten lost in Charlotte the first time I drove there, so I'd memorized one specific way to get to each of my favorite landmarks. It never occurred to me that there might be a better way—or a "pretty" route, as Paul described it.

"Go however you wish," I said, reaching down for my briefcase. "I'm going to be busy. Just get me to the campus by 11:30."

"Roger." The car moved out of the driveway.

For miles we rode in silence, interrupted only by the rustling of my papers and the scribbling of my pen as I underlined words on my typed speech. No doubt about it: I liked having the entire back seat on which to spread out papers. I was a fast study, and I thrived under pressure. I reviewed my introductory remarks and made written notations before committing them to memory. I closed my eyes and pictured myself on stage, visualizing gestures. A speech coach from my student days at Carolina had taught me well, and through the years I had become totally at ease in front of a microphone.

Now I delved into my work, head bowed over my papers. The car sped south along a four-lane highway that linked Hurley to the busy interstate southwest of Charlotte.

To this day I don't know what inspired me to raise my head at the exact moment I did. I only know that suddenly I looked up, and in those few seconds I caught Paul looking at me in his rearview mirror. Our gazes intertwined. Then his eyes flicked away, staring straight ahead as the car hummed along.

How long had he been watching me? There it was again—that fluttery, off-balance feeling that welled inside my stomach and twisted. I hated its quivery sensation. What was wrong with me? *Stop it!* I scolded myself for the second time that morning.

"How's Lennie's coffee? Still hot?" Thankfully, Paul broke our silence. I had completely forgotten about the coffee. I busied myself with the thermos, pouring the steaming brew and handing Paul a Styrofoam cup over the back of the seat.

"There's no sugar or creamer," I said, half-apologetically. "Lennie knows I drink it black."

"Can't drink it without sugar," said Paul, grasping the cup with one hand while focusing on the driving. Then he met my eyes again in the mirror. "Just kidding. I take it black, too. Lennie asked me earlier," he added, mimicking my apologetic tone.

I broke into a huge smile, in spite of myself. It felt good. I poured myself a cup and settled into the leather cushions, enjoying the coffee's deep woody aroma and permitting myself a view of the countryside. The highway median was filled with massive expanses of lance-leafed *Coreopsis* and spreads of pink catchfly—all products of North Carolina's highway beautification program. We passed two-story white frame farmhouses, dilapidated gray barns with sunken roofs, and red-clay fields whose rows of head-high corn seemed carved with sculptural precision.

"The houses look smaller from the back seat," I remarked idly. Paul's face wreathed into a smile.

A comfortable silence filled the car as we moved into Charlotte's fast-flowing traffic. Paul turned off the interstate onto Billy Graham Parkway. We passed the airport complex and the Charlotte Coliseum, home of the wildly popular Hornets, the NBA's newest professional team. We crossed over I-77, a truck-studded interstate I avoided whenever possible, and followed Woodlawn Road through newer commercial sections. We drove through the intersections with South Boulevard and Park Road and eventually turned left onto Selwyn. Soon we were cruising along the spacious residential street leading to Queens College.

The neighborhoods were spectacular; I could not contain my delight. Every home and yard was a new treasure: graceful Georgian homes with artful shrubbery, and Tudor Revivals with angular gables and narrow-paned windows of leaded glass. Most were set back from the street in oversized yards graced by towering hardwoods and manicured bushes. Slender ramrod trees lined the curbs. It was hard to believe I had visited this neighborhood without "seeing" it from this approach.

As Paul neared campus and the entrance to the Burwell Hall circle, I reclaimed my professional demeanor. Paul jumped out and came around to open my door. I ducked my head as I emerged from the big car.

"See you here at 1:30," I said, holding up my briefcase in a little wave. I gazed around at a well-tended campus of brick buildings trimmed in white.

"Don't be late," Paul deadpanned.

Two hours later, I was amazed at how good I felt. My audience had been packed with educated women who yearned to return to the workplace after raising their children. They had ventured in from all around the Charlotte area, including towns like Kings Mountain and Rock Hill. I shook so many hands afterward that my wrists were sore.

"Important topic," one lady said. "And you expressed it beautifully." The praise was humbling, especially in light of the hunger these women expressed for finding fulfillment. I knew this "fulfillment" issue was a timely subject among young families.

Now, burrowed in the back seat of my car, I savored the afterglow. At my suggestion, Paul turned the radio to a classical music station. Symphonic grandeur filled the car, and I settled back to the richness of Mozart's *Symphony No. 40*. I relaxed completely, closing my eyes.

It seemed only moments had passed before Paul was shaking my shoulder, leaning over me and saying, "Nap time's over, Prez."

I groped dazedly for my belongings. "How long did I sleep?" I asked. I stepped onto the sun-dappled sidewalk in front of Wellstone Hall and stared about in disbelief.

"Well over an hour," he said. "You dropped off like a rock. So glad you liked my driving." There it was again—that self-deprecating sense of humor.

I stood completely still, seduced by the afternoon breeze. The fragrance of nearby foliage was pungent in the air. I felt almost betrayed at the thought of having to return to work. Mellowed by the gentle haze of sleep, I wanted to linger forever in this comfortable cocoon.

"Thank you," I said simply. "We're doing this next week. Thursday again, I think. Yes, Thursday the fourteenth, to Chapel Hill. Board of Governors." My mind was flipping rapidly through next week's schedule. "It will take us all day, so clear your calendar."

"I look forward to it," said Paul. This time he said it without mockery or even a grin. Instead he smiled, his eyes looking deeply into mine and holding the gaze for several seconds. It was a different kind of look, one I had not seen earlier. Again I felt the flutter. This time, however, it was more like a kick that launched its way upward until it landed in my throat. It constricted so tightly I knew I could not speak.

Reluctantly, I turned and headed up Wellstone's wide concrete steps.

Chapter 6
TRAGEDY ON CAMPUS

Early the next morning, the ring of the phone jarred me from my sleep. I reached my bare arm from under the sheets and fumbled for the receiver. The neon dial on my alarm clock beamed 5:03.

Paul Stafford was on the other end.

"Katherine? Sorry to wake you up so early." He had no need to apologize. I sat up instantly, every nerve alert.

"Hi." Later, recalling the scene, I distinctly remembered saying nothing professional—just "hi."

"Bad news, I'm afraid."

I sucked in my breath.

"Suicide, apparently. A male student jumped—or rolled, it's not clear—from his dorm window. It probably happened about two o'clock. His roommate discovered the open window when the flapping blinds woke him. He saw the body below and called us."

"Which dorm?"

"Richardson."

"Who's been notified?"

"Jake Mooney was on the scene immediately, and he asked me to call you. He's called the family. They're from Raleigh. The student was a sophomore—a Sig Ep, although not in the house—good student and nice kid, from all I've heard. Name is David Weise. Everyone's in shock, of course. The family wants answers. No one saw this coming."

"Dreadful." My voice broke.

"The coroner's on the scene now. Cause of death will probably be blunt trauma. The kid didn't drink at all, from what I understand, but there will be toxicology tests with the autopsy. The body is being taken to Piedmont Memorial."

"Is the family coming?"

"Yes. They're expected by midmorning and will go straight to the hospital, then here. Would you like to meet with them?"

"Absolutely. Have them come to the house. They can use the back guest room during the afternoon. That will give them a telephone and as much privacy as they need. How's Jake handling this?"

"He's a pro." Paul uttered a sound that was nearly a chuckle. "The guy is at his best in a crisis."

"Jake has a crisis plan for everything. He'll have counselors on the scene for students. Ask him to call me at his first opportunity."

"Right. Where will you be?"

"In my office by eight. Please have Jake relay my deepest condolences to the family. I'll tell them in person when they get here. I want updates throughout the day, Paul."

"Roger that."

I burrowed under my flouncy bedding to digest the tragic news. My mind darted from one sad image to another. I thought about the young man's desperation, his stealthy tugs to raise the window, his anguish as he faced the black hole below the sloped roof. I envisioned the father's contorted face when Jake shattered him with the news before dawn. I felt the terror of the mother who heard half a conversation from her side of the bed.

Enough. I dressed for the day, made coffee, and wrote out special instructions for Lennie. At seven I started phoning the news to my cabinet members. As a courtesy, I also called Carrington, who I knew would already be up with the *Charlotte Observer*. He grunted when I told him the sad story.

"Got to keep control, Katherine," he admonished me. "This won't look a bit good in the papers." I heard a newspaper rattle in the background, as though he were punctuating his comment with an exclamation point.

Then I headed for my car. I was fixated on the idea of observing the scene, getting a clearer mental picture of exactly what had taken place. I backed out of the garage and circled around the top of the broad driveway, pointing the nose of the car forward. I ventured several blocks through the back side of the still-sleeping campus toward Richardson Hall.

The dormitory, ironically, was the newest building on campus, having opened doors for its first students only two weeks earlier. It was named in honor of Stephen Richardson, a wealthy businessman who owned five Ford dealerships in the Carolinas and Virginia. His wife, Sheila, was the daughter of one of Wickfield's charter alumnae—class of 1892—and in the mother's memory they together had contributed ten million dollars toward the new building. Their wealth had been accumulated through years of frugality and dogged determination.

Nailing down the dormitory gift had been Bob Atterbury's biggest success to date as Wickfield's chief fund-raiser. After nearly two years of discussion with Steve and Sheila, he had finally sealed the deal on the private-gift agreement. He had correctly assumed that Sheila Richardson would want her name included as a prime donor to the building—indeed, he had built his gift request around this premise. The strategy had worked.

Of the twosome, Sheila had been by far the more difficult to handle, harping on every detail.

"Hell, Steve just wants to sign the dotted line," Bob had told me when I asked why the agreement was taking so long to close. "If we let her, Sheila will bake the bricks and mix the mortar herself." An Asheville artist was completing an oil painting of the couple, to be unveiled during the building's dedication in late October. Special lettering that spelled out "Richardson Hall" had been ordered for the side of the building that faced busy Merritt Street.

Now the building stood silent in the early morning amber. Its rose-brick walls soared straight up for eight floors, an amazing match to the Neoclassical style of much of the campus. The rigidity was softened by dormer windows and mansard roofs. I drove along Jordan Drive, the main interior street, observing the yellow police tape and the presence of both Wickfield and City of Hurley police cars. I did not see Paul and imagined him inside with Jake. I visualized the shock being felt by students as they awakened. I returned somberly to my driveway, parked outside the garage, and walked over to Wellstone. There I holed myself in my office. It was impossible to shake off my desolate mood.

Not surprisingly, I thought of Daddy. Suicide had been an anathema to him. During his thirty years as dean of students at Arden, he had encountered very few student suicides, but each had devastated him to the core.

"It's the worst thing—absolutely the worst—that could happen to a family," I remembered him saying when I was a teenager. Murder, drowning, plane crashes, death in war—he ticked off the most hideous ways of dying and defied anyone to tell him they were more costly to the human spirit than the endurance of a loved one's suicide.

As a little girl I had adored my father, and for the first few years of our young lives, he seemed a nearly perfect father to me. As the third consecutive daughter, I was the one whose gender was most disappointing at birth, so it surprised the family to observe that Daddy doted on me as much as he did the others. I was scarcely four when he began teaching me how to tie my shoes, often seating me on the running board of our old Pontiac to demonstrate. I would watch in fascination while he made the big loop, my nose nearly touching the shoe leather when looking for the hole where the string should poke through. Daddy was patient, coaxing my too-young fingers to bend and hold and push at the right juncture.

Breakfast was another time I'd loved with Daddy. He showed me how to pull apart the sections of a tangerine, each segment plump in my hand before exploding in my mouth in a surge of sweet liquid. He taught me how to sprinkle an exact amount of sugar on top of my Wheaties so that it glazed onto the flakes when softened by milk.

But when it came to his attitude about the family bathrooms, Harold Embright had been an enigma to all. Our two-story Victorian house was large by normal standards, with a formal living room, a dining room that seated twelve with the extra table leaves, an airy kitchen, a breakfast room with a bowed window facing the backyard, and a parlor where the piano stood and the ironing board was stored. The four bedrooms were spacious even with two persons in a room.

The two bathrooms, however, gained the most attention.

"One for the men, the other for the ladies," Daddy would say to female guests when explaining why they had to climb the stairs to use the bathroom. The gentlemen's bathroom—the one downstairs, the one coveted by the six females in the house—he had deemed to be his alone.

To be accurate, there was a third bathroom of sorts, a tiny stall behind the kitchen pantry that the builder had included as a maid's bathroom. It held only a toilet and sink—not even a mirror—and had barely enough room in which to maneuver. Although there was no ventilation, we girls sometimes ventured in if the upstairs line grew long. If truth be told, this tiny bathroom was almost luxurious in comparison to similar arrangements in my friends' homes. Sally Gordon, for example, lived in a rambling turreted house that had a freestanding maid's toilet in the basement. The porcelain base stood in the open next to the washing machine, with the unfurled toilet paper perched on the dank cement floor.

Until Benny's death, Daddy's obsession over the family bathrooms had been something of a joke within the Arden community, but when he lost Benny and turned reclusive, the joviality ceased. Town gossips said our family had lost our father as well, and I knew there was some truth to that. I had been thirteen that wretched summer and had grieved as hard as any of my sisters. For three short years Benny had been a treasure, a blessing who added heart and soul to all of our lives. For Mother, who was forty-one when he was born, the relief of giving birth to a male child was immeasurable. For all of us, there were picture books to read and colors to teach. We adored our baby brother.

"Get the ball, Benny!"

I shook myself from my reverie. Death stalked my thoughts this morning. With little activity yet in Wellstone, I decided to take solace by walking through the quiet halls. According to Wickfield legend—the campus was full of century-old lore—Wellstone Hall was inhabited by ghosts. I usually dismissed such rumors as nonsense, but I remembered them now as I climbed the stairs to the fourth floor in the eerie stillness. This top floor was my favorite, in spite of the fact that it was off-limits to the public and used mainly for storage. It was the silent statues that attracted me. Around the turn of the century, when Wickfield was training many of the state's future educators, the school's then-president had become convinced that Wickfield's women needed exposure to the classics. He'd promptly ordered a large shipment of Greek and Roman statuary from Europe, some carved from authentic marble, others in plaster cast. Some towered eight feet or so in height. At one time these reproductions, including a bare-breasted Venus de Milo and a starkly muscular David, ornamented the top of each stairwell in Wellstone Hall.

After a refurbishing in the mid-sixties, however, when indignant alumnae objected to nudity on a now-coed campus, even if sanctified as art, Venus and David and scores of other statues were spirited from public view to the now-defunct fourth-floor hallway. When I first discovered this secret repository, I was drawn to it instantly. Sometimes when I needed a break from my desk, I slipped up to the sanctuary of the fourth floor. I liked to roam the hallway's entire length and linger at favorite statues. I especially admired the lovely form of The Bather and sometimes rubbed my hand over the maiden's modest draping. My plan was to move the statuary to the forthcoming School of the Arts—a pet project of mine—that would be housed in the domed Marcus Building. I loved visualizing this vast collection in its future home a year from now.

Today, however, the sculptures brought little comfort as they stood in the half-light of the musty hall. I paused at Adrianne, noting her exquisite stance as she stood with her water jug. I moved on to Eros and Psyche, arms stretched out to each other in passionate longing. I studied the young lovers, remembering the ancient mythology that forbade them to look at each other. My hand lightly brushed the tip of one of Eros's wings. Like the granite of a tombstone, its chiseled marble was cold to my touch.

A shiver passed over me. I turned to the stairway and fled downstairs to my office, reaching for the banister between the fourth and third floors as I footed the ancient cupped stairway steps. Jackie had arrived and was making coffee in the kitchenette, and I welcomed the burbles of the perking pot.

Soon after nine, an unshaven and somber Jake Mooney settled heavily on my settee and filled me in on details. No, David Weise had shown no outward signs of depression before taking his life. No, he was not known to be on drugs. Yes, he had many friends, and no, he had not broken up with a girlfriend recently. He was not far enough into the semester to be failing any subjects. Indeed, he had been in unusually good spirits during the few days before the suicide.

"His friends are shocked beyond belief," Jake said. He mentioned a core of three inseparable friends—Michael, Jay, and Zander—who were nothing less than bewildered. I also fielded a couple of calls from the press, wishing desperately that our new public-relations officer were already hired and well-versed in duties. Carl, the previous director, had moved to a college in South Carolina, and his position was not yet filled. In spite of my ease before a microphone, I was never eager to talk to reporters for fear of being misquoted. Still, words flowed easily today. I lamented the futility of having a young life snuffed out so tragically, and I quickly deflected one caller's suggestion that the university had failed in its responsibility to protect its students.

"Wickfield University most certainly provides and maintains a robust environment of security for our students within our gates," I said. "The health and security of our students is of utmost concern at all times. Even so, we recognize that as a public institution we are also part of a larger society and part of all the influences, good and bad, that society brings to our students."

In spite of the formality of my institutional quote, I felt hot tears pricking my eyes when I hung up the phone. Beyond all my high-flung prose like "robust environment," the images that most deeply touched me were those of a dead son, a lost brother, and a broken family.

Chapter 7
DEALING WITH DEATH

The rest of the tragic morning moved quickly. Paul called. The Weise family had arrived and had met with Jake and a group of David's closest friends. Now they wanted to meet with me.

"Bring them to the Chancellor's House at noon," I said.

Later, as I walked back to the house to meet them, I reflected on words to say to this crumpled family. My own family's reaction to Benny's death was blurred in my memory—clearly a defense against visiting that terrible space. But I did recall the horror at the park where the accident had occurred, the ghastly and ghostly blinking lights, the caterwauling sirens, and the frantic ride to the hospital behind the ambulance.

Even worse were those desperate summer nights in the weeks after the funeral. Our grieving family had counted on sleep to diminish our nightmares. What we had yet to endure, however, was the cadence of each other's darkest weeping. Bedroom by bedroom, our grief burst forth. The Embright home was wracked that summer with the bereavement of an inconsolable family.

The Weise family had not yet reached that terrible nadir. Watching from the curtains of an upstairs bedroom, I saw Paul's police car pull into my driveway, followed by a black Honda Accord. I observed what appeared to be an ordinary man and woman and teenage boy alight and gather themselves in a tiny huddle before following Paul onto the breezeway. I greeted the family at the kitchen door, assuming they would appreciate the privacy of the secluded entrance. I saw then the pain-struck father, the mother bent with sobs, the brother stooped in silence. They followed me into my formal living room.

"The entire college campus shares your loss," I began. I waited to take my cues from them, and gradually the questions came.

"Why? Why on earth did this happen?" Jeffery Weise, the father, appeared lost and bewildered.

"Why did no one see this coming? David was excited when he left home two weeks ago. He couldn't wait to get back to Wickfield." Amy Weise's misery was so acute in her face that I was forced to look away.

"When a death is as futile as David's, there are no clear answers, at least not at this point."

As our brief conversation continued, I realized my presence was helping very little. This family was pierced to the core with raw grief. I paused while Amy Weise blotted her eyes with a fresh Kleenex.

"Whatever it takes, the university will find some answers to what took place last night and why. We will talk to David's friends and classmates and professors—everyone and anyone who might help us ascertain what led to his death. We may not know the whole truth for a long time, but we will keep trying. I know promises won't bring back your son and brother, but they might spare other families from the tragedy you're experiencing." We sat in silence, each of us struggling with our emotions. The grandfather clock in the foyer, whose tones normally rang mellow, seemed to interrupt now with a clang.

Finally I stood. There was nothing more to say. The family slowly rose to their feet, and I embraced each of the three silently. I ushered them onto the sun porch, where Lennie stood waiting with potato soup and egg salad.

In the kitchen, Paul was sitting at the table, eating a sandwich that Lennie had served him. He stood when I entered.

"They're in terrible shock," I told him, leaning against the sink. "This must never happen again here. I feel we've failed them. We need a better way to identify those students who are vulnerable."

"Don't be so hard on yourself, Prez." I was startled to hear Paul call me that curious nickname again. No one ever called me Prez, especially since I was a regional chancellor. Chancellor sounded a tad fancier than president.

"You're not to blame, and neither is Wickfield. We're only two weeks into the school year. Whatever triggered this tragedy could have been planted years ago. You'll spook yourself into illness if you feel personally responsible for kids like David."

Paul's words were rational, and I felt new respect for this man who had received my disdain only yesterday morning. I was relieved that the day's events demanded total professionalism. Yesterday's off-balance feeling had vanished. I had made strong leadership decisions all morning, totally in charge every step of the way.

I thought about Alex. Although he was coming tomorrow for his weekend visit, I craved hearing his voice yet tonight. He would be a good listener if my dinner party ended in time. We rarely talked late at night, since Alex's surgery schedule required strict bedtime hours. Still, since Chicago was an hour earlier than my East Coast time, we might yet steal a few moments.

During the dinner that evening, surrounded by translucent bone china and crystal goblets in my formal dining room, I pushed the suicide to a distant corner of my mind. I let Bob Atterbury carry much of the conversation with the prospective donor, a silver-haired and somewhat pompous CEO of a major New York investment company. Susan Atterbury and I tried with limited success to converse with the wife, a portly woman with over-permed hair and wrists weighed down by massive rings and bracelets. I found the couple unbearably boring. They had adult children in their forties but no grandchildren, and I wondered silently what sorts of joys sparked their marriage. I had a sudden image of sterile lives, as empty as inky-stamped passports from annual cruises that led nowhere.

The miserable evening finally ended. I closed up the downstairs and headed straight for my bedroom phone.

Alex answered on the first ring. Dear Alex. He listened sympathetically as I summarized my day. This was our third conversation of the week, each seemingly more dramatic in nature than the one before. As I had predicted, the conversation eased my angst.

"How did your day go yesterday?" Alex asked just before we hung up. He asked it almost like an afterthought.

"Yesterday?"

"You know. Your trip with the chauffeur."

"Oh. Okay, I guess. He gave me my space. I slept all the way back."

"Atta girl. Can't wait to see you, Kat. It should be a good weekend. Even if USAir couldn't give me an aisle seat."

"Be safe, Alex."

As we signed off, I recognized exactly how much I needed this weekend with Alex. In fact, I needed Alex more than ever *right now*, I thought emphatically, reaching for a padded suit hangar as I prepared for bed. He was supportive when I craved it most, and he was a good companion. Besides, it was good for the college community to know that Alex was a mainstay in my life. I knew the campus gossips wondered aloud about the nature of our relationship, but I didn't care. Somehow Alex had defied becoming a problem.

I studied my image in the mirror as I went through my bedtime routine. I would turn fifty in four months, and I was increasingly sensitive about my looks. "Damn good-looking woman" was how Alex liked to describe me. Long ago I'd realized that my height at five feet eight inches—an embarrassment in my gawky early teens—was a captivating asset. When I wore heels, I commanded even more presence. There was something about being as tall as many of the men in a room that suggested an extra measure of authority.

Yes, I decided, tossing my robe at the foot of my bed, Alex was more important to me than ever. Sometime later this fall when he visited, I would have some colleagues over for steaks on the grill—maybe the cabinet and deans. It wouldn't hurt to remind them that I had a special and faithful man in my life.

As I turned out the light, my thoughts flickered to the Weise family and today's campus sadness. I was exhausted. So much had happened this week. Was it really only four days ago I had been stranded on the parkway in Virginia?

Then there was Paul. Paul Stafford. His name turned over in my mind. He had certainly turned out differently from the way I anticipated. Paul...

For the second time in three nights, Paul Stafford was the last thought on my mind before I fell asleep.

Chapter 8
ALEX

Alex called early the next morning and cancelled for the entire weekend. I was already dressing in eager anticipation when my bedroom phone lit up.

"Doggone it, Kat, I can't make it. We've got a heart transplant and have to move fast. They've called in both teams. We could easily go into night. But, hey, let's shoot for next weekend. I can make it work."

Doggone it yourself, I thought as I hung up. I was keenly disappointed. I sank onto the edge of my bed, absorbing the abrupt change that had just blown my way. I hated sudden letdowns. Alex's cancellations, few though they were, had thrown me out of balance in the past.

Immediately, I thought ahead to "next weekend." That would be the weekend of the faculty-staff family picnic, held in front of Wellstone Hall on the broad lawn that bordered Grove Boulevard. It was an ideal spot, because traffic on Grove could see our families queuing up for Southern barbecue and seated at cheerfully decorated tables. I encouraged the idea of creating a strong public image of camaraderie. Even more important, the event was hugely popular within the Wickfield community. Each year we featured a special attraction for faculty children, like a big-footed clown that danced with balloons, or a docile pony that gave rides while clopping around the Wellstone fountain.

During my two earlier years as Wickfield's chancellor, Alex had not attended the affair. He had been present at other events, and he had met my closest circle of colleagues, but his visits had never coincided with the picnic. I did not mind attending such gatherings without a partner—especially this particular picnic, which was one of my favorites among annual campus events. I tried to review the attendees' list in advance, re-memorizing spouses' names and recalling faces.

Now that Alex would be here, too, I would let him circulate on his own. He wouldn't mind. He would prefer introducing himself here and there rather than have me drag him through every gaspy hug. Besides, once word circulated as to his identity—"It's Katherine's doctor-friend from Chicago!" they would whisper—many would doubtless approach him on their own. Some might even saddle him with a personal medical question unrelated to his expertise as a surgeon.

"So much for having a few people over for steaks," I muttered to myself. "Might as well have the *whole campus* see the man in my life."

Amazingly, I now found myself facing an empty weekend. I had cleared my calendar intentionally, looking forward to waking up with Alex tomorrow and stealing another round of lovemaking in the drowsy languor of Sunday morning. Alex, who was handy in the kitchen, usually made breakfast: Canadian bacon, scrambled eggs with grated Parmesan cheese, buttered wheat toast, juice. Then he would carry it grandly on a tray to the sun porch, where he would find me buried in newspapers.

"Happy Valentine's Day," he would say, bending over for a quick peck. He said it whatever the time of year—February, July, or November, it didn't matter. *Valentine's Day* was his code for "I love you."

On this morning, without Alex, I found myself strangely restless. I had a whole Saturday to myself, a luxury I fantasized about in my moments of deepest fatigue. Now that it was here, I was unprepared. Time yawned before me like a gaping mouth. I wandered into the living room, skimming my fingers through rapid arpeggios on the baby grand's keyboard. I rubbed my hand over the inlaid panels on an antique chest with droplet handles, a family heirloom.

In the dining room, I found myself drawn to the crystal collection behind the glass doors of my walnut hutch. I opened the doors carefully, tugging a tad to release them where they stuck, and reached for the tall cut-glass pitcher etched with roses. It had been a cherished wedding gift to my mother, who had filled it with sweetened iced tea and freshly sliced lemons whenever company came.

There was something about being surrounded with beauty like crystal pitchers that was as essential to me as air itself. I sucked it in like oxygen. The Chancellor's House fit me perfectly. I never called it "my" house but always "the Chancellor's House" in a breathy sort of way that revealed my enormous respect for its century-old grandeur. Others might think it strange that a single woman would live alone among its spacious twelve rooms, but I reveled in it. Every niche was a treasure. I loved the grand staircase, the wainscoted walls, the tongued grooves in the doorsills. I knew every architectural nuance and had studied the home's history in detail.

The best feature was the plethora of bathrooms—five of them. "There's one for each Embright sister," I realized gleefully, remembering the bathroom dilemma of our childhoods. I had tried to organize a family reunion that first summer, but my sisters, although excited at the prospect, had not been able to meet at the same time. Next summer, they promised. Now the third summer had passed, and I had yet to get my entire family under the roof of the Chancellor's House.

I eventually found myself in my favorite room—the bricked-in sun porch. Its wide windows beamed out onto the landscaped side lawn with the sunny rose garden. Suddenly I was inspired to spend my newfound day of freedom here, surrounded by my current books and magazines. I roamed from room to room to gather them, unloading a pile on the floor by the couch. I cranked open the windows and turned on the ceiling fan to pull in the outside breeze. Then I filled the crystal pitcher with lemonade and ice and stretched out languorously. I read fast, in snippets, switching by the hour from fiction to gardening magazines to a popular new business book on management styles. By late morning I had dozed off.

It was the day of the picnic, and I was standing alone, holding a plate of barbecued pork and looking at the milling crowd. Alex stood on a little hill in the background, looking down at me. I waved and smiled, and he waved back. Then Paul Stafford appeared, seated next to me on a wide concrete step, plate in hand. He was eating grilled sirloin steak, and I kidded him about rejecting my choice of menu for the picnic. "I like your food," Paul said. "It's the boyfriend I don't like."

I awoke sharply and stared up at the spinning fan. Paul would meet Alex next Saturday, and vice versa. What was so strange about that? Why this silly dream? It perplexed me. I was sure Alex and Paul would like each other. Alex already approved of Paul, if *approved* was the appropriate word. If they didn't bond, so what?

I fretted the rest of the day, unable to concentrate on my reading. This wasn't like me. I always found plenty to do. I thought about going to my office—my desk and daily planner were like wine to my soul—but the idea of work repelled me today. I ended up going to bed early. I tossed and turned all night, my body resistant to the benefits of sleep.

The next morning, I slipped into a side pew at Grace Episcopal Church for the eleven o'clock service. I loved attending the little stone church with the terraced landscaping and wide circular front driveway. I was entranced by its rich stained-glass windows and the intricate carved partition that separated the nave from the chancel. I had begun attending Episcopal services with Tim soon after we'd married. I found the stately hymns and formal Episcopal worship so similar to the Lutheran rituals of my girlhood that I adapted quickly.

"You do church well," Tim used to tell me. That was a stretch of a compliment for Tim, like admitting I "did" cooking or laundry well.

Today, I tried to find a sense of calmness for my restive spirit. I closed my eyes, letting the power of the choir-led music envelop me. *Why, dear God, am I so distracted? I have so much work to do. Help me use my time today well. Help me to be productive. Help me to help Wickfield. Help me to be the best possible leader. Show me how, Lord. Use me.*

Prayer came easily to me. My earliest childhood memory involved the recitation of "Now I lay me" before Sarah and I turned out the lights. Instead of the scary "if I should die before I wake," our parents had taught gentler words: "May angels watch o'er me this night, and help me do whate'er is right." Mealtime prayer was similar: "Thank you, Jesus, for this food. Help us always to be good."

"The Embright girls could only have been sterling kids," I joked once to Alex. "We had a straight line to goodness."

"Too bad," he joked back. "Good girls don't have fun."

As for my soul, I was almost blasé. Heaven was an obvious goal, an easy destination. God and I had always been on close terms. *Forever and ever, amen.* If there was one thing in life I was sure about, it was my afterlife.

But today, uneasy, I had a childhood memory of watching my mother in church, her eyes closed in deep meditation, lips moving with the memorized texts of the liturgy. I was looking up from my crayons and scribbled bulletin and wondering why this mother, the exemplar of all that was good, prayed so much. Sometimes Mother brushed away tears while she knelt.

Come on, Lord, I muttered to myself as I drove home. *Get me out of this funk.* Saturday's dream flashed through my mind again, and I suddenly found myself wondering what Paul was doing today.

CLAIRE

Alex called again Sunday, apologetic about the cancellation. I explained about the upcoming picnic. "We won't have a lot of time alone," I warned. "I'll be in work mode."

"Tiger, not kitten," Alex teased. He knew how intense I became when energized by my work. All of my senses were heightened.

I ignored the intimate reference. "So, try to come Friday night," I said.

"No problem. Jack will cover me. No beeper. Promise."

Later that evening I reviewed the remaining applications for the public-relations position. This was a key position, a significant hire. It was important to find an exemplary writer with an engaging personality who could work well with the public. Managerial experience helped, since the position came with an office assistant. It was a difficult combination to find, and the right candidate had eluded me so far.

But there was one more to go, a young woman from Pennsylvania who had been turned down by the search committee on the first cut. "No experience," someone had penciled on the resume. One of my former Maryland colleagues, who coincidentally served as a personal reference for this applicant, suggested she be given a second chance.

"Claire Matthews is sensational," she had told me when I phoned her. "Young, yes, but a quick learner. She will take on everything you throw at her." As a result, I was bringing her to campus Wednesday for interviews—including fifteen minutes with each cabinet member.

"Yes, she's a neophyte, but I hear she's a crackerjack writer, and we can work together on her managerial skills if she's short there," I told the cabinet Monday as we reviewed the schedule. "You already know how important this hire will be to each of your positions, so check her out carefully. Contact me as soon as you've talked to her, and give me impressions."

Claire's first interview Wednesday would be with me during a seven-thirty breakfast at the Chancellor's House. I liked watching candidates during a meal, observing how well they conversed under pressure while also making decisions about food. It was the perfect test of leadership.

"Serve those crackly breakfast rolls, the kind that spread crumbs when you break them apart," I told Lennie. "We'll see how she handles that."

"You bad, Miz Katherine," said Lennie, rolling her eyes.

I knew Lennie would serve a lovely breakfast. Visitors were always impressed with events in the Chancellor's House, comparing our hospitality with the best of Charleston's historic inns. All of Wickfield, in fact, reeked with Southern graciousness. I insisted on meticulous detail at every public event—a trait my staff sometimes chafed at—and a good public-relations officer would need to know the drill by heart.

When the doorbell chimed early Wednesday, I opened it to find an attractive blonde woman staring down at, of all things, her feet—minus her shoes. She glanced up with a hesitant smile, then bent over to tug one of the shoes from the metal grate in front of the door. Quickly, she stepped back into both shoes.

"Hello, Chancellor Embright," she said, holding out her hand. "I'm Claire Matthews. Sorry. My shoe got stuck in the grate," she added with a little laugh.

"Katherine Embright," I said, extending my hand and looking in wonderment at the floor of my porch. "Come in." No one had ever gotten stuck at the entryway before.

"They're new shoes," Claire added, stepping inside. "Oh, how beautiful!" She gazed in delight at the massive foyer and the stately staircase that ascended in front of her.

The incident momentarily unsettled me. I wasn't sure whether to apologize for the grate or be miffed at the strange introduction. I decided to ignore it.

At least I liked what I saw: late twenties, stylish short haircut with soft side bangs, hazel eyes, and an expressive face. Claire's smart caramel-colored suit set off the dark print blouse and black accessories. The new shoes were plain pumps with a high, narrow heel.

"Yes, this house has lots of history," I said, leading Claire into the living room. "It dates back to the late 1800s. Five different presidents have lived here. Before we started calling them chancellors." I placed Claire's umbrella and purse on a side table. "We're eating in here," I said, walking past the grand piano with its framed family photos and into the beautifully appointed dining room.

Claire glanced around, her eyes holding for a long second on the brocaded burgundy drapes. She joined me at the table, smiling directly at Lennie when she appeared with coffee. She said little at first, letting me lead the conversation. She ate without fanfare, politely turning down the offer of the hard rolls when Lennie appeared with a doily-covered basket.

"I almost felt as though I were the one being interviewed," I lamented to Marilyn later in the morning. "She answered my questions but asked a lot in return. She's apparently single; no wedding band. I couldn't ask, of course, but my friend from Maryland didn't mention a husband. I can't quite get a handle on her."

By the end of the day, I knew much more. According to Dan Jones, Claire had joked with him about meeting the chancellor in her stocking feet, but she also emphasized the importance of faculty research so she could match professors and expertise with media inquiries. She told Jake Mooney that the school's most challenging moments with the public would probably come within his area of student affairs. "The media pivots on fraternity misbehavior and student demonstrations," she said. She agreed with Bob Atterbury that positive press coverage was essential to his ability to raise funds. "Success creates trust," she said with a maturity that surprised Bob. And she told Pud that his teams' ability to win was as important to a positive public perception as anything she did in her department.

"I found her refreshing," Dan said. "She is bright and professional. And she doesn't take herself too seriously."

"She may not have a lot of direct PR experience, but she has good instincts," said Jake. "She knows her stuff."

"Alumni and donors would like her," Bob said. "Charming young woman. Very impressive."

"I liked her candor," Marilyn said. "And she had done her homework. She knew more about Wickfield's history than I did."

"She's definitely a looker," Pud said. I should have known he would use a word like *looker.*

As for her writing ability, I had nothing but confidence, based on samples submitted with her application. Bob Atterbury, who as head of Advancement would be Claire's direct supervisor, spent the next afternoon calling references on the list—including my friend who had referred her to us.

"We love Claire," she told Bob, much as she had told me earlier. "Would hate to lose her, but for what seem like personal reasons, she's eager for a change in setting."

By the end of the day Thursday, Bob had offered Claire the job.

"She officially starts in three weeks," I told Marilyn happily, "but Bob talked her into coming next week for a few days of crash training. He wants her up and running by Homecoming. Bob says she's thrilled with the job and that she felt connected to us the first moment she stepped on campus. 'Except when I *mis*-stepped on campus,' she told Bob, and then she laughed."

"Sounds like baptism by fire," said Marilyn.

"I'm betting she'll take us by storm!" I said.

I had no idea at the time how literal my prediction would turn out to be.

Chapter 10
BOARD OF GOVERNORS

Of all the challenges that beset me during those opening weeks of school, the most unwelcome one involved my growing awareness of Paul Stafford. When I was honest with myself, I had to face what was becoming more and more obvious to me: inappropriate personal thoughts about a Wickfield employee. A *married* Wickfield employee.

"Forget it," I scoffed to myself whenever Paul's face flashed before me. "Utterly, utterly ridiculous." The very idea that I could harbor such misguided feelings appalled me. I was, after all, known for my discipline, my need for order, my appropriate behavior choices. Not only that, I was a mature woman—forty-nine, to be exact. In January I would face my fiftieth birthday.

Fortunately, my good sense came to the rescue. I was glad that Claire's visit occupied my mind that Wednesday—the day before the Board of Governors meeting at UNC-Chapel Hill. Paul would be driving me there—or so we had discussed the week before. Before Wednesday was over, I needed to nail down details about our trip.

"Call Officer Stafford and have him pick me up tomorrow at seven," I directed Jackie. "Tell him to park in the driveway and come to the kitchen door." Although I had not discussed the new driving arrangement in detail with Jackie, she knew enough to handle the situation efficiently—and discreetly. I had no plans at present to reveal the "Carrington plan" to others.

Fortunately, the ride the next morning began smoothly. I was intentionally professional in my demeanor toward Paul. I sat in the back and studied the "BD of GOV" reading file Jackie had created for the trip. I reviewed the minutes of the June meeting and read through a mass of committee reports due for discussion. Paul was largely silent in the front seat until, almost two hours into the trip, we began passing landmarks for Winston-Salem.

"What about a rest stop, Prez?" he asked. "We have a little time to spare. There's a Cracker Barrel at the exit coming up."

A break was a great idea, I decided, quite bored by now in the back seat. That's how I found myself facing Paul at a Cracker Barrel table, letting him take the lead in conversation while I observed. He had revealed little about himself to this point, but this morning he mentioned casually that he was attending night-school classes in law.

"Law school?" I was thunderstruck. Paul managed a career, a family, and *law school*? Besides, he had to be at least fifty, a mature age for launching a new career. I studied him over my coffee cup. My first impression had been that he was a large man—wide-shouldered and thick of neck. Now I realized it was raw, compact muscle that filled him out.

"Where?" I managed to ask.

"Charlotte. Just once a week, Wednesday nights. Last night. Got home before 11:30."

It had never occurred to me that our out-of-town trips might interfere with Paul's personal life. I was quite certain Carrington knew nothing about Paul and law school. Such commuting required strict discipline and could be a major constraint on job performance. Last night, apparently, Paul had scarcely gone to bed before he had to get up to be on the road with me this morning.

As if reading my thoughts, Paul tried to ease my concerns. "Don't worry about Wednesdays. I can miss a night here or there if I have to."

As we resumed our travel along the interstate, I found myself thoughtful in the back seat. Paul never ceased to surprise me. He was uncommonly bright, that was obvious. He was—nice, darn it. Maybe too nice. These trips could be easier if he were boring enough for me to ignore him, or at least slight him with some mild disdain. "Nice" seemed trite, but I had been reared in a home that rewarded good manners. Okay, so he was also charming. Charm was not new to me. I had encountered charming men all my life and had learned when to be wary. But Paul's hangdog, boyish charm seemed genuine, not contrived.

And his eyes! What was that distinctive thing about Paul's eyes that made me want to lower my own a second too quickly when speaking with him? I decided it was the way they started to smile before his mouth did, hinting of a merry thought working its way to the forefront. It caught me off balance, as though he could bore through my skull and read my most private thoughts.

I observed him from my oblique rear view, taking in his strong profile. I had to hand it to him: he was actually quite handsome. Years ago I had stopped scoring men in terms of their physical attractiveness, preferring to judge them on their intellectual strength or depth of character. Surely women noticed Paul. For one thing, he had a great head of hair for a man in his fifties. It was turning gray around the temples, yet it was thick on top and in back, and the waviness contrasted neatly with his short, crisp sides. Why was it that men got better-looking as they grew older while women struggled with the process? Graying hair and facial creases made attractive men look wiser. Distinguished, even. Rugged. What kindly words described a handsome woman with graying hair and facial creases? Mature? An aging beauty? A lovely older woman? It all seemed pitifully unfair.

By now I was eager to get through my long day of meetings to begin the return trip with Paul. In spite of my promise to be cautious, I wanted to learn more about this intriguing man. For starters, I could be friendlier. I *would* be friendlier! I would engage him in conversation. I would get him to talk about himself. Hey, I might even sit in the front seat! I smiled to myself at the thought.

Finally we wheeled into Chapel Hill on the 15-501 bypass, turning southwest and spotting the signs to the UNC campus. "The University of North Carolina. Founded 1795," proclaimed an historical marker. Had we turned northeast we would be passing signs to Duke University, Duke Gardens, and Duke Chapel. The nation knew these two universities as academic powerhouses and arch-rivals in basketball, but few outside of North Carolina knew that their outer campuses lay a mere eight miles apart. Both schools were highly ranked in more fields than I could count, and both claimed athletic supremacies that others merely dreamed about. Yet their contrasts in profile were distinctive. One was United Methodist and handsomely endowed; the other was nationally historic and ensnared by state politics.

Those state politics would doubtless permeate today's meeting—perhaps subtly, but they would influence the speed with which our discussions moved. Most board members were distinguished: business executives, entrepreneurs, educators, attorneys. Their expertise was respected and valued. Not surprisingly, there were also those on the board who, like Carrington, were consumed with inflated pride. Hopefully the blusterers would be kept at bay today.

"We should be out by 4:30," I noted as Paul turned into the parking lot of the General Administration Building. "You might want to explore East Franklin Street while you wait—lots of quaint shops and restaurants. Did you bring a book?"

Paul held up a yellow legal pad from the front seat. "Last night's class notes right here. Thought I might find a quiet bench somewhere. Any suggestions?"

I almost laughed at his question. UNC's main quad was famous for its canopy of trees and breeze-cooled benches.

"Just enter the campus anywhere from Franklin Street and follow the sidewalks. You'll find a bench, guaranteed." I thought about mentioning Silent Sam—surely Paul would pass the famous statue—but thought better of it. Campus legend swore that the beloved Confederate soldier fired his gun every time a virgin passed.

With little time to spare, I found my way to the board's meeting room, pinned on my plastic name badge, and studied the day's agenda. As newest chancellor in the state university system, I was still learning my way through the ropes with the Board of Governors. I enjoyed a bit of notoriety as a woman and as a relative newcomer to the enclave. There were sixteen campuses within the state's network, and chancellors were expected to attend as many board meetings as possible. Although we had no vote, we did have voice. Our meeting locations rotated among the campuses.

Today's meeting was laboriously long. As usual, there were committee reports upon reports: budget and finance, university governance, university health, public affairs. Although I usually raked in information with interest, today's agenda seemed like much ado about nothing. I found myself impatient, wanting to advance both the schedule and the clock.

Yet one report caught my attention as utterly fascinating, and it came from the Committee on the Future of Technology. Its chairman gave a dramatic description of an impending system of electronic mail for universities. He explained how professors at the University of Minnesota had developed a communication technology—they named it "Gopher" after their campus mascot—which allowed professors to send digital messages directly to each other on their computers. The technology would be easy enough to access, and future implications were staggering: conversations through the computer screen not only between offices but even between campuses! If Wickfield computers were equipped with the same technology, students and professors could discuss assignments, even grades, by the mere click of a computer key.

At the end of the presentation, the chancellors buzzed with questions and dominated the discussion. We had been hearing snippets about this electronic mail system—"e-mail," as it was being dubbed—for months. Dan and I had already speculated on a timeline for Wickfield, hoping to have campus e-mail within the year. I made a mental note to have Kevin Merriweather, Wickfield's director of technology, update the cabinet.

Many on the board, I noticed, had little to say in this discussion. In fact, as a group they seemed unable to ask appropriate questions about e-mail. Most were telephone communicators, I realized, contemplating their various professions. The telephone played a major role in their control of power. Writing was not necessarily a major priority. Many had secretaries who made grammatical decisions involving their dictated letters.

If this new e-mail were to become the wave of the future, the power in communication skills would shift to those who wrote well—not to those with blustery voices. This was an interesting discovery, and I surveyed the room with a little wave of shock. I tried to envision a Board of Governors meeting five years from now, wondering which powerhouses around the table would become the new bastions of authority.

Change was coming, and quickly. Without a doubt, this new e-mail would not be welcomed by all.

Chapter 11
THE DINER

It was well after 4:30 when I emerged from the Board of Governors meeting. The late afternoon sun was pouring into the parking lot where Paul was waiting. He walked around to the passenger side as I approached my Victoria.

"Nap time?" he asked, gallantly swinging open the back door.

"Second-wind time," I said matter-of-factly. I handed Paul my briefcase. "How about tossing this into the back seat."

Paul set the briefcase on the floor of the back seat and quickly switched his grip to the front passenger door. I was grateful he didn't feign surprise or make a smart comment—he merely grinned as I climbed in.

"First time I've ever ridden in this seat," I commented as he slid in next to me behind the steering wheel. "It's roomier than I thought."

We encountered heavy congestion as we headed out of Chapel Hill. I knew well the treachery of traffic in a crowded college town, where pedestrians ruled the streets and rarely gave way to oncoming vehicles. Paul drove deftly as he maneuvered between lanes. I was acutely aware of him next to me—his wide shoulders, the light wool fabric of his suit jacket, the stylish black-tinted sunglasses that blocked his face.

"I talked to Lydia Weise," I commented. "Called her during the lunch break."

"How are they doing?"

"Still grieving hard. She said friends have been wonderful. Lots of out-of-town relatives came for the funeral. The church was packed, and a large group of students showed up. The family liked that. Jake went, you know. Took a carload."

"That family will never be the same," Paul said quietly. "A crisis of that nature changes them for life."

He turned on his blinker to merge into the interstate, heading west. "How's *your* family doing?" he asked, changing the subject.

Perhaps it was the casual way he asked the question, as if he had known the Embright family for years. Perhaps it was the way he looked into his left rearview mirror, head turned away from me, that inspired me to fill the space. Perhaps it was simply his comfortable physical presence.

Whatever the trigger, I began to talk, and I continued to chatter for the next thirty miles. It was as though a stopper had come unhinged from the top of my throat. I described the old family house in Arden with its wide verandah and front-porch swing, the foyer's sparkling chandelier, the stained-glass window on the landing where the stairs reversed themselves. I mentioned the backyard fig tree whose low sturdy branches made a secret bunker for my summertime reading. I talked about growing up with four sisters, our carefree adventures on the nearby campus, and the influences of the red-doored St. John's Church at the bottom of Ingleside Drive.

"Which sister did you fight with the most?" Paul's teasing tone suggested I had omitted certain stories.

I mulled that one over. I was closest in age to Sarah, who was not even two years older, but we had not been close as sisters. Sarah had resented sharing toys as a child and refused to share clothes as a teenager. Mother tried to mediate our cat fights, often without success. Daddy usually took my side in a dispute. Even as an adult, Sarah was cool toward me.

Marianna, on the other hand, was both level-headed and compassionate. As the eldest, she had felt it her responsibility to mentor the rest of us, and I had often benefited in the process. There was a gap of nearly five years after me before Emily was born, followed soon by Jane, then Benny a year later. "I birthed two generations," my mother often joked. I was in college and graduate school when my younger sisters were teenagers. I had missed much of their upbringing.

"We had our normal squabbles," I answered. It was too complicated to explain my awkward relationship with Sarah. "Some of us have grown closer as adults. I guess I'm closest now to Marianna, who lives in Richmond, and Emily, who's in remission from cancer. Sarah still lives in Arden— never moved. Jane's in California. Her husband's in the Navy, a lieutenant commander. We don't see them that often."

"Where's Emily?"

"She and her husband live in Florida. Jacksonville. It was breast cancer, and the doctors see no sign of recurrence. But it was touch and go there for a while." I grimaced as I recalled those frantic times. I didn't mention Benny. That story would save for another time.

"Are you as hungry as I am?" We were nearing an exit east of Greensboro. "We're still two hours from home. What kind of food do you like?"

"I'm starved," I admitted. "You pick it. Just find a place with real silverware."

"If you like good country cooking, I know a place that's off the main road, but it's worth every extra mile. Trust me?" He flipped his right-turn blinker.

"Sure." The idea of a country inn was appealing. And, I had to admit, so was the idea of a quiet meal with Paul. The man had stirred much more than my curiosity. I tried to quell an inner flutter of anticipation.

The drive was full of twists and turns, but I sensed we were going north, then west. We drove a full ten minutes on two-lane roads. We passed fields of late summer corn, soon to be cut as fodder for livestock, and fields abundant with dark-green leafy tobacco. The early evening sun was sinking on the horizon, hanging golden shadows on the rolling landscape. We both lowered our visors.

Paul finally slowed as we approached a small red-brick building fronted by a sign reading "Wendell's Place." He turned into the gravel lot. I stared in disbelief. This place was scarcely more than a wayside diner. Two Exxon gas pumps in front were anchored by wooden barrels of faded pink petunias.

Paul noticed my dismay. "Now, Prez, where's your sense of adventure? Doesn't look like much, but wait until you taste the food." He reached over and gave my hand a perfunctory pat. "No plastic forks. I promise."

I recovered quickly. From the outside, at least, the restaurant appeared to be clean. It was also private. No one would know us here—not that there was anything wrong with our eating together in public, I reminded myself. I had eaten countless times with Dan or Bob or Jake at favorite Hurley restaurants.

Inside, we passed restroom doors marked "Mens" and Ladie's." I spotted the requisite North Carolina Department of Health sanitation card, located in plain view as we entered the dining area. The score, written in large block numbers, read 94.5%. A waitress in a mauve-colored uniform waved us toward a booth. In spite of being overdressed, we were completely ignored by the handful of diners. I scooted across my cracked vinyl seat and reached for a plastic-covered menu.

The waitress followed with glasses of ice and a pitcher of water. "Y'all doing okay?" She didn't wait for a response. "Specials are on the wall," she said, gesturing to a giant blackboard with her elbow. Her name, according to the clip on her blouse, was Shelba. "They're $5.25, including beverage and cornbread or biscuits. But you can order from the menu, too. Coffee?" She disappeared to get the pot.

The specials were simple: pepper steak with rice, baked ham with pineapple sauce, fish strips with tartar sauce. Vegetables were mashed potatoes with brown gravy, black-eyed peas, and okra with stewed tomatoes. It wasn't clear whether one vegetable or all three came with the special, so I simply ordered the ham. Paul ordered the pepper steak. Shelba poured decaffeinated coffee and vanished again.

"How did you find this place?" I asked as I watched Paul tear open a packet of sugar.

"We low-lifers know all the back roads." I realized with a start that I still knew little about Paul. I had done all the talking today. How had that happened?

Shelba reappeared, this time with savory platters of the specials along with family-sized bowls of all three vegetables for us to share. The potatoes were heaped up like a snow drift, and the peas and tomatoes smelled fragrant and spicy. Shelba returned a minute later with smaller bowls of fried okra and sliced cucumbers in sour cream, which we had not ordered, and a plastic basket piled with golden hot biscuits and cornbread. They were warm to the touch.

"Cook says to eat up, looks like a slow night. Want some honey with your cornbread?"

She trotted off to find the honey pot, and Paul held up his sweaty water glass. "To your health," he said grandly, as though toasting me with a rare champagne. I clicked my glass against his and smiled. So far, so good.

True to Paul's prediction, the food was spectacular, cooked and seasoned to perfection. "You'd think Lennie never fed me," I observed. Usually a light eater, I was sampling everything on my plate with relish. Paul watched, pleased.

"Dessert's the best part," he warned.

We spoke easily of many things, and I savored every moment. I liked observing Paul when he bent over his plate, then connecting with his eyes when he looked up. I still hadn't figured out exactly why I enjoyed his company. I only knew I was becoming as comfortable with him as with Alex. How long had I known this man? Surely in some distant kingdom where lives merged like streams into a river, Paul and I had known each other well.

We lingered over homemade blackberry cobbler and whipped cream. Shelba brought more coffee. There was something intimate about sitting across from Paul, even more so than sitting next to him. It's the eye contact, I thought as I fished in a dish for a container of half-and-half. And his voice, too. It was deep and rich and floated directly toward me. I had always been attracted to men with strong speaking voices. Actually, I had married such a man. Tim had been a Radio-Television major at Carolina when we met.

"Think we'd better hit the road again?" Paul was looking at me, waiting for my cue. It was close to eight o'clock by now, but he wasn't rushing me. The check was lying casually on the table between us. Was he as reluctant to leave as I?

I sighed. "It's nice to be completely anonymous." I wondered how many people understood the stress endured by someone in the public eye. I longed to talk another hour in this refuge.

"Everyone needs a getaway," Paul said. "I've spent many an hour here. No one bothers me. No one cares, actually. It's the place where I can be my most honest self."

He reached for the check, and I reminded him that the meal was to be recorded against my travel budget. Back in the car, I mused over his words: *My most honest self.* As we passed darkened homes with muted lights in the windows, I wondered about the honesty in lives everywhere. What secrets were hidden behind these walls, where hard-working people were taking respite from the day? Were they engaged in family conversations? Sprawled in front of television sets? Connecting behind closed bedroom doors?

"You're quiet," Paul commented as we approached the interstate.

"Just thinking about my staff," I admitted. "I work with them so closely, and I think I know them well, but sometimes I wonder."

"Anyone in particular?" Paul's voice was casual.

"All of them. I count on them totally, I trust them explicitly, yet I'm certain they have elements in their personal lives that would totally surprise me."

"Count on it," Paul said.

"You sound like someone in the know."

"That's my job. I know every nook and cranny of the campus, I know whose car is parked where, I know what time people come and go. It's what you pay me to do."

An uneasy moment passed over me. How much did Paul know about my own private life? "Guess you keep an eye on my house, too." I said it as a statement, not a question.

"You bet. Yours is probably the safest spot on campus. I know when that boyfriend of yours shows up from Chicago, for example. He always rents a Lincoln at the Charlotte airport."

My jaw dropped. "You know that? How can you tell?"

"By his license tag. All rental car tags are coded." He entered the left lane to pass an eighteen-wheeler as we began an incline. "And don't forget the surveillance cameras. One is located on your garage."

It was true. I had always known that exterior cameras watched the grounds, but it never occurred to me they would capture such personal information.

"I'll make sure my lipstick is on straight when I go for my car." I sounded slightly annoyed. "Should I wave next time?"

"You always look great. You don't need makeup." Paul sounded sincere, almost reverential. I was extremely surprised.

"The boyfriend is Alex Wentworth, and yes, he's from Chicago. Not too many campus folks have met him. He's a surgeon. His time is limited, so his trips are short." I paused. "He's coming tomorrow night, actually, assuming he can get away. For the picnic Saturday."

"I just hope he treats you well." Another personal comment. Once again, Paul's tone seemed genuine.

"He does. Absolutely. We've been together a long time, ever since my early years at Keck College, but our careers keep us separated."

We drove in silence, both immersed in thoughts.

"What about you?"

"No girlfriend in Chicago," Paul said with a chuckle. "June and I will have our twentieth next year. Two great kids. They don't drive yet, so they keep her hopping. She's a hostess at Peter's on weekends." He referred to a popular restaurant on the north side of Hurley.

"She must be a patient one, to put up with your schedule."

"She's the perfect wife." Paul said it matter-of-factly. "She never asks questions. She's been married to a cop long enough to know how that works. She keeps clean socks in my drawers and hot meals in the oven when I'm late. That works for me."

"I remember meeting her last year at the picnic. She seems like a lovely lady."

"June's a great little gal." I could hear the pride in Paul's voice.

It was interesting what that one comment did for me. That he was happily married gave me a sense of safety—that is, attractive though I realized he was, I felt we were in no danger of usurping a strictly professional relationship.

Not that I was worried in the slightest, I reminded myself. I watched the silver night slip away as we pressed on toward Hurley.

Chapter 12
PAUL

It was nearly ten when we pulled into my driveway from Chapel Hill. It had been a long day—fifteen hours, in fact, since Paul had arrived to pick me up. Yet it had been a good day. I felt replete.

"I'll check inside." Paul waited as I unlocked the door. He flipped on lights, watched me punch in a code to disengage the security alarm, and walked through the kitchen into the adjoining hallway. I followed him into the living room and noticed that he also entered both the dining room and the sun porch, scrutinizing every detail within his gaze.

"Everything looks okay. Want me to check upstairs?"

I suppressed a laugh. I knew Paul was merely being solicitous, but I was amused by the image of walking toward my personal quarters with Paul in tow.

"No, thanks, I'm fine. Surveillance cameras, remember? This place is a fortress."

"So it is. Well, then, goodnight."

"It's been a lovely day, Paul. You have great taste in dining." We both laughed, looking at each other.

"Sleep well." He held his look for a long moment before exiting through the kitchen. He had given me that look before, the day we went to Queens.

Although I was exhausted and should have retired instantly, I found myself curled up on my sofa on the sun porch. Paul had surprised me once again. During the last hour of our ride, he—much as I had done earlier in the day—had become the consummate storyteller, gracefully unraveling family tales with candor and humor. I realized I now knew as much about Paul Stafford as I did any of my cabinet.

His name, for example: Paul Ogden Stafford. He was named for his great-grandfather, Ogden Blair Stafford, who had survived the Battle of

Gettysburg at the age of nineteen. That fact alone had made Ogden a hero throughout Ogden County—in fact, the county had been named for him. "And since I grew up in a county that bore my name," Paul added, "I strutted my family name with pride. When I was ten, I asked everyone to start calling me Ogden, but that didn't last long."

After the war, Ogden had drifted into the mountains north of Georgia, where he married, farmed, and raised seven children. Paul's grandfather, the oldest child, had a good head for numbers and opened a mercantile store. Years later, Paul's father grew up with the understanding that he someday would attend college. He ambitiously set his sights on Carolina, but in the end traded Chapel Hill for Western Carolina, in Cullowhee. That's where he met Paul's mother. They settled near Murphy, where together they managed the local Woolworth's.

Paul seemed to enjoy spinning his tale, and I marveled at his ease with me. "From childhood, my future was laid out before me like a blueprint," he said. "I was supposed to get a business degree and return to Murphy to help run the family business. My older brother, Jeremy, had no aptitude for business—none. But he took piano lessons with a teacher in Andrews and showed some real talent."

Paul, on the other hand, had the traits of a leader, or so I figured from his story. As a four-year-old, he'd been able to kick the ball harder than any other child in his play group. In the third grade, his teacher had proclaimed him school treasurer, meaning he counted the money for that week's snack breaks. In the seventh grade, he won handily as class president, encouraged by heady cheers when he walked to the auditorium microphone. From that day forward, he won every class election that came his way.

When Paul was twelve, he moved into the attic room being vacated by Jeremy, who was headed to college on a music scholarship. Paul filled his new space with posters, sports trophies, and favorite books. He played baseball in empty pastures and fished in the cold creek that carved through the nearby woods. Sometimes he played alone, talking to invisible gnomes who lived in the tall cottonwoods by the backyard fence. Murphy was a rural community, hemmed in by mountain ranges that extended from Georgia to Pennsylvania. Travel to larger towns was limited.

"Once a year or so our family visited Atlanta or Chattanooga," Paul recalled. "We shopped at the new malls and ate ice-cream sundaes in tall glasses with fudge sauce." I knew those concoctions. Daddy used to fix them for the family on Sunday nights.

Because of his geographical boundaries, Paul began to read voraciously at a young age. He devoured works by Sir Walter Scott, James Fenimore Cooper, and Herman Melville. He consumed Arthurian legends and Greek mythology and chronicles about outer space. Books fed his imagination, empowering him to sail skies to exotic lands and move through time to distant events. "There was nothing I couldn't do," he recalled, his voice confident. "I explored ancient cities in Europe. I tangled with ogres. I fought in some of history's most famous battles."

I listened without comment, captivated as he described images that exploded upon the screen of his mind's eye. I could picture him propped on goose-down pillows, reading by yellow lamplight on the narrow bed in his loft.

Girls liked him. Paul chuckled when he told this part—how girls began to leave notes under his books when he was fourteen. Having no sisters, he found girls captivating with their flouncy hair and good smells.

During his junior year he excelled in baseball, pitching a no-hitter in a play-off series that caught the attention of college scouts. As a senior he was on the list of every major recruiter in the Southeast. He won a full-ride scholarship to Florida State, where he surprised his coaches by choosing a major as challenging as business.

Then he discovered FSU's criminology department, and his life changed dramatically. He switched majors and devoured courses on human behaviors, crime detection, and the courts. He quit baseball, picking up instead an Army ROTC scholarship that taxed both his intelligence and physical stamina through rigorous summer training. When he graduated in 1960 as a commissioned officer, he committed to four years as a field artillery officer, convinced such an experience would eventually enhance a civilian career in law enforcement.

"My father was keenly disappointed in my career choices," Paul said. His voice slowed down with the memory. "Mom worried about my safety, especially when Vietnam heated up. I was one of the first battalion leaders in the field, commanding raw recruits. We trained in mock Vietcong villages at Fort Polk, where those marshy bottomlands were similar to 'Nam."

Near the end of his tour, Paul met a French-born Eurasian woman. That's all he said about her, other than the fact that he toyed with the idea of marriage and that, in the end, he returned to the States to wonder a thousand times if he had left the best part of his life behind. He met June on a blind date when he was thirty-one—"a confirmed bachelor many times over"—and was in his late thirties when their firstborn, Marcy, arrived.

I thought about Paul a long time, remembering his spiel. It seemed fascinating how our life stories had intersected at this point. He had come to Wickfield after more than twenty years as a narcotics detective in Tallahassee and Columbia, yearning for less stressful assignments than the undercover pursuit of hard-core criminals. He was burned out, weary, ready for a different kind of challenge. He wanted to spend more time with his teenagers, and although he didn't say it, he doubtless hoped to be heir to Sam Sutton's position of chief.

Now, simply because I had run out of gas on a Monday afternoon, he was driving me around the interstates and back roads of North Carolina. It seemed incongruous, somehow—mysterious, perhaps—but not entirely crazy. My earlier coldness had been inappropriate, an anger triggered by Carrington and misdirected toward Paul. I realized that if I remained open and fair-minded, I could learn a lot from this intelligent, engaging man.

I declared my little war with Paul officially over, and I headed upstairs to bed.

PICNIC

When I heard Alex's rental car drive up Friday night, I met him on the breezeway. We embraced for a long moment, our heads shielded from the driveway by the long trails of my Swedish ivy baskets.

"So I'm finally going to meet the whole family," Alex said, rubbing his face in my hair. "Think we'll start any rumors?"

"Don't make things more complicated than they are," I said, eagerly kissing him. I was glad to see him. We talked late into the night.

Saturday afternoon, the party was already well in motion as Alex and I strolled from the Chancellor's House to the lower lawn in front of Wellstone. Alex had surprised me by dressing in Wickfield's "red devil" colors: dark navy slacks and a scarlet polo shirt. The strong hues contrasted nicely with his thick graying hair and silver-rimmed glasses. We made a handsome couple by anyone's standards. More importantly, I hoped we looked happy.

A banjo band was warming up near an ancient live oak tree as we entered the picnic area. Low rows of folding tables were covered with cherry-red tablecloths and pots of ruby chrysanthemums. Other tables were covered in white butcher paper for the caterers, who were handling vast metal containers of food. ATO fraternity brothers, wearing matching polo shirts with their fraternity logo, were positioned at key locations as greeters, and Kappa Delta sorority women were shepherding the younger children to nearby games.

Alex and I approached the registration table, where we were given paper name tags by Lana Underwood, Dan's new secretary in Academic Affairs. Lana's sandals and brief white shorts showed off her perfectly bronzed legs and red-painted toenails.

Dan and his wife, Mimi, saw us coming and greeted us as we joined the milling crowd. Mimi, whose horn-rimmed glasses and salt-and-pepper hair complemented her no-nonsense personality, pounced on Alex. "It's about time you tore yourself away from all those Yankees," she said.

"Chicago is in the Midwest," corrected Alex, smiling. He was struggling to peel his name tag off its paper backing.

"North of Virginia, it's all the same," retorted Mimi. "You're a Yankee." She reached for Alex's errant tag and pried off the backing, grinning as she slapped the sticky side onto his shirt.

Susan Atterbury appeared and gave me a hug, which I quickly returned. "Those are great colors on you," she said, referring to my multi-hued paisley jacket. Of all the cabinet wives, Susan was the closest to being a true friend. Gracious in demeanor and smart as a whip, she was the epitome of all I admired in women.

Jake Mooney showed up next and wrapped one arm around my waist and the other around Susan's, asking if he could get us drinks. For some reason, I stiffened at the overly familiar gesture, in spite of the fact that I usually enjoyed Jake's banter. The banjo band began to play, strumming a lively tune. The party broke into full swing, and I used the moment to escape the group. I flipped Alex a little wave, which he answered with a high sign of his own, and began to work the crowd.

Although I was the unofficial hostess for the picnic, Jake's office and staff were doing the major legwork. My main role was to mingle with the guests and make sure everyone had plenty to eat. I admit I loved this part of my job the most—the rush, the power, the recognition. I felt the warmth of the crowd as I made my circle, chatting and laughing among the families while encouraging them to move toward the food lines. I ran into Carrington and his wife, Edith, both looking uncomfortable amid the noise and chatter. I spoke as briefly as possible without appearing rude. I didn't want Carrington asking about my new driver.

"Hear you brought the handsome doctor tonight." The voice belonged to Edna Hemphill, the red-headed wife of the music department chair. She had slipped up behind me and was bearing a plate loaded with pork barbecue, red slaw, and hush puppies. "About time." She winked at me. I smiled back politely. I scarcely knew Edna, and the remark seemed out of place. I moved on to the farthest tables, which were filling fast.

"What was Dan thinking when he hired that model as his secretary? Who really cares that she tested with perfect typing scores?" This time the voice belonged to Marilyn, who, like Edna, had moved in behind me unseen. She spoke conspiratorially into my ear. I turned in surprise.

"Really? Is Lana really a model? She's tall enough, I guess." I laughed in spite of myself. I enjoyed Marilyn, even though she was a disaster not only at protocol but also fashion. This evening she was wearing a powder-blue polyester pants suit that she had apparently owned for years and still wore much too often.

"She certainly doesn't hold back, does she?" Marilyn wandered on, but the disapproval in her tone made me turn back to face the crowd. I gazed over a throng of heads toward the registration table.

Suddenly, someone else was standing behind me. I felt a hand land lightly on my shoulder.

"Well, Prez, you certainly know how to throw a great party." I stood perfectly still. The invisible party was Paul.

"I threatened the hired help," I replied, without skipping a beat. "When did you get here?"

I didn't turn as I spoke. I looked straight ahead, inhaling his closeness. He had recently showered; I could smell the freshness of his soap. Zest? Irish Spring?

"Just arrived. Both kids had school affairs. Blair can't make it, but June and Marcy are here somewhere."

The jangly music wafted over the voices of those eating, as did the pungent smell of the vinegar-spiked barbecue sauce. My eyes continued to scan the crowd. That's when I spotted Alex. He was engrossed in conversation with Lana, his hands firmly on the registration table as he leaned in toward her.

As though following my sight line, Paul's hand tightened briefly on my shoulder. "Going to eat soon?" he asked.

I kept my tone light. "Yes, it's time to round up Alex and sample the food. The barbecue smells wonderful, and I know he'll go for those biscuits." The true crowd-pleaser each year was a huge supply of Southern fried biscuits, served hot with apple butter.

I continued watching Alex a moment. Lana flashed him a toothpasty smile and spoke a few words, and Alex puffed out his chest and laughed as heartily as though he were watching an episode of *Cheers*.

"Come on," I said, inspired by the moment. "I'll introduce you."

We started for the registration table, me leading the way. In spite of the fact that I hadn't yet looked directly at Paul, I was aware of his presence with each step. Paul's wife, June, caught up with us along the way. Her eyes gleamed in open admiration as she greeted me. I had forgotten how pretty and petite she was. The top of her head scarcely reached Paul's shoulder.

As we approached the table, Alex spotted us and quickly turned toward me, his back now to Lana. "*Here* you are!" he said, as though he had been searching for me for some time.

"I was about to say the same thing," I replied evenly. "Alex, I'd like you to meet Paul Stafford and his wife, June. Paul, June, this is Dr. Alex Wentworth."

I was looking directly at Paul now; it was the first time I remembered seeing him in casual attire. He was wearing crisp gray Dockers and a yellow polo shirt with gray vertical stripes. I noted his clean-shaven face and the silky swatch of hair that poked through the open vee of his collar.

The men shook hands, eyeing each other squarely. They continued to shake hands longer than necessary, I noticed. Looking closer, I saw that Alex was gripping Paul's hand in a hard crunch, wringing it slowly while smiling into his eyes.

Then the strange moment was over, and we all turned toward the dinner line. Paul and June moved through first and headed with their plates toward a distant table to join Sam Sutton and his wife.

Alex and I loaded our plates and crossed to a long table that Marilyn was holding for the cabinet members. We found an animated Jake Mooney in a one-way conversation with a pipe-puffing Bob Atterbury. Susan was laughing over a story Alma Earle Mooney was telling about an amusing incident in her first-grade class. Alma Earle had been teaching in the Hurley city schools since she and Jake had come to Wickfield, much to Jake's consternation. He wanted her to be a stay-at-home wife.

We had missed our beverages as we went through line, so Alex left briefly in search of the iced-tea kegs. I used the moment to look around me. This should be the culminating moment of the evening—great friends, terrific food, perfect weather, the start of a new year. I knew I looked and felt the picture of health—people had been telling me that all evening—and I had Alex close by my side. What more could I want?

Even so, something seemed suddenly awry—not with the party but with an inner sensation that began to engulf me. I felt it before I plunged into my food, before I took my first sip of iced tea, before I tried to recapture the good feelings Alex and I had shared before the party. The sensation was one I'd rarely experienced, but from years of living alone I knew its symptoms well. It was loneliness. It was the wretched kind, and it was closing in on me like an early morning fog. In spite of the lively conversation and music, this fog began to grip me so intensely that I grabbed my iced tea and forced down a hard gulp.

Still, the fog remained. That's when I realized it had surfaced the instant Paul and June moved to their distant table. The minute Paul had turned his back and walked away, I missed the strength in his simple presence. Throughout the rest of the meal, even as I ate and drank and laughed and conversed, I felt a loss. It intensified when I later saw Paul and June get up from their table to leave, his hand steadying the back of her chair as she rose.

They're leaving early, I thought, disappointed. *They're going to pick up Blair.*

I felt bleakly alone. The feeling was not the sharp pain one experiences with sudden grief. It was more like an emptiness, a confusion, an imbalance. The feeling left me terrified.

Help me, I whispered fiercely to myself. *I think I'm falling for Paul. It will make me miserable. Please help these feelings pass.*

Worst of all, I recognized this as the wicked kind of loneliness, more treacherous than shock. This loneliness was insidious. I had not expected it tonight, nor created it, nor invited it. It was known to slip up from behind, attacking its victims with a stickiness that would not let go. Without a doubt, it had sneaked up on me tonight. I was astounded at its power. And I knew from long years of singlehood that the more I might try to wrench away, the better armed would be this loneliness to jerk me back.

Chapter 14
BIRTH OF A MONSTER

The monster—for it would topple forests and rip babies from their beds— was conceived in heat.

It was the meanest kind, rising from the searing ethers of the Sahara Desert and merging into light winds that flowed west across the Ethiopian mountains and the Atlas Mountains of Morocco. From there, the winds blew over warm tropical waters north of the equator, gulping up moisture and boiling into unstable currents that, within days, fueled vigorous thunderstorms. These, in turn, formed a tropical depression, a huge indentation like a gigantic coffee cup in the sky.

When air rushed in to fill the cup's hollow, it interacted with the mechanics of Earth's rotation. Like spinning ice skaters who pull in their arms for that final outburst of energy, these currents raced tighter and faster as they reached the center. Laden with moisture and rising vertically into the atmosphere, they condensed and descended as rain, heating the air so that it rose again, faster, causing more air to rush in behind to equalize the decreasing pressure. Over and over the cycle repeated itself. The winds accelerated even more tightly as they approached the storm's center until finally, unable to go further, they spewed into boiling-white eye walls of towering cumulous clouds.

Thus, on September 11, 1989, two days after its detection as a cluster of thunderheads, the monster was born. It was named Hugo by the National Weather Service—the eighth tropical storm of the season. It grew in intensity as it moved westward, maturing over the Gulf Stream's warm waters and nearly destroying a reconnaissance aircraft with its ferocity. Surface winds were over 160 miles per hour.

Hugo churned onward, smashing into seaports like a crazed speedboat on an erratic course. It barreled into Guadeloupe on September 17, then

Montserrat, the U.S. Virgin Islands, and St. Croix. Everywhere it struck, it decimated villages and left a trail of lethal destruction and misery.

On September 19, Hugo pummeled Puerto Rico, leaving 30,000 more people with roofless homes and tumbled walls. It emerged into the Atlantic with a snarl, picking off tiny islands with deadly fury. The list read like a travel brochure: St. Kitts, Nevis, Dominica, Antigua, St. Martin.

On September 20, the Hurricane Tracking Center in Miami recorded Hugo's winds at 105 miles per hour.

On Thursday, September 21, the Hurricane Tracking Center in Miami issued a hurricane warning for the Carolina coasts. By noon, thousands of residents were evacuating coastal and low-lying areas. Hugo—a Category Four as massive as the entire state of South Carolina—had sets its course upon historic Charleston.

Its projected landfall: midnight.

In those days when Hugo was devouring the Caribbean—the week after our faculty picnic—the newsy information about the storm swirled around me like distant hot winds. For those of us two hundred miles inland, a wandering hurricane was scarcely a blip on the weather screen. That Monday before it strode ashore, however, the subject did come up at our weekly cabinet meeting.

"It will be interesting to see where Hugo lands," Dan said conversationally as we assembled in the conference room near my office. The room was my favorite gathering place, whether we assembled formally for scheduled meetings or informally for coffee chats. The staff had dubbed it the "Oval Office." I rather liked that name. It provided a sense of power and order, and it commanded respect from those who met with me there. The gleaming mahogany table, twenty feet from end to end, was flanked by sixteen padded chairs and was regularly polished to a high gloss by the custodial service. It had originally been designed for Board of Trustees meetings, but I encouraged its use by other groups. Why should such elegance gather dust except for four quarterly meetings a year?

"Probably the Outer Banks," said Bob Atterbury, cupping his hands as he struck a match for his pipe. "They get these storms all the time."

"That's too far north," Marilyn said briskly. She and her mother were avid television watchers. "They're saying Florida, Georgia, or South Carolina."

"Sounds like Hilton Head," offered Pud, breezing through the door at the final moment and catching the last words of conversation.

"How troubling for those with schools near the coast," I mused. I was thinking of The Citadel, the College of Charleston, and Coastal Carolina. "At least *we* don't have to worry." The comfortable piedmont where we lived sometimes caught snow and ice storms, and remnants of hurricanes brought much-needed rains. Beyond that, our location bore few weather problems.

"But we could get a hard blow," Dan said cautiously. "This one's a giant. If it hits anywhere along the Carolina coasts, it could swamp either state with its size. Or both."

"Okay, Jake, what's our latest crisis plan for a hard blow?" I asked, smiling. Jake was always prepared for campus disasters, large or small. I nodded to him as I arranged my meeting notes in front of me.

"It's standard," Jake replied, speaking slowly. Surprisingly, my question seemed to have caught him unprepared. "We'll continue to watch the path. If the storm hits South Carolina, it will probably track north and could catch us with heavy outer winds. And rains. Maybe flooding; depends. Thursday. Or Friday, maybe."

"What's 'standard?'" asked Marilyn. It was a rhetorical question. This group had been through crisis plans before.

"Early curfew. No candles in the dorms, that kind of thing. I'll review the RAs about loss-of-power procedures, just in case." RAs were graduate students who managed residence halls in exchange for free tuition.

On Wednesday, I addressed the approaching storm in a phone conversation with Sam Sutton. He brushed me off.

"I know they're calling it a monster, but hell, Katherine, we're way more than two hundred miles inland." His cavalier attitude irritated me. As usual, I pictured the disheveled police chief in his scarred swivel chair, drawing on a stubby cigarette and daring the protruding plume of ashes to fall before he reached the ashtray.

That night on the phone, Alex echoed the police chief's sentiments. "I just saw it on CNN, and it's headed straight for Charleston, maybe Myrtle Beach. Man, they're in for a bad time. You'll be fine in Hurley. But I wouldn't take any midnight strolls tomorrow."

I teased back, but I felt a stab of uneasiness. I, too, had seen the video clips of Caribbean destruction. Once a hurricane reached land, it usually dissipated into a tropical storm, but its impact could be felt for months.

And how I hated high winds! I had been only seven when I saw Dorothy's house sail through the air in *The Wizard of Oz*, young enough to harbor deep fears of any objects that hurtled out of the sky. These fears may have been irrational, but they were firmly ingrained within me. Tornado sirens made me think of air-raid sirens, which in turn made me think of night terrors from my childhood when Europe was hammered by German bombers. I had overheard my parents talking in those days, looking sad, and one girl in my first-grade class, Linda Lipe, had told a disturbing story about naked children and mothers killed in showers that sprayed poisonous gases. I didn't believe her, but Daddy confirmed the story, although using more sanitized images. Still, sirens to me were harbingers of deadly powers that rained down from above.

Early the next afternoon, Paul surprised me by dropping by my office. He had never done that before. In fact, he had never been in my office.

"Nice digs," he said, glancing around the elegant room as Jackie ushered him in. I watched his eyes rake in the Queen Anne furniture, the vivid floral watercolors, and the potted white chrysanthemums on the coffee table.

"What's up?" I said, keeping my voice level in spite of my suddenly sweaty palms. In one brief second I inhaled every detail of his presence: his ease of manner, his confident stride as he crossed the room, the strength in his arms as he placed them on my desk and looked steadily into my eyes.

"Thought I'd do a once-over at your house." His voice was unhurried. "To make sure it's airtight. We'll be feeling some strong winds by morning."

"Really? You think it's going to be bad?" I felt real concern for the first time.

"Depends. South Carolina is going to get major damage, that's for sure. The storm has intensified. It's a Category Four now. Could be a Five when it hits, but even a Four spells disaster for the coast."

"Well, they're certainly not worried in Charlotte, even though it's on the state line. All their TV crews are headed south to Charleston. The whole coast is evacuating, all the way up to Cape Fear and Wilmington." I had watched the reports that morning at home.

Even as I spoke, Paul was reaching into his inner coat pocket. He unfolded a road map of the two Carolinas and spread it, rattling, across my desk. I pushed aside my planner and coffee mug.

"Got a ruler?"

I fished around in a drawer and pulled out a wooden one. Paul laid it diagonally across the map, with one end on Hurley and the Appalachians northwest of our foothills. He angled it downward across North Carolina and South Carolina in a straight line to the Charleston harbor. The ruler's end jutted like an enormous timbered pier into the blue print of the ocean.

"Here's Hugo," he said, pointing at the end with his right hand. "Here's Charleston. And here's one projected path of the storm." He lightly tapped with his left fingers while holding the ruler tightly to the map. "Notice anything?"

I studied the ruler's position. "Hurley!" I exclaimed. "We're all in a straight line!" I looked up at Paul in wonderment. "We're directly in the path!"

"Well, if it doesn't veer and keeps its current track, we are," Paul said. "It depends on how far north it goes and whether it then tracks north or northwest." He refolded the map carefully, flap against flap. "Our region will certainly get rain, maybe flooding. Maybe tornados, even. A lot depends on the speed of the storm. Right now it's plowing along at a good clip. Once it spreads over land—who knows?" He shrugged as he tucked the map away. "Better be safe than sorry, I say."

I stood. "You're welcome to check the house, Paul. I'll call Lennie. I have a meeting in twenty minutes, or I'd come with you."

"No problem. I called Odell, but he's already on it, battening down the hatches all around." Odell Evans was director of Wickfield's physical plant.

"Good. And I'll alert my staff. Beyond that, there's not much we can do, right?"

"Nope, unless you want to send your staff home early. The next twelve hours are critical."

As soon as Paul left, I picked up the phone and dialed Jake's number. For the sake of our resident students, it was important to alert him that the storm appeared more threatening at this hour. When he did not answer, I left an urgent message. "Please return the call immediately, Jake. Need to reconsider our precautions regarding Hugo. Call me at home if you miss me here."

The afternoon ticked on, and a perverse mood took over the administration building. I felt the nervousness, thick and tangible, as I walked Wellstone's halls. It was funereal solemnity mixed with the electric excitement of a holiday eve. I noticed it even as Jackie cleared her desk shortly after four. Usually Jackie worked well past five, but I had urged her to leave early. The Human Resources office frowned on such a gesture for support staff, but tonight seemed a clear exception.

"I'm filling the gas tank and hunkering down with my TV set," Jackie told me, poking her head into my office, keys in hand.

"I'm on my way myself. Be safe, Jackie."

I said the words automatically, but they hung in the air as she scurried down the hallway toward the parking lot. Be safe! There was no doubt that thousands of lives near the coast were, at that very moment, undergoing rapid transformation. I pictured frantic fathers nailing plywood over windows, harried mothers yanking cans off grocery shelves, fretting youngsters too young to feel frenzy but old enough to sense alarm. I visualized flurry in hospitals, confusion in nursing homes, and jams on highways.

By nine o'clock, inured to the hype of TV reports and exhausted by angst, I headed to bed with a book. Jake had not returned my call, which was not only frustrating but curious as well. Was I overreacting? Wickfield's dormitories were all-brick structures that had defied the elements countless times in the past. Alex was right. I probably worried too much.

I checked television reports once more before turning out the lights. The storm by now was pounding the coast with heavy rains and tempests; landfall near Charleston was imminent. As I tossed my flannel robe over the end of my bed, I paused to peer behind the blinds of my south bedroom window. I shuddered slightly. The campus beyond was darkly lugubrious, marked only by the glow of ghostly gas lamps.

It was beginning to rain.

Chapter 15
HUGO

It was Christmas Eve. I lay still in bed, listening, waiting for Santa Claus. I knew he would come. Daddy had promised. And I had been a very good little girl, proper for sure, eager to make my parents proud. Oh dear, except for those tiffs with Sarah! I strained, anxious for any sign, and then he was there, stomping across the roof of the house, his booted footsteps solid from one end of the bedroom ceiling to the other. And the reindeer, too, their prancing lighter: a steady drop, drop, and then swishing as they sprang into the air and back down, dancing across and up, and landing hard once more, and again, and again . . .

I stirred, half awake. There really *were* people on my roof! Had a tree fallen? Was Odell Evans on top of my house? With a crew? In the middle of the night?

Then I was completely awake, springing from bed and racing to the window. Torrents of rain gushed past me, not flowing downward but slapping in waves against the glass. Everything was in motion: trees, clouds, air. The incessant noise came from flying debris--leaves, branches, anything hurtling through space at the moment, all thudding and bouncing and lifting up again.

As I watched, transfixed, the sky exploded in a solid surge of light, exposing hideous pea-green clouds heaving above the horizon. The sheet lightning persisted, without thunder. The racket overhead pierced like a fusillade of rocks.

I turned on my bedroom television set, grabbed my robe, and fumbled urgently for slippers. There! I could see Charleston on my screen, blurry trees whipping through a watery camera lens, a hanging stoplight swinging wildly on overhead wires like a trapeze artist. Wait, no! What was the announcer saying? I turned up the volume. This was *Charlotte*? No way! It couldn't possibly be!

But it was. Charlotte was getting hammered, pounded with a ferocity that had not been forecast. A television truck was crawling at a snail's pace along water-clogged streets, capturing uprooted trees and mangled signs in its lights. Whatever Hurley was feeling at the moment was only a foretaste of imminent fury headed our way.

I flew through the house, flipping on lights as I passed. At least we still had electricity! Downstairs, I turned on the television in the sun room. It helped, somehow, to keep a human voice nearby. I hurried into the kitchen to scrounge up candles and matches. The power could go out at any second.

That's when I heard new tapping sounds—a measured rat-tat-tat at the breezeway door. I moved toward it quickly. Through the window towered Paul Stafford, his nose pressed against the glass, his yellow slicker shiny with raindrops.

I quickly unlocked the door. Paul stepped inside.

"Saw your lights so I figured you were up. You okay?" Paul seemed to study me closely. The water from his slicker pooled onto the kitchen floor.

"What time is it?" I demanded. In spite of all that was unfolding, it was the only rational thing I could utter.

"Nearly three. A tree has crashed into McInnery. It went through an upstairs window and clobbered a bedroom. The two girls are all right, we think. The whole dorm has been herded downstairs. But I'm headed over there. Thought you should know."

"I'm going with you." My words were instantaneous.

"Absolutely not," Paul said flatly. "Nope. No way. There's a monster outside these doors. There's stuff flying everywhere. You have no idea."

"I'm going." I was resolute. "Give me five minutes to pull on some clothes."

"Lady, you won't make it twenty feet to my cruiser without tree limbs in those curls of yours."

"Well, *you* made it to *my* door," I replied tartly.

"I don't have curls." Paul stared at me, silent. I glared back.

"Besides," I added, breaking the impasse, "McInnery has an overhang in front." It was true. McInnery, of all the residence halls on campus, had a portico at the front door, like a vestibule fronting a nice hotel. Paul could pull his car up to the entrance.

Paul shook his head. "Impossible. Crazy. The drive will be the worst five minutes of your entire life."

I smiled slightly. He was relenting. "I bet I can be ready in three."

Paul sighed. "Okay, Prez. But dress for the weather. And skip the details." I was already headed to the stairs as he spoke.

"Nice bunny slippers," he added to my back.

I paused on the stairwell, glancing at my feet. My pink bedroom slippers had been a Christmas gift from Marianna, whose presents often played on my childhood name of "Kat." And these slippers bore pointed ears and long whiskers.

"They're kittens," I shot back over my shoulder.

Upstairs, I threw on a warm-up suit, pulled on sturdy socks and sneakers, raked a brush through my unruly hair, and flashed a toothbrush. I slapped on some lip gloss. There was no time for makeup, but who cared? I ran down the stairs to my hall closet and pawed into a back corner for a long poplin trench coat. Paul watched approvingly as I pulled the hood over my head and snapped the metal fasteners. I clicked off the TV in the sun room but left lights on for my return. If, of course, we still had lights.

"Stay close," Paul said as we headed toward the back door. I paused to snatch a flashlight from a kitchen drawer. Then I felt Paul's arm tighten around my shoulders as we stepped onto the breezeway.

The screams of the storm engulfed us. Although Paul had parked the cruiser only feet away, both of us were pounded with water as we dashed to its doors, bound like Siamese twins. Paul literally pushed me into the front seat before slamming the door and feeling his way to the driver's side. I huddled in my wetness, shaking slightly while taking note of the police car's interior. It was a cockpit of crackling radios, blinking colored lights, and enigmatic buttons.

"Lots of bells and whistles," I observed as Paul piled in, his slicker glistening with rain. He buckled himself in tightly, then reached over and tugged on my belt.

"Hope we don't need them. Stay alert now. And if I tell you to duck, then duck."

Paul nosed the car cautiously into the howling night. The sound of the wind was overpowering. The paternal oaks moaned in anguish with the buffeting. The younger trees with limber trunks flipped their top branches to the ground and then whipped back up, bobbing like slender damsels shaking their hair dry.

We drove without speaking. The racket obstructed any attempt at conversation. Debris ricocheted and crashed around us. The sky, when lit up, remained that lewd shade of putrid green.

About a block from the house, as we headed toward the back campus, Paul suddenly leaned forward, peering intently through the windshield wipers.

"Damn!" He slammed on his brakes. The car squealed and jerked.

Ahead, a massive tree lay horizontally across the street, directly in our path. We stared through the blurry glass at its hulking mass.

"Afraid of this," Paul muttered, shifting into reverse. He began to turn around, cautiously rocking his long car backward and forward in the narrow street. At least there were no cars parked on the sides.

I silently scolded myself as he maneuvered. The havoc around me was indeed terrifying. I had been oh-so-reckless to place myself in such danger. A tree could crush our car—yes, crush my skull!—at any moment. Paul and Carrington were right: I was foolhardy and impetuous. In the wavering headlights I could see the tree's gigantic root ball, tentacled and ugly. Its naked roots dangled in midair.

Paul retraced our route, passing the Chancellor's House without comment. This time he headed in the direction of Wellstone. The old administration hall with its stately clock tower stood like a watchman in the stormy night. The front lawn and its mélange of trees were visible only through intermittent flashes of lighting. Thudding sounds continued, but it was impossible to see what damage was occurring. We inched on, turning left at the massive College of Arts and Sciences building and on past the Lineberger College of Business toward the back streets of the campus. Every building bore inky-black windows—that is, until we rounded a corner that took us toward a tangle of residence halls. Each one of these was ablaze with lights.

McInnery was the last dormitory in the grouping. Paul pulled up under its portico and parked. I could imagine the fluster within, with students rousted from sleep and directed to lower levels for safety. When Paul and I stepped inside the spacious front parlor, sodden and windblown, we found a galaxy of young women in assorted nightwear crammed into the middle of the room. Some were draped over chairs and sofas; others were sprawled on the massive plush carpet with bed pillows. The girls cheered loudly when we entered, and I was pleasantly surprised, assuming the applause was for me. Then I realized it was a raucous welcome to Paul.

"Man on the hall!" voices hooted happily. McInnery was a "closed" women's dorm, meaning men were not allowed after closing hours.

Lisa, a graduate resident assistant, immediately pounced on us and helped us shed our soggy coats. She did not register surprise at seeing me—only gratitude for our sudden appearance. Paul, unruffled by the catcalls, disappeared with another RA to assess the damage from the fallen tree.

"We're fine," Lisa assured me when I fired away with questions. "Everyone was nervous at first because of the wind. You could almost feel the building sway. And when that tree hit, we were terrified. Now that we're together, it's at least tolerable."

Indeed, the camaraderie eased the stress of the storm. There was something comforting about being in the middle of the fortress-like building. The girls who greeted me were friendly. Some were sitting cross-legged on the floor in front of the TV, which was tuned to WSOC-TV in Charlotte.

I quickly sought out the students whose room had been struck by the tree. Lisa led me to two girls ensconced on a sofa and surrounded by a circle of friends. When the tree fell, the girls were away from the windows, preparing to shift quarters to the downstairs lounge. Neither had been harmed, although both had been clearly shaken by the earth-shattering boom.

"The room's a disaster," one said somberly. She described a scene of chaos: limbs and leaves on top of their beds, shattered glass, and a clobbered dresser. The other student prattled nervously about a buried typewriter and books.

As the girls chattered on, the lamp next to the sofa began to wink. I held my breath. It flickered again. Seconds later, all the lights blinked out. The room was plunged into inky darkness, followed by high squeals from the girls.

"Use your flashlights!" Lisa's calm voice called out with authority. Long yellow beacons soon darted around the room. The girls inspected walls and ceilings and shone their lights playfully into each other's faces.

Now I was deeply concerned, my worries far beyond one damaged dorm room. Loss of power meant major trouble. My thoughts raced as I sat in the ominous blackness, grateful I didn't have to converse. I needed time to assess the storm's enormous impact. Clearly, Hugo's deceptive speed had overpowered the region, swindling millions of residents of their last shred of security. No one had foreseen a catastrophe this far inland. How extensive was it? Could commuters get to class? Some lived as far as fifty miles away. What about faculty and staff, many of whom lived at a distance? And vendors? Could they reach the Wickfield campus?

As for the internal community, I felt less alarm. Like the local hospital, Wickfield had emergency generators to provide electric power. Odell and his crew could rev them up quickly. But Wickfield was not a self-contained domain, in spite of Carrington's hot-bellied outbursts about the need to protect it from the outer world. Wickfield depended on hundreds of outside resources to fulfill its mission as a university. And it counted on them to deliver with speed and efficiency.

Even as my thoughts tumbled, I saw the flickering flashlights of Paul and the resident assistant as they reentered the parlor. I turned on my own flashlight and groped my way through the furniture, stepping gingerly over girls and pillows.

"The damage is limited to the one room," Paul reported. "It's extensive. The two girls will need new quarters. There's nothing more we can do tonight. We'll be lucky if this is the worst."

I was suddenly exhausted. The rain continued to fall in torrents, but the wind sounded less frightful, and the girls were settling down to try to sleep. Paul and I made a quiet departure. As we drove back through debris-strewn streets, we caught glimpses through the downpour of more felled trees. Classes today? Forget it. With power outages and extensive damage, it was senseless to even consider them.

Back in my darkened kitchen, Paul helped with wicks and matches and carried a lighted jar candle into the sun room. "I need to cancel classes," I told him when he came back. Cancelling classes was a big deal. Usually only the governor could make such a decision for state campuses, but chancellors could supersede the governor in the wake of an "act of God." Thank goodness I didn't have to wait on the governor to make such a call, as was the case in many states.

"Believe me, everyone will stay home of their own accord," Paul said. "And remember, they can't hear an announcement without power."

"But we don't know how extensive the outage is. We're just assuming it's widespread. Anyway, we have to make it official." I was a stickler for going through proper channels.

"It's widespread, count on it. How many Duke Power trucks do you think it will take to manage this damage?"

I didn't answer. I was spent, too fatigued to try to grasp the full impact of what had befallen Wickfield. It was obvious that, unlike Dorothy's storm, this one did not lead to the Land of Oz.

"The troops will rally," Paul said as he placed another lit candle near the kitchen wall phone. He noticed my fatigue. "You run a well-oiled machine, Katherine. Why don't you grab some quick shut-eye?"

It was after five. The idea of sleep was appealing, but I dared not slow my momentum yet. While Paul took off with a flashlight to check the house for damage, I pulled out my campus directory from a kitchen drawer and dialed Dan Jones's home number. Dan answered instantly. I gave him a dire description of the battered campus.

"Wait another hour or so to call the deans about classes," I told him. "And have them call each of their faculty members to check on them, no matter how long it takes. At least we have phones. God bless BellSouth." I said it grimly, like a solemn prayer.

Dan volunteered to call the other four cabinet members. "What about an emergency staff meeting?" he asked.

"Absolutely," I said. "I'll be in my office by eight, and I'll meet at ten in the Oval Office with anyone who can make it in. Spread the word. Fact-gathering. We'll compare notes and create a plan." I was still curious why Jake—the proud gatekeeper of all campus crisis plans—had not returned yesterday's call.

Then I called Claire, who was staying in campus guest quarters for the week. "Baptism by fire," I thought as her phone began to ring, remembering Marilyn's earlier prophesy. The true measure of a new employee, in my estimation, was reaction to the unexpected.

"I'm so glad you're all right," Claire breathed. "I can't stand this wind." She had been awake for half the night, trying to read under the covers to alleviate her terror. She was armed, however, with a list of "inside numbers" for area TV and radio stations. Like Paul, she was worried that very few would hear the cancellation.

"Some will try their car radios, but your office will be swamped as long as the phones hold," I warned her. "The earlier you make it to your desk, the better, assuming it's safe enough to get out and walk. Be careful! Look out for downed wires." Smart girl, that Claire. She was prepared.

"You'll hear a lot of war stories," I continued. "Everyone will have their dramatic little tale. The university will try to be flexible in accommodating those hit hard, but make no promises to anyone. Take notes to cover yourself. Be sympathetic, but absolutely no faculty home numbers to the public unless I okay it later. I'll feed you new information as decisions are made."

It was still raining hard. Paul waved a silent goodbye from the kitchen door as I continued on the phone, and I raised a hand in return. Hanging up from Claire, I stumbled into my living room. My couch looked like a pallet of sheer pleasure as I sank wearily into its cushions.

Enough. I would nap briefly before dealing with the next onslaught of decisions.

Chapter 16
AFTER THE STORM

It was nearly 10:15 before I slid into my seat in the Oval Office and faced a ragtag ensemble of employees. Without exception, all appeared to be staggered by last night's storm.

My morning was already a blur. It had begun a few minutes after eight, when the incessant jangling of the phone broke my deep sleep on the living-room couch. I had raced to the hallway phone, clearing the grogginess from my throat before lifting the receiver.

Carrington Hall was on the other end. "No one answered the phone in your office," he groused. "Who's minding the store, Katherine?"

Carrington, you are incorrigible! I fumed to myself. I responded by inviting him to tour the campus with me in twenty minutes. It was a bluff; Carrington never ventured from his gargantuan home before nine o'clock. He mumbled something about being unable to open his electronic garage doors manually. That fits, I thought, still miffed at his churlishness. Carrington's home and grounds were run by hired help. He would have to fend for himself today.

Jackie had called soon afterward, upset because a fallen tree was blocking her driveway. Her husband had left to borrow a chain saw from a neighbor. It would be a day of crises, I realized as I dressed hastily in khakis and walking boots. My spirits were as gray as the morning. Although electricity had returned in a blaze of lights—how had I slept through that surge?—I was in no mood for coffee or toast. At least the wind's awful yowl had abated. I steeled myself as I cracked the front door to check the yard. The front lawn, usually a lovely landscaped expanse of St. Augustine sod, was now a soggy mess of leaves and limbs. The feathery little Japanese maple had blown down into some bushes. But the saucer magnolia near the curb—a showpiece of wax-pink blossoms each spring—stood intact.

Buoyed by that small blessing, I grabbed an umbrella and departed through the kitchen door, fending off the yet-drenching rain. But nothing had prepared me for the devastation I beheld as I slogged along toward Wellstone. In the full light of day, the campus resembled a war zone. Uprooted oaks lay like corpses at odd angles to each other, their root balls lifted toward the wet heavens next to gaping craters. Wooden benches had tipped over, their metal legs awkwardly askew like old men who had fallen on their backsides. Against one lamppost was a tumbled pile of trash containers that appeared to have hurled themselves like missiles onto the ground.

Heartsick, I paused at the Wellstone steps and gazed across the mangled lawn toward Grove Boulevard. The street was empty, as though all of Hurley was paralyzed into silence. The picnic area was rampant with sweet gum balls. The front campus appeared to have lost at least a third of its beautiful old trees, perhaps half. Hauntingly, I could hear my voice telling trustees months ago how the removal of select trees would enhance the public's view of the campus. I could also hear echoes of Carrington's opposition. Well, I had won this round. These deciduous warriors had fought their last battle. Thanks to a mighty wind, Wickfield now had an "open" campus.

Fifty yards away, I spotted Odell Evans standing with a cluster of workmen—or were they students?—near a severed tree. Knowing Odell, he'd probably been here since daybreak, despite the hard winds. I shivered in the cool drizzle at the thought of the cleanup ahead. Overwhelming powers had wrought their might upon this site.

Yet, in that same moment, I caught a distant glimpse of the patriarchal "Sweetheart Tree" and was lifted by a moment of hope. After two hundred years, the famous campus tree was still upright. It was an impregnable live oak, endowed by Mother Nature in its formative years with a large natural opening between twin trunks. Its massive branches dipped low enough for students to sit on them. The tree's photo appeared in every admissions view book. It represented the heart of campus culture, breathing magic into the heart of every coed who kissed beneath its canopy.

I was tempted to explore the grounds further, but that could wait. Jackie's phone was ringing when I fumbled with my keys at the outer door to my suite. For half an hour I fielded one caller after another. Most were faculty inquiring about classes. Some were anxious parents.

Shortly after nine, a cheery Mimi Jones showed up with Dan and held high a sack of powdered donuts like a battle flag. "Rations!" she exclaimed. "How can I help?"

I pointed to Jackie's desk. "Take over," I said, grateful. "And check on Lennie at her house. I haven't heard from her."

I felt even more relief when Jake Mooney appeared at my door, pen and planner in hand. I studied him quietly as he settled into my office couch. It was the same place he had sat three weeks earlier when he'd reported on the David Weise suicide.

As usual, Jake was well groomed, almost dapper in jeans and sweatshirt. He had even managed a shave. Today, however, he seemed—well, subdued. I was surprised, in spite of the duress of the morning. Nothing seemed to upset Jake. "No-shake Jake," his friends called him. He was well known for his ebullience and charm. Both men and women found him attractive. Jake and Alma Earle were the social divas of the cabinet, easy hosts who lit up their gas grill at a second's notice. I had enjoyed various evenings at the Mooney house, always punctuated with laughter and high spirits.

"Where were you yesterday afternoon?" I asked testily. My annoyance was crystal clear.

"Out of town," he replied. "Sorry. Got back too late to return your call." He offered no further explanation. I decided to drop the issue for the time being, although cabinet members customarily alerted me if they had to be out of town. For now, there was too much to do. I filled him in on my trip to McInnery Hall.

"Why didn't you call me?" he asked, incredulous as he pictured my trek through the storm. His was a fair question. As vice president for Student Affairs, Jake would normally have been alerted.

"Well, you hadn't answered my earlier call," I reminded him. "Besides, it was too urgent. And I was closer. What's our crisis plan for today?"

"There isn't one," he admitted, shaking his head. "Hugo is a new kind of challenge."

In the Oval Office, finally, an odd assortment of nine people was assembled around the conference table. Dan reported on those missing. Bob Atterbury was directing his teenagers in a massive attack on their yard, which had major tree damage. Pud would be in "later." A traumatized Marilyn, whose family farm was a hundred-acre spread, was "staying put with Mama."

Wisely, Dan had rounded up others. A tobacco-pungent Sam Sutton—the one who had brushed off my Hugo concerns Wednesday—sat sullenly in his seat and refused to meet my eyes. Marla Caldwell, the famously fashionable director of Alumni Affairs, wore jeans and a baggy sweatshirt. School photographer Joey Coffin sat with his camera in hand, eager to scout out every square inch of grounds for pictures. John Sigmon, the always-cheerful business-school dean, was present, along with Kiley Crenshaw, head custodian. I sent Mimi to track down Claire and Odell.

"Good morning, survivors," I began, smiling at the haggard faces around me, "and congratulations on making it in today." I paused, warming to my subject.

"Clearly, Wickfield is in a state of shock. What we experienced last night was not supposed to happen. Somehow Hugo surprised us all, even the weathermen. Our campus has endured a great loss in terms of tree and structural damage, a loss that affects our pride and assaults our emotions. At the same time, our Wickfield community has suffered no loss of life nor limb, as far as we know, and for this we are very grateful. We are especially fortunate that there was no *human* injury when a tree crashed into McInnery last night."

No one spoke. I continued. "It's now incumbent upon us to secure the future safety of our students and staff. Today's cancellation of classes is indicative of our pursuit of this goal. At the same time, we will use every ounce of energy among us to reopen our classrooms as soon as appropriate."

I stopped. Why such formality? Why was I sounding so professorial, so doggone dreary? I sounded like Carrington when he was trying to impress. I was known for an easy conversational style and the ability to put people at ease. This didn't sound like me. It was as though the awesome nature of the storm had endowed me with an artificial reverence.

When I paused, everyone began to talk at once. There was such a torrent of conversation that I called for order and asked for individual comment. It was obvious that all of us had experienced a frightful night. Everyone had lost electricity, and many had lost hot water. Those with electric pumps on their wells had no water at all. Local phone calls connected, but long-distance calls did not. Fallen trees were intertwined with power lines. Some wires were live. The water beneath Penny Point Bridge was at highway level. A pickup truck had blown over near the Wickfield gymnasium. Trees of all sizes were down in every nook and cranny of town.

During the discussion, Claire slid into an empty seat and reported a "deluge" of phone calls. "One young woman sobbed on the phone for at least five minutes," she said. "She was convinced she was going to die and spent the night under her bathroom sink. Everyone wants to focus on their homes and yards. That's all they can handle right now."

Just then Odell Evans entered the room with two male resident students in tow. I welcomed them, pleased to have student voices included. They reported that students from badly stricken areas couldn't reach their families. Many were scrambling for rides home. The thought of losing campus students to their home bases had not occurred to me before now.

I made fast mental notes as the stories unfolded. The city of Hurley was in the middle of a disaster, yet Wickfield had power. The dual meaning of "power" was not lost on me. Clearly, Wickfield could become an oasis to the general public if needed. But the welfare of Wickfield's students and staff had to come first under every circumstance. Otherwise, I would face a public-relations nightmare.

I turned urgently to Odell. "How long to clear the campus to a state of near normalcy?"

Odell had never been big on words. He studied his calloused thumbs carefully. "Depends on manpower," he finally said. "Just 'pends."

Impatient, I eyeballed each person around the table. "It appears we have a unique dilemma," I said. "Here we are with the electric power to operate—but only our residential students are able to utilize this luxury. The other thirty percent must travel to get to us. This doesn't include our faculty and staff. We must anticipate everyone's needs and constraints— everyone from delivery-truck drivers to dining-hall workers.

"We certainly have the capacity to hold classes Monday. After all, our lights burn, our water runs, our ovens bake, and our toilets flush. In some ways, it would be terrific if the world could point to Wickfield and say, 'See, they were prepared; nothing stops education! Kudos to Wickfield.' Yet Dan doesn't know if he'll have adequate faculty, and Jake doesn't know if we'll have enough students in seats to make the effort worthwhile."

I turned to Chief Sutton. "Sam, I want a typed assessment of the condition and safety of the entire campus as affected by the storm. I want it on my desk by 4:00 p.m. today, sooner if possible. Current and future safety.

"Odell, pull together whatever crews you can for clearing—sidewalks and parking lots first, lawns second. Give me a verbal progress report by day's end, along with a better projection for completion. Coordinate with Jake if you use student labor, and make certain everyone is supervised as appropriate.

"Jake, check on dorm conditions. Relocate those two McInnery women. Contact their parents immediately on my behalf. Look for volunteers among the service clubs. Think through all safety parameters—no accidents with chain saws! And think through next week's events calendar. If we cancel classes next week, we'll need to reassess scheduling for every group on campus.

"Dan," I continued, turning to him on my other side, "I need an assessment of the entire faculty and how they've been affected. Again, work through the deans. And review the entire academic calendar in case we lose more time.

"Marla, check on upcoming alumni events—mailers, facilities, anything that might need adjustment for the short run. Joey, treat this as an historic event. Don't skimp on film. Work with Claire on stories.

"Claire, continue to think in terms of damage control regarding the media. Stay neutral about next week's classes until further notice. Downplay last night's tree crash, but make sure the media knows we've been a direct hit. We need all the sympathy we can get, especially from our legislators.

"To the rest of you, thank you for your input and participation. It's good to be together on this morning of . . . mourning."

When I spoke again, my tone was quieter. "One more thing. It's possible we may become a resource for services. Hot showers in our gym, for example. Hot meals in the dining room at a nominal cost. Much depends on how long folks are without electricity. It could take weeks. Any or all of you may be called upon for double duty should we become involved. The bottom line is, we have facilities that work and the capacity to share. I'll know more after speaking with Mayor Barnhardt.

"Finally," I said, winding down, "do be careful. As a university, we are *exceptionally* fortunate. Trees can be replanted. Windows can be repaired.

Let's keep our priorities straight and appreciate our homes, our families, our jobs, our very lives."

I removed my glasses and closed my vinyl folder. "To all of you here this morning, thank you for time and participation. Now—let's get to work."

The room was silent. Suddenly, en masse, the group began applauding. I was stunned. In my twenty-five years in higher education circles, this kind of spontaneous recognition was a rarity.

And Jake, I noticed, was the one who led the plaudits.

Chapter 17
RECOVERY

By early afternoon the rain had stopped, and sunshine glinted upon the campus. The high-pitched twang of chain saws ripped the air. Clusters of students wearing caps and work gloves moved in tandem in work crews. They cut trees and hauled heavy branches. Instructions had come from city officials to stack limbs along the edge of the street. We watched in morbid fascination as a low thicket swelled along the Grove Boulevard curb.

New information filtered in all day about Hugo. The storm had followed the Blue Ridge Parkway into Virginia and was tracking toward Washington, which was now bracing for a treacherous rush hour. State forestry services were clearing fallen trees. Charlotte was a wreck, devastated by hundred-mile-an-hour winds. Its one fatality was a baby, killed in its crib in the suburb of Matthews. The city was ninety percent without power. Duke Power reported three hundred utility poles down and ordered employees to pack overnight bags. BellSouth's long-distance lines were out of service. People in the storm zone could not reach out-of-town loved ones, nor could they *be* reached by frantic family members outside.

I wondered how the disaster looked on national TV. The whole country was watching our crisis while *we* waited for electricity. I thought about my sisters glued to TV sets—Marianna and Sarah in Virginia, Emily in Florida, and Jane and her brood in California. I considered calling Marianna but had little hope of getting through. And Alex! Alex must be frantic! He avoided Friday afternoon surgeries whenever possible, and I pictured him, worried, in front of the doctors' lounge TV.

By early afternoon, Mayor Jay Barnhardt and I had mapped out a joint plan that encouraged local citizens to take advantage of Wickfield's electric power. Claire, excited to publicize free showers in the gym and budget meals in the dining room, helped us shape details. We would begin the plan tomorrow, Saturday, after the media circulated the information.

"I just hope we're not moving too fast," I told Jay cautiously. "It's one thing to be generous of spirit, but we haven't thought of all the problems the public could throw at us."

"Katherine," he sighed, "folks will be so happy to get hot water and food that they won't care about efficiency. Mark my words, you'll have few problems with the public."

To help regarding classes, Charlie Pettigrew in Chapel Hill contacted those of us most affected by the storm—UNC-Charlotte and Wickfield had been hardest hit—and granted us complete latitude to cancel if safety were an issue. Relieved, Dan and I cancelled Monday classes in consideration of our widespread families in crisis.

With these decisions firmly in place, I went home midafternoon to a quiet house. I was utterly exhausted. I thought briefly about checking on others but scarcely knew where to begin. Lennie? Her hands were full today caring for her daughter's family, including six-year-old Robert, the grandson who often stayed at Lennie's house after school. Carrington? Ridiculous, I chided myself. There was nothing bad enough that could happen to him. I stretched out on my queen-sized bed and fell asleep.

The evening news was sobering. I watched in sadness as Charlotte television stations showed chilling images of damage throughout both Carolinas. I couldn't get CNN—cable service was out—but the local news teams were on top of regional coverage.

As for Hugo's freakish invasion of our area, national weather experts were calling it a "two-hundred-year event." Two air pressure systems, unrelated, were to blame. A Charlotte weatherman explained the science: "A high-pressure system over New England blowing clockwise, along with a low-pressure system turning counterclockwise over the Deep South, created a narrow river of air that channeled Hugo northwest." He used swooping motions with his arms as he pointed to two circles of arrows moving in opposite directions. "These systems energized the storm with moisture at the very time it should have lost its ocean fuel. That's why Hugo's eye was still intact as the air masses approached our area."

At day's end, there were no reports of injuries from students or staff. Odell declared the campus safe by foot and vehicle, and Claire produced colorful directions to the gym and dining room. I slept well that night, grateful for fragrant clean sheets at a time when hordes were left homeless.

Saturday afternoon I walked the entire campus. It was a beautiful day, empowered by sparkling blue skies and crisp air. The noise level was an entirely other matter. The clamor of chain saws was so pervasive that it was hard to remember how life had sounded before the storm.

The sun had shifted slightly west as I approached Whitely Hall, the temporary home of the School of Education. It housed our largest group of faculty, who had moved into Whitely during the summer when renovation of their regular building began. I suddenly smelled amazing aromas wafting through the air: grilled beef, onions, and fragrant spices. At that moment, a small woman in shorts and T-shirt emerged from Whitely's front entrance, bearing a tray of assorted cookware. I recognized her instantly as June Stafford, Paul's wife. She saw me and stopped, beaming.

"Chancellor Embright! You're just in time! We have a huge feast inside!"

I greeted her back, noting to myself her short modish hairstyle. "Cooking contest?" I asked.

"We're saving our refrigerators! Just go to the conference room at the end of the hall." She lifted the tray. "I've been cooking all morning. Need to get these to the car."

I wandered into the building, where the intriguing smells enveloped me. The building had originally been constructed as housing for married students. As a result, each professor's office included a kitchenette: an electric stove and oven, a refrigerator with a small freezer, and a full-sized sink.

I followed a trail of laughter. As soon as I appeared at the conference room door, a rousing cheer went up. I was astounded at the potluck meal spread out on tables: Omaha steaks, loin roasts, baked chicken, casseroles, homemade soups, salads. All had been prepared by faculty families from their melting home freezers. I gathered that friends and neighbors were part of the group. Apparently that's how June and Paul Stafford had been invited.

Yes, Paul was there. I had spotted him the very minute I was dragged into the party. It was the first time we had connected since our escapade in the storm. He waved across the room and came bounding over with a can of Diet Coke for me. Beyond that, we had little interchange. I watched as he ate with June and his two teenagers and helped pack up their belongings at the end. He and June worked well as a team, I noted. Paul seemed especially attentive to his daughter, Marcy. She was tall like her father and strikingly pretty, with bright, clear eyes.

I returned to the Chancellor's House laden with enough foil-wrapped food to carry me through several days. At this point, more than anything, I wanted to connect with family. I dialed Marianna's number again, then Emily's. I tried Alex again. Long-distance lines out of Hurley remained down.

The next day I read in the paper about Saturday weddings at local churches and wondered if they had actually taken place. The society-page stories were often written well in advance, and I felt swells of sympathy for the brides-to-be who surely had wept in despair Friday. One bride, according to the paper, wore a white satin gown with Schiffli band collar, leg-of-mutton sleeves, and Sposabella lace-trimmed train. I could almost smell the *Gypsophila*.

No way, I thought—there was *no way* such an elaborate event could have taken place yesterday, when roads and bridges and parking lots were in chaos! It would have taken the bridal couple half of Friday to track down their wedding party of sixteen attendants. What were the legal ramifications of declaring someone married in print when, perhaps, they were not yet wed?

It was an intriguing legal question, the kind Tim and I had enjoyed haggling over early in our marriage. I would have to ask Paul. After all, he was a law student. I stored the story mentally for my next trip with him. He was becoming, in short order, a quasi-advisor on legal matters. I found myself looking forward to our trips.

In spite of cancelled classes, I insisted the cabinet meet as usual Monday, and I was pleased to see that each of my staff was dealing well with the crisis. Overall, the university was functioning decently. Paul was right—Wickfield was a well-oiled machine. I was surprised, however, at the small public turnout for the free showers. Evidently numbers of families with gas-powered homes had shared their facilities with friends over the weekend. Jake and Alma Earle had even hosted "shower parties," proffering glasses of cold wine to their guests as they took turns behind bathroom doors.

Or so I gathered from fragments of conversation I overheard. "How many glasses did my wife have?" I heard Bob Atterbury ask jokingly of Jake. I had just dismissed the cabinet meeting and was leaving the Oval Office. "Susan was half-smashed Saturday when she got home. I told her it was probably the longest shower of her life."

"Longest and best," I heard Jake say agreeably.

It was Tuesday, the fifth day of our recovery, before I finally got through to Alex's surgical service. The receptionist offered to have him paged, but I was afraid he would be in surgery. "Just tell him I called and ask him to return my call at his first opportunity," I said. I knew he would respond in a flash as soon as he got the message.

But Alex was between patients when he reached me, and he seemed rushed. Our long-awaited connection became an awkward moment. I had mentally rehearsed storm dramas with which to regale him. This was clearly the wrong time for such sagas. And, in moments of true candor with myself, I knew there were other reasons I'd retreated once his familiar voice had come through the lines. I was a Hugo warrior who had survived hardened battle, and survivors create bonds of intimacy with those who share their experience. Alex had not shared my experience. Paul had. When describing our drive through the storm to the cabinet, I had downplayed the details, even though it was the stuff of lore in every sense. Paul and I had defied thrashing skies and crashing trees and lashing winds. Perhaps I feared that sharing the drama might strip it of its power and diminish its gilt. Only Paul and I could fully understand the private connection that had been forged that night.

So I merely told Alex that I was well, that the campus was damaged substantially but that recovery was in full gear. It was a strange conversation for two people who had been trying to reach each other for five days. I heard loud clangs in the background and the strident nasal drones of the hospital PA system. I hung up quickly, an interloper in an alien world.

No, Paul was no longer my enemy, and I welcomed the friendlier times we were now sharing. My personal worries these days involved Alex. Even before the storm, I'd sensed his phone calls becoming fewer, his conversations shorter. And there had been that abruptly cancelled weekend, the one that had suddenly dropped at my feet with the story about a heart transplant. I had never had reason to doubt Alex in the past, but, for whatever reason, I seemed to view him with new eyes these days. Something was afoot, it seemed; I could smell it like rancid perfume through the miles.

Fortunately, Thanksgiving would be approaching soon enough, and Alex already had invited me to visit him that weekend. If I could get through this Hugo crisis and the month of October, I would soon enough get to the bottom of whatever was happening in Chicago.

The holidays lay just beyond.

Chapter 18
INA ROSS EVERWINE FARTHINGALE

Hurley's electricity crisis continued into the next two weeks. Strain was etched tautly into faces everywhere. Adding to my own stress was the speed of academic flow that invariably hit in October. Paul drove me to a day-long meeting at Duke University early in the month, after our campus routine had returned to normal. The Duke group, although small, was composed of women administrators from both the privates and publics in North Carolina. Our mission that day was to "network"—the new catchphrase of the day—as we connected both in body and spirit. I had known many of these women for years, having bumped into them at workshops and conferences. In our discussions through the years, we had struggled with issues regarding gender inequality in the workplace. In higher education, these injustices seemed rampant. I was convinced that each woman around the table that day could perform her job every bit as well as her male counterparts—if not better.

For the past year or so, I had been outspoken within this group as an advocate for academic reform. I was pleased that these women liked my latest tinkering with Wickfield's tenure policies. In particular, I was examining new ways to advance faculty through the promotions process—always a sticky wicket. My proposal—one Dan Jones was supporting—was to allow specific experiences in service and leadership to serve as "research" credit to advance faculty to full professorships. For those lacking time to conduct traditional research that led to academic publishing, my proposal was significant.

"Why not?" I said to the women around the table that day at Duke. We had been relegated to one of those utilitarian rooms that exists on every campus in the country: a functional gray table and matching folding chairs, with a requisite philodendron in the corner. The room choice was a disappointment, since Duke's gray limestone campus was an aristocrat of the South. I had hoped we would be tucked away in a gracious stone building with arches and wainscoting—and carpeting! At least our coffee bar was catered well.

"After all," I continued, "any number of faculty, both men and women, are exemplary leaders in areas that have a scholarship proponent not related specifically to academic studies. For example, some serve on training teams that teach and administer AP tests and thus require strong backgrounds in the sciences or humanities. Many of these leaders have exhibited experience appropriate for advancement."

The women loved the idea and pummeled me with questions. The afternoon flew.

I hated to tear myself away from the group, but Paul was waiting when I returned to the car. I was always struck with the ease with which Paul and I connected. He was a good listener whose comments sometimes offered a wise perspective on an issue. I never tired of hearing him describe lectures from his law classes. Sometimes I fished in my purse for a pen to jot down main points.

Paul, in turn, made me feel witty by chuckling at my stories at exactly the right moments. He enjoyed, for example, my impromptu impersonations of Carrington's grumpiness. I welcomed the release provided by my irreverent theatrics, even though I was clearly breaking the code of professionalism by mimicking the idiosyncrasies of the Wickfield board chairman.

Carrington, however, was not the only trustee who was a thorn in my side. Ina Ross Everwine Farthingale was also a handful. For starters, she answered to both a first name and middle name, running "Inaross" together as if one word—like "Suellen" Ewing, J.R.'s colorful wife on *Dallas*. Ross was her mother's maiden name, such as was commonly given to infant daughters of well-bred Southern families. Everwine was her own maiden name. The tricky part was that Ina Ross insisted on using all four names. They were a mouthful to pronounce.

My Wickfield predecessor had named Ina Ross to the board for her money. She was, after all, fabulously rich. She dressed to the nines, even for campus picnics, and changed husbands with the speed that some use to buy new cars. She was currently married to number four.

In spite of her well-flaunted marriages, Ina Ross was also smart. Her cleverness came naturally: her father was the founder of the Brandyshine furniture empire headquartered east of Greensboro. People in Hurley knew all about Brandyshine sofas and chairs. One of Hurley's biggest textile mills produced their upholstery.

The fall Board of Trustees meeting took place the second Friday in October—three weeks after Hugo hit—and Claire was working overtime to prepare what I was touting as "a printed historical record" of Wickfield's survival of Hugo. On the agenda was also a walking tour so that trustees could survey our damaged trees. The entire meeting promised to run several hours. My head ached just thinking about the swirl of the day.

The headache accelerated when my bedroom phone rang early the morning of the board meeting. My heart sank when I recognized Ina Ross's familiar coo.

"Katherine, darling, I am so sorry to bother you at this impossible hour, but I have a gargantuan problem that I know you can help me solve." I huddled in my bathrobe on the edge of my bed, preparing for the worst.

"I have to meet two contractors at eight—it's an emergency, you understand—so there's no way I can make 10:30 by car, and I do so dearly want to hear every word of our meeting, especially your storm report." She paused, probably for dramatic effect. *Get to the point*, I hissed under my breath, thinking that "storm report" sounded like something Tim would say on the news when handing off to the weatherman.

"So I'm taking our company plane to Hurley, but I will need transportation from your little airport to campus. I know you don't have a shuttle, of course"—her voice tittered—"but surely you can send someone to pick me up?" Her high-pitched chatter scratched my ear.

"Of course, Ina Ross," I said briefly, chasing through a mental list of available staff. Bob Atterbury was the ideal choice, or Claire, with her conversational skills—but both were making critical reports early in the meeting. I couldn't chance a delay for either. The round trip would take close to forty-five minutes, and the driver had to own a respectable car. This was no time to send Odell in his white pickup truck.

"Well, then, ten o'clock? Harvey thinks he can fly it in forty-five minutes, but it all depends on the winds."

"Someone will pick you up at ten," I said with finality. I hung up quickly, irked at facing a curved ball before I'd had my first cup of coffee. Maybe a taxi would be easiest—impersonal but efficient. Ina Ross liked efficiency.

That's when I thought of Paul. He had the charisma, and Ina Ross would love the attention of riding in a police cruiser's front seat. The main problem would be Paul's schedule—no doubt a busy one with trustees on campus. I called Sam Sutton's answering machine and prayed for a quick response. Nothing would be worse than a trustee stranded at the airport—especially one with a yappy mouth.

Fortunately, Sam responded quickly and agreed to send Paul to the airport. I marveled with relief over the ease of the plan. Ina Ross actually flounced into the board meeting a full ten minutes early. I stared a long moment at her stylish chocolate-suede suit. It was trimmed in velvet at the collar, with a thin border of faux fur on the cuffs. Her maxi-skirt flared just enough at the ankles to reveal glossy brown boots. When she spotted me, she floated to my side.

"Thank you for arranging the ride, Katherine, dear, but really"—and here she lowered her voice—"you need to keep your eye on that driver you sent."

"Paul?" I asked, visibly startled.

"Yes, that's the one, Paul. He was delightful at first, quite cheery, but really, I never would have taken him to be a player." Her disapproval shocked me into silence. Then she yoo-hooed across the room to Frances Culpepper, another trustee from Alamance County, and slipped away while her words donged in my head.

A player? Paul? No way! The word was derogatory, describing men whose goal in a relationship was merely that of sex. "Players" by definition were often seductive in their romantic overtures but quick to vanish as soon as their women showed signs of attachment. These women were often left distraught at being "played" by men they had trusted.

Players could be single men or married, and Ina Ross had made it clear that Paul's wedding ring was no barrier to his pursuit of women. My mood plummeted at this revelation. Was this strong connection between Paul and me nothing more than a magnetic charm felt by scores of other women? Was I in danger of falling for a "player"? Was Paul using his role as my driver for personal power? I made a stern mental note to watch every single future thought I shared with Paul.

Even as I made such a vow, I felt sad. My shoulders actually sagged as I processed these thoughts. To recast Paul as a potential rogue would mean a huge hole in the rapport growing between us. I sighed mentally as Carrington called the meeting to order.

In the days that followed, the opportunity to ask Paul about the airport incident eluded me. I was busy beyond belief. There were days when I simply turned to Jackie at her desk and said, "Next?" She would hand me a printout of the next meeting's agenda and point me in the right direction. Beyond faculty meetings and staff assignments, I spoke to student groups, alumni gatherings, and community leaders. Words came easily, inspired as I was by people who loved Wickfield as much as I did. I redeemed little time for myself during that interlude, and there were no out-of-town trips. Paul and I had limited contact.

Late in the evenings, however, when I slumped on my sun porch with a glass of wine, I thought about Ina Ross's words of warning. They seemed completely out of sync with what I had perceived in Paul. I was highly disappointed that I had allowed my growing friendship with him to veil this darker side. What in the world had Paul done to Ina Ross? Had he made a pass, done something truly offensive? Heaven forbid! Yet never in our weeks together had Paul been anything but sterling in words and behavior toward me.

The longer this mystery lingered, the more my confidence in Paul teetered—such was the power he exerted over me. I vowed to get to the bottom of the story. In the process, I would make Paul as uncomfortable as needed to get him to explain himself.

GHOSTS

Hugo's aftermath continued to dominate the news. I reflected over and over about Wickfield's good fortune in enduring the brunt of the storm. In spite of being a century old, our original buildings, hand-built with infinite care, had dodged major damage. In contrast, huge areas of both Carolinas were reeling from catastrophic loss.

Later in October, in events unrelated to the storm, some of Wickfield's most prominent buildings unfortunately suffered a different kind of desecration.

The first problem involved pigeons. For decades these birds had roosted in the eaves of some of Wickfield's most splendid old structures, which ranged in styles from Tudor-Gothic to Romanesque and Classical Revival. This turn-of-the-century architecture created a rooftop hodgepodge of towers and gables. I personally found this skyscape quite charming.

When their breeding seasons peaked, however, pigeons descended on these lairs in mass invasions. The birds were dramatic interlopers. They swooped in at day's end, wings raised at an angle as they navigated the thermal drafts. After landing on our turrets and ledges, they chattered and preened, necks bobbing like exuberant choristers.

"They're almost like good company," I told Claire one day in my office, "if you like cooing, that is, and don't mind the scratching."

I had called Claire to my office to update her on Wickfield's dubious history with pigeons—mainly because they had caused me all kinds of problems with the media last spring.

"But they're filthy, really, and their droppings cause disease and deface our buildings. That speeds up deterioration and increases our maintenance cost. The birds are back, and I'm determined to beat the *Herald* to the punch this season."

"What happened last time?" Claire asked. Goodness, she was a *pretty* young woman. I marveled at her wholesome looks once again, noting her coloring as the afternoon sun splayed through the windows onto her lavender sweater. I was continually impressed as well with her professional work. She was definitely a good hire.

"Two pigeons flew into a classroom. The professor had opened the windows for the breeze, and these birds hopped right in and joined the class. The students loved it and whooped loudly enough to scare the birds, which then flew into a frenzy. They fluttered and batted around every corner of the room, trying to escape. Since the class was so badly disrupted, the professor sent for Odell, who showed up with another worker bearing a broom—and, of all things, a baseball bat."

Claire began to giggle, anticipating the story's end.

"In trying to shoo the pigeons out the window, the men somehow ended up clubbing them to death—a grisly demise, as it was described to me. The students had gone pretty wild by now, cheering for the birds and booing whenever the men struck them. It was disaster run amok."

Claire was laughing hard now. "How did the paper get the story?"

"A couple of students called it in. The headlines were unkind: 'Pigeons Perish in Classroom Clubbing.' And one student wrote a letter to the *Daily Wickfield* describing how sickened she felt while watching the poor birds pummeled in slaughter. The Charlotte papers didn't pick up on that one—we were lucky there."

"What do we do now?" Claire asked, wiping tears of laughter from her eyes.

"Odell has been working on a new battle plan. Talk to him for the details. He's fastened sheet metal onto some of the eaves to discourage roosting. He's adding mechanical prongs that repel the pigeons when they try to land. We tried netting last time, but the pigeons trampled it. There's also a sticky goop, but it's too expensive for our size."

Claire snapped her notebook shut. "I'll get right on it," she said. "Would you like to see a draft of the release?"

"In this case, absolutely," I said. "We'll need to be proactive with the media—before they call us with a problem."

As Claire stood up to leave, she spotted a photograph of me that had been taken last year during the 1988 presidential campaign.

"That's you!" she exclaimed. 'With President Bush!" She crossed over to my side table and picked up the framed color photo. It had been taken in Charlotte well over a year ago, when George Bush, then the Republican candidate, was stumping throughout the South. Some state Republican legislators had pulled me aside after he'd spoken and introduced me.

"He gave a great speech," I said, remembering. I joined her at the table, feeling my spirits rise as I looked at the picture. It always gave me a rush. The president and I were smiling in tandem into the camera, leaning in a bit toward each other. "He was very charming, and Claire, he's incredibly good-looking in person." I felt myself coloring a bit, my voice growing girlish as I described the scene. "He put his hand on my shoulder and spoke a couple of words before the camera clicked, but I can't for the life of me remember what he said." I laughed almost giddily, and Claire looked up at me rather oddly.

"I guess I thought you would be a Democrat," she said as she returned the picture to its place. "Lots of academics are."

"Oh, I am," I said hastily. "You know me. Social advancement for all." I laughed again, but this time it sounded clacky to my ears. I wondered why on earth I had made my description so personal, and I ushered Claire out rather crisply.

The other desecration had far more serious repercussions, and it threw me together with Paul, although not in any way suitable for a discussion of Ina Ross. It involved our newest men's residence hall, Richardson, the scene of David Weise's recent suicide. The building was to be formally dedicated on the last Monday in October, which also happened to be the day before Halloween. Paul had warned me that campus incidents could occur during that weekend.

"It's always worse when Halloween falls on the weekend or shortly after," he said. "Weekends give students more time to get into trouble."

For years I had felt uneasy whenever Halloween rolled around. It sometimes filled me with so much distress that I had come to understand the *dis-ease* in the word "disease." In short, I had an irrational fear of ghosts, a phobia that had begun in my young adulthood. The thought of a world filled with invisible specters chilled me beyond explanation. The malady persisted well into my middle age.

Related to my ghost fixation was an abnormal fear of the dark. A particularly upsetting incident had occurred soon after I had arrived at Wickfield. The night Dan Jones had given me my inaugural tour of

Wellstone Hall, he flicked lights on and off as we entered each office area with his master key. We started in the basement, where wooden scaffolds from the building's early convict labor leaned against the faded brick walls. A bit later, as we ascended those tricky narrow steps to the fourth floor—the one with the Greek and Roman castings—Dan fumbled with unfamiliar light switches, accidentally shutting down all the lights at the very moment we entered the hallway. Terror grabbed me as blackness descended. I steadied myself against a wall.

In that exact moment of panic, I was convinced I saw large white apparitions looming eerily in the corridor ahead—not just one, but several. All had definitive gleaming shapes that grew more distinct as my eyes adjusted to the darkness. I reached for Dan's shoulder, pressing my fingers into his suit jacket and feeling a shriek rise within my throat. Then his hands found the proper switches and flipped on the lights, revealing to me for the first time the unique hallway of statuary. The statue closest to me was young Athena, wearing fish-scaled armor and a Corinthian helmet. I stifled my scream and caught my breath, but Dan seemed to sense my nervousness and hurried me through the tour. We never spoke of the incident again.

On the Friday before the dedication ceremony, Bob Atterbury and I went over every detail of the Monday ceremony. Bob had labored for months, rewriting the script countless times and choosing careful gifts for every member of the Richardson family. Steve and Sheila Richardson, along with their adult son and daughter and spouses, would be attending from several points around the country.

But it was the signage that had caused Bob the greatest angst. The architects had recommended two-foot-high lettering to spell RICHARDSON HALL across the north end of the building. This side faced Merritt Road, a busy thoroughfare that intersected with Grove Avenue east of the dormitory. The charcoal-gray letters were a highly polished aluminum manufactured by an Atlanta firm, a company that Bob had finally settled on after numerous weeks of bids and discussions. The firm was sending a team to install the letters this very day. Bob was a nervous wreck.

"It's a five-pipe day!" I remarked to Jackie that afternoon, and she laughed. Everyone knew that Bob switched pipes frequently when he was especially high-strung. I drove past Richardson that evening to admire the results.

RICHARDSON HALL was spelled out handsomely in dramatic letters. The signage was like icing on a cake—the final addition to a splendid building.

The next morning I arrived early in my Wellstone office, taking advantage of a quiet Saturday to catch up on paperwork. A sharp knock on Jackie's locked outer door startled me, mainly because few people were in the building on weekends. I opened it to find a workman—a member of Odell Evan's physical plant crew—outside. He was breathing heavily, as though in a hurry, and his pained expression caught my attention.

"Yes, Wayne? What is it?" I waited. He appeared thoroughly distressed.

I tried again. "Come in, please." I ushered him into my private office, and he stood silently in front of me, tongue-tied.

"Wayne?" I asked it urgently this time.

"Chancellor Embright, I'm sorry to bother you, but Officer Stafford—"

Paul! My heart raced. Wayne had stopped midsentence.

"Yes?"

"Officer Stafford wanted me to tell you that there's a . . . something happened at Richardson Hall." I held my breath. "He wanted you to know he's working on it right now, before you heard it from anyone else."

"What kind of incident?"

"Some students . . . " He started over. "Somebody messed with the letters on the side of the new dorm. Richardson. Some of them is missing. It happened during the night." He stopped. "But Officer Stafford thinks it's students in the dorm, just a prank, and he's talking to them now. He's shut down the entire building to get to the bottom of it. Odell thinks the letters can be put up again if we can find them."

"How many letters?" My mind was racing. Timing was everything. The dedication was two days away, scheduled for 2:30 p.m. "Is the building surface damaged?"

"Not really, ma'am, nothing that can't be covered up if we find them letters. But it's causing all kinds of traffic problems on Merritt. Officer Stafford didn't want you to find out by driving by. He sent me to let you know he's working on it."

"Has Bob Atterbury been notified?" The story was very strange. I struggled to sort out the facts.

Wayne shook his head. "I really don't know, ma'am." He shuffled, seeming eager to leave. "I really need to get back—"

"Wait a minute." I stood deep in thought, still puzzled. "Why is there a traffic problem? It's just missing letters, right?" Although the lettering was in plain sight of drivers on Merritt Road, I couldn't understand a traffic jam. The wall was not in the direct sight line of cars waiting at the light.

Wayne suddenly turned bright red. I stared at him, hard. "Wayne?" He looked down at his feet and shifted his weight.

"Wayne? What's going on? What letters are missing?"

Wayne continued to shuffle. "It's four letters, ma'am."

"Which letters?" My voice was harsh. "Tell me exactly what the wall says right now."

Wayne looked as if he would prefer dental surgery to this conversation, but I held my ground.

"The R is missing," he began. "And the I. And the C."

"Sounds like they were going for the whole word," I mused. "What else?"

Wayne reddened again, and I waited, perplexed.

"And . . . the S." He stopped.

"The *S*? Interesting. R, I, C, and S," I repeated slowly. I didn't get it. Richardson Hall. I tried to arrange the remaining letters in my mind's eye. It was like playing a mental version of hangman.

Then, in a flash, I did understand, and my mouth fell open. "Dear God." I sank into the nearest chair.

At my reaction, Wayne seemed eager to speak. "At first, bunches of students was hanging out of the windows with their shirts off, waving them in the air and pointing to the letters and cheering at the cars below. And cars was honking like crazy, and folks was waving back. It was kind of wild there for a while. That was before Officer Stafford got there."

"Thank you very much, Wayne," I said, keeping my face straight. I herded him to the door and began to close it on him. "Please thank Officer Stafford and ask him and Odell to report to me as soon as this is under control. I'll be in my office."

Wayne exited, and I closed the door, leaning against it. I clapped both hands over my mouth and shook hard for several seconds in outrageous mirth. But even as I was doubled over with laughter, I knew I was facing a crisis rife with major repercussions.

Could this really be happening? And on my watch?

Chapter 20
CULPRITS

There are times when the whirl of life is so unpredictable that it sucks you into its vortex. It spins you silly until you are spat out in a crumpled heap well beyond your control.

That's the way I felt upon hearing about the Richardson Hall vandalism. It seemed impossible that any of our Wickfield students could have committed such an immature act—desecration upon a beautiful building—and with such a dire sense of timing. The dedication was only two days away. The entire Richardson family was coming to the event, and currently their gift of a dormitory was a crude dirty joke, quickly becoming the butt of humor throughout Hurley. Worse, it was occurring under my tenure. The situation was incredibly serious.

Fortunately, I was able to quickly regain my composure. I paced my office floor, the facts tumbling fast. If the letters on the wall could not be retrieved, Wickfield could be facing a catastrophe. We might have to remove the remaining letters before Monday's ceremony, but then we'd have a terrible void on the building, which would be embarrassing for the university and totally unfair to the Richardson family. Even if we found the letters, was there time to rehang them? Could Odell's men do it adequately, or would we have to fly in the Atlanta firm? And would they come on a Sunday? A *Sunday?*

And what about Bob! I knew Bob Atterbury would be horrified, yet he must be informed as soon as possible. I gazed out my west window toward the back campus, trying to envision the scarred wall and its message. Of course this story would spread rapidly through town. People were doubtless already cruising by Richardson just to see the sight for themselves. They would either howl in hilarity or despair on Wickfield's behalf—or maybe something in between, depending on age and maturity and sensibility.

I dialed the Atterbury's home number, still considering my approach in delivering this news to Bob. Susan answered; Bob and the boys were out getting haircuts. She gasped when she heard the story. "Oh. Oh, God. Oh, no." That was all she could moan as I unraveled the details.

"Tell him as gently as you can," I said, "and have him call me immediately for an update. Perhaps we'll have better news by then."

Unbelievably, when Paul Stafford knocked on my office door less than an hour later, he indeed had better news. Yes, he had nailed the culprits and recovered the letters. Just like that, after all my angst! I listened like a wide-eyed child as Paul perched on my settee and rolled out his tale.

"Four students were involved," he reported. "They managed to unhinge the letters, working with just enough shadows and darkness to avoid being seen. The passing cars couldn't see them directly, and two of the guys knew how to remove the letters without breaking them. Each agreed to hide one letter."

"So you searched the entire dorm and found them?" I asked.

"No, I used an old Army trick. We corralled all the guys in the dorm and ended up with a hundred guys sitting on the floor in the main lounge, or however many were present when I sealed the building. No one could leave. No bathroom breaks. Jake positioned staffers at each door. If a resident tried to enter the building, he had to join the crowd. Visitors were turned away. We sat there until the guilty parties 'fessed up."

I gaped. "Just like that, they 'fessed up? Just like that?"

"Well, not quite." Paul looked at me thoughtfully, as if deciding how much to tell. "I made everyone turn in their car keys and room keys and told them they'd get them back as soon as we found the letters. Someone from Jake's staff checked them off against a master roster and kept track. I had notified Sam early, by the way, and he actually showed up. I put him to work alphabetizing the keys while I talked to the guys."

I laughed aloud at the image of our aging police chief playing with bunches of key rings, like a kindergartner with Legos. "Did you give the guys holy hell?"

"Not at all," Paul said. "I was very pleasant. Told 'em we had all day and night, if that's what it took. I told a few bad jokes, the worst ones I could think of. I threatened to sing to them." He grinned. "Oh, and I had the RA turn off the air-conditioning. Works every time. Then peer pressure took over, and there were some pleading speeches and lots of general disgust against those who did it. That was interesting, since a couple of the speakers had participated in the shirt-waving. I saw them when I first pulled up in my car.

"The guy who broke first—his name is Barry, the kid from Asheville—stood and spoke to the other three directly. I frankly think they were all glad to get it over with. They left one at a time to get the letters while everyone waited. One was in a closet, another in a car trunk. One guy had hidden his letter in his girlfriend's room in another dorm, so Jake sent someone to pick it up."

It was hard to believe Paul had accomplished so much so quickly. My thoughts were whirling as he stood to leave. The next hurdle would be to find a way to reinstall the letters. We had only forty-eight hours before the dedication.

As Paul departed down the hall, I spotted Bob and Jake entering the corridor from the far end. I watched as they paused to speak to Paul and saw Bob actually slump against the wall in what was obvious relief. As they continued toward me, I thought about how much emotion these two men put into their work for Wickfield. Bob probably knew as much about fundraising as any Advancement vice president in the region. And Jake—well, I usually trusted him beyond words when it came to finesse in dealing with students.

Until now, that is. Now, I hardly knew where to begin with him. I ushered both men into my office. "How did this happen?" I demanded, glaring at Jake as I paced. My patience was running thin. "Security alerted us to be extra cautious this week! These vandals were almost in plain sight of the public! How did they get away with this?"

"I think it was part luck and part daring," said Jake, ducking under my harshness. "It was a lark, a last-minute idea when they saw the letters go up. They thought it would be cool and funny and attractive to the girls. They obviously didn't think it through very well—just the part about stealing the letters. It never occurred to them that they'd be caught so easily. A couple of them are pretty remorseful."

"Katherine, excuse me, please, but if I may say so, it was partly my responsibility," began Bob. "I thought I had every angle of this dedication covered, but I'll be doggoned if I didn't overlook the idea of vandalism. It never occurred to me. I was concentrating so hard on getting the materials here on time from Atlanta that I—"

"It's not your fault, Bob. These young men have committed a serious offense, one worthy of expulsion. It's important that we stay focused on our role in either punishing them or rehabilitating them—or both. I like the latter idea best. I'll have more to say on this Monday at cabinet. Where are the young men now?" I turned to Jake.

"Waiting in my office."

"Okay, do your usual process, let them sweat, keep them grounded over the weekend. When do you notify the parents?"

"After I meet with the students."

"Okay, but remember, they're forbidden to leave the dorm all weekend. Be absolutely clear on that. I've been thinking through several approaches, and here's what's first on my list: I want all four men in coats and ties at the dedication Monday."

Jake looked stunned. "Why? Isn't that rewarding them? Letting them go to the dedication?"

"We're not 'letting' them do anything. They won't be there as honored guests," I said. "I want them in a group near the back, with you on one side and Sam Sutton on the other. Afterward, I want them to meet Steve and Sheila and as many family members as possible at the reception. You and Sam will walk them through line and introduce them as ordinary students. The family isn't to know about any of this, of course, assuming we can get the letters reinstalled in time. Hopefully the Richardsons will never *ever* hear of this incident."

Jake began to smile. "Do I sense another amazing Katherine Embright scheme in the works?"

"Not at all," I replied. "But I don't want to waste four young lives, and this just may be an opportunity to ignite them. I'll need complete files on all four men this afternoon—also full write-ups on the calls to the parents and another copy of the Steve Richardson profile."

Jake nodded. "Garbage Can?"

"If I'm not home." Jake was referring to a decorative gardening container I kept at my breezeway door for emergency staff drop-offs. Everyone on the cabinet used it for last-minute reports or messages. During my two years at Wickfield it had acquired its affectionate moniker.

As we were talking, Odell showed up at my door, breathless and sweaty. "Excuse me, Chancellor, but I think I've figured out how we can get them letters back up. The guys told me how they got 'em down. The mounting hardware is still on the wall, so it's not that big a deal to rehang them. My men are on it."

Bob and Jake and I actually cheered. "Bob, go home, put your feet up, and give yourself a proper Saturday. You deserve it. Jake, go handle the students. Remember, let them sweat, and don't tell them what we're planning. We'll hash out more details Monday. Trust me. The day will go well."

The next day at church, my heart was still full of thoughts about our young vandals. *"Please guide me, Lord, in steering their lives,"* I whispered as I knelt. *"Give me wisdom in my leadership. Give me courage."* It was not that I felt weak as a leader, but I wanted no missteps. As usual, prayer was my companion that day.

When I read the background reports on the four culprits, I was surprised at their talent and promise. None had been in trouble at Wickfield before. All came from seemingly solid middle-class families, and each had shown potential to rise to true leadership. Hal Baldwin, the ringleader—the one who had conceived the idea and climbed the ladder—had worked summer construction jobs at sixteen. Jerry Hulsey, his sidekick and roommate, was a business major with a B average. Robin Lee played lead trumpet in the marching band. Barry Bannister, the first one to confess, had been president of his high school's Key Club. I puzzled the most over him.

By the time I went to bed Sunday, I knew I wanted a personal audience with the four students. Such a meeting was highly out of the norm. The student honor council routinely handled disciplinary cases, and the chancellor rarely saw offenders face to face. This case, however, was different. It required immediate action. I would exercise executive privilege by recommending probation without expulsion, and I would speak to the men personally.

The cabinet unanimously supported this the next morning, and Jake promised to have the men in my office at eleven, well before the dedication. Jackie bent over her desk to rework my morning schedule.

At the hour of eleven, the miscreants filed in, somber at the formality of my office and caught off guard at this surprise gathering. They were dressed casually, and three—all but Barry—were unshaven.

"Gentlemen." I acknowledged them coolly, maintaining eye contact, and pointing to the settee and chairs. They took their seats. I remained standing.

Yet in spite of the solemnity, my words were simple. I was betting that the men were amply mortified by what was now being viewed throughout the campus as an act of sheer stupidity. I had decided to appeal to their parental upbringing. From what I had researched, all four had had basic values instilled in them long ago.

In short, I talked about conscience and character.

"I'm sure you realize how serious a situation we have on our hands," I began. "Each of you has confused your priorities. You have succumbed to the false idea that sexual prowess and popularity are what really count in life. You have betrayed your parents and grandparents and every good thing they ever taught you. You have betrayed yourselves and every good thing you once imagined for yourselves."

The men sat slumped, staring at the floor.

"Let me tell you a story. In your eagerness to show off and look like heroes, you lost sight of the fact that there are lives behind the name you tore off that wall. The Richardson name has been synonymous with integrity for decades.

"Still, things weren't always easy for Steve Richardson. He grew up in a town in eastern North Carolina that's so small it's not even found on most maps. When he was a child, his father gave him an area of the family garden to call his own, so he grew big red tomatoes and loaded them into his wagon to sell to summer lakeside residents. It was his first job. He was eight.

"After his father died in an accident, Steve Richardson worked in a factory near his hometown. He manned the three-to-eleven shift after school, hitching rides with a neighbor since he couldn't drive. In spite of all, he still maintained grades high enough to get him into Carolina on a scholarship. Steve didn't mind work. He'd been working for years, and he was thrilled to find he could major in business and get paid for what by now was easy to him. He didn't have a lot of money for dating, but he had charm, and he enchanted a pretty brown-eyed brunette named Sheila from Meredith College by singing corny songs to her until she agreed to be his girl. Eventually, she agreed to be his wife.

"Then, because he was smart, and because he knew the power of sweat and he followed the rules of ethics, he brokered all kinds of deals as a salesman, working terrible hours to make sure his family had the things he didn't get to enjoy growing up. Today he owns *five* Ford dealerships in both Carolinas and Virginia—yes, five—and he's big enough of heart to give Wickfield several million dollars so that young men like you can have a comfortable and attractive home while you study. He made all this possible so that you will make good grades and have successful careers and, like him, enjoy life in prosperity and joy."

The men remained silent.

"Steve Richardson is very excited about the ceremony that will take place here in a few hours. So is his entire family: Sheila, his son Trey and Trey's wife Laura and their teenagers, his daughter Michelle and her husband Peter and their young sons. This day is a dream come true for a man who forty years ago didn't have an extra nickel in his pocket and who had to wheel and deal to borrow a car so he could drive from Chapel Hill to Raleigh to sing corny songs to a pretty brown-eyed girl."

I waited several seconds before shifting to a more informal tone.

"For today, I'm sending you back to the dorm to shower and shave and change into coat and tie. If you don't have a tie, borrow one. I'm asking Vice President Mooney to escort you to the dedication so you can witness how a university honors generosity. Maybe in the process you can learn a bit about honor yourselves. As you listen to Mr. Richardson's words this afternoon, I want you to think about the years of hard and honest work he's encountered since he was your age. Try to imagine the pride he will feel when he sees the words RICHARDSON HALL as he drives past the building today.

"Think also about how he would have felt to find his name desecrated in ridicule."

The room was hushed. The only one who met my eyes as they filed out was Barry, whose shy smile wobbled somewhere between remorse and gratitude.

Chapter 21
TURKEYS IN CHICAGO

The near fiasco with the Richardson Hall dedication rankled with me long after our afternoon celebration. Steve Richardson's voice had cracked at the lectern, and his emotion had not been lost upon our bright but misguided students. Even so, I churned with uneasiness. The vandalism reminded me of the precarious nature of human beings in the crosshairs of critical thinking. Even the best of us could make foolish decisions—myself included.

And it was in situations where men were involved—affairs of the heart—that I was probably the most vulnerable. That thought hung over me like a dark veil as I faced the upcoming holiday with Alex.

Alex and I had been a couple for nearly four years when I left Chicago for Wickfield. We had met in the student dining hall at Keck College. I had been emerging from the faculty-staff corner during a fast-paced lunch hour, holding a plastic tray bearing the remains of my meal and heading toward the nearby conveyor belt. "Katherine!" a voice called out, and I glanced over toward the exit door. Jarvis Briggs, chairman of the Biology Department, was standing there with another man, tall, slender, and bespectacled. Jarvis beckoned me with his head, and I detoured over, still holding the tray.

"Katherine, I'd like you to meet Dr. Alex Wentworth from the Filburn Medical Group in Highland Park," Jarvis said, looking at me meaningfully. Jarvis and I were faculty lounge buddies; he had heard me spout off more than once about love, marriage, divorce, and the futility of finding perfect love. "Dr. Wentworth is serving on the panel for this afternoon's symposium on athletic injuries."

I looked into a set of smiling gray-green eyes and instantly recognized that old stomach lurch—nearly nonexistent since my early days with Tim. I was suddenly grateful for the plates smeared with spaghetti sauce and Italian dressing. I was able to return the smile while keeping a casual distance.

"Hello," I said coolly, my eyes sucking in the well-groomed man in gray suit, splashy tie of red whorls, and clear-rimmed glasses.

Alex called me at home that night—Jarvis answered his pleas for my phone number—and we talked for nearly two hours. I knew several doctor-friends socially but none that were surgeons. He spoke that night in his fast Midwestern clip, sprinkling the conversation with multisyllabic words like *laparoendoscopic* and *diverticulosis*. His medical jargon was like a foreign language, yet I found it fascinating.

We fell in love quickly. I soon absorbed Alex's world of medicine, while he learned my cosmos of higher education. Ours grew into a comfortable relationship where marriage was assumed to be a natural but not imminent destination. We met each other's professional colleagues. We shared movies and football games and expensive vacations. My sisters welcomed Alex to our holiday gatherings.

When Wickfield came knocking on my door for the chancellorship, Alex was astounded—and deeply hurt. It had never occurred to him that I might prefer a fulfilling professional career to a comfortable life as a surgeon's wife. The truth was, even throughout the years of our heady romance, I'd known full well that I would never stalemate my career. Indeed, I'd been constantly aware of opportunities to advance it. I had often huddled with the weekly arrival of the *Chronicle of Higher Education*, studying the advertised positions for college presidents with much more than a casual eye.

That's where I'd spotted the distinctive display ad for the chancellorship at Wickfield. The University of North Carolina was a luminary among public universities, and the mere thought of being a part of its massive organization was intoxicating. I quickly applied, all the while knowing I was probably too young for the position and that competition would be fierce. Yet, after passing the initial phone interview, I was invited to meet several administrators on the Wickfield campus. I assumed the final candidates would be named soon after, and the search committee, to my relief, asked me to return to Hurley for "one more round of conversations." That was the trip during which Carrington grilled me to such a painful point that I felt real doubts about the wisdom of leaving Chicago.

In the end, however, Fate prevailed. Carrington recommended me to Charles Pettigrew in Chapel Hill, who officially hired me.

In loving Alex and learning about his profession, I made an amusing discovery: physicians and business-school professors had much in common. It wasn't just that they were both well heeled—business professors were well known at Keck for holding the highest faculty salaries. There was something more, something subtle regarding their personalities and chosen fields of specialty. Like pediatricians, the marketing professors were gregarious, even noisy in their friendliness. The accountants were like internists, single-tracked and focused, and the management wizards were as curious and diverse as psychiatrists.

But surgeons? They were hard to pigeonhole. Some had hearts and souls as big as the earth—but many, sadly, had egos to match.

I remarked on this to Paul during another trip to Chapel Hill in early November—a week after the Richardson Hall dedication and our first trip in several weeks. We were returning from a meeting of the chancellors—a periodic gathering that took place in Charlie Pettigrew's office in the General Administration Building. I thoroughly enjoyed these discussions; they were times of free-wheeling conversations unique to us as regional chancellors. Charlie—he insisted we call him Charlie—promised he would never take a policy to the Board of Governors for a vote without discussing it with us first.

"Alex, for example, sees the world from a very narrow perspective," I said to Paul quite seriously. "It's as though he wears blinders. He lives his life in snippets. He goes to bed early and gets up early. Sometimes he catches the news and sports, but most of the time his schedule is so irregular he simply concentrates on what he knows best, which is surgery. He enjoys his medical journals the same way most men enjoy *Sports Illustrated*. Surgery is everything. When he looks at people in general, he sees scientific anatomy. He doesn't have much of a social life." I sighed, feeling a bit sorry for Alex. "Really, little at all, except when we get together."

Paul took his eyes off the road to give me a swift sideways glance. "You don't really believe that, do you?"

I took offense at Paul's unexpected tone. "Alex doesn't have time for other women, if that's what you mean. He works too hard."

Paul said nothing as we hummed west along I-40. His question was an uneasy reminder about Alex's recent sporadic communications. My Thanksgiving visit to Chicago was only two weeks away.

The rise in my pique offered the moment I had been seeking regarding Ina Ross's recent comment.

"By the way," I said, changing the subject smoothly, "how did things go for you the day of our board meeting? You know—that mission of mercy to pick up our stranded trustee at the airport."

"Ina Ross, you mean?" Paul's voice was even. There was not the least bit of worry in his tone.

"Yes. She's very colorful."

"I'll say."

"What do you mean?"

"She's a confident woman. Knows what she wants. Nothing shy about that lady."

"Did something happen?" I had to ask; Paul's tone suggested nothing less.

"Nothing important enough to talk about."

"Come now, Paul, what does that mean? You can't drop a comment like that without explaining it." Paul was a good enough friend that I could actually confide in him a few personal thoughts, but, with the exception of my occasional stabs at Carrington, we spoke lightly where Wickfield people were concerned. In this case, however, something almost alarming in Paul's tone made me press forward.

"Really, it's not important." Paul seemed uncomfortable for the first time. We were approaching heavy rush-hour traffic on the outskirts of Greensboro. He toyed with the handle that adjusted his rearview mirrors, as if reminding me he needed to concentrate on his driving. Even so, I kept on.

"Well, for the record, Ina Ross did not seem particularly impressed with your chauffeuring skills that day."

"I'm sure." A smile tugged at his mouth in spite of his caustic tone. I said nothing, waiting.

We drove on another couple of miles in silence. Paul glided in and out of traffic with his usual expertise. I watched cars slow a bit as drivers followed the overhead green traffic signs and chose lanes for either Winston-Salem or Charlotte.

"Ina Ross is not a lady used to hearing the word no. At least that's what I figured when I said it to her," Paul finally said, his eyes focused on the road. "When I delivered her to the front door of Wellstone, she asked if my work ever took me to her neck of the state. She handed me her business card when she said it. Her personal phone number was circled. There was no doubt about what she meant—it was apparent in the way she laughed when she said 'work,' meaning just the opposite. That's when I said no. That's all I said—simply no—no explanation. She reacted as if I had slapped her. She didn't thank me or make the usual pleasantries in saying goodbye. She yanked the card out of my hand and reached for the door handle before I could open it for her. I recall she slammed the door as she marched off."

I said nothing at first, mulling over his story and imagining the scene.

"Well, that explains why she was so hard on you once she showed up at the meeting. As they say, hell hath no fury like—"

"Like a woman scorned," finished Paul.

"She misread you," I said thoughtfully, still reviewing the scene in my mind. "She saw a handsome man, a friendly one, and assumed you would succumb to her money and charms. She didn't consider that you might be a happily married father of two teenagers who refused to be tempted."

I turned my head as I said these words, sneaking a peek at Paul's profile.

It was a view I liked: a sensuous mouth that birthed utterances both humorous and wise, and a solid physical frame.

That Paul had been wrongly implicated by Ina Ross came as a relief, but it also reminded me that the frequent hammering of my heart needed to be put to rest. I well understood the pitfalls of falling for a married man, much less a Wickfield employee. The constraints were cemented in my girlhood when my core values were formed. Through the years I had prided myself on maintaining those values.

So, after that revealing conversation about Ina Ross, I silently berated myself whenever the subject of Paul surfaced in my internal conversations: *Enjoy the charm, Kat, but keep it in check.* Our ease of conversation was the most curious draw between us. I marveled time after time about that. It added an intimacy to our relationship that neither of us sought. It was simply there, both a gift and a peril. I understood well the need for caution.

Fortunately, Thanksgiving loomed as an antidote for this distracting schoolgirl crush. Alex began showing real interest in my visit. He called one night, unusually eager, to describe our social calendar for the long weekend.

"We're invited to Ted and Myra Lambert's home for Thanksgiving dinner. They've finally moved into their new house on the lake. It's a stunner; you'll love it. Friday we'll relax at my place—drive around the Keck campus if you like. Since you want to shop Water Tower, Saturday might be better than Friday, since it's Black Friday—although Saturday will be crowded, too. Think about where you'd like to go. We'll do the art museum, too."

Christmas shopping along the Magnificent Mile in Chicago! How long had it been? I closed my eyes, envisioning Michigan Avenue with its fairyland of tiny white lights and its street musicians who puffed wreaths of frost as they sang carols. It was the perfect remedy for the tension from my frenetic Wickfield pace. I was exhausted. It had been nearly two months since Hugo had hit, and I had to admit that I had never known a semester so physically demanding. My sleep these days reminded me of my childhood slumbers—long and very deep.

"Wonderful!" I told Alex, and I meant it. Thanksgiving in Chicago would be stupendous! I was so weary that night that I scarcely had the strength to reach up to turn off my bedside lamp. But the trip was a little more than a week away, and I could hold out until then. I folded my pillow in half lengthwise and cushioned it under the back of my neck.

As I drifted off, I realized that at this point in time, Paul Stafford was being tucked safely away into a distant corner of my heart.

Chapter 22
THANKSGIVING

In hindsight, I probably should have taken my fatigue in November more seriously. I dismissed it, as do many women, blaming it on the unusual stress the fall semester had thrust upon me. One major stress factor was the time I was putting into the new WHCC task force. WHCC was the acronym for the new Wickfield-Hurley Community Collaboration task force, a product of our unified efforts after Hugo. I had pronounced the acronym "Whichy" when we formed it in early October. Mayor Barnhardt had wanted the Hurley name first in the title, but, for a myriad of reasons, I argued strongly for Wickfield as the anchor name. "Besides," I said reasonably, "you can't pronounce anything that begins with an H and a W."

The catchy moniker stuck like a marketing stamp, and the mayor was placated with coverage in the *Hurley Herald* that made him look heroic. I was immensely pleased with this "town-and-gown" project. It was a direct outgrowth of my conversations with the mayor after the storm. It gave form to a vision I had long held but never had the opportunity to develop—the city and university working together in mutual support.

As for Carrington's tiresome grousing about Wickfield's need to "protect against the world," the Whichy project became the solution. What could be better than to have Wickfield tied closely to the city as a partner? The trustees loved the idea of an alliance with Hurley's city fathers. At the board's October meeting, following the campus tour, I had provided detailed reports of our post-Hugo efforts. They voiced unanimous support for the project.

To my relief, Carrington said little in opposition to the project. "He's mellowing in his old age," I crowed to Paul during one of our trips.

"Maybe he knows he's outnumbered," Paul chuckled back.

To head Wickfield's arm of the collaboration, I picked Susan Atterbury. "She's the perfect choice," I told the board, enormously pleased with myself for selecting her. "She's smart and articulate, she has the time to apply to the project, and she's worked with the mayor in earlier projects." The fact that she was married to a Wickfield administrator was a bonus.

During October I had devoted hours to shaping Wickfield's part of this collaboration. In the end, I added Jake to the committee to represent Wickfield. He was, after all, gatekeeper of our student civic volunteers.

The effort, however, had taken a physical toll. It was good to put these affairs behind me by boarding a late-afternoon flight to Chicago the day before Thanksgiving. My USAir aircraft looked like a huge hammock ready to rock me to sleep. Once buckled into my window seat, I relaxed like a wilting flower that drooped from its vase. I wrapped myself in an airline blanket and fell asleep as soon as we were aloft. When I awakened to preparations for landing, I gazed below upon a small starry kingdom of fairyland lights.

Alex met me at my gate. I sank gratefully into his open arms while he pecked me on the mouth. I was happy to let him guide me through the massive terminal, which was teeming with holiday passengers lugging heavy coats and shopping bags. I loved O'Hare's international hustle. It hinted of a larger cosmos outside the glass walls. I had to admit, a bit ruefully, that life in Hurley, North Carolina, was prosaic at best. My most exotic trip this fall had been a car ride to Chapel Hill.

Next, a surprise awaited me, one for which I was totally unprepared. Alex directed me through the airport garage to his pickup truck, a secondhand vehicle he had purchased a year earlier. I hadn't questioned the purchase at the time, especially since its four-wheel drive maneuvered well on icy side roads during Illinois' frozen winters. Now he helped me in without apology, merely saying he didn't want to expose his new car to the heavy traffic of the city.

"New car? You never mentioned a new car," I said, startled. "What was wrong with the Lexus?" I felt a stab of loss. The silver Lexus was a glory of luxurious leather seats and a state-of-the-art stereo system. I loved that car. It had felt safe, and it was stylish and good-looking. Now I had to squirm to get comfortable in the truck's narrow front seat.

"Nothing, really," he responded as we wound through the airport's maze of departing lanes. "I liked the new one better."

We entered the flowing stream of traffic, which seemed faster than usual from my perch high in the truck's cab. I exclaimed over the lights of the city, and the subject of the new car was dropped. Alex lived in the exclusive suburb of Highland Park, and we spent the hour-long drive catching up on news.

The new car, I discovered soon enough, was spectacular. It was a wine-colored Jaguar that gleamed like a jewel in the lights of our truck as Alex pressed the remote control button that lifted his garage door. Again, I was jolted. Alex rarely discussed his finances except to recommend an occasional investment, and since we both had attractive salaries, we took each other's comfortable lifestyles for granted. But this—this car was pure *extravagance,* easily worth a dozen Wickfield scholarships. I wondered about the attraction of surgeons to sports cars, recalling the jaunty red Triumph I had ridden in to fetch gas that day in the mountains. That, too, had belonged to a surgeon.

I didn't try to analyze Alex, however. During my four days with him, I enjoyed the flashy low-slung roadster, succumbing for the time being to its gaudy symbolism of power and ego. It carried us to Lake Forest for the elegant turkey repast at the Lamberts' estate overlooking wind-chopped Lake Michigan. It took us through gorgeous old neighborhoods I had known well during my years at Keck College, past handsome Tudors and colonials with established trees and lawns and sidewalks. They reminded me of Charlotte and the drive to Queens College that first day I had traveled with Paul. My heart lurched a bit at the thought of Paul. It still did these days, even when I was with Alex.

I thought little else about Wickfield that weekend. True to his word, Alex created diversions that I eagerly absorbed. Early Saturday we took his truck into the city—he was afraid of damaging the Jaguar in a parking garage—and shopped at Saks and Neiman-Marcus and Crate 'N Barrel. We ate an elegant lunch at the Ritz-Carlton. Back on Michigan Avenue, we stood outdoors in an incredibly long line to purchase bags of piping-hot caramel corn. We were still licking our fingers after stashing our empty sacks in a public trashcan.

For our trip to the Art Institute, I had assumed we would walk from the Water Tower down Michigan Avenue, as we had done in earlier times. Alex and I had strolled through this area many times in our past. The walk would take us past the amazing Chicago Tribune building, constructed of flinty Indiana limestone, and the gleaming white Wrigley Building at Wacker Drive. Both edifices dazzled like treasures in gorgeous old European cities.

In the end, though, my head throbbed and my feet hurt, so Alex hailed a cab. As our taxi approached the museum, now shadowed by afternoon sun, I caught sight of the gallant bronzed lions that marked the entrance. The majestic cats usually made me pulse with excitement, but today I felt a wearing down. Even the wondrous Asian and Impressionist collections failed to ignite me. Somehow, my soul rejected antiquity. My one pleasure was the Thorne Rooms of architectural miniatures—rows of tiny houses representing periods of European and American history, re-created in perfect detail. The precision was astounding—right down to the furniture, wallpaper, kitchen sinks, and porch swings. The intricacies of time and art produced a calming effect.

"So beautiful," I whispered as Alex and I peered over the rails at the exquisite replicas. I repressed a surprising sob in my throat. Beauty did that to me.

For dinner, we decided on Berghoff's, a longtime favorite. It held special memories for us. Alex had first professed his love for me during an evening several years ago at this popular German restaurant. Now we walked the two blocks from the museum through gathering darkness. Rich aromas greeted us, and a black-jacketed waiter led us to a small table near the wall. The festoons of sparkling Christmas lights set off the polished dark wood and stained-glass windows. I kicked off my shoes under the table, eager for the solace of sauerbraten and home-brewed beer.

"Feeling better?" Alex asked, his eyes studying me across the table.

"Much. The shopping undid me. I'm used to a desk," I teased. The waiter set two mounds of rye bread before us.

"You've looked tired this weekend," Alex said. He busied himself with the warm loaves, cleaving each with precise surgical slices.

"Could well be," I replied lightly. "In the past three months alone, I've tangled with Mother Nature, fought with my board chairman, entertained scores of students in my home, driven over half the state of North Carolina, played hardball with our city mayor—and that's just for starters."

Alex passed me a hefty piece of buttered bread. "Not that kind of tired. It's your eyes. I don't like those purple hollows. You getting enough sleep?"

"Actually, I'm sleeping more than ever. Forget Johnny and *The Tonight Show*." I was enjoying the banter. "Are you asking as my boyfriend or my doctor?"

"Right now, I'm both. I'm serious, Kat. When did you have your last physical?"

"One's coming up in January. My birthday, remember?" Of course he remembered. I would be turning fifty on January 25. The subject of my "Big 5-0" had surfaced in recent conversations.

"Move it up to December. Ask for a complete blood panel. I'll write out what you should request. Do it before the holidays."

Alex and I would be spending our first Christmas apart this year. At the last minute he had been asked to present a paper at an international conference of surgeons in Hawaii. I, of course, would be in Richmond for the Embright family reunion. Alex and I had decided to postpone our personal Christmas until my birthday. Tonight would be our last evening together for nearly two months.

But if I had hoped for tender romance this evening, it was not to be. I fell asleep as the truck jounced back to Alex's house, my chin jerking into the collar of my coat. Alex tucked me into his bed like a child.

In the morning I awoke to empty sheets, inhaling the elixirs of bacon and coffee that drifted up the stairs. When I wandered downstairs in my robe, I found Alex engaged in front of a skillet. What remained of the Sunday *New York Times* was folded in neat little stacks near the fireplace.

Before we left for the airport at noon, Alex wrote out exact instructions for a medical workup. "Give this to your doctor," he said, eyeing me sternly over his kitchen table. "Before the holidays."

Even more disappointing, there was no tender embrace at the house or airport—only another sweet peck at the USAir gate. The aircraft climbed into November's bright-blue ether, its powerful engines freighted with silent melancholy. We leveled out over the sprawling metropolis. Chicago's skyline and waters glittered briefly before disappearing into hazy brown fields.

I was reflective as I settled into my seat for the two-hour flight to Charlotte. Alex had been attentive, even if not passionate. There had been no mysterious phone calls or unexplained errands. If there were intrusions in our relationship, which now seemed unlikely, they were safely tucked away.

Yet if loving and being loved is the greatest joy on earth, I thought achingly, why was my heart not singing?

Chapter 23
MADRIGAL DINNER

Whatever disappointment stalked me when I left Chicago was lost in the aircraft's vapor trails. Back in Hurley, work engulfed me. With the advent of December I was overwhelmed with end-of-semester events. Dan Smith's Office of Academic Affairs was preparing for winter commencement—as he reminded us in a meticulous summary the Monday after Thanksgiving.

"It's twelve pages this year," he said as he handed out neatly prepared packets at our cabinet meeting. "Two more than last year. This year's includes a flow chart for the faculty procession."

I groaned aloud, flipping through Dan's detailed pages and recalling last year's near-debacle during winter commencement in the gymnasium. The student marshals had failed to count out enough seats for faculty—someone had forgotten to tell them that part-time faculty were also marching. As a result, an entire row of professors was left stranded in the aisle, shifting uncomfortably in their robes and tasseled velvet hats while gazing about for seats. There was last-minute scramble as extra chairs were rushed in and the stragglers were squeezed in among parents on side aisles. I had watched from the stage, appalled, as the scene unfolded before me.

"Everything's covered," Dan assured me, as if reading my thoughts. "We've added the Wickfield flag to the North Carolina and American flags." This was a new touch I had requested. "We've hired a signing specialist for the deaf." Again, my request. I had insisted on considerations for the "hearing impaired," which was the politically correct term of the day.

"And the *a cappella* choir will sing traditional ballads in honor of Dr. Murchison's British background." I nodded my approval. Rachel Murchison was our keynote speaker, a renowned child-advocacy expert with Scotch-Irish ties to North Carolina. I had been thrilled when her Washington DC office called to accept our invitation for her to speak. As part of our ceremony, we would hood her with an honorary Doctor of Humane Letters degree.

However, my most pressing concern after Thanksgiving was holiday décor for the Chancellor's House. Immediately after the commencement ceremony, I would be hosting the platform party at the house. Since the group included the entire Board of Trustees, I demanded nothing from my staff short of magnificence. Odell and his grounds crew arrived at the back door one frosty Friday morning, filling the driveway with their trucks and hauling in massive boxes of decorations. Lennie rose to her role like a peripatetic traffic cop, directing the men as they moved furniture and carried ladders in and out of the high-ceilinged rooms. In spite of a day of chaos, I loved this annual festooning. It reminded me of the greening of the church from my childhood, when parishioners had filled the nave with fresh-cut spruce trucked in from nearby Virginia mountains.

At day's end, the Chancellor's House was flooded with the crisp, pungent scent of evergreens. A twelve-foot spangled tree filled a corner of the living room—every bit as grand, I felt, as the stunning tree I had admired at Crate 'N Barrel in Chicago. I moved judiciously in and out of rooms, tweaking bows and garlands, scrupulously adding my personal touches to the yards of burgundy plaid ribbon that trailed the front banister. Pots of coral *Camellia sasanqua* banked the staircase base, blending beautifully with taller crimson poinsettias. The double doors facing Oakland Avenue bore bountiful wreaths of fir intertwined with pine cones. They had been donated by an alumna in Boone who crafted them each year to fit within the doors' massive frames.

With my family shopping completed in Chicago, I now concentrated on an appropriate gift for my immediate staff. Last year's country ham had been a hit—Susan Atterbury said she'd cooked up their final frozen slabs last summer at their Ocean Isle cottage—but this year I wanted to give something more personal. Jackie inadvertently gave me the idea of the madrigal feast—another Wickfield tradition—when I overheard her chatting about the banquet menu.

"Okay, maybe it's not really a boar's head," Jackie was saying to a student office assistant, remembering an earlier time she had attended, "but they have an actual creature carried out on an enormous tray. You can see its eyes and ears."

"How creepy!" said the student, slicing open the morning mail.

"But it's worth the shock of the moment. The rest of the food is out of this world. And the costumes are fantastic. So is the music."

The madrigal feast was a sumptuous roast-pork dinner held each year in Garner Hall. The building's hammer-beamed ceilings had been designed in the Tudor style, and its main room resembled the grand hall of a medieval castle. In its early years this space had served as Wickfield's dining room, where the women students ate family-style under the massive timber system. A huge wood-burning fireplace flanked one end. Another wall featured small stained-glass windows atop tall panes of clear leaded glass. The room was constantly in demand for alumni gatherings.

Partly because of Garner's unique appearance, the music department long ago had introduced the madrigal feast. The event was a grand showcase for our music majors, who wore Elizabethan costumes and served as singing waiters. I loved to boast about the banquet's success to other college presidents. I had attended the previous two years, each time as a guest at someone else's table. This year, I decided, I would return the favor by reserving my own table and treating my entire executive staff. It was the perfect solution to my gift dilemma.

With that, I picked up the phone and invited each member of the cabinet to attend as my guest, along with their spouses. All but Marilyn accepted. "Mama won't travel at night, and I can't leave her alone," she said pointedly; her aging mother was still recovering from the shock of Hugo. Pud assured me he would bring a date. Counting Jackie and her husband, plus Lennie, we would be a party of twelve. It was the perfect number for an extra-long reserved table.

As I made these arrangements, I suddenly thought of Paul. Was he part of my immediate staff? *Of course not*, argued one indignant voice in my head. *He belongs to Sam Sutton's staff. He's part of your current life only because Carrington intervened. Besides, you don't want others to know about that silly driving arrangement and Carrington's ridiculous hold on you. Why invite speculation?*

Wait! argued another voice. *Paul is, at the least, a temporary part of your staff. He was assigned to you. You spend as much time with Paul*

Stafford as with any member of your executive team—sometimes more. Besides, he is increasingly valuable to you as both a sounding board and a source of information.

These dueling voices crisscrossed my heart. For a brief moment I tried to imagine Paul at our table, solicitous with wife June as he held her chair and bent his ear to her mouth in the noisy banquet hall. I pictured her flushed in the candlelight. And suddenly I knew with absolute certainty that I did *not* want to include Paul and June. *Stupid idea,* I scoffed.

Yet on the evening of the dinner, Paul and June and I actually arrived at the entrance to Garner Hall in tandem. I had not known they were attending. In fact, Paul and I had not traveled together since mid-November. He was wearing a full-length winter dress coat for the chilly evening—charcoal grey. Their sudden appearance startled me so acutely that I was momentarily speechless.

"Nice timing," Paul said calmly, but I saw the surprise in his eyes. He raised a gloved hand to hold the opened door. I caught a moment of his aftershave and averted my eyes, feeling heat rise in my face. I concentrated my greetings, instead, on June, who beamed as usual when she saw me. Her short blonde hair was combed straight back in soft waves, setting off a lovely pair of dangly pearl earrings.

"Ooh," we breathed in unison as we absorbed the transformed interior of Garner Hall. Wooden candelabra lit the aisles, their tapers descending in staggered heights. Ropes of greenery cascaded from the coffered oak beams. Fresh spruce branches were laid like cradles in each windowsill, centered by glass globes that shielded glowing candles. A seated string quartet—violin, viola, cello, and bass—were tuning instruments on a side platform. At last year's banquet, I recalled, the group had played gorgeous baroque numbers—Bach and Corelli and Vivaldi.

We separated, Paul taking our wraps to the coat check. I merged into the mammoth room, greeting guests as I made my way to the reserved table. It was situated on the right side, close to where the pageantry and singing would be staged. I was pleased with the intimacy of our setting and chose a seat on the end where I backed up to the wall. From this vantage point I could overlook the room without feeling conspicuous.

My guests soon streamed in, and I moved quickly to seat Dan and Mimi Jones on my left and Bob and Susan Atterbury on my right. Then the evening's revelry began in earnest. Piebald court jesters in spiked hats leapt into the room, and one made a straight line for our table. I quickly braced myself for a moment of merriment—possibly madness, remembering the pranks of past years—but apparently Pud was this year's target. He sat at our table's far end, opposite me, and I gathered from the peals of laughter that he had come close to having his wassail mug laced with food coloring.

"That would have turned his entire mouth green," commented Dan under his breath to me. "Not a pretty sight for his new date." Pud had arrived earlier with the statuesque Lana on his arm, and heads had turned.

"Those music majors have it in for the athletes," I noted. As for Lana being a "new" date, I wasn't sure. Pud's personal life was apparently the stuff of men's fantasies. I heard he had dated most of Wickfield's single female employees under the age of thirty—the attractive ones, at least. His philandering on campus made him either well loved or deeply detested, depending on which woman was claiming his attention at the moment.

The food was sumptuous and gallantly served. I enjoyed the chatter around our table and surveyed the group with the quiet pride of a Mother Superior. An animated Lennie busied herself talking to Jackie's husband, Rod. Jackie and Lana were deep into a private conversation, and Jake Mooney was entertaining the Atterburys with one of his famous student stories. Susan, I noticed, looked stunningly beautiful, as always. I gathered that she and Bob had driven with the Mooneys, and I was pleased the two couples were such good friends. Their closeness puzzled me, however. Susan and Bob, involved in activities with their church and three teenagers, seemed more settled to me than the carefree Jake and the somewhat insipid Alma Earle. Jake and Bob, moreover, often disagreed during cabinet discussions.

It wasn't until later that I discovered Paul and June seated at the table to my left. The evening up to this point had been full of medieval ritual. A manor lord and wife—Dean Gordon Hemphill and wife Edna in brocade jackets and pleated ruffs—had welcomed their subjects to the holiday celebration. The boar's head—a real boar shipped from Purdue University with a cloved orange stuffed in its gaping mouth—entered on a stupendous tray borne by courtiers. Mimes and jugglers entertained. Near the end, I recalled, troubadours would serenade us with madrigals. I could not have been prouder of Wickfield's students and faculty than I was at this moment. The magnificence of this evening would be hard to surpass.

Sated with the vapors of food and wine, I leaned my head against the wall behind me. It was in one of these moments of relaxation that I spotted Paul. He was seated at an angle so that he fell directly within my sight line if I turned my head. I marveled that I had not noticed him before. He was speaking animatedly to the couple across from him. I studied his profile in the softened light and absorbed yet one more time his rugged good looks. *Darn!* I thought. *Darn, darn, darn!* I turned back to my guests and reached for my wine goblet.

Not until the madrigals began did I glance Paul's way again. These tender love songs, both joyful and poignant, were the perfect conclusion to the evening. To my surprise, the musicians, singing *a cappella* and pure-voiced in the stillness of the room, stirred emotions that penetrated me deeply. Tears flooded my eyes as the minstrels sang words of cherished devotion. For a few seconds I felt a rush of closeness to dear ones whom I had cared for deeply yet who had brought me some form of pain: Benny, my father, Tim, Alex—and Paul.

Oh yes, Paul. Most absolutely Paul.

That's when I blinked back the wetness and turned my head in his direction. And through the glow of the dancing lights I saw that Paul's eyes were fixed steadily on me. How long he had been gazing, I did not know, but I knew he had seen my tears. I also knew that our eyes locked and held in that candlelit corner for what seemed an eternity. Ours was not an innocent look, nor was it casual. Nor was it, if I were truly honest with myself, unexpected. The language of the moment spoke clearly of words withheld, of feelings repressed, of heartbeats unchecked. It was as though we had both known of this inevitable instant, that we had both been certain beyond the shadow of a doubt that this juncture in time would appear, and that, in bittersweet acceptance, we would bow to its arrival.

I reluctantly broke the gaze to join the applause. The guests rose to their feet, cheering as the musicians returned for several bows. I joined in, clapping in unison with the crowd, but in truth I was wrapped into that single instant when Paul and I had connected through the glowing candles. The moment felt so surreal that I scarcely heard the flurry of voices as the lights rose again.

To calm myself, I set myself to doing small tasks. I sent Dan for my coat and, when he returned with it, pressed it against my breast like a blanket. I said goodbyes to my guests, thanking each couple individually for coming. I sought out student performers to congratulate, even stepping into the huge polished kitchen to thank the serving staff. At long last I dared to glance around the emptying hall and found, to my utmost relief, that Paul and June had departed.

I don't remember that short, brisk walk back to my house from Garner Hall. I only recall that, once safe in my living room, I piled logs from the brass holder into the fireplace, turned the pewter key of the gas lighter, and watched tongues of flame leap into life. I curled into a kitten-ball on the couch, covering myself with an afghan and tucking it in around my feet, and I listened to the syncopated cadence of the crackling wood. Every molecule of my being was alert as I lay there, motionless. I pictured Paul again as he approached the Garner entrance and held the door, his eyes bright with possibilities. I remembered how he'd conversed with others at his table, his hands stabbing the air as he made his points, an energetic man at the peak of his life. I saw him as he gazed longingly at me from his chair, his face mere inches from the back of June's hair.

How long did I lie on that couch, anchored by my thoughts? One hour? Two? I lost all rhythm of time until nudged by the sound of shifting logs. I watched them jostle into new positions. They were like sleeping lovers who relinquish their grips on thighs and shoulders, tucking into empty spaces and nestling together for another spell.

Still deep in thought, I closed the iron screen of the open hearth and grasped the banister to pull myself upstairs.

Chapter 24
CHRISTMAS

Commencement—that traditional and stirring event which officially marked the end of fall semester—"commenced" without a hitch. Promptly at eleven, the December graduates marched into the auditorium to the wild cheers of an expectant crowd. The faculty had plenty of space, with seats left over. The hooding ceremony proceeded flawlessly. Dr. Murchison's speech was perfectly balanced between information and inspiration. I breathed a sigh of relief as I hustled from the auditorium to the Chancellor's House for the trustees' luncheon.

Surprisingly, Carrington and Edith Hall were the last to arrive. They were, in fact, overly tardy for this type of event. At Wickfield, punctuality was highly valued. Earlier, Carrington had sat on the commencement platform, imperious and invincible as he eyed the crowd with his hawkish chairman-of-the-board gaze. It now occurred to me that his wife might somehow have missed the ceremony and that he'd had to detour home to pick her up.

"Merry Christmas, Edith!" I beamed, helping with their coats in the foyer and handing them to the student attendant. I projected my voice in spite of the visible hearing aid that dominated Edith's outer ear. I gave her a little cheek-to-cheek hug and promptly caught a whiff of bourbon breath.

"Carrington!" I turned to him and braced for his perfunctory kiss on the cheek. "I'm so glad you both could come!"

I led the Halls to the dining room, where a line had formed around the buffet spread. The house gleamed and twinkled. Savory smells of ham and cinnamon emanated from the kitchen, and the whir of conversations blended with the clink of glasses and the scrape of silver against china. At the living room baby grand, a student pianist rendered a softly jazzed version of "Silver Bells."

To facilitate dining, I had stashed small tables and chairs throughout the downstairs rooms. I personally disliked eating in a crowd while standing up. One table on the sun porch was designated for Rachel Murchison and the Halls. I joined them, eventually, with my own plate. Carrington was pontificating about the recent fall of the Berlin Wall, an event that had filled the news for the past month. Dr. Murchison was listening to him silently while buttering her Parker House roll. I let the conversation flow while I plunged into my food. I was famished. I realized with a start that this was my first solid meal in two days.

It was somewhere in this conversation that Claire Matthews appeared at Dr. Murchison's side, waiting to speak until the older woman looked up.

"Sorry to interrupt," Claire said politely, "but I'm letting you know that your driver has arrived. He says there's no rush at the moment but that you should be leaving for the airport in approximately twenty minutes."

I was caught off guard by this information. Claire had been put in charge of Rachel Murchison's travel plans, and, according to what had been discussed earlier, Claire would be driving her to Charlotte to catch a four o'clock flight back to Washington. Claire needed this one-on-one time to elicit details for an alumni magazine story. I had personally walked Claire through the steps of reserving a university car.

"Who's the driver?" I asked. I put down my fork.

"It's Paul Stafford from University Security," explained Claire. "He called me and volunteered. He thought it might be easier on us all if he took on this detail." She observed my frown of confusion. "Dr. Murchison and I have agreed to discuss the magazine story by phone next week," she added.

"Well, then," said Rachel, shaking out her green-plaid napkin and scooting back her chair, "since time is flying, I really must get to the dessert table. That pecan pie sounds like the best treat south of the Mason-Dixon line." She laid her hand on my shoulder. "Everything is simply lovely, Katherine." Edith Hall followed her to the dining room.

I turned my head toward the kitchen. So Paul was here. He was probably nibbling leftover rolls and whatever else Lennie would be heaping on him in the kitchen. I had not seen him since the madrigal dinner a week ago. I scooped my fork into the green bean casserole on my plate, suddenly conscious that I was alone with Carrington.

"I understand, Katherine," he began, clearing his throat, "that the driving arrangement with you and Officer Stafford is working out well. Sam Sutton says he has no complaints. I'm very pleased, Katherine." He cleared his throat again. "Very pleased."

"It's total nonsense, Carrington, and a huge waste of Officer Stafford's time." I hoped the edgy flatness of my voice would camouflage any betrayal of body language. The very second Claire mentioned Paul's name, my inner emotions had reacted.

I've wondered over the past months how my life might have altered had Carrington simply agreed with me that day. He could have said, "All right, then, Katherine"—he always drawled it out as "Kath-uh-run," in three slurred syllables—"if you're certain you won't accept any more rides from strangers, perhaps we can close the issue at this point." That would be tantamount to him saying, "If you've learned your lesson, and if you will be a good girl, I believe we can drop this now." Winning, to Carrington, was essential.

But at that point Rachel and Edith returned with desserts, and a student waiter appeared at my side to pour coffee. The issue was left unresolved, and I ended up escorting Rachel to the kitchen for her back-door exit. I found Paul leaning against the kitchen counter in his overcoat, his keys in one hand and a glass of orange juice in the other. Our eyes met directly. Our gaze held a full three seconds, but I could read nothing. The look was vapid. Indeed, Paul and I were like strangers who nod a taciturn greeting. I watched the back of his head as he departed down the back sidewalk with our distinguished guest. I could not be sure whether I felt relief or distinct disappointment over our empty moment.

Alex called that night. He was preparing for his trip to Hawaii, sorting through slides for his presentation and managing last-minute shopping. "Just try finding swim trunks in Chicago in December," he griped. But he was in good spirits and sent greetings to the entire Embright family. "I hate to miss the reunion, Kat. We'll make it up in January, I promise you. Christmas and birthday, all at once. And do I ever have a surprise for you!" He offered a little Santa-like *ho-ho-ho*. Alex could be amusing, no doubt about it.

In spite of my pleasant musings about Alex, Paul still invaded my thoughts. Driving to Richmond two days after Christmas, my Neiman-Marcus family gifts piled safely on the back seat, I felt once more the weight of crisscrossed emotions. Since the evening of the madrigal banquet, Paul and I had not had a personal moment alone. At the very least, it would have been appropriate for me to wish him and his family a happy holiday, to thank him for his services during the fall months, or to invite him to drop by our Wellstone staff party for Russian tea. Was that candlelit moment to be frozen in time? Would it be recalled only in fleeting whispers of memory?

I switched my thoughts to the family reunion ahead. During the week after Christmas, my sisters and their families would be together for the better part of two days—twenty of us, including children in age from two to twenty-three. Marianna had arranged for most of us to stay at a Hampton Inn, negotiating for a group rate, but our meals and gatherings would be in Marianna's sprawling Victorian home. Gifts would be opened the second day of the reunion, after Jane's husband, Ron, arrived from California. Since he was a lieutenant commander in the Navy, his duties kept him confined on base, and Jane was preceding him by flying cross-country solo with their four children. I found it impossible to imagine myself packing gifts and clothes and traveling with four youngsters in tow. The task of managing airport restrooms would in itself be huge. Jane, however, had organizational skills that exceeded even mine, and Benjamin, the oldest at ten, was able to help with the middle siblings—Holly, seven, and Christopher, five.

There had been times in our girlhoods when we Embright girls had pretended to be the four *Little Women* sisters. Before Jane had been born, friends had frequently compared us to the fictitious March siblings, and one Christmas when we were older we re-created favorite scenes and acted them out in the living room for our parents.

"Christmas won't be Christmas without any presents," grumbled Jo, *lying on the rug.* I remembered verbatim these opening lines from Louisa May Alcott, as fresh in my memory as my recent remarks at commencement.

"It's so dreadful to be poor," sighed Meg, *looking down at her old dress.*

"I don't think it's fair for some girls to have plenty of pretty things, and other girls nothing at all," added little Amy, *with an injured sniff.*

"We've got Father and Mother and each other," said Beth contentedly *from her corner.*

We spent hours that Christmas experimenting with Victorian hairstyles and makeup, creating hooped skirts from layers of crinolines underneath long bathrobes. In later years I marveled over how each of

PREZ: A STORY OF LOVE

us had identified with a character whose history was similar to the lives we eventually lived. Marianna, for example, played the role of Meg, not just because both were wise and mature but because Meg's "small, white hands" inspired a personal beauty regimen that Marianna continues yet today. Sarah, whose ability to get along with others was a shortcoming in her youth—even today, I noted—identified with feisty Amy, a spoiled youngster who incurred the constant ire of her sisters. Emily picked Beth, the long-suffering sister who died in her early teens, never dreaming that she herself would brush death in her thirties.

I, of course, became Jo—not as a tomboy, which I definitely was not, nor even as a writer, which I enjoyed being, but because I admired her take-charge spunk and never-say-die courage. I loved her defiance when she stood up to grumpy Aunt March, and I empathized hugely with her rejection of platonic Laurie as a suitor. To my immense satisfaction, Jo eventually found romance with Professor Baer—not a wealthy man, not even handsome, but a priceless diamond in the rough who completed all of Jo's expectations for true love.

As soon as I arrived in Richmond, I put Wickfield behind me entirely. I was the last of the sisters to arrive, in spite of living only a few hours away. It had been several years since all five sisters had managed a reunion with children without the prompting of a family wedding or funeral. The minute I entered Marianna's living room, Katie, Jane's youngest, flung herself around my leg. "Aunt Kat!" she crooned in her sweet baby voice, suddenly shy as she gave me a candy-sticky kiss on the cheek.

"Dear Katie, look at you!" I exclaimed, hugging her tightly. "You've grown! You're a big girl now!" I had been astounded when Jane told me three years ago that, if the new baby were a girl, she would be naming her after me. I had managed to fly to California last year for Katie's first birthday, and I hung onto the beautiful child much of the rest of this December afternoon. For dinner, we were divided among a children's table, a teens' table, and two tables of adults. Even better, Ron arrived on an early flight from San Diego just as we were sitting down. Sarah popped up to take pictures of us in various stages of eating, and I held up my overloaded plate for the camera.

Later that evening, I found myself in the kitchen, wrist-deep inside the carcass of the denuded turkey. To bone leftover fowl was messy, a job I preferred to avoid because of the slippery pull of the meat against the slimy hull. Tonight, however, with sisters for company, it became a bearable task. I listened from the kitchen to the conversation in the adjoining room.

"And the way Daddy was always pruning the yard just the opposite of the way Mother wanted it," Sarah was saying to her sisters. They had been reminiscing about our mother's frustrations with Daddy, whose need to control his wife had superseded even his powerful hold on his daughters. "Remember how she would tell him to leave the new shoots under the crepe myrtle tree, to fill out the space around the trunk? And how he would ignore her and trim them back every time?"

"That's because he liked the trunk with its bare gray bark," recalled Marianna. "The tree was supposed to be perfectly smooth all the way up to the branches, but its nakedness somehow made Mother nervous. I don't remember why. What was it she said it reminded her of?"

"Pretty ladies without their undies," I piped up from the sink, and we all shrieked in hysterics, remembering.

Later, with the younger ones bedded down and the rest of the family watching football in the den, we five sisters grew almost melancholy with girlhood memories. Perhaps it was the flames that licked the living-room hearth, or the pulsating lights on the tinseled tree, or the lull of after-dinner liqueurs. Whatever the impetus, sentiments ran deep.

"Benny would be forty this spring if he had lived," ventured Emily. She swirled the amaretto in her snifter. The rest of us absorbed that thought as we watched shadows dance off the logs. It was impossible to create a forty-year-old face from that of a lovely child. I tried to picture the adult Benny among us. He would have a wife, of course—my sister-in-law. Probably adolescent children.

"How old would Daddy be now?" asked Jane. She had been a young teenager when he died; her memories of him were vastly different from mine.

"Seventy-something," said Marianna. "Seventy-six." She remembered the birth date and birth year of all the family members. "Thank goodness he died when he did. He suffered horribly at the end."

Daddy's death from pancreatic cancer had been traumatic for all of us. I had been in college and clearly remembered his fast decline.

"No one should have to suffer pain like his," I remarked.

"Agreed," said Emily softly. Silence fell again.

"We all have secrets and silent pains," said Sarah to no one in particular. It was a curious statement, and, although she spoke in a normal tone of voice, her words bounced off the walls and hurtled toward me like nails. I shot her a glance across the darkened room. She was looking directly at me, glaring. I glared back.

Then, abruptly, I untangled my long legs from my reclining position on the couch and set down my drink. "Excuse me." I exited toward the hallway bathroom.

I stayed there a while, long enough that Marianna eventually knocked. "Kat?" she called quietly. Her mouth was close to the door.

"In a minute," I said loudly through the wall. I ran water noisily in the sink and pulled a towel off the rack before I opened the door.

"You okay?" she asked. She looked at me closely. I was rubbing my face briskly with the rough nub of the dampened cloth.

"Allergies," I said briefly. "Probably your cats." I hung up the towel and fluffed my hair with my hands. She studied me dubiously before leading us back to join the others. It was hard to fool Marianna. She had no doubt detected I had been crying.

The following day, shortly before we began to depart, Jane proposed a photo of all the sisters. We had been taking pictures for two days, clowning with our opened packages and capturing the children leaping through the mountain of torn gift wrap. But those had been informal shots. "I want a posed one," Jane said. "In front of the fireplace." She looked briefly subdued. "I wish I could see you all more often."

I later framed the picture we took that day. Considering the haste with which we posed, it turned out splendidly. I stood in the middle as the tallest, Marianna and Sarah on each side of me, Emily and Jane like bookends. Our arms were draped over each other. We smiled grandly in our jeans and bulky sweaters. Our faces belied the scrapes and scabs of our pasts and spoke only of five close-knit women facing the realities of modern adult life. We looked happy. We looked healthy.

As we completed the photo, a distant commotion sounded from the kitchen. As if on cue, the rest of the family floated into the living room, and children's voices burst into song. Walking slowly behind a frosted cake with lit candles came Benjamin, followed by his brother and sisters moving as a pack. "Happy birthday to you," they chorused in off-key unison. "Happy birthday to you! Happy *Birth*-day, dear Aunt Kat. Happy birthday to you!" The rest of the family cheered.

"But it's not my birthday yet," I said, thunderstruck. In spite of my mild protests, I was enormously pleased. Birthday with my family! The cake bore ten candles. Stuck into the middle of the white icing was a large number five made of decorated sugar.

"We didn't have fifty candles, Aunt Kat," said Holly, jumping up and down in excitement. "Do you like it? I helped Mama stir." She looked up at me, eyes shining.

Fifty! A half century! In a matter of weeks I would be fifty years old. In a flash I remembered Alex's urgency about a medical checkup. I had done nothing about it. In fact, I wasn't sure at the moment where I had placed those instructions he had written. *I'll make that appointment when I return*, I promised myself, blowing out the candles while the children clapped. Bowls of chocolate ice cream appeared. The sisters produced gifts in pastel-colored bags stuffed with crinkly tissue paper. I laughed in sheer glee, tossing the paper like confetti while the children swooped it up.

Then Jane tapped on her ice-cream dish with her spoon and hushed us into silence.

"We have something to tell you, everyone!" she announced. She was standing in front of the Christmas tree as she spoke, her diminutive figure framed by the uplifted branches. I tried to read her face. Ron appeared by her side holding Katie, who playfully lunged at her mother. Jane reached out to hoist her into the crook of her arm.

"Well, you won't believe this, folks." Her voice was flat, her expression blank. She looked down at her three older youngsters, who were watching expectantly, then up at her six-foot-three husband. "We just found out, actually. We told the children on Christmas." Now I caught the emotion in her voice. I suddenly swallowed hard.

"Surprise!" In a flash Jane was smiling, sparkling her happiness upon us all. She flattened her hands against her waistline and threw back her head with an exuberant belly laugh.

"We're expecting! Again!"

Chapter 25
SNOW

It's true, as we're warned in our youth, that we never forget the power of our first love. I pondered this mystery after the Christmas reunion as I drove home through Virginia.

It was Emily who had triggered some unexpected memories of my former husband, Tim. "We saw Tim last night," she'd told me that first evening in Richmond—meaning, of course, that she had seen him on television. "He still has his looks, but he's getting pretty gray, Kat. His sideburns have turned nearly white since we saw him last." Emily and Edward stayed in a north Georgia motel on their trips from Jacksonville to Virginia and, perhaps in morbid curiosity, faithfully watched Tim's Atlanta channel for the nightly news while traveling. They had reported "Tim sightings" before.

Tim Bernay was not only my former husband but also the first man who had fully captured my heart. Andy Parker counted only as my first kiss, and that was during a sixth-grade kissing game in the coat closet at Sally Gordon's house. Bob Boniface counted as my high-school boyfriend— we dated from my sixteenth birthday until I left for college, steaming up the windows of his blue '56 Chevy every Friday and Saturday night. He treated me like a princess, and I adored every minute we spent together. As we headed to different colleges, however, we became more like brother and sister, to our mutual disappointment. We even quarreled like siblings at the end.

At Hollins, an all-woman campus, I dated frequently, enjoying the steady stream of male visitors who swarmed in from Roanoke College, Virginia Tech, and Radford. One of them, Baldwin—I referred to him as The Bald One, even though he had thick curls like mine—taught me how to French kiss as well as how to smoke cigarettes. Smoking never became a habit, and I gave it up quite easily before I married. Still, I thought myself quite elegant at ATO parties as I pinned a cigarette between my index and middle fingers, inhaling deeply with my chin cast upward just so before extending my elbow straight out toward the ashtray. I loved to fell that hot gray clump with a genteel tap of my forefinger.

Tim and I met in Chapel Hill in the spring of our junior year, but I fell in love with his voice months before I saw him in the flesh. He was well known as the "afternoon talk" man on a local radio station, meaning he was a DJ who played easy tunes and light rock for loyal listeners like me. Between musical numbers he indulged—perhaps a bit too much—in casual banter and self-deprecating jokes. When listening to him, I'd had no idea he was a fellow Carolina student. His voice was lazy but resonant, almost growly in its deepest dimensions, and in my fantasies he bore the commanding muscles of Charlton Heston and the wise, safe face of William Holden.

We fell into conversation one day while waiting for carry-out at a popular fried chicken restaurant. Uncomfortable as always with the silence of strangers, I made the first overture, remarking on the lengthy wait. The instant he responded and I heard that magical voice, I gasped.

"You're Timber Nay!" I exclaimed in excitement. Tim was instantly flattered. He slouched against the chrome counter and began to chatter, oblivious to customers in line who were forced to listen. It never occurred to me until much too late that none of his conversation showed concern for me. At the time, it somehow seemed appropriate that a popular radio personality should talk solely about himself.

And he thought it quite charming that I thought his name was "Timber."

"It's the way you slide your voice when signing off," I tried to explain, a bit embarrassed that I had called him "Mr. Nay."

"What do you mean?" he asked, but he smiled into my eyes when he spoke.

"You say, 'This is Tim'"—and my voice rose slightly upward, like legs climbing a small hill—"ber Nay.'" I held the "ber" a scant second longer before voicing "nay," sliding down the scale on the last syllable. To me it seemed perfectly reasonable that I had heard "Timber Nay."

We married immediately after our June graduations and honeymooned cozily at Cape Cod, despite a drippy air conditioner in our beachfront cottage. When we returned to Chapel Hill a week later, a bit smug in our new roles as wedded adults, we established housekeeping in a garage apartment rented from a faculty widow named Mrs. O'Steen ("Call me Ruby"). We each held a coveted graduate fellowship—Radio-TV and English—but we were destitute enough those first few months to eat vegetables only on even-numbered days and to forgo breakfast entirely. Ruby, either by instinct or by kindness of heart, surprised us with bubbly casseroles precisely when our spirits ran most needy.

Still, those early years had been good ones. I recalled that we had laughed a lot. I edited Tim's master's thesis, and after my doctoral committee approved my dissertation and I passed my orals, Tim and I held an impromptu ceremony in which we lugged a bulging plastic trash bag through the wooded area behind our apartment. It was crammed with cardboard shoeboxes stuffed with my 5 x 8" research index cards. Pulling his arms back with a mighty swing, Tim heaved the bag into a hulking metal dumpster while I cheered lustily, my arms flailing. Then I improvised a provocative dance step in the gravel, gyrating to imaginary music while my hips swung back and forth. Tim watched and grinned wickedly.

Like me, Tim was now approaching fifty; his February birthday followed mine by three weeks. I wondered whether Rosa, his wife, would surprise him with a party. *I should send him a card,* I thought, *even if he forgets mine. It's a zero birthday, a half century. It's important.* A moment of tenderness tugged.

I continued my drive, reminiscing about the love that had surrounded me at Marianna's and smiling once more over Jane's baby announcement. Another Embright! New life in the family! My thoughts flashed ahead to next Christmas, when all of us would meet the newest member. The baby would be four months old when we gathered again.

I continued my trip west through counties with historic names like Powhatan and Appomattox, skirting south of Lynchburg. I noted familiar signs to Hollins College as I passed Roanoke and finally emerged onto the interstate. When I eventually approached the town of Arden, I impulsively turned off the main road for a quick detour by our old house. I drove down Main Street with its enclave of quaint sites: Dot's Diner of the famous meat loaf, the shabby bookstore that smelled gluey like the basement in my grammar school, and the giant cone-shaped clock with Roman numerals in front of Gilbert's Ice Cream Shoppe. I passed the brick gates of the east entrance into campus and the garnet-red doors of St. John's. I began the climb up the hill toward our old house, slowing as I passed the comfortable homes of families I'd once known well: the Gordons, the Llewellyns, the Hillmans, the Browns.

I braked when I came to the house where we had lived. The front door was now an unfamiliar forest green, but at least the porch swing still faced sideways down the hill toward town. The yard seemed unusually large with its bare limbs and barren flower beds; crushed chrysanthemum stalks had keeled over into crunchy brown leaves. The gnarled fig trees and crabapples stood silent against the yellowed grass. The backyard pushed into a cliff of scraggly underbrush, which, in today's overcast light, looked like a massive coil of black barbed wire. I suddenly shivered in spite of my coat, my engine idling. Above the cliff, cars climbed Pinnacle Drive, the street that led steeply to the city cemetery atop the highest point in Arden. "I promise I'll visit you next time," I whispered, apologizing silently to my parents' tombstones that awaited there. A gusty breeze slapped my windshield. When a red SUV paused behind me, I moved on.

The snowstorm that hit Hurley a few days later arrived suddenly. It was accompanied by the usual fanfare for a Carolina weather event. Dan Smith was the first to warn me of its size and power. The entire executive staff was back at work in those days immediately after New Year's, taking advantage of the one-week lull before the students' return from the holidays. Because I had scheduled the staff for an overnight retreat in Charlotte, the threat of inclement weather caught my attention. The weather report described a fast-moving Arctic blast that threatened to dump several inches of snow upon our low-flung Piedmont hills. The meteorologist chilled me with his dramatic maps and sweeping charts. Unlike my Chicago, Charlotte and its outlying cities were ill-prepared for winter's hazards. For starters, there were few salt trucks. Even worse, Southerners drove very badly in snow—partly out of sheer terror.

The next day, Wednesday, I cancelled the retreat. Anticipating the worst, I sent Lennie to Food Lion to stock up on supplies. The snow was forecast for Thursday, and the granite skies were threatening that morning as I bundled up. I dug deeply into the coat closet for my rubber-soled boots; I would need them later for my walk home. I had given Lennie the day off and looked forward to a quiet evening in front of the fireplace.

Wellstone was already humming when I arrived. The mood was expectant, not unlike the anticipation we had felt before Hugo. A beaming Susan Atterbury unexpectedly stuck her head into my office.

"Susan! What brings you to campus?" I asked. I was delighted to see her.

"Well, you know my Bob. He's a true Southern boy. Hates to drive in the snow. I offered to play chauffeur so I can drive us home in the snow this afternoon. But I came prepared. See? Christmas present." She held up a copy of Anne Tyler's *Breathing Lessons*. "If this turns into a blizzard, I'll prod him out of his chair early. We're not spending the night here with the Wellstone ghosts."

"Anyone who gets snowbound can stay with me," I laughed. "Remember, the Chancellor's House has five bathrooms."

Then came the snow, silent and stealthy. Huge ragged flakes began to pelt the campus, tumbling and dancing as they fell from the leaden sky. I found it hard to concentrate on my work. Jackie came into my office to inspect the scene from my large picture window. We stood together, entranced like children.

"'The woods are lovely, dark and deep,'" I quoted. Once in a college lit class I had read Robert Frost aloud in a voice that had actually quivered with the richness of his words. Now we were watching our own campus woods fill up with snow.

"'The only other sound's the sweep, / Of easy wind and downy flake.'"

"'But I have promises to keep,'" sighed Jackie. "I remember *that* line." Reluctantly she returned to her outer desk and I to mine. Today, with two unexpected days to catch up on work, I was eager to move ahead.

In spite of my good intentions, however, I could not concentrate. Frustrated, I closed my eyes, my hands pressed to my temples, trying to push away an unwelcome image that kept surfacing. It was the face of Paul Stafford from the night of the madrigal dinner. I saw again his eyes riveted on my face and remembered how I had locked mine on his and refused to look away. I had not seen Paul since the commencement luncheon, but today I half-expected him to show up with a problem. Earlier this morning I had asked Jake to check safety issues with Sam Sutton and Odell—parking lots, sidewalks, every surface that might cause trouble. The dormitories were still closed for the holidays, so problems should be minimal.

Still . . .

I rose abruptly from my desk. *This is crazy*, I admonished myself; *this is not me. It's just snow, for heaven's sakes.* Crossing through Jackie's office, I strolled into the main hallway. Staffers had burrowed like rabbits into their offices. Restless, I found myself headed toward the stairs. *I'll watch the snow from the upper floors*, I decided. *The campus view will be spectacular, and the climb will clear my head.*

But upon reaching the Alumni and Public Relations offices on the third floor, I found myself passing them by. It seemed almost presumptuous to barge in just to look at snow. Instead, I found myself clambering up those rickety steps toward the creaky fourth floor and the statue gallery I so dearly loved. The area would be deserted. Those high front windows would overlook the frozen fountain and copse of trees beyond, and I would have a front-row seat to a scene that would be nothing short of magical.

As I entered the long tunnel of the fourth floor, I was startled as always at the museum-like expanse of statuary. The sculptures stretched down both sides of the dark hallway. I rubbed Adriane's marbled head with affection as I passed her on the left. Approaching the double French doors that led into the former conference room, I pushed on the doorknobs. They seemed stuck at first, so I nudged them with my hip. They burst open, squealing on their stiff hinges, and I adjusted my eyes to the dim light of drawn shades.

Then I gasped—out loud! Two people, a man and a woman, were standing near the opposite wall. The woman did not turn but stood like a mannequin at a window, peering out through a raised slat of the aluminum blinds. The man faced me squarely, an odd smile playing about his mouth. "Hello, Katherine," he said.

It was Jake. And the woman, who remained motionless with her back to me, was Susan Atterbury.

I froze, uncomprehending. "Jake! You scared me!" I stood there, a gawking stranger, confused, my mind whirling. Idiotically, I almost felt the need to apologize, as stupidly as if I had found intruders raiding my unstocked refrigerator. Only two hours earlier, Susan had been heading to a comfortable corner to read. And Jake—wasn't he on the other side of campus with Sam Sutton?

Then I did comprehend. Jake's color rose as he deciphered my stricken face. Silent Susan appeared to be memorizing the snowfall.

I turned wordlessly and walked out of the room. I don't remember rushing down those treacherous cupped steps, nor do I recall encountering a soul as I fled to my office. I only know that an hour later Dan found me transfixed, unmoving, staring out my big window at the snow. He urgently pressed me to dismiss the entire Wickfield staff at once.

The snowfall, he reported, was gaining in intensity. It was now considered a full-blown blizzard.

Chapter 26
SUSAN

The whiteness of the afternoon gripped me. I was its captive. Safely now at home, I watched the world fill up with snow, riveted to my bedroom window as though a powerful magnet in Earth's core anchored me to that one spot. Had I not felt so forlorn, the snow's stark beauty could have soothed me. After all, I mused, staring at the trees in white robes, cotton is white and feels soft. Sugar is white and tastes sweet. Brides wear white and look radiant.

But the lack of color depressed me now. I blamed it on the shock I had experienced that morning. White connotes death in certain cultures, I suddenly recalled. In old Japan, mourners usually wore white to funerals. In *Moby Dick*, Captain Ahab had pursued an albino whale that became the pursuer. In teaching that novel, I had learned to shudder at the whale's utter whiteness.

As I gazed through the window, I was startled to spot a dark figure trudging through the snow below. At first I thought it was Odell and assumed the roads had become too treacherous even for his truck. The campus, by now, was virtually deserted. For the past hour only a brave driver here or there had slithered down Grove Boulevard. I watched the bundled shadow loom larger along the sidewalk from Wellstone, struggling head downward against the whipping gusts.

Nearing my backyard, the footsteps turned into my driveway, and the blurb of a coat became a bright turquoise ski jacket. I recognized it instantly. I broke from the window, dashed down the staircase, and burst through the kitchen to the back door. I flung it open and stood in the windy breezeway while Susan Atterbury stomped up the bricks steps, kicking snow from her boots and pushing the wet hood from her head. Her face was bright red and puddled, but whether chapped from the cold or enflamed by tears, I couldn't be sure.

"Come in!" I ordered, holding open the door against the howling blast of air. "Quickly!" Susan avoided my eyes but followed me into the toasty kitchen, where she shed her dripping outerwear and ran a hand through snow-edged hair.

"I was about to heat the teakettle. Won't you join me?" I flinched at my prim voice. I sounded like Mrs. Bennet in *Pride and Prejudice* inviting a neighbor in for a spot of tea.

Susan paused. "Got any alcohol?" she croaked. She sounded as if she had a bad cold, and her face looked so tragic that I resisted the tug of a smile.

"Two hot toddies, coming right up." I moved quickly, filling the teakettle and setting out spice bottles of cloves and ground nutmeg. I ushered Susan to the sun porch. On my way back to the kitchen, I stooped to the lower door of the liquor cabinet and grabbed a bottle of Wild Turkey.

Once settled in front of the fireplace with our steaming mugs, Susan and I groped to regain our normal selves. I spoke first. "So. What's new, Susan?" That was as good a place as any to start—a little levity, a bit of neutrality. *Throw the ball to Susan*, I thought. I had no idea where this conversation would take us.

It took a full half-minute before she began, and I watched the struggle on her face. Then the tears emerged. "Oh, Kat, I'm so horribly sorry. I feel terrible. Absolutely horrible."

"Where's Bob?"

"In his office. Still working. I couldn't get the—him—to leave."

I thought she was going to say, "I couldn't get the idiot to leave," but she stopped.

"Does he know?"

"No. Oh God, no. This would kill him." The tears increased. I left momentarily to slip into the bathroom for a box of Kleenex, which I placed discreetly on the coffee table.

"How much do you want to tell me? You can tell me all or nothing, Susan, but choose wisely. Your story impacts two members of my staff."

As she opened up to me, her pink-socked ankles crossed neatly on my ottoman, I studied her striking sandy-blonde looks. Susan had been a Miss Poconos or something of the sort during high school. Through the years she had matured from a comely teenager into a stunningly handsome woman. Her pink turtleneck sweater would have gone well with my dark hair, but on Susan it looked sensational. She wore it like a model promoting an Oregon ski lodge. Two rows of full-fashioned cable stitching etched themselves down the bodice like birds' wings; a slim pink stripe trailed down her navy sweat pants. Wherever she went with her three boys—band practice, soccer games, or Scout programs—Susan seemed the epitome of success. Each of her boys favored her in appearance and manners, and I sometimes felt stabs of mother-envy when I glimpsed her perfect family. Now I watched this myth dissolve as she described her increasing unhappiness with the often-absent Bob.

"He's absolutely married to his job, Kat. But it's not just that he puts the job over the family. He's a fussy little woman about everything. He hovers over every single detail, like which brand of car tire to buy, and he changes his mind constantly in fear that something else could be better. He drove the family whacky over the Richardson Hall event. You should have seen his face when I told him about the vandalism. It was like watching a neon sign flash colors—white, then red, then purple. But at least he showed some *life*." She cupped her mug with both hands and blew on the surface.

"When did this start?" I was referring to Jake, not Bob.

"After Hugo. After Whichy and all those long meetings. He gave me rides sometimes." The words came out in slow jerks. She leaned her head against the back of the chair and gazed at the ceiling, sighing. "Okay, so it probably really started during the summer, I don't know how long ago. Jake is fun, Kat, and I can talk to him. He distracts me. He makes me laugh and laugh. I've always liked being around him—everyone does—but I never expected it to get out of hand." She reached for a Kleenex.

"Bob and I never laugh. The boys and I tiptoe around him, but it really doesn't matter. I don't think he hears us or sees us, either way." She honked noisily into her tissue, tucking the damp wad into the wrist band of her sweater. Then she wrapped her arms around herself, rocking back and forth in place.

"I'd give anything to not be here right now."

"Jake and Bob are friends." I said it as a statement, not a question.

"Jake does like Bob," Susan said. She started to continue but stopped. It seemed there was nothing, really, to say.

We sipped from our mugs, our silence buoyed only by the soughing wind under the house eaves. Susan seemed content to simply sit, letting the peaceful confines of the room wrap her like a chrysalis. I was struck by the drama of what was being left untold. It seemed impossible to picture intimacies between her and Jake, and I pushed away any such images when they leered into place. What hurt me most was the way Bob was being isolated within the story, cast aside as idiosyncratic.

"So, what do you plan to do?" I finally asked.

Susan turned tragic eyes on me. "I thought *you* would have some answers."

"It sounds as though you have a lot to sort out," I said quietly. "Tell me again how you and Bob met. Philadelphia, right?"

She nodded. "It was my junior year at Rosemont. Bob had just started at Wharton. We met on a blind date and clicked right away, but we didn't see much of each other that first year. God, we studied hard!" She laughed wryly at the memory. "Wharton was competitive as heck, and Rosemont had strict rules about hours off campus. We had to sign in and out of the dorms, and those nuns could make us feel guilty just by breathing on us. But the city was great—galleries and museums and all kinds of parks. We did a lot of exploring, most by public transportation. Bob finally got to the point where he could take a Saturday afternoon or evening off, or even both, without worrying about his grades."

"So you knew even back then that his work was a high priority."

"Yes. I guess so. He couldn't stand the thought of failing. Even now he can't tolerate mistakes."

"And how does that make you feel?"

"Inadequate. Not able to meet his standards of perfection."

"And Jake?"

"He just lets me be me. He's wonderful, Kat."

"And Alma Earle?

Susan was silent. I rearranged myself on the couch, stretching my legs up onto the ottoman and tossing the crocheted afghan over my feet. "Let me tell you about the Bob I know," I began.

Susan listened without comment as I described the Bob Atterbury whom I had hired soon after coming to Wickfield. We had clicked instantly. I had given him a day to get settled into his new environment and then, rather than scheduling our first meeting in my office, I had gone to his. I wanted to see him in his professional work space—to observe where he placed his telephone and how he worked his incoming and outgoing files. I not only inhaled the instant aroma of Bob's custom-blended pipe tobacco—black cherry and vanilla—but also noted that a framed Woodberry Forest forensic award was hanging between his Duke and Wharton diplomas. A small frame of a younger Susan—long tresses trailing in the breeze as she gazed from a lake pier—sat at a corner of his leather executive desk set.

Professionally, Bob's credentials were sterling. Prior to coming to Wickfield, he had overseen a successful campaign at a small private college in Georgia, nearly tripling their endowment within five years and, in the process, gaining national attention from the Council for the Advancement and Support of Education in Washington. At Wickfield he was connecting well with both alumni and corporate donors, scoring on gifts both large and small and raising the giving level for the university to a record high.

"In short, Susan, I can't say enough good things about Bob's leadership and long-range vision for Wickfield. I value his opinions completely. When he asks me to entertain a certain donor in my home or even travel cross-country to request a gift, I do it. He has the education and fund-raising skills to be a future college president. I've been privately grooming him since I first met the two of you."

My voice grew thoughtful. "In fact, I've often thought that if I were to be killed on the highway tomorrow—perish the thought, but I suppose it could happen—Dan Jones and Bob Atterbury together could lead this university forward without missing a beat."

Susan stirred. "Oh, be serious, Kat. Everyone knows you are a chancellor *extraordinaire*. These guys couldn't hold a candle to you."

"Of course they could. I may be the orchestra conductor, but Dan is the concertmaster, and Bob is first-chair trumpet. I treasure him partly because he makes me look good! Some of those very qualities you say drive you crazy—his propensity for details and accuracy, for example—are the very attributes that make Bob so successful at his work. Eventually they will carry him far beyond what he has already achieved at Wickfield. He needs a few more years of experience, like this current campaign, but his future is wide open."

I paused. "Of course, he's going to need a good woman by his side as he moves forward. Those search committees love to find a sharp spouse as part of the package."

I reached for Susan's empty mug and carried it with my own to the kitchen. I realized we had scarcely mentioned Jake. As much as I yearned to paint a more realistic picture of him, something far beyond Susan's glorified version, I could not and would not. To speak of Jake's shortcomings would not only transgress my professional boundaries but also betray my personal impatience with him. Susan would need to reason through this triangle on her own. It would not be easy. The classic head-versus-heart debate was as old as the Bible, and I myself was as vulnerable as anyone. I thought of Paul and felt the familiar stab as I rinsed dishes at the sink.

Susan followed me into the kitchen and began rummaging through her outerwear, which still lay in a heap on the floor. "Kat, tell me one thing," she said. "Did you know Jake and I were in that room before you opened the door? Jake is convinced you followed us."

My surprise at her question was clear. "Not at all. I merely chanced upon you." I frowned. "Espionage is hardly my style, Susan."

"But why else would you be on the fourth floor?"

I hesitated. "I go there sometimes to get away. To think. It's quiet, like a museum. I like the statues. There's something about being part of all that antiquity . . . "

"But it's dirty, maybe even dangerous. No one ever goes up there, or so Jake says. That's why . . . " Her voice trailed off.

"So that's why *you* go there?" I asked, my voice a bit edgy. "The excitement of the risk?"

Susan worked on her parka snaps and pulled up the outer zipper.

"Now I have one for you, Susan. Where were you the afternoon before Hugo?"

Susan's face flushed.

"That's what I thought," I said to her silence. "I really needed Jake that day." I dried my hands on a tea towel and faced her squarely.

"Susan, you asked for my advice. Here it is. First of all, understand that you are not the first woman to become infatuated with a co-worker. Jake fills a temporary void for you, you are inspired and grateful, and you elevate him to an imaginary pedestal where he appears to be wondrous. In short, you are bewitched. Accept that. Then take a moment to be grateful that you and Jake got caught. Now that someone else knows your secret—and I will guard your secret as long as you and Jake do—I think you'll find the excitement greatly diminished. In fact, I can almost guarantee that in time—hopefully very short—this hero worship will wear off.

"Next, go home, turn on a hot shower, and take a long look at yourself in the bathroom mirror. You are a stunningly beautiful woman. You have a successful husband, and precious children, and a lovely home. And you have much more leverage over the happiness of your marriage than you think you do. If you think Bob is rejecting you because he does not love you, you're wrong. He's merely scared. Some men get frightened to death, Susan, when things are going well, out of fear they will mess up and lose it all. They worry that their kids will have wrecks and their wives will get cancer. They worry they will forget to pay the insurance bill on time. And ironically, in the process of all this fear and worry, they create the very scenarios they fight against. It's the fulfillment of the old perception-becomes-reality law. In short, insecure men often dig their own graves."

Susan teared up at my words, and I was afraid for a second she would fall into another weeping spell.

"Dry your tears, Susan. Go find your husband and get him home, and start working on your marriage. Today. Try to find the little boy behind Bob's façade, and cater to it. Be nurturing and reassuring. Try to love him with all your heart, Susan. Just try. I think it will be easier than you think.

"As for Jake, stay as far away as possible. No more rides. No more get-togethers. If Alma Earle or Bob suggest getting together, find an excuse. Get friendly with other couples." Susan closed her eyes, making a deep furrow between them, and turned her head away from me.

"I know that right now you want to run to him and bury your head on his chest or do whatever it is that you two do. But unless you want this affair to blow up in your face and haunt you for years, you need to cut this off right now. You *can* let him go, Susan."

She opened her eyes and stared hard at the kitchen floor; tears were just beneath the surface. I cleared my throat and resumed my professional voice.

"I'll replace Jake Monday on the Whichy committee," I said briskly. "Needless to say, we will have a very sobering talk. As for you, you need to get back to Wellstone immediately and see if you can't pry that husband of yours out of his chair." My kitchen phone rang shrilly at the exact moment I finished my sentence. I raised my eyebrows as I reached for the receiver on the wall.

"If it's Bob, I'm on my way," Susan said, heading for the breezeway to retrieve her boots.

"Hello? . . . Yes, Bob, she's here. Sorry if I've detained her, but we've been talking like magpies. . . . Do be careful driving home. I'm worried about that hill at the entrance to your neighborhood. . . . Meet at the car? Yes, I'll tell her. . . . Well, you might want to think that through again. I've filled her up with warm bourbon." I laughed merrily, my voice tinkling. "Perhaps *you* had better drive. . . . Yes, she's heading for the door now. Have her call me when you get home so I know you made it safely." I hung up.

"What did I tell you!" Susan sputtered, tucking her hair under her knit cap. "How many men will tell their boss they want their *wife* to drive because they themselves are scared to drive in the snow?" She tossed her white wool scarf around her neck, letting the ends dangle loosely in front.

"How many men have enough self-confidence to let themselves be vulnerable?" I countered gently. "Take it as a sign of his love. He wants you both to be safe. And so do I." I reached out to hug her, swaddling and all. "Be loving, Susan," I whispered in her ear, suddenly feeling my own eyes well. I opened the kitchen door and lightly nudged her out onto the breezeway.

"Don't forget to call!" I caroled into the crisp air. The snowflakes were smaller now, their descent less profuse. The afternoon was starting to dim. I watched Susan's turquoise jacket grow smaller as she crunched down the driveway.

It was nearly two hours before Susan called. I was heating leftovers in the microwave when I picked up the kitchen phone.

"Thank you, Kat. I can't thank you enough for listening to me. And not judging. I feel a lot better now that I'm home. And I'm heading for that hot shower."

Before we hung up, I had one last thought. "Who drove, Susan?"

I heard a faint laugh; it was almost a giggle.

"Bob drove. He made sure I was buckled in tightly, and then he crawled like a snail, sticking to the tracks in front of us. We slipped a lot here and there, it was crazy, and I started laughing and making swooping noises as if we were crashing, but we didn't. The worst part was our hill. We stalled about halfway up, but the boys saw us coming and ran out to meet us and pushed us right into our driveway. They had been out in the street since getting home from school, helping neighbors as they tried to gun up the slope. One of them tipped with a twenty-dollar bill. Right now they're squabbling over how to split it three ways." There was another giggle.

I thought about the Atterburys as I ate a solitary supper at my kitchen table. I pictured Susan frying spicy sausage and stirring up a huge batch of pancake batter, perhaps in her white Turkish bathrobe with hair still wet from her shower, and Bob drawn into the kitchen by the aroma just in time to watch perfect circles form in the skillet and bubble around the edges. I thought about the Mooneys—Jake downing a bowl of chili in front of the television and grunting to Alma Earle as she prattled during the news.

And, darn it, I thought about the Staffords, in spite of myself. I tried to imagine June's kitchen, maybe almond-colored appliances and tapioca-colored paint on the walls, with wallpaper strips of trailing grape clusters and cheerful matching curtains. I pictured her preparing dinner for Paul, lifting the steamy lid of a crock pot to spear the pot roast she would have started that morning—rich bubbly meat dressed in self-made gravy, chunks of tender peeled carrots and thin-skinned red potatoes. She would have dimmed the lights to accentuate the inside coziness, while Marcy would set the table with everyday stoneware and embossed paper napkins. I wondered if Paul were still out in the bitter night. Perhaps he was clearing neighbors' driveways with the front-end snowplow that mounted onto his pickup.

How ironic, I thought as I turned in for the evening, that I had fled to the fourth floor to escape thoughts of Paul. The truth was, today's events had led me to think of him all the more. I understood that despair on Susan's face—the crumpled look that overwhelmed her when I advised her to break with Jake. I understood it because I knew it myself.

In spite of all that was clearly wrong between Jake and Susan, I nonetheless felt the shadow of their loss.

Chapter 27
ROSES IN A CORNFIELD

Monday's meeting with Jake did not go well. For starters, I did not sleep well the night before. I had retired early, exhausted, only to find myself at 2:30 as wide-eyed as though I had slept a blissful seven hours. I tried staring down the numbers as they dropped in the alarm clock's dim light—3:23, 3:24, 3:25. Although I finally dozed off, I overslept on the other end, which put me on edge once I arrived at the office. I was brusque with Jackie when I asked her to immediately cancel our 8:30 cabinet meeting "until further notice." It was an unusual move, and Jackie's face showed surprise as she quickly swiveled in her chair to make the calls. I disliked the abruptness of the moment, but there was no way I could face Jake and Bob in the same room, knowing what I now knew—at least not until I had spoken to Jake privately.

Then I sent for Jake.

Even now I feel a slow burn as I recall the confidence with which he entered my office that morning. He arrived within five minutes of the call, and he strode in and seated himself on my couch without hesitation. I seared him with my most forbidding look, but he responded impassively. He did not seem surprised at my stern voice and measured words—he scarcely blinked—but he did react strongly when I told him I was naming Claire Matthews in his place on the WHCCC committee.

"Claire's too new—she's still learning the ropes," he protested. "She doesn't have the breadth or long-range perspective I have regarding the college. She certainly doesn't have a grip on our history, and she doesn't have the connections I have." Jake didn't mention that he was a full-fledged vice-president while Claire was a lesser public relations officer, but I sensed his disdain. He appeared highly agitated, but whether this was due to the demotion or the loss of his proximity to Susan, I could not be sure.

"The committee needs someone who can represent the college well," I responded. "Claire has represented us splendidly every minute of her brief employment here. What she hasn't yet learned, she can find out. Besides, she is connecting quickly and ably with the Hurley community. They like her. She's smart. She's responsive. She's responsible.

"That having been said, Jake, let me make sure you understand why you are being removed from this committee. It has nothing to do with talent or experience and *everything* to do with the fact that Susan Atterbury is chair of this committee." I paused and watched his face flinch. His reaction told me my instincts had been right—that Susan and Jake had not had a chance to meet since Friday's snow and that Jake did not know she and I had discussed their relationship. A weekend phone call between them would have been too risky.

"Jake, let me be perfectly clear." Mine could have been verbiage out of a TV script, but I didn't have time to be original. "I cannot simply stand by and watch two families within my cabinet get torn apart by careless and indiscreet behavior. Assuming your relationship with Susan is a mere flirtation"—here I fixed him with a granite stare—"then it should be easy enough to put up proper barriers to dissuade things from progressing. Removing you from this committee is one contribution I can make from the chancellor's desk." Jake, sullen, said nothing.

"Please understand, Jake, that I value you and the contributions you make to Wickfield. You have been a steady force within the administration. But I need someone whose judgments are wise and sound. I need you to think maturely. I need you to be focused. I cannot afford—the *university* cannot afford—the kind of distraction that a scandal would produce. And Jake, no matter how innocent your relationship may be at the moment, it would be perceived by the public in the worst possible light if known to others. You do understand, right?"

Jake nodded.

"Now, about Bob," I began, but Jake interrupted.

"Let's not go there. I totally understand."

"You understand what? That Bob would feel betrayed beyond words if he knew? That he might say he could never work with you again? That his anger, and his grief, could dismantle his performance? Or worse?"

My voice rose, and Jake raised his hand as if to steady me. "Look, Katherine, Bob is not going to know, if that's what you're worried about. Susan and I have promised each other."

I didn't like the intimacy of "Susan and I."

"What about Alma Earle?"

"She doesn't know, and she won't." Jake's voice was flat.

"Get your affairs in order, Jake." My words were a slip, an unintended pun, but my flinty eyes gored into Jake's and would not let go. "My cabinet must be composed of persons of the highest integrity. I need to be able to sit across the conference table from you and Bob at the same time and know you are both thinking productively. I need you both in top form. We can't afford a schism or distraction or a breakdown of staff performance. Wickfield is at a hugely important juncture right now."

Jake nodded. "I understand, Katherine." But he did not apologize, not then and not later, nor did he show remorse, as Susan had.

"For now, I am putting you on notice, Jake. Consider your job on the line." I dismissed him coldly and packed him off to meet with his staff. Today marked the return of our residential students from the holidays. Jake faced a full schedule.

As for me, I was headed for warmer weather. Friday I was to fly to Fort Lauderdale to join a small group of women college leaders for a working weekend at a colleague's home. Our hostess, Laura Parkinson, herself the president of an affluent private college, had issued a personal invitation at an American Council on Education meeting last spring. "Come spend an early January weekend under our sun," she had cajoled us one morning as we'd gathered in our hotel coffee shop. Our group was so small that we were all able to fit around a single table.

The invitation tempted me sorely. Laura described it as a weekend of problem-solving and socializing, a time to gain strength and compassion from each other as female compatriots in a male-dominated profession. There were so few of us women among the nation's several thousand presidents and chancellors that we stood out—"like roses in a cornfield," we joked among ourselves.

I thoroughly enjoyed this conclave of women. We were a collegial group who sought each other's opinion in confidentiality. It would be appealing to discuss sensitive campus issues from a poolside chaise longue with a piña colada in hand.

As I prepared for my trip, I realized that Jake and Susan had given me my own "sensitive" campus issue to digest. Perhaps the weekend discussion would give me better insight into how better to handle each of them—especially since their responses had been so different from each other's.

Plans for travel brought Paul to mind: I needed a ride to the Charlotte airport. Not that I really *needed* the ride, I admitted to myself. I could easily enough drive to the airport parking garage without running astray of Carrington, especially after his softer remarks at the Christmas lunch. In truth, of course, I *wanted* to see Paul. Our time in the car, both going to Charlotte and returning to Hurley, would give us ample time to express anything that might, well, need expressing. I knew I needed to give it a chance to surface so that I could gently head off anything even remotely out of line.

But the ride to Charlotte did not go as I had envisioned. Paul had been friendly—but not too—on the phone when I called about the ride, and he'd hauled my suitcase to my car trunk with his usual jokes. "How many pairs of shoes, Prez? Different sandals for each day on the beach?"

What surprised me, rather, was my own reaction to him. The instant I saw him, my world steadied. In fact, I was so delighted to be in his company again that I found myself almost babbling as we drove. I told him about our Embright Christmas in Richmond: how we had filled Marianna's house with our laughter and stories, how we sisters had shagged to fifties' music in front of the living-room television, and how the men had anchored themselves in the basement den to watch football. By now Paul had each of my sisters and husbands fixed in memory; I was surprised at how well he remembered names and relationships.

It seemed only minutes before we were pulling up in front of the Queen Charlotte statue that faced the entrance into the airport terminal. Black-tinged snow was piled in smudgy hedges around the cleared sidewalks. Although eighty-degree weather was less than two hours away, I felt a sincere reluctance to leave Paul's company.

He seemed to sense my hesitation. "Be safe, Prez. I'll be here Sunday when you return. Five-fifteen." He set my suitcase down in front of the curbside attendants and gave me a little salute.

Perhaps it was confusion over my feelings for Paul that led me to stay low key when our group assembled on Laura's poolside patio. Six of us had made the trip, one from as far away as Montana. I allowed myself to be assertive during our lively conversation that first evening. The discussion centered on the ongoing—often exasperating—need to achieve balance in our personal lives. Three of us were single and thus without the traditional spouse. It was a sensitive topic.

"Of *course* there's more expected of us as women," I nearly snorted in response to the president from Massachusetts; she felt that our ability to raise money was the only relative measurement of our success as executives. "That's the way we've been socialized, and it's naïve to think otherwise. We have to consider earrings and hair and makeup just to dash to the store for a can of cream of mushroom soup." Laughter broke the tension.

On Saturday, as the waning sun sparkled on intracoastal waters and graceful yachts slapped the water with their bows, our conversation shifted to more personal topics. A woman from a private Midwestern university mentioned the name of a rival institution in her city. "Rumor has it—strong rumor—that their president is having an affair," she remarked.

I reached for my sangria glass.

"Well, consider him gone," responded the Montana president, certainty strong in her voice. "Every school that has faced a presidential affair has seen a resignation. He'll either resign voluntarily or get forced out."

"Who's the woman?" asked Laura.

"Well, again, this is just rumor, but the word on the street is that she's his executive assistant. She's in her forties, maybe even fifty, but very attractive. There has been any number of sightings, I understand."

I was surprised at the gossipy turn of the conversation. "Isn't it possible they've simply been thrown together because of their work?" I asked. "That could account for 'sightings.'"

"Those in the know think otherwise. Of course, I'm just the messenger," she added hastily. I gazed thoughtfully from behind my sunglasses at thick white ankles that ballooned over the rims of her canvas shoes. Her legs were crossed and her slacks rode high, exposing webs of spidery red veins in her right calf. In that tottering moment I decided not to share my Jake-and-Susan story with this group, even though the door had been opened for such a discussion.

We covered many other topics that weekend, everything from anti-aging skin creams to disparate salary levels. Before we left Sunday, Laura feted us with an elegant breakfast: honeybell oranges that we peeled at the table, creamed shiitake mushrooms over toast points, and omelets dressed with asparagus spears. As a parting gift, Laura crossed to the far side of her patio and plucked fresh grapefruit from a tree drooping over her pool. We stuffed them into the empty spaces of our suitcases as mementoes from Florida. Carrington and Jake and my work-heaped desk seemed a distant world away.

Paul, on the other hand, was a welcome sight when he met my gate in Charlotte. I tried to look "professionally friendly"—an expression we had coined at Laura's—when he greeted me, grinning from ear to ear. I was newly aware that we could be the subject of a "sighting" ourselves.

Our drive back to Hurley was quiet. After my weekend of high stimulation, it was good to simply ride through the countryside in pleasant silence and enjoy the comfort of Paul's presence. I commented once on the snowy cornfields, still tightly bound with a solid white sheet. Paul noted the profusion of road kill from wildlife in search of food. The unspoken moment from the madrigal banquet hung suspended between us, silent but unthreatening. I relaxed and enjoyed the ride.

It was Paul who brought up the subject of my approaching birthday. "January 26?" he asked.

"The twenty-fifth. A month after Jesus." My little joke was irreverent, but Paul smiled.

"Family coming?"

"Oh, no. Too far, and besides, they celebrated my birthday early. In Richmond."

"Not even the boyfriend?" His tone was teasing now. He always referred to Alex as "the boyfriend," as though he were an inanimate object.

"Oh. Yes. Alex is coming the weekend after. We missed Christmas together because of a medical conference in Hawaii."

I didn't think of Alex as "family," exactly.

Paul's mention of my birthday reminded me that my annual physical exam was on the calendar for next week: Friday the nineteenth. I had not taken time for the early blood workup that Alex had been so insistent about, but it could wait until this official visit. I probably would have to ask my doctor for it specifically, since my annual exams only included the routine checks: heart, lungs, vital organs, urine test, Pap smear. I had an excellent health record. Through the years, additional lab work had been ordered only when something seemed out of kink—like the nosebleeds I'd had a few years ago. Blood tests had revealed nothing untoward, and my doctor had merely added Vitamin K to my supplements. It was no big deal.

I looked forward to my medical visit, actually. The lab results would come back just in time for me to celebrate my good reports along with my birthday.

Chapter 28
BIRTHDAY

George Hoffmann had become my internist soon after I'd settled in Hurley. His personality had irritated me long before I became convinced of his brilliance as an interpreter of the body's ills. At first his overquick smile made me think of an eager college student dressed up in the demeanor of a forty-five-year-old. But he was suitably professional during his examinations, when he poked and prodded and pressed upon my anatomy from every conceivable angle. The only thing I didn't like was the little reassuring pat he gave each time the exam was completed. It seemed patronizing, as though all it took was a small forgive-me gesture to make it acceptable to invade the most private wells of my body.

But overall our relationship was good, and it transcended professional lines into the social. That was not surprising in a small city like Hurley, where the university dominated the town's economy. George Hoffmann's wife, Paige, was a fund-raiser on Bob Atterbury's Advancement staff. I called George by his first name. He called me Katherine.

Now, following my exam, we moved into his office, and he leaned back in his oversized desk chair to review my file. "Well, Katherine, you appear to be a very healthy female," he said. "Still taking the calcium?"

"Yes," I said. The small talk made me impatient. I quickly moved the conversation to the lab work I wanted.

"You remember my surgeon friend, Alex, from Chicago. I introduced you at the faculty-staff picnic. He wants me to have a blood count, a chemistry panel, and a thyroid check." That was the shortcut version I remembered from Alex. I hadn't brought the notes that he had written in his kitchen before I left Chicago.

"He's worried about you?"

"He thought I was looking extra tired when he saw me at Thanksgiving. And he was right—I was totally exhausted. Other than a conference in Atlanta in October, that Chicago trip was my first real break since Hugo and all that cleanup stress afterward."

"Yes, you have definitely seen more than your share this fall." The doctor lifted his phone receiver, pushed a button, and snapped out some brief orders.

"You're probably just fatigued, but Gwen can certainly run a CBC. The score on your blood count can tell us a lot of things—whether you're anemic, for example. The blood chemistry panel tests twenty-one things—your liver function, your kidneys, your electrolytes, things like your potassium and fluoride and salt levels. The thyroid screen tests your TSH. If your score is high, your thyroid is underactive. If it's low, you're overactive. It's an inverse relationship," he added, almost apologetically.

"Where's the test that scores my level of Hugo stress?" I was trying to keep my sense of humor, but I probably sounded petulant.

"We'll know a lot when we get the numbers. My staff will call you. Now, on another matter"—he hesitated briefly—"you're about to turn fifty, I see." He looked up from his file. "Congratulations! That's a record milestone."

I sighed. "So they tell me."

"It's a good idea to get a routine colonoscopy after fifty," he continued, scribbling an order on his pad. "You can have it done through the medical center here. Dr. Stewart Colby is the one I recommend. I think you'll like him, Katherine. If something's amiss, he'll figure it out." He chuckled. "Stew and I were Chi Psis together at Carolina and in the same med class. He's a good man."

I wrinkled my nose at the thought of a colonoscopy. "Getting old isn't easy, is it? You guys really dish it out to us seniors."

"You're not old, Katherine, not at all. In fact, I'd say you're at the prime of your life. My exam showed nothing abnormal. We'll wait to see these lab reports."

"Any rush on this?" I asked, holding the colonoscopy order at arm's length and waving it by its corner like a dead mouse.

"Not really. You'll need to take a day off, so work it in at your convenience this spring. And it's a fairly simple procedure these days. Just call that number, and a nurse will walk you through the prelim. You'll be sedated, no pain. Most patients say the anticipation is the worst part."

I left the doctor's office a bit indignant. A colonoscopy! It was not what I'd expected, certainly not what I wanted, but at least it would be something concrete for Alex's medical mind to react to—that test plus my lab results. We could discuss those next weekend when he came for my birthday.

Throughout the week I received family birthday cards from Virginia and Florida and California. My uncontested favorite came from Benjamin, Jane's ten-year-old in San Diego, who was developing serious talent as a cartoonist. He had sketched a charming caricature of a giant female insect—an ant—that had sprouted the perky ears, whiskers and long tail of a cat. She was perched on a stool, smiling beguilingly through small eyeglasses and mascaraed eyelashes while dark curls dangled from her antennae. The stool stood on top of a three-dimensional number fifty, like a bust on a pedestal.

It was labeled "Ant Cat."

On Tuesday, Dr. Hoffmann's technician, Gwen, called the house with my lab reports. Lennie's note said I was to call her back "to discuss." It was the next day before I could place the call. I watched the sun glint through the blinds onto the wall's wainscoting as I waited for Gwen's voice. This was the last day I could think of myself in my forties.

"Dr. Embright?" Gwen came on the line. "I have those numbers for you." I scribbled furiously on a pad, knowing they would make perfect sense to Alex.

"A twelve on the CBC?" I repeated. "Is that good or bad?"

"Twelve is a good score. You were a 13.2 last year, but you're still pre-menopausal. A nine or an eight would have given us concern. In fact, all your scores are quite acceptable, although Dr. Hoffmann wants to test you again in three months on the thyroid. It seemed a bit high, and if the numbers continue to climb, he may put you on medication."

Although I had not expected bad news, the report was a relief. It kept my spirits high through the dreary rain that began that afternoon. As the temperatures plunged at nightfall, dropping from the forties into the high twenties, the freezing rains continued. When I awoke on my birthday and pulled my bedroom drapes, I beheld a thin layer of ice that fanned the pine tree boughs outside my window into elegant little whisk-brooms. On the berried shrubs below I could make out a lovely shape to the dropping water as it froze, intact, on the arching branches. This was not one of those treacherous Piedmont ice storms that broke the backs of majestic trees and caused havoc with power lines. It was a spectacle of sheen and shine. I was eager to see the frozen fountain in front of Wellstone. It surely would be a marvel of stalactites.

I entered my office with a jubilant stride, but when Jackie delivered her normal greeting, I was secretly disappointed. Jackie certainly knew today was my birthday; in fact, last year she had given me a lovely card and a stunning pair of droplet earrings. But I had been silent through the weeks about this milestone birthday, and so had she. Perhaps I had overdone the silence. A cheerful "Happy Birthday!" would have felt good.

The morning sped along with its usual routines, and to my secret dismay I saw the noon hour approaching and realized I had nothing special planned for lunch. Weird, I thought. I had purposely kept the hour open, hoping for a bit of levity or celebration. Now I was annoyed with myself for not planning better.

That's when I heard a light knock on my door. I whirled around from my computer to see a beaming Paul Stafford in the doorway. Jackie, obviously, had cleared him to see me.

"How are you doing?" He continued to smile.

"Come in, Paul." I pushed papers to the side. My temples suddenly felt moist.

He strode over to my desk, half-shutting the door behind him. "Do you have an extra forty-five minutes today? Come on, Prez, tell me you do. There's something I want to show you."

Suddenly I was in my eighth-grade classroom again, watching the open door for that cute Steve Lasorda with the curly black hair to make his daily 11:53 a.m. pilgrimage to his student assembly post. I couldn't believe the giddiness that captured my spirits. My surge of emotion was, quite simply, ridiculous. I fought for composure, hoping my eyes did not betray my internal upheaval.

"I don't know, Paul," I hedged. "Today is my birthday and I—"

"Exactly. I have a birthday surprise, all wrapped up in a sparkling white bow. After work? What about now? It's lunchtime. Do you have plans?"

"Well, no. Not exactly." I laughed with embarrassment because I was turning fifty and had no plans. And because Paul was so insistent.

"Good. I'll meet you in your driveway."

We agreed to meet in ten minutes. I heard him speak briefly to Jackie before he left. I carefully closed my office door and slipped into my private bathroom to freshen up, primping like a schoolgirl before a big date. *Stop it!* I commanded myself. I recalled speaking to myself in similar fashion the first time Paul and I had driven to Charlotte.

On my way out I looked for Jackie. I wanted to alert her that I would be back well before a 1:30 meeting, but she had evidently stepped out for the moment. I simply walked from my Wellstone office to my driveway, where Paul stood waiting beside a mud-splashed black pickup truck. I smiled in spite of myself, remembering Alex's surprise conveyance from O'Hare. What was this special love affair between a man and his pickup? This would be my second truck ride in two months.

"No police car?" I asked.

"Not official business. You get the limo today." He opened the cab door for me. I pulled myself up and swung my long legs in, buckling my belt and observing the wide front seat and roomy leg space. *So this is Paul's fishing truck*, I thought in surprise. It was incredibly neat—no leaves on the floorboards, no Snickers wrappers in the ash tray. Was he a natural neatnik, or had he vacuumed the cab in advance?

We left town via a back street and in minutes were on a two-lane highway heading north. The sun had emerged; the day was turning gorgeous, with a Carolina-blue sky. The crystalline trees sparkled in the sun, mocking the softening fields now lumpy with earthy patches. We passed frame houses with gray tendrils curling from chimneys. We circumvented a plodding postal truck with a driver perched on the right-hand side. In time we turned off the highway onto an obscure rural road. The terrain became hilly and winding.

We spoke sparingly along the way, and while I was curious about our destination, I did not cajole Paul for information. He was totally focused on his driving. I, in turn, had faith in this venture—*adventure*, I should say, because the farther we drove, the more remote became our surroundings. Eventually there was no traffic to speak of, nor houses, nor signs of another living soul. When Paul finally turned off the pavement onto a narrow ice-packed lane, I realized why we had come in his truck. Up to this point I had felt perfectly safe, but the swaying of the truck along the furrowed road gave me momentary pause.

"Hey, lumberjack, you sure you know how to get us back home?" We had just passed a No Trespassing sign nailed to tree.

"Home is twenty miles behind us. Hang on." Paul kept his eyes on the tracks as he navigated the winding trail. Another vehicle had cut through in recent days, but last night's rain had added a slippery glaze to the path. Thin trees lined our road on both sides, sagging slightly with the weight of the ice. Underbrush grazed the sides of the truck as it crowded through. The trail rounded a deep curve to the left, and I swung in my seat belt toward Paul, my shoulder hitting his. Then the road seemed to end, and Paul drove straight ahead into a small clearing and braked. I drew in my breath sharply.

Directly in front of us were the crystal waters of an exquisite lake, pristine in the coldness of winter's grip and cradled in a well of stunning shoreline and sunlight. The water's surface was a mirror of thick-laced evergreens that cascaded from descending bluffs and rippled in shades of blue and charcoal gray. Bare-branched trees girdled the water's edge. They stood silent, etched in white diamonds against the noontime sun. Icicles shimmered like wind chimes, released by the invisible breeze.

Paul cut the ignition and we sat, motionless. We had come upon this scene so suddenly that its beauty left me speechless. I felt the rapture of early explorers—those who had travelled a stream that became a river, or followed a whir that roared into a waterfall. The glorious spectacle left me shaken. We had stepped backward in time to the world's beginnings, when God first created it and made it perfect.

Paul opened the driver's door for a few seconds and held it steady, an arm's length wide. "Listen!" he said. At first I heard nothing but absolute quiet. Then I felt the rustle of the wind and heard soft plops of falling ice.

"The silence gets me every time," he said. "You can actually hear it." He closed the door carefully.

"How on earth did you find this?" I finally asked. Like Paul's, my voice was reverent.

"I fish here, summers. Friend of mine, Jay, owns the land. As far as I'm concerned, it's the closest to paradise I'll ever get."

"How often do you come here?"

"Every chance I get. And not just to fish. Sometimes I walk the shoreline. Sometimes I sit and watch the water." He pointed to a juncture of nearby trees. "Jay sets up a hammock in the summer, right over there. Best naps in the world. Great sunsets. This place has saved me more than once."

So Paul had a hideout, a secret retreat. It didn't surprise me, actually. I had long suspected he had haunting memories that stemmed from his Vietnam years. My throat constricted. Beauty could make me weep as suddenly as sadness, and here I felt dazed by both. The vast wild solitude and its deep white peace were overwhelming. I leaned my head back against the seat and closed my eyes.

"It's . . . the perfect gift."

"Knew you'd like it," he said. His voice was husky. Together we sat in silence, drinking in the splendor. It was, truly, perfect. I had somehow been favored to experience one of life's special gifts.

Then Paul reached over and picked up my hand, holding it in both of his. I did not pull it back. I heard a click and felt an arm slide behind my head. He scooted toward me in one swift move and pulled me as close as my seat belt would allow. I turned my face up to his and closed my eyes and, as though I had rehearsed a thousand times, I found Paul's mouth. Ours was not a clutching, passionate kiss. It was, rather, a slow-paced moment of such exquisite tenderness that I was undone by Paul's touch, his lips, even the air of his breath. The fleshy part of his mouth was soft and wet and jolted me into thinking of the deepest and most intimate moments between man and woman.

When he released me, Paul pressed his forehead against mine and held me tightly. I drank in his closeness. It was the closest we had ever been physically, and I inhaled the moment. After he pulled away, we simply sat there, immersed in the private pounding of heartbeats.

"Happy birthday, Prez," Paul finally said, covering my hand again with his own. "You deserve the finest day possible." I interlaced my fingers and squeezed his hand. There was nothing else to be said, really, so I placed his hand on the steering wheel. He started the engine, turned the truck around in the clearing, and headed back down the snowy lane.

How did I feel on that ride back to campus, with Paul by my side and his kiss seared into my brain? Did I feel wicked? Remorseful? Angry at myself? Angry at Paul? Had I transgressed an unforgivable line?

The truth was that I felt closer to Paul than I had ever thought possible. The kiss had sealed a special coupling, the dimensions of which loomed far beyond collegiality and friendship but whose depth I was not yet ready to explore. Our conversation was easy and natural, void of the restraints of earlier times together. It was an instantaneous extension of the closeness we had forged the night of our wild ride through Hugo's winds. Our unspoken dance of past months now had texture and shape.

What remained unanswered was how we would deal with it in the future.

Paul delivered me to my driveway—not to Wellstone's concrete steps, as he offered—and I walked back to my office with a new exuberance. I had not eaten, yet I was bursting with energy. It was shortly after one o'clock when I charged down the wide hallway toward my office, eager to prepare for the upcoming meeting.

"How was lunch?" I said conversationally to Jackie as I entered her outer office. *Mine was terrific!* I wanted to shout. Instead, I reined in the brightness of my voice.

"We missed you," Jackie replied, shuffling papers. She did not look up. "Where were you? Your calendar was clear. I checked it all week."

I paused. Something was awry. "I left campus for a while," I said. I looked around her office, noting her usual furniture and plants, and glanced inside my door. "What's up?"

Jackie finally eyed me with a flinty look behind her dark-rimmed glasses. "The staff came to surprise you. We brought food. The leftovers are in the fridge." She gestured down the hall and managed a half-smile. "We saved you some birthday cake. Check it out. Oval Office." She bent back over her papers.

I stared. Jackie had never before used such a terse voice with me. I swept out of her office and down the hall to the twin doors that guarded the Oval Office. I opened them slowly and peered inside the darkness, fumbling for the light switch. The room was empty. And for the second time within the hour, I gasped aloud.

Festoons of dark-blue and red streamers fanned down from the chandelier. A vase of deep blue iris and garnet lilies centered the table. The wastebaskets overflowed with paper plates and napkins. A lovely antique glass cake stand, one I recognized as belonging to Susan Atterbury, stood at one end of the table and bore the skeletal remains of a chocolate birthday cake. Only the cake's center remained. "Life begins at fifty!" read the burgundy script that laced the creamy white frosting.

The table on one end had been reset with a single plate and napkin and fork. Next to it sat a neat stack of greeting cards addressed to me in handwritings of people I knew well: Dan and Bob and Susan and Marilyn and Jake and Pud and Claire and—whose was *this*?—oh, dear lady, *Lennie*! Tears hovered.

Next to the cards was a long box several inches high, beautifully sealed in joyous birthday wrap and encircled with a wide satin ribbon and bow. I tore off the paper and discovered a simple banker's box. Lifting the lid, I felt a shiver of shock. Inside were dozens and dozens of envelopes— probably well over a hundred. Each was addressed to "Jackie Barnes, Project Director." Jackie! The "project director" title was an obvious code for this birthday card shower Jackie had organized. I fingered through the top layer, each card tightly packed one behind the other. Several bore stamps and out-of-town postmarks. I sank into the chair in front of the plate.

So I had not been forgotten. My friends had reached out for me with love, but I had not been here to receive it.

I sat down at the solitary plate, reached across, cut a generous slice of the remaining cake, and placed it before me. It would make a lonely yet lovely feast. I picked up my fork.

I must tell Paul, I thought as I leaned forward for the first bite.

That's when I noticed that my piece included some iced words. I turned my plate slightly so I could read them. I read the garnet script, then read it again, and suddenly I put down my fork.

The message said simply, "Life begins."

Chapter 2

COLD WEEKEND

Near the end of the afternoon on my birthday, I received a surprise call from Chapel Hill.

"Katherine!" boomed a familiar throaty voice that made me smile. "My tickler file says you are a lady of high priority today. I hope those Wickfield folks are giving you the birthday you deserve."

UNC President Charles Pettigrew had built his popularity partly on his attention to personal detail. Frankly, I was delighted to hear from my University of North Carolina boss today. I pictured him in his office, probably standing by his secretary's phone with his briefcase prior to splitting for his next appointment. Indefatigable, he had created more state legislation on behalf of the university system than any president in recent memory. In the annals of the University of North Carolina, Charles Pettigrew was becoming a new legend among legends.

"Charlie, I have a king-sized carton of birthday cards to read. Jackie must have contacted the entire Board of Governors and every legislator on every key committee. I may have to take a day off just to read."

"Well, now, Wickfield's First Lady deserves a day off. We won't even count it as a vacation day." Charlie enjoyed the banter as much as I did. The conversation lasted less than two minutes but topped off my day. A real class act, that Charlie. I mentally gave him extra credit for mentioning that his wife, Wanda, sent greetings as well.

Before the afternoon ended, I called Susan Atterbury to thank her for her part in my surprise party.

"We waited and waited before we ate," she reported, "and Jackie was embarrassed many times over because she had been convinced she could detain you if you tried to head out. Where were you, anyway?

Jackie said Paul Stafford came into your office, and then you suddenly disappeared."

This was significant information—the group connected my absence with Paul. I weighed my words carefully. "Yes, something came up that needed me. Unfortunate timing, I guess. Anyway, I'm glad you went ahead without me, and I love the cards and the thoughts behind the beautiful notes."

Jake, I gathered, had not attended, telling Jackie he had a "prior commitment" off campus. And Susan had apparently known this in advance, before she arrived with the cake stand and server. I seized this opportunity to acknowledge—and applaud—her efforts to separate herself from Jake. From what little she had told me, I gathered she was forcing a painful end to the relationship.

"But I do miss Jake," she said, almost as an afterthought. "This isn't easy, Kat. I think about him all the time. Believe me, I hurt all over."

I assured her that I understood.

Alex called that night to give me his flight schedule for the next day. "Happy birthday, Beautiful! How exciting was your day?"

Exciting? There was no way I could tell Alex what this day was beginning to mean to me. I described the party I'd missed, leaving out all mention of Paul, of course, and emphasizing the huge carton of messages I was eager to wade through.

But I was unprepared for the apathy with which I privately approached Alex's visit. Since we had not been together since Thanksgiving, I expected to feel some personal excitement, a high level of anticipation. Instead, I felt something akin to dread. Were he to call and cancel as he had in September, I would have been relieved.

The reason, of course, was The Kiss. That's how I thought of it now—that instant when Paul had pulled me against the supple softness of his leather jacket and delivered those gentle moments of intimacy. I relived them over and over in my memory, each time feeling that hot stir of blood. To be sure, the kiss was not a serious kiss—not the kind I imagined Susan exchanging with Jake, clinging to him in their secret lairs, kisses as hungry and driven as passion itself. Paul's kiss suggested something deeper—so indefinable that it vaguely disturbed me.

So when Alex's rental car arrived in my driveway that night, I fought the confusion in my chest as I awaited him on the breezeway. I wondered fleetingly whether Paul were monitoring the campus security—perhaps on purpose—and exactly how much activity could be picked up on the exterior cameras. Alex, sporting a bronzed Hawaiian tan, received only a perfunctory kiss as I quickly led him into the house.

But Alex looked great, as always, and he seemed relaxed in spite of his travel. We swapped Christmas stories and photos. Even more curious was the fact that I found myself postponing bedtime. Alex solved that problem by pleading fatigue and falling asleep before I had closed up the house for the night. I carefully slipped under the covers next to a soundly snoring man, his left arm hooked behind his left ear. He was unaware of anything other than blessed sleep. I rolled over on my right side, my back to Alex, and drifted off.

On Saturday we devoured the last pieces of birthday cake. Alex then helped me delve into the carton of cards, slicing the envelopes with a letter opener and returning them to the box. We sat at my dining-room table, the carton in the middle, and as I read each note I placed it into a category: faculty, staff, students, alumni, Wickfield trustees, Arden College trustees, board of governors, legislators, donors. I finally started a new pile that included miscellaneous people—the rector at Grace Episcopal, my manicurist, even the flower vendor who sold me fresh-cut bouquets each time I visited the downtown square. I had referred to her only as "Maria," but Jackie had actually sleuthed out her stall. Jackie had covered nearly everyone I knew.

"Looking for someone specific?" Alex asked. I was pawing through the yet-unread envelopes like a secretary thumbing through an index file.

"Here it is!" I exclaimed. I had been looking for Carrington's distinctive handwriting, whose bold lettering leaned to the left and tracked downward to the right. His envelope was light blue, UNC's color. Intentional? Maybe. I was curious as heck to see what kind of message he would choose.

"It's something religious, I'm betting. Nothing smarmy, not humorous." I made a clean cut with the slicer.

Alex watched my face change as I mouthed the message to myself. "Well?"

"Well. I'm not believing this." I paused to digest Carrington's words. "It's a very nice message."

Alex took the card, read it, and laughed. "His wife must have bought it."

"But look, Alex, he added a few words of his own." The personal script had grabbed my attention: "*A well deserved milestone to a deserving colleage.*" The message was scribbled in his hand, and the signature read "Carrington and Edith Hall."

"However, he misspelled *colleague*," I noted. "And he forgot the hyphen, and he used the same word twice."

"Forget it, professor." Alex moved over to kiss the top of my head. "So he's had court reporters writing for him. Give the old man a break. Now it's my turn."

Alex pulled me out onto the sun porch, poured me a glass of Riesling from a bottle in the refrigerator, and tucked a pillow behind my back. Then, with great fanfare, he presented me with two packages: one wrapped in Christmas paper, the other in a colorful design of balloons and fireworks.

"This one first," he said, thrusting the Christmas package in my lap.

I confess I was almost childlike when it came to gifts, perhaps from being the youngest during those years before Emily was born. My mother described me as a precocious child, impish and sociable, so gifts seemed to come to me in a steady stream. I loved the thrill of examining the bulk of the package, the artistic design of the paper, the curl of the bow. I opened this one carefully, sliding my finger under the tape to save the beautiful green-and-gold wrapping.

Inside was a Neiman-Marcus box—surely straight from Michigan Avenue—and laid out inside the crisp tissue paper was a beautiful silk sports outfit. It looked outrageously expensive. Included were beige tailored slacks with a slight textured nub, a lustrous braided belt, and a coordinated floral top in wild colors of mountain grape and rosy mauve. I pulled each piece gingerly out of the box and spread them on the couch next to me.

"Gorgeous, Alex!" I exclaimed, absolutely delighted. The outfit was in my correct size and spoke of elegance in every way. "Love it!" I rose from the couch to endow him with a generous kiss—my first real kiss of the weekend. He returned it with a wet, smacking kiss of his own.

"Now this one." He shoved the birthday package toward me. It was much smaller, like a jewelry box, and my first thought was that it might be a necklace or bracelet. Again, I carefully removed the tape and paper. Alex watched closely.

The box, however, was for a Buxton leather wallet—a man's—and I realized that Alex had packed this one himself. "Aha! A disguise!" I lifted the lid slowly.

Inside was a brochure for a Fort Lauderdale cruise company, with a photo of a sleek white ship on the cover. When I picked it up, out fell two tickets.

"Alex!" I was completely stunned. A Caribbean cruise! The thought of separation from the stresses of Wickfield produced an unexpected lift and sent my spirits soaring. I studied the tickets closely; even the slick cardboard felt exciting.

"It's for Thanksgiving week, but if you prefer July or August, they'll switch for a different cruise." Alex seemed genuinely excited himself. "I wasn't sure of your summer schedule. There's a sailboat cruise off of Maine in August. We need to decide soon, though, so I can claim vacation time as well."

"Alex." I swallowed hard, feeling contrite. I was truly overwhelmed. This was a lot to comprehend all at once. I rose once more to kiss him, and this time the kiss was gentler, sweeter, longer. I'd had no idea that Alex would pull a lovely surprise like this.

And yet, in spite of the jolt of the gift and the exotic pictures it conjured—gleaming luxury liner, glittery cocktail receptions, winter sunshine—my images fell short of pure enchantment. The fact that I did not feel romantically enthralled left me vaguely disappointed. Was ingratitude on my part separating me from true happiness?

For the rest of Saturday I tried to be highly attentive to Alex. I even half-apologized for the evening I had planned. The Theatre Department had given me tickets to see Thornton Wilder's *Our Town* in Wellstone Auditorium; it was the last night of the production. Perhaps, I suggested with a sly smile, Alex might prefer an intimate evening in front of the fireplace rather than a student theatrical performance.

Alex surprised me. He voted for the play, and, once we settled in our seats, he quickly absorbed both the acting and the script. He concentrated on the dialogue and applauded with enthusiasm. I might have even detected a tear when Emily's painful monologue lamented her return to heaven—he flipped his nose casually with the back of his knuckles, the way men do when trying to conceal their emotions. Afterward, he joined me backstage to congratulate the cast.

We were both in good spirits as we walked back to the Chancellor's House from Wellstone. It was a chilly evening. Yesterday's ice had long melted away, but a cold wind fronted our faces. Alex wrapped his arm around my thick coat and pulled me close. He pulled me close again in bed as we reached for each other under the blankets, and I relaxed in his arms, anticipating the long series of slow kisses to come.

But it was not to be. Once again Alex fell asleep, snoring almost instantly as I lay my head on his chest. The side of my face rose and fell as his chest swelled with deep intakes of breath, then dropped with snorts of release. I lay there, pondering the meaning of it all. Why would he lavish such devotion on me but lack the drive to make love? He was leaving early in the morning to catch his flight home.

Was I the one who was disappointed, or was it Alex? Okay, so his behavior had seemed weird at Thanksgiving. I could overlook the obsession with his Jaguar. But his Christmas trip to Hawaii had caught me by surprise, a late decision that had wounded me in spite of my seeming support. And now his libido seemed swallowed up in his need for sleep. Could it be that Alex was ill?

Ill! Suddenly I remembered that blood lab report and those numbers from George Hoffmann's nurse. I had forgotten to mention them, nor had Alex asked about them even once. I felt momentary relief. Whatever had concerned him in November must have been a false alarm. I would mention my good scores in the morning over breakfast, and we would swap little rakish jokes about the upcoming colonoscopy. That would be that.

It didn't turn out to be that easy.

"Actually, your eyes still look hollow," Alex said over toast and coffee early the next morning. He buttered his toast with long, clean strokes. I sat opposite him in my robe with my scribbled notes from Gwen.

"And you look thin, Kat, scrawny. Your hip bones felt sharp as rocks last night. You don't have as much meat on you as I remember."

"Is that what's bothering you?" I retorted. "I'm suddenly too skinny?" My voice grew harsh. "You scarcely touched me·last night, Alex. I'm surprised you noticed."

The nastiness of my words surprised us both. Alex and I seldom feuded. But he had hurt my feelings by calling me scrawny, creating a sting that burned all over. I hated my sharp words. They made me sound like a petulant teenager.

Alex leveled his eyes at me over his coffee cup. "No need to get testy." When he set the cup down, it rattled in its saucer. "I'm a physician,

Katherine. I observe. That's what I'm supposed to do. And yes, you do seem thinner than when I saw you last." He picked up the sheet and studied the numbers.

"Have your doctor run the tests again in two months. If something's wrong, it hasn't shown up yet, but it should by then." He wiped his mouth with his napkin and pulled back his chair. "Gotta run, little one. Never understood why the airlines want us an hour in advance. Thanks for a lovely weekend. All too short."

He planted a java kiss on my mouth. "And let me know about the tickets. Call me as soon as you check your calendar."

He disappeared upstairs into the bathroom, and I heard water running. He emerged with his overnight bag. We embraced—this time in a mist of Crest—and he slipped through the breezeway into the darkness of the early hour. I stood and watched his taillights disappear from the drive.

Although I had no idea at the time, that would be the last time I saw Alex.

CHURCH

I have always been fascinated with the way a person's choice of religion shapes other life perspectives. Some of this observation came from my parents' own religious bias. I recalled an argument with Sally Gordon when we were six or seven. In my anger at a small injustice, I had lashed out. "You just say that because you're a shabby Catholic!" I'd protested heatedly. That's how close our friendship was—we could fight like tigers and then love each other again, all in the same day.

"I am not shabby!" she yelled back. "My clothes are as nice as yours!" Her face reddened as she put her hand on her hip and stomped her brown oxford on the sidewalk.

"You are, too! My Daddy said so! He said Catholics are *shabby*!"

"Am not!"

"Are too!"

As it turned out, two local city councilmen, both well-known as Catholics, had been accused of laundering money in connection with a land deal for a new regional hospital. I'd overheard my father one night describe their politics to my mother as "shabby." The confusion got straightened out after Mrs. Gordon, white-voiced with anger, called my parents. They promptly disciplined me for calling Sally names.

"You must apologize to Sally," my mother insisted, appalled that I had dared to insult a neighbor's child—and in the name of God!

I did. I apologized the very next afternoon. I told Sally I was sorry I had called her a shabby Catholic. "At least you're not a Baptist," I said consolingly. "They dunk their babies."

"They do not! My grandmother is a Baptist! She was ten when she got dunked! She told me!"

I had forgotten that detail about the grandmother. Wary of another tangle with Mrs. Gordon—she of the Baptist mother—I tried the tactic of evasion.

"My mother says what is most important is the love in our hearts. If we love Jesus and each other, we'll go to heaven. God doesn't care about the details."

Our mother's Swedish heritage was the reason we had all been raised Lutheran. She had not taken it well when I'd become an Episcopalian. Christ Episcopal Church was a mere block from Keck College and the campus church for many of our students. In fact, a number of Keck College weddings took place in the high-arched sanctuary early each summer.

"The Episcopal liturgy is almost word-for-word Lutheran," I explained to Mother in self-defense. "In fact, the Anglicans probably stole it from us." I had no idea whether this were true or not. I based my glib statement on the fact that Martin Luther's protests against Rome had inadvertently started the Protestant Reformation. I figured that when Henry VIII separated the Church of England from papal authority, he and his Anglican followers probably modified Luther's German worship to suit their English tastes.

"I don't know, dear," she sighed. "Those Episcopals have bishops who wear tall hats, and they call their ministers priests. It's good that Grandpa Larson has passed on."

"You didn't get this worked up when Sarah became Methodist," I replied tartly. Sarah's "defection" had scarcely caused a stir.

"But you're . . . the *smart* one, Katherine." I should know better. That's what she meant.

This Embright family history was scarcely in my subconscious that morning as I drove to Grace Episcopal for the nine o'clock worship. I was a regular eleven o'clocker at church, but Alex's predawn departure that morning had given an early start to my Sunday. Today was a beautiful winter morning of sun-slicked skies. I parked in the main lot beside the berm of fluffy Leyland cypress trees and entered the narthex from a side door. The vestibule embraced me instantly, and my eyes adjusted to the dimmer indoor light.

The ushers, as always, provided friendly nods of recognition. Ken Clark, a longtime staffer in the Wickfield Admissions Office, handed me a bulletin, his carnation boutonniere fanning a spicy fragrance in my direction. He leaned into my face to ask if he could show me to a seat.

"No, thanks, Ken. I'll just fill in," I whispered back. We had been through this little charade a dozen times: the ushers always asking and I always refusing. I preferred to stand at the entrance into the nave and search out the largest empty space where no one was sitting. Then I would proceed to seat myself—alone, without benefit of usher—in the middle of the gap. It was my little contribution to making the church appear filled, a trick I'd learned from Eva Krueger when a teenager. Eva, our minister's wife at the time, had always waited until the last possible moment to seat herself. "That way the church will look its fullest when Karl first turns around at the altar to face the congregation," she'd confided to my mother. "It gives him a little boost."

Today's most noticeable gap was about two-thirds of the way down. I sidled along the far-left aisle under the twenty-one rows of jewel-colored stained-glass windows. This led me past Carrington and Edith Hall, seated in what they considered to be their permanent pew—not because of benevolence or family history but because they had staked their claim years ago. Legend had it that one Sunday when a visiting gentleman had accidentally strayed into their pew, Edith stopped in the middle of the aisle as she approached and whispered something to the usher. The usher hesitated. The visitor, not exactly sure of his misstep, merely scooted over. As a result, the Halls ended up sharing the pew with Wickfield's new visiting mathematics professor from Egypt.

It was told later that Edith had strong words with the priest about the incident, insisting that the professor's presence had "distracted" her from worship. Seemingly to appease her, the priest agreed to include in the next week's bulletin some wording to address the situation—and he did. It appeared as a warm welcome to "all of our brothers and sisters, regardless of race, nationality, or creed, who choose to worship among us in the unity of Christ."

In her subsequent outrage, Edith threatened to move their membership to Main Street Presbyterian, but that never came to be. Carrington had the last word. Edith and Carrington Hall remained members at Grace Episcopal and continued to "pew" near the center aisle.

Now I passed beyond them, down one, two, three, four more rows, and slid into the pew marked by the pane with the lily and the butterfly. In that exact instant, the organ burst into the stately chords of "Praise My Soul, the King of Heaven." The choir began its sweep down the aisle, and

I grappled for a hymnal. I found the page, fingered my place in the words, and joined in.

> Praise, my soul, the King of Heaven;
> To his feet thy tribute bring;
> Ransomed, healed, restored, forgiven,
> Evermore his praises sing:
> Alleluia! Alleluia!
> Praise the everlasting King!

I relished this majestic Anglican hymn of joy and forgiveness. Queen Elizabeth II, I had read, had loved it so much she had used it as her wedding processional. The words were tender, describing God as "slow to chide" and father-like as he "tends and spares us." These seemed written specifically for me. For the final verse, the organist pulled out the trumpet stop:

> Alleluia! Alleluia!
> Praise with us the God of grace.

Good beginning, I thought as the hymn ended. I swapped the hymnal for the red *Common Book of Prayer.*

"Blessed be God: Father, Son, and Holy Spirit," intoned the priest.

"And blessed be his kingdom, now and forever. Amen," the congregation responded.

"Alleluia! Christ is risen."

"The Lord is risen indeed. Alleluia."

So began our liturgy. The familiar rite, filled with beautiful words of praise and response, carried me along. We stood, sang, sat, and knelt.

Yet God seemed to elude me throughout that hour. I heard little of the sermon and followed none of its organization. In listening to speakers through the years, I'd usually looked for a thesis of sorts, an announcement of main points of argument. I liked to ride on the tide of rhythm, noting strong vocabulary and turns of phrase.

Today, my mind was mush. The overwhelming experiences of the week spun and jumbled. The quiver of organ pipes tugged at my emotions. I thanked God for my recent birthday and for his providence of fifty years.

Thank you, Lord, also, for my good health report and for the excellent health and prosperity of my sisters and their families. I added this last part with fervor, although my head was beginning to throb with the overtures of a headache.

And what about that birthday kiss—the forbidden moment when I trespassed into new and slippery territory? When the priest invited us to prepare ourselves for the Confession, that birthday kiss leaped into the forefront of my mind. I had known this would happen. All weekend those images had crept in, even when I'd been enjoying time with Alex. All I had to do was close my eyes to return to the front seat of Paul's truck. In silence I re-absorbed the soft touch of his mouth, the earthy smell of his truck's cab, the deep quietude of our forest-clad cloister.

Now that stolen moment left me humpbacked with guilt. Even worse, I felt Carrington's eyes, four rows behind me, burning into the rear of my very existence. It was as though he could see into my soul. I shifted in my pew.

"Let us confess our sins against God and our neighbors."

The clacking of wooden kneelers filled the nave as the congregation lowered them in unison from their upright positions. I scooted forward until my knees met the needlepoint cushion.

"Most merciful God," we read in unison, "we confess that we have sinned against thee in thought, word, and deed, by what we have done and by what we have left undone."

I had always loved these specific words, especially the concern about leaving things undone. They had always given me pause. Today, however, I concentrated on the "what we have done" part.

The chorus of voices continued: "We have not loved you with our whole heart; we have not loved our neighbors as ourselves."

Well, that was certainly true, now, wasn't it? June Stafford, for example. I had not loved her as myself.

"We are truly sorry, and we humbly repent." Okay. That one worked, too. I was truly sorry if I had offended God by kissing Paul.

"For the sake of thy Son, Jesus Christ, have mercy on us and forgive us, that we may delight in thy will and walk in thy ways. To the glory of thy name, amen."

There. That was done. I sucked in a deep breath.

The priest continued praying, granting us forgiveness in the name of Christ, and my thoughts drifted once again as I knelt. I pictured Paul relaxing over the Sunday newspapers. I thought of Alex's plane winging north over the black-green hills of Kentucky and snow-patched fields of Indiana. I wondered about Susan and Bob and their boys, about Jake and Alma Earle. I reflected on my huge responsibility to the Wickfield community and my niche as a role leader for women. I was subdued with all that had invaded my life this week.

Then came the moment when we passed the peace, a brief ritual in which worshippers greet each other informally in the pews. The wooden kneelers thudded again as we returned them to their upright positions and turned to face each other. The soft echo of "Peace!" rippled through the air. As we spoke, we pressed the hand of whoever was close by, or smiled at acquaintances at a distance. I sent a wave across the pews to Carrington, not sure if he could see my gesture. But he responded with a curt nod as we sat once more.

Peace. Yes, that was what I needed today. I had not felt this restless in a long time. I felt the need for greater strength, and I prayed silently for courage well beyond my reach. By the time those in my pew proceeded to the altar rail for Communion, I felt properly prepared for my moment before the Cross. I waited in line in front of the carved rood screen that separated the nave from the altar.

Even then, I failed to receive an answer.

I knelt at the altar rail, my hands cupped to receive the holy bread, and watched as the priest pulled a ragged tuft from the greater wheat loaf. I dipped my piece into the chalice. The bread sopped up the wine. I swallowed it whole, wiping away a drop of juice in the process. The organ played softly. My eyes took in the white marbled floor behind the altar rail, the platform surrounding the altar, and the vivid green altar hangings for the liturgical season of Epiphany. The priest's resonant voice rang out a blessing, his arms extended, palms open and fingers pointed down. I remained kneeling, head bent, waiting for a shining moment to comfort me.

It did not come. I felt no fireworks from heaven, no clear direction from God. Did I feel, as the hymn promised, "ransomed, healed, restored, forgiven"? I could not be sure. I rose from the kneeler and returned to my pew.

Yet as I prepared for the recessional, I suddenly felt a small, still breath, one that fanned my face and neck, released my heavy shoulders, and cooled me with focus and purpose. I stood like a statue, listening to that stillness. In those moments I knew I was, at last, feeling God's forgiving presence.

How like God, I thought, my hand groping in my purse for a Kleenex while the choir sailed by. How like God to sneak up on me like that, to nudge me with a simple puff, to speak to my heart and open my eyes with the simple power of his grace.

I bowed my head for the benediction.

Chapter 31
THE BLEEDING

When I noticed it that early morning in my bathroom, the blood did not frighten me. It startled me so that I sucked in air with a breathy gasp. I would describe it to George Hoffmann that afternoon as angry-red, bright in freshness and intensity.

I remember the date I discovered it—February 15, a Thursday—because it was the day after Valentine's Day. Wednesday, Alex had sent me two dozen spectacular pink roses, long-stemmers whose perfect unfurling buds spoke volumes about their quality. These were hundred-dollar roses, a pink rainbow of hues ranging from pale powder to deep magenta. He had them sent to me at Wickfield, where they landed on Jackie's desk. Before I knew they were intended for me, I opened our adjoining door and entered her office.

"Oh, gorgeous, gorgeous! That husband of yours never misses!" I laughed in delight and played my hand across the puffy baby's breath that studded the arrangement. "Look at those colors!"

"I wish. They're yours. Just arrived." Jackie pretended to sigh as she picked up the sturdy vase and carefully handed it to me. I was headed down the hall at the moment, but I took time to carry the flowers into my office. I removed a potted peace plant from my Williamsburg plant stand and replaced it with the showy bouquet.

In truth, I was thrilled with them. They brightened the room and piqued a spark inside me that had been waning over the weeks since Alex's visit. There was no doubt that Alex was sending mixed signals. He plied me with expensive gifts but played me coolly when expressing affection. The confusion was curious, but right now I didn't have time to figure it out. I decided to enjoy the beauty of the roses and let the rest take care of itself.

As for Paul—yes, he of the exquisite kiss—I intentionally kept my distance. The kiss had been a one-time moment, a special message of friendship and respect. Yet my heavy sense of honor kept me alert for a future moment when I could speak of it—a simple word to make absolutely sure he understood the limits of our relationship. *Just keep it light, Kat,* I admonished myself whenever I rehearsed that moment in my mind. *Use humor, perhaps. Whatever you do, don't go heavy.*

That kiss, no doubt about it, had wrapped itself around me, inside and out. Paul floated constantly in my subconsciousness, as real as if we he were present in the same room. Those fluttery sensations had grown into a roll, like heated water ready to burst into boiling. I thought about Paul as frequently as though his photograph were pinned inside my blouse. At times I snapped my head up from my paperwork, half-expecting to see him stride across the room.

But January rolled into February. There were no major trips out of town, no campus crises to legitimately draw us together. "All for the best," I assured myself. I was deeply entrenched in nagging decisions for the school. I would soon be announcing three new trustees to replace those rotating off the board in April. I had not yet nailed down a speaker for spring commencement. In spite of its gray dampness, February demanded huge bursts of energy to propel us to May commencement. Because of January's intense snow, this February was drearier than any I remembered. I sensed its bleakness within my staff. I felt its bluster when I walked on campus.

That is why the bleeding, when it first appeared, startled me more than frightened me. I had already reached an emotional nadir, a weariness that sapped my usual urgent stride. Abnormal bleeding? It was just one more thing to sort through.

Still, as I stood on my peach-tinted bath mat and watched the unwelcome blood flush away in a swirl, I felt a chill. My morning shower massaged my head, neck, and back, yet uneasiness lingered as I reached for my terry bathrobe. This was not menstrual blood. Whatever it was, it puzzled me.

I heard Lennie's rustlings in the kitchen, and the Mr. Coffee was gurgling on the counter when I entered, dressed and ready for work. I glanced at the morning headlines laid on the table—the *Charlotte Observer* and *Hurley Herald*. Each was part of my morning routine. I fished for a coffee mug and reached for the pot.

"Early meeting?" asked Lennie, her lovely brown face wreathing into smiles as she greeted me. I enjoyed her daily companionship. She sensed when I welcomed conversation but had learned to respect my moods of deep thought. This morning, I was reserved.

"Early desk work," I answered, more curtly than usual. Suddenly I didn't want to wait for breakfast. "Make it a scrambled egg sandwich on toast. I'll eat at my desk."

Lennie's hand stopped in midmotion as she unscrewed the cap to the orange juice. I knew a lecture was forthcoming.

"Miz Katherine, breakfast is you most important meal of the day. You can't skimp on calories, 'cause you gonna work 'em all off by noon anyway." Lennie regarded her role as far exceeding that of a housekeeper. She admonished me on my wardrobe, supervised my nutrition, and oversaw my general health. She fussed a blue streak whenever I strayed from her homespun advice.

"Just wrap it in foil," I added, ignoring her. "Okay, I'll take the juice, too." She was stooping into a lower cabinet for a clean peanut-butter jar.

I emptied my coffee mug into the sink and bolted upstairs for my final routine. Back in the bathroom, I checked once more for bleeding. Nope, no sign. Good. False alarm. I studied my hemline in the long mirror and tugged the cuffs of my blouse.

Once in my office, still dusky with early-morning darkness, I turned on my desk lamp and flipped through my Rolodex. Dr. Hoffmann's nurse would not be in yet, but I dialed the office number and waited for the recorder to beep for my message. "This is Katherine Embright at Wickfield," I said into the receiver. "Please ask Dr. Hoffmann's office to return my call at ——." I recited my direct-line number, repeating it distinctly since the nurse had only Jackie's number in her files. Although I didn't suggest an urgency to my call, I knew a nurse would call back promptly.

She did. She called at 8:34, which is how I found myself that very afternoon facing George Hoffmann in an examining room. He asked all kinds of clinical questions, each increasingly invading my sense of privacy. Still, I was surprised at the ease with which I answered—and my gratitude for his professionalism.

"Sounds as if we need to speed up that colonoscopy, Katherine," he said finally. "Fortunately, Stewart Colby is a superb surgeon and a good friend. We were frat brothers at Carolina. Chi Psi. I'll call him and set up a colonoscopy right away. How's your Monday?"

So he was giving me the weekend. He must not deem it that urgent, I thought with a spark of hope. But my mind was flashing beyond Monday.

"And if the colonoscopy finds something awry?"

"If he finds something small enough to remove on the spot, he'll take care of it then. If there's something large—like, say, a mass of considerable size that is bleeding—he might need to schedule separate surgery." He saw my stricken face. "Inconvenient, of course, Katherine, but very necessary. If something doesn't belong there, it needs to come out as soon as possible. Dr. Colby operates at Piedmont Memorial, so that part would be easy, at least."

"Terrible timing," I muttered, mostly under my breath. My mind was whirling.

"Who's in Charlotte?" I suddenly asked, looking at him directly.

He looked back blankly.

"Who's the top surgeon in this field in Charlotte?"

George blanched. "You won't find anyone any more skilled than—"

"But Charlotte is more private. I would need complete privacy if I had surgery. No one must know, George."

Now George looked earnestly pained. "You would need friends, maybe your staff, to help you in recovery. You could share this information within your inner circle, surely. And colon surgery, if that is what is needed, is very commonplace. There's nothing to be . . . embarrassed about, if that's of concern. Stewart is—"

"It's not the intimacy of the surgery. It's the simple fact of surgery itself. It's important that I be perceived as well—*well* as in 'not sick.'"

George actually laughed aloud. "Even college presidents get sick, Katherine. There's no shame in that."

"But most college presidents are not women." I held my gaze without blinking.

George stared back for several long seconds. "Excuse me. Let me see if I can get Dr. Colby." He walked toward the door. "You can get dressed. Help yourself to magazines."

So he wants to call his frat brother from another phone, I thought, scooting off the examining table and stepping behind the screen to sort through my clothes. I eventually settled into a chair with a *Good Housekeeping*, flipping through Pert shampoo and Spic 'n Span Pine ads while wondering if all doctors buddied up with referrals. Good old Chi Psi. I had dated a Chi Psi when at Hollins, Larry Somebody from Randolph-Macon or some such school. He had driven a black Ford Mustang with wide leather seats.

I had switched to a copy of *Redbook* and was deep into an article about menopause when George reentered the room.

"Sorry for the wait. Stew was in surgery. He recommends"—he pulled a slip of paper from the pocket of his white coat—"Dr. Wayne Witherspoon. His office is off Providence Road, and he operates out of Hillcrest, which would be a good choice for you if we need to do surgery. Stew says he's the best colorectal surgeon between here and Atlanta. Knew him during residency." He scribbled an address and phone number on his prescription pad.

"We're set for Monday at Hillcrest. Ambulatory surgery—outpatient. Call this number before five today. A nurse will walk you through the prep. It's easy—something you buy at any pharmacy. You will mix it with water and sip it slowly Sunday evening. And you can't eat or drink anything else after you start the prep."

"What time is my appointment?" *Please, God, don't make me have to cancel another cabinet meeting.*

"Ten thirty, but you report in a full hour in advance. And you'll need a driver." He looked at me sharply to make sure I understood. So much for privacy! "You'll be groggy for at least an hour afterward."

Then he smiled, one of those George Hoffmann killer smiles that denied the agony writhing inside me. "The good news is that you'll lose only one day. You'll be back at the ranch Tuesday."

If all goes well, I thought glumly. I was numb as I drove back to my office. I had just been handed marching orders that completely shot next week's schedule, not to mention that of my entire cabinet. To reschedule our cabinet meeting meant raising Jackie's curiosity. In fact, I would need to shift appointments for the entire week.

Uppermost was the fact that I would need a driver. Who could I ask to take me on such a personal errand? Susan? No, of course not. She was married to a cabinet member, which could jeopardize my need for secrecy. Marianna? Sarah? No. Richmond and Arden were too far away for such an imminent event.

Then I thought of Paul. I squirmed a moment at the thought of sharing such a delicate experience. After all, an intimate kiss scarcely qualified him for the intimacy of a colonoscopy.

In the end, my sense of humor took over, along with the urgency of the situation. If Paul could keep one secret, he could keep two.

I picked up the phone and dialed his number.

Chapter 32
COLONOSCOPY

Paul picked up his phone on the first ring, thank goodness. I had had visions of tracking him down during the weekend.

"Officer Stafford."

"You are hereby invited to participate in an excursion of deep intrigue and subterfuge," I intoned in a low voice.

Paul burst into instant laughter. I smiled as I listened to his hearty voice cutting through the lines. His voice was a warm massage. This was my first uplifting moment since yesterday morning, and I closed my eyes as I soaked up his presence. I gave few details, only the Hillcrest Hospital address and our arrival time.

"Monday will be a long and boring day," I said, warning him to bring work with him. He agreed to pick me up Monday at eight. He was still chuckling when he hung up.

Dr. Witherspoon's nurse, on the other hand, was chatty, full of details. She told me the product name for the prep, exactly how many ounces were to be mixed with water, and how I was to time my consumption. She warned that I would be hungry Monday morning but not permitted to eat. "It tastes rather nice, like lemon. Just sip it slowly. This will clean you out real fast, dear."

Great, just great, I groaned to myself. Without a doubt, this trip would be the true test of solid friendship with Paul. I envisioned emergency restroom stops all the way to Charlotte.

As it turned out, the trip went well. Lennie saw us off in bewilderment, since she'd known nothing about this unscheduled trip until she walked into the kitchen early Monday. She found me bending over a chair, wearing a purple jogging suit and tying the laces on my tennis shoes. I merely told her I was going to Charlotte for a routine colonoscopy.

"Well." She often said that single word when she was startled, as if it covered a complete sentence. She knew something was afoot, of course, but I figured I would share details only if merited by the results of the test. My Thursday bleeding had not recurred. Surely something minor had triggered it. George Hoffmann had said there was a myriad of possible reasons. This test would clear up the mystery. I was eager to return to more important matters.

As for Paul, I offered nothing beyond the bare essentials of our destination, nor did he inquire. He bundled me into my Ford Crown Victoria and set off south toward Charlotte. The sky overhead was gray but not dismal. The highway before us ran straight and open as we left Hurley and Wickfield well behind. Stress dropped from my shoulders as we sailed past muddy-red farmlands and open, barren fields. I felt free, almost carefree. It felt good simply to be with Paul, to be at his side, to drift comfortably back and forth between easy silence and conversation. With him, life always seemed easier.

When we approached the Hillcrest Hospital campus, I spotted the clinic set back to the right—a one-story building with huge letters hanging from the yellow brick. Colorectal Cancer Center, they read. Dear God, did they have to scream the names of body parts with such indiscretion? Dr. Hoffmann had not mentioned the word *cancer* even once. The sign was unsettling, even shocking. It was clearly not a warm welcome, especially for those of us arriving for a mere screening.

"There it is," I said, pointing out the building. "Turn here." We wound our way through Hillcrest's parking lot to an empty slot.

"So you're a patient today," Paul said cheerfully as he pulled into the space. "Colonoscopy?"

Paul made it so easy on me—acting as nonchalant as though I were about to buy a new handbag.

"Your job is to get me home in one piece," I said. "I have to sign you in as my driver, because I'll be groggy afterward. I'll probably sleep all the way back."

"Will you talk funny and tell secrets?"

"Be serious. There's no truth serum involved. This is ambulatory surgery. It's merely a rite of passage for new fifty-year-olds." The comment was a reminder of my recent birthday, which in turn brought to mind The

Kiss. I sat perfectly still in the front seat for a moment, reluctant to go inside and begin my ordeal.

Paul reached over and grabbed my hand, lacing his fingers through mine. "Well, you're going to do great, and by this time tomorrow it will be a fuzzy memory. I went through one of these deals a couple of years ago. The hard part's behind you." *Behind* me? I wasn't sure whether he were attempting a bawdy little joke or not. I simply sat and held his hand— it seemed like the most natural thing in the world to do—and wished fervently that a normal "tomorrow" were at hand.

It had never occurred to me that Paul might have been through a colonoscopy himself. That would make him about fifty-two, an age I had guessed earlier. As we walked across the parking lot and entered the brightly lit lobby, it struck me that had I not been so hung up on privacy issues, Paul could have relieved much of my uncertainty about the procedure. A discreet description of his own experience would have been perfectly appropriate conversation during our drive to Hillcrest. *Darn!* Too wise, too late. I stepped to the receptionist's window, signed myself in, entered Paul's name as my personal contact, and followed a nurse to a door.

Before entering the hallway, I turned to look at Paul. He had unloaded his *Charlotte Observer* and briefcase onto a green vinyl sofa near a coffee urn. He saluted me with his empty Styrofoam cup and gave me a huge grin. I returned the gesture with a little wave.

The rest is a blur in my memory: the curtained-off cubicle with scarcely enough space for two technicians around the gurney, the wrinkled blue cotton gown with stringy ties in back, a blood pressure cuff on my right arm, a plastic catheter on the back of my left hand for the anesthetic, a butterfly clip on my index finger to monitor blood oxygen. The cubicle was in a holding area, and I was aware of swishing gray curtains, the murmur of voices, and the scuffing of soft-soled shoes. Apparently the feet passing by the bottom of my curtains were supporting patients in various stages of preparation. There seemed to be no great deluge of patients, which surprised me. George Hoffmann had suggested that colonoscopies were beginning to be "favored" in the public eye.

An attendant in green scrubs arrived to push my bed to the room where the colonoscopy would take place. I was tranquil from medications as the gurney rolled down a long gray hallway. The room for the procedure seemed surprisingly small. It was dominated by a low-hanging television monitor that caught my eye. A nurse tinkered with my catheter, and a bespectacled young doctor with a mop of black hair perched himself on a low stool at my side. He introduced himself with a friendly smile, giving a name I did not retain. He mentioned that he was a gastroenterologist conducting the colonoscopy as a member of Dr. Witherspoon's practice and assured me Dr. Witherspoon would assess my results promptly. I liked him instantly. He asked a couple of questions about my bleeding history and joked about the five feet of twists and turns that he was about to navigate. "It's as though I'll be driving the gorge between Asheville and Knoxville, only without the beautiful scenery," he said. *Very clever,* I thought sleepily from the gurney. But I never responded.

My next memory was back in my cubicle, where a nurse stood by my shoulder and told me clearly to wake up and get dressed. I nodded, comprehending, and she left. I closed my heavy eyes and dozed off. The nurse returned, more urgent this time, and held up the plastic bin containing my clothes and purse. She pulled me into a sitting position and admonished me to dress quickly, because the doctor was waiting to speak to me.

I slid into my jogging suit and was sitting on the side of my gurney tying those darn shoelaces again when the doctor with the flopping locks entered. Someone else stood at the flap of the curtain with his back toward me—rather like a sentry guarding hallowed ground.

I said nothing. I was dimly astonished that the procedure was over and much too groggy to conduct a conversation. The doctor began speaking, and I sat on the side of my cot, listening in a half-stupor to words like "three centimeters" and "too large to remove" and "bleeding" and "surgery." Dr. Witherspoon's name was mentioned several times, and I remembered then that this young doctor was a physician with Dr. Witherspoon's practice. He turned to the sentry, and the two of them exchanged some clipped words.

That's when I recognized the second man to be Paul.

It was all surreal. I ran my hands through my hair, trying to shake some sense into what I had just heard. Was I still sleeping? The two men left, and the nurse returned to hand me some saltines on a napkin and juice in a plastic container. She waited while I ate and drank, chattering about inane things that did not matter. She was much too cheerful for my mood.

Finally, she pulled the curtains back, revealing a shiny wheelchair. "Mrs. Embright, this is your ride. You get to ride out that door over there to the sidewalk. Your husband has gone to get the car. Is this your coat?" She helped me slide my arms into my overcoat, draped my scarf around my throat, and then guided me into the wheelchair. "You're ready to roll."

She placed my purse in my lap and smiled much too hugely. A young man in green scrubs appeared out of nowhere to wheel me away.

Then I was in open air, where the chilly wind caressed my face and hair. I saw my champagne-colored Ford approaching the curb. Paul snapped out on his side, motor still running, and bolted to open the passenger door. Then his arm was over my shoulder, helping me into the front seat.

"Comfortable?" he asked, adjusting my seat belt, and I nodded mutely. He closed my door and slipped back behind the wheel. We rode away in silence. I tried desperately to stay awake, to make sense of what was happening, to formulate at least one coherent sentence, but the effects of the anesthetic overpowered me. My chin bobbed down into my chest, then snapped up again as I jerked awake. I was faintly aware of stoplights and merging traffic signs and the swish of passing cars. Once homebound on the interstate, I slipped into a dreamless sleep.

When I finally jolted awake, my mind was perfectly clear. From the wide curve we were rounding—the one near the low-set white farmhouse that had flooded during Hugo—I knew Hurley was less than half an hour away. I reached over for Paul's hand; it covered mine instantly.

"What's going on?"

"How much do you remember?"

"Very little. Something about surgery." Now I understood why Paul had been called to my bedside. My driver, I had been told earlier, should be someone with whom the doctor could discuss the results of the test. I listened, disbelieving, while Paul described the tumor the doctor had found in my lower right intestine. It was roughly three centimeters in diameter and was leaking blood. The doctor had snipped a part of the tumor tissue for a biopsy, as well as tissue from the colon wall; the results should be back late Wednesday. Dr. Witherspoon would notify Dr. Hoffmann, who as my personal physician would discuss the findings with me in his office.

Paul made it sound so simple, but I was still confused. My recent blood tests had shown no sign of blood loss. "Twelve is good," Gwen had told me.

I remembered writing down the twelve and doodling short straight lines around it, like a halo.

"What did he say about Dr. Witherspoon and surgery? And why did he call the mass a tumor and not a polyp?" A polyp, I knew, was a noncancerous growth.

"I asked more or less the same thing. The doc said a tumor by definition was an abnormal growth of cells. He called the mass 'progressive.' As for Dr. Witherspoon, he specializes in resectionings of the colon. I gather he can cut out the tumor and stitch your colon back together."

That meant he could fix it. He could do what Alex does every day—cut out the problem, make it go away, send the patient off to heal. Slice, snip, remove, close. Easy as pie, Alex had once said early in our relationship. At the time he had been showing off, trying to impress me with his vast medical skills, but I knew surgery was never easy as pie. Routine, maybe, but always with a factor of risk.

So Thursday would be the day—the day I would find out whether I had cancer. Cancer. The Big C. The word that had terrorized Emily and terrified our whole family twelve years ago. The disease that had ravaged my father and driven him insane with pain. The word had lurked in the back shadows of my brain from the moment I'd discovered Thursday's bleeding. Now I had to confront it.

From Paul's description, surgery sounded likely. I didn't have time for surgery, but at least I had tomorrow to think through my calendar to find the most advantageous opening. I would squeeze the surgery in somewhere, maybe next month. February was simply too busy a time to interrupt.

Paul released my hand as we approached Hurley. "You haven't eaten!" I said suddenly. It was nearly midafternoon. "Paul, you must be starving!"

"I'm okay. Vending machines and Lantz crackers work wonders."

I thought quickly. How should I best handle Lennie? She must be having a fitful afternoon. She would ask a ton of questions, none of which I felt like explaining.

"Lennie can make you a sandwich, and while you're eating, explain to her what you just told me. No more, no less—just the basics. Lennie knows to say nothing to anyone, but it's okay to remind her that this is . . . " I trailed off.

"A time of 'deep intrigue and subterfuge'?" he asked. I heard the grin in his voice as he mimicked my Friday phone call.

"Exactly."

"By the way, Prez, the doctor said you might have some, ah, bleeding, and, if so, it's to be expected. Something about the tissue he cut out for the biopsy."

"Lovely, just lovely." I no longer needed to have that conversation with Paul about drawing the line. The events of the past few days had thrown us into a whole new kind of relationship and an unexpected brand of intimacy.

We approached my house from the back street, avoiding the route past Wellstone. As expected, Lennie was waiting in the kitchen. "Give this man anything in the house he wants to eat and drink. He's famished," I said as we entered.

"What 'bout you?"

"Not hungry. I'm heading upstairs for a nap. Wake me up at four."

"Dr. Hoffmann's office called, and a lady from Charlotte left a number." *Dr. Witherspoon's office*, I thought. Word was already out; the forces were in motion.

"I'll call them later. Thank you, Lennie," I said.

Then I turned to Paul. "And thank *you*." He gave me his ROTC salute, clicking his heels, and I managed a sad smile before trudging upstairs. I heard Lennie firing away with questions before I reached the top step.

Chapter 33
DIAGNOSIS

To feel the executioner's sword through the inward eye—that, I think, defines terror.

Although my execution was not at hand, it might as well have been. My dread of what Thursday would bring was so intense that I thrashed in bed Wednesday night. I tried to be reasonable. I stared at my mitered cornice boards in the weak gray light, shaming myself into reminders that fears of tomorrows had wracked women of far truer courage than mine. I thought of martyrs like Joan of Arc and Saint Margaret of England, waiting for dawn and death while shackled in irons. I thought of mothers sending too-young sons into war. I thought of battered wives, bruised and mute, holding their broken ribs while waiting for the dawn.

My anxiety, I realized, was based on the unknown. As chancellor, I functioned daily by interpreting data. I listened, read, mused, and discussed. Now I faced a dearth of information. If I were diagnosed with cancer tomorrow, I would regard it as a kind of failure, a tacit understanding that my body had somehow not achieved and, in failing, had prevented me from attaining major goals. I willed my eyes to go beneath my skin into the composition of my most minute cells. I realized my illness was not an infectious disease, yet I pictured my interior teeming with microscopic invaders. Were they infiltrating my colon walls, crawling like termites into my lymph vessels, gnawing my organs at this very instant? I envisioned infinitesimal warriors in battle positions, aiming spears and cannons to fire a fusillade of destruction at the nub of my existence. Cancer is often described in combat language: "Dr. Katherine Embright, chancellor of Wickfield University and the nation's youngest woman to head a state university campus, lost her battle with cancer this morning . . ."

I thought of unfinished business that could not endure distraction—bills to be paid, clothes to be purchased, decisions to be sealed. I envisioned the struggle that might well lie ahead: surgery, pain, drugs, therapy, loss. I heard the haunting cries of my father as he writhed in the vise of pancreatic cancer. I remembered my sister Emily, assaulted for over a year by the ravages of breast cancer, her already-slim body growing so thin that her arms could wrap around to the middle of her back.

I rose and walked barefooted through the house, the plush of the carpet soft beneath my toes and my shadows looming larger than my own self in the dim light of the downstairs hallway. I drank a glass of milk. I watched an idiotic television infomercial touting magical cleaning cloths that could be restored like new with a simple dip in soap suds.

Eventually I drifted into the back bathroom, the one at the end of the hall that I often showed guests. It was charming and spacious, a feminine Victorian solitude in pink and purple florals. Its bathtub walls still bore original white tiles. I squared myself at the sink and gazed directly into the gilt-framed mirror. Staring back was the pale face of a fifty-year-old woman with tousled hair and haunted eyes. "Damn good-looking woman," Alex liked to call me when spurred by brief moments of appreciation. I pulled up my blue pajama top, gathering it under my breasts with one hand while slightly lowering the band of the trouser bottoms with the other. I pulled in my breath and studied my smooth belly. It was amazingly flat—flat for a woman of any age. No fat, no ripples. There was little of that bulging band that older woman acquired after childbirth and menopause—neither of which I had experienced. Mine was still a bikini-worthy body, although I reasoned modestly that such a blessing came partly from my height and legginess, partly from my Swedish genes, and partly from my workhorse mentality that brimmed with adrenaline.

I rubbed my hand lightly from my navel down. If I needed surgery, this picture-perfect plane of skin would soon look like a hot-red zipper. Alex had once described in detail this kind of lower abdominal incision: the midline vertical cut that went straight down from the belly button. I pictured the parting of skin and muscle wall, the forceps that would extricate the tumor, the scalpel that would sever lengths of surrounding tissue, the intricate stitching of the various layers, the elaborate gauze dressings, the blazing scar. I wondered how Alex would react to such medically altered skin. Would he subconsciously see me as a patient rather than a lover? Would he view me as a correction of surgery rather than the perfection of his fantasies?

But the one vanity that I treasured, far more than my yet-firm body, was my bountiful hair. In my first-birthday photo, sitting in my high chair in front of a white-frosted cake, I showed early tendrils that trailed at my nape. While I was still a toddler, Shirley Temple curls had sprouted from my head like wire springs. When I was four, ringlets had hung like rolled silk around my shoulders, and strangers had stopped Mother on the street to comment on their thick profusion. Partly to keep the locks at bay, Mother had plaited the lengths into braids, even teaching Marianna, who was almost eight, how to dress them with bright-colored ribbons.

As a teenager I'd kept my hair long, having learned that greater length would achieve looser, softer curls. I joined my sisters in battles with metal hair rollers, foam-covered curlers, and electric hair driers with bouffant hoods that sat on our heads like plastic bonnets. I had tried a myriad of gels and sprays to tame my hair, but by adulthood I'd learned to let it be. Now it fell in rivulets around my face, a medium length of thick, natural waves. Women were paying a hefty price for salon perms that achieved this very look. Many doubtless assumed I spent a small fortune to replicate this trendy style.

Now I ran my hands through my curls, digging my fingers deeply into their mass and letting the hair web through my fingers as I lifted it straight up at the scalp. Chemo did terrible things to hair. I shuddered as I pictured my hair falling out in chunks, piling up at the shower drain in heaps of dark locks. I became almost ill at the thought, and I sat on top of the toilet lid for a couple of minutes to catch my breath.

The grandfather clock in the entry chimed four o'clock. Tomorrow I would be sleep-deprived, an added insult to the challenges ahead. Because Jackie had rescheduled our cancelled Monday cabinet meeting for Thursday, I was now saddled with a nine o'clock cabinet meeting followed by my eleven o'clock medical appointment.

Close to sunrise I returned to bed and finally slept. Lennie knocked sharply on my bedroom door to rouse me. I was distracted during the cabinet meeting, but only Dan seemed to notice my desultory mood. My mind heavy and numb, I let Marilyn prattle longer than usual and failed to silence a heated discussion between Bob and Jake. Dan interceded at exactly the right moment, allowing me to bring the meeting to a graceful close.

After that, I found myself behind the wheel of my car, driving the ten blocks to my appointment, failing to respond to the friendly receptionist and treating her, instead, like a stranger in line at the post office. I faced a stricken George Hoffmann across his desk, watched him pick up his ballpoint pen and put it back down, heard him use the C word and describe the tumor as malignant. And I sat mutely, stupidly, full of questions that would not form words, finally admitting to my quaking heart that I absolutely had known he would speak as he did.

"Many people think that cancer is their fault, the result of some error in judgment or a faulty lifestyle. The truth is, yours probably started several years ago as a simple polyp called an adenoma, and over time it became cancerous. You have an adenocarcinoma." I tried to picture the word spelled out.

George's voice labored along about how colon cancer could be painless and asymptomatic for years. The show of blood was the first telltale sign.

"How far—?" I stopped to clear my throat, which sounded as though I had acute laryngitis. "How far along am I?" The words sounded insipid, as though I were newly pregnant.

"The good news is that you're probably at a Stage I or II. Stage I means the cancer is contained within the inner layers of the colon, the mucosa. If it's Stage II, it will have spread through the muscle wall but not into the lymph nodes. That's why we need to remove this cancer immediately. If it spreads further, say into the lymph nodes, it can also spread to other organs of the body."

He picked up the snow globe on his desk, tipped it over, and set it back down. White sparkles whirled and settled to the bottom.

"Did the biopsy indicate how . . . what condition the tumor is in? Can you tell how fast it is growing?"

"It was determined to be about three centimeters and moderately aggressive. That's a Grade 3."

"I thought you said a one or a two."

"Stage I or Stage II. Those are the levels of disease progression. The condition of the tumor itself is marked in grades. Yours was friable and fruncated. That's why it was bleeding." I had no idea what "friable and fruncated" meant, but I pushed on.

"Why did this not show up in my blood work?" The raspy laryngitis had relented. Now I was demanding hard answers.

"At the time of the blood test, you had evidently not been bleeding that much or for very long. Microscopic bleeding may not show up in healthy patients like you. You eat an iron-rich diet and you take iron supplements. However, Gwen will do another blood panel today. You will doubtless show a lower hemoglobin level than last time. As I said, the tumor is friable, so it's fragile and prone to bleed."

He moved on to discuss the surgery—an ordeal I found hard to face. He described a midline lower-abdominal incision, one that would leave me with a red-zipper scar. Wayne Witherspoon would extricate the tumor, which was located in my ascending colon. He would also remove small lengths of colon tissue on both sides of the tumor, along with surrounding lymph glands, which would be biopsied. Then he would reattach the two new ends and stitch me back up.

George made it sound simple and clean. "There are, however, some risks, as is always true in surgery." He proceeded to warn about the possibility of infection, or a leaking of the incision, or the emergence of scar adhesions. He really didn't need to spell out the details. I had heard Alex's war stories from the operating room.

In all of this, however, there was a sliver of good news: I would be hospitalized for a week or less and be on my feet by the second week, able to maneuver around the house. My mind was making acrobatic leaps with this information. This meant I could easily enough be absent from Wickfield for a week or so and then make staged appearances to present a normal front. This surgery might be easier to manage than I'd thought.

George, however, seemed to read my thoughts. "But it's important that you take it easy until you are completely healed. That will take a full six weeks. You can work from home during that time. I strongly advise it. Meet with your staff at your house."

He made it sound nonthreatening, and I had a flash of his wife, Paige, preparing documents for Bob Atterbury to bring me at the house. After all, Paige worked for Bob in the Advancement Office. But such a plan would mean involving the staff—and eventually the entire population of Hurley, considering the speed with which news moved through a small Southern town—in the most intimate details of my disease and recovery. The thought was anathema to me.

"You know what a private person I am, George," I said. "Until I say otherwise, no one, including my staff, is to know anything about this." I eyeballed him, and he managed a grin back.

"Understood," he said cheerfully, reading to perfection my unspoken message. "Paige will hear nothing from me."

"Now," I continued. "About scheduling this surgery." I had already removed a small calendar notebook from my purse and was flipping through its scribbled pages. "The timing couldn't be worse. February is nearly over, so we're heading into the semester home stretch. March and April are booked!" I shook my head in dismay, looking for a week I might squeeze free. It was impossible.

"Tuesday," said George.

"*Tuesday!*" I was thunderstruck. That gave me only two work days to meet with staff and finish projects before being out for a full week.

"It's all set," he continued, projecting a calmness that astonished me. "Three o'clock Tuesday. Dr. Witherspoon and I conferred earlier this morning. You'll check in Tuesday to consult with him and the anesthesiologist. Surgery will be first thing Wednesday. Seven o'clock." He ignored my shocked face. "He's shifting other surgeries to accommodate us," he added.

"Impossible," I moaned, scanning through the appointments that I would have to cancel.

"Katherine, hear me on this. Whatever is on that calendar can wait. It *must* wait. Look at me, Katherine." I reluctantly lifted my face, and he held my gaze fiercely until my eyes dropped again. I sat like a statue, thinking through this rapid change of priorities. I hated changes I couldn't control. And I heard the silence of the room. George said nothing; he only waited.

I was suddenly filled with something far greater than anger, a feeling more akin to despair. My doctor could not grant me the dream of extended time. He could not even give me a tad of meaningless hope.

My tears hovered below the surface.

"Okay," I said finally, accepting reality. "Let's fix it."

Chapter 34
PREPARING FOR
SURGERY

The minute I returned home from George Hoffmann's office, I phoned Marianna in Virginia. She listened without interruption while I revealed my disturbing news. I kept my tone calm and matter-of-fact. "There's no need to be alarmed," I said. "This is a quick fix-it job, the kind Alex does all the time."

After hanging up, I huddled on my quilted bedspread and embraced the comfort of her words. Marianna had been the perfect antidote, as I had known she would be. I knew that, even now, she had begun dialing our three sisters and would have contacted them within the hour. One of them, she had promised, would be at my side throughout my surgery. They would immediately compare schedules to decide who would join me at the hospital.

Lennie, on the other hand, was not quite the rock I had expected. I sat her down at the kitchen table, aware that worry was spilling from her face like water from a leaky bucket. She listened gravely, snuffling through her Kleenex as I described the diagnosis and the need to move quickly with the surgery. She shook her head several times as I spoke. "Well, Miz Katherine," she murmured over and over, dabbing at her eyes and nose.

In one particular manner, however, Lennie rose mightier than a thousand soldiers: She vowed to protect my secret. "No, no, Miz Katherine, this be personal. No way will nobody know. No way." She spoke with such fervor that I knew she was genuine. There truly was "no way" anyone—not even Marilyn with her intrusive questions—would get a speck of information from Lennie without my instruction.

Jackie was yet another I would take into my confidence, but that could wait until tomorrow. Today I merely called her from the house to indicate I would be late returning to the office. I also had her cancel two out-of-town visitors on next week's calendar, telling her to apologize on my behalf.

As for my cabinet, I would tell them at our weekly Monday meeting. How much I would share, I did not yet know. I would figure that out between now and Monday.

With these conversations in hand, I did a curious thing: I stretched out on my bed and took a long nap. The stress of the past twenty-four hours had left me exhausted, and I slept soundly, without compunction. The nap would be the first of many I would snare over the next six months. Although I sometimes had taken cat naps after lunch at the house, I had never interrupted my work routine for solid daytime sleep.

I was back at my desk before five, somber but refreshed. That's where Paul found me at day's end. He entered through Jackie's outer door, which I had asked her to leave open as she was closing up. When he tapped on my office door and stepped inside, I knew before looking up that his would be the face I would see.

I took a deep breath and met his eyes.

"Well?"

Paul had never before appeared so enormous, so hulking. His visage and body hovered in front of my desk like a giant eagle. His nervous energy was palpable. Gazing at him, I felt momentarily light-headed.

"Well??" He said it again—demanding, urgent, almost angry.

"Malignant."

Paul recoiled as if hit by a slingshot. He dropped into my wing chair, slumped and silent. The color plunged from his face.

"Bummer." His voice was strangled.

"It's in the early stages. The surgery will be just a resection. I'll be out only a week."

"When?"

"Tuesday for pre-op. Surgery Wednesday."

"Where?"

"Hillcrest."

"Good."

"I want you to take me."

"Of course."

There was a clatter in the outer hallway as departing employees called goodbyes to each other.

"Who knows?"

"Only Lennie so far. And my sisters. Marianna is calling them." I paused. "I'm thinking less information is better. But I have to tell the cabinet something."

"Maybe more is better. It cuts down on speculation, gossip."

"Perhaps. I'll think about it." I smiled at him rather sadly. Paul suddenly looked much smaller, as though he had shrunk in size in front of my eyes.

"It's good you caught it early."

"Yes."

We sat in silence again. An emergency vehicle hustled along Grove Boulevard, its siren wailing. I didn't tell him that we were actually in Stage II and that we were rushing to remove the tumor before it invaded my lymphatic system.

But I didn't need to. Paul understood.

"How's Katherine doing?" He asked it gently, leaning forward in his chair with a smile that crinkled the corners of his eyes.

"Stunned. Terrified. It's all happened so fast. I need to catch my breath."

"Maybe Alex can help." He said it as a statement, not a question.

Alex. I was surprised first of all to hear Paul use Alex's first name and, secondly, to have him bring up the name of someone I sensed he did not like.

"I haven't told Alex. Not about any of this."

"No? Why not? Seems this is his thing."

I hesitated. How could I explain my inner turmoil where Alex was concerned—especially since Paul himself was part of the reason for my confusion? If a bolder truth were known, I had already discounted Alex's reaction. I was certain, without hesitation, that he would shoulder his way into my case completely. He would consult with George Hoffmann and, in particular, the Charlotte surgical team. He would offer his opinion and insist—not suggest, but insist—on procedures or treatment or therapy that might be in opposition to theirs. He might become a general nuisance, an annoying gadfly who would hinder more than help. Whether he would be at my side was questionable—maybe even doubtful, considering his surgery schedule—but he would certainly project his voice and opinion—yes, his very ego—into every step involving my care.

I continued to think about Alex long after Paul had left and long after I had picked through the roasted chicken Lennie had left in the oven. Marianna called to tell me that Emily would fly to Charlotte Tuesday to be my bedside companion. Sarah called from Virginia and asked what Alex had advised me. Jane called from California, her voice agitated, and also demanded to know Alex's opinion. I stalled, merely telling them both that Alex was still on my list to call.

When Emily called from Florida, we cried a little, both of us remembering the long days and nights we had spent together during her own cancer experience.

"We'll get you through this, KitKit." Emily's term of endearment forced me to smile. She was the only one in the family who still used that moniker, one she had created as a two-year-old. Emily was my treasure. I was deeply touched that she had rearranged her schedule to be with me. She did not mention Alex.

The next morning I called Jackie into my office and revealed the simple facts about my upcoming surgery. She blanched only once, and that was when I first used the word *tumor*. She bent her head, scribbling furiously on her notepad, and left the room when we finished without looking at me directly. I thought it odd until I saw that her mouth was tight and crooked and moving in tiny jerks.

Tears dominated much of my weekend. I alternated between bouts of self-pity and periods of surprising serenity. Childhood memories that had long lain dormant popped up without warning. One was a flashback to a family trip the summer before I started kindergarten. We were visiting a state park, one with a huge fish hatchery and a tall observation tower that was open to the public to climb. Daddy and Marianna scampered up the iron steps with ease, while Mother followed with Sarah and me. About halfway up, six-year-old Sarah parked herself on a step and sat with her arms folded, skittish of the new heights as the land fell away beneath us.

"Go on, Harold!" Mother called up through the metal scaffolding to Daddy. "I'll wait here with the girls!"

But she didn't count on my spunk and daring. I slipped past her and clambered up the steps on my own, determined to catch up with the two above us. Mother yelled for me to come back, but Daddy and Marianna stopped and watched through the slats, cheering with encouragement as I tugged the railing and puffed my way onward. When I reached the top, Daddy swung me onto his shoulders and told me to hold my arms straight up. As I did, I gazed out onto blue sky in front of me. I felt myself at the threshold to heaven, high enough to catch a passing bird or drifting cloud. When Daddy set me down, I leaned over the rail and waved to Mother and Sarah. They looked like tiny ladybugs below.

In another memory I was about the same age, playing alone in the front yard on a carpet of green grass. I spun myself around until dizzy, my eyes shut tightly, pretending that all the world as I knew it would disappear into oblivion until I commanded it to return. "I am Queen of the World!" I crowed while I spun, arms and fingers extended, and when my balance had righted itself and the pounding in my head had settled, I opened my eyes and imagined that everything I now beheld—house and cars, trees and skies—had returned to their places through my powers.

By Sunday I was tired of games and sadness. I slipped into church at the last minute and left before the final hymn. I spent four hours that afternoon in my office, working ahead on next week's duties, reading documents waiting for review from the staff and making lists for each member of my cabinet.

"This is overkill, Katherine," I muttered as I crowded yet one more item onto Dan's list. But I always felt better when I knew things were under control. That was my problem, I told myself as I walked back to the house in the gathering darkness. Control. I was losing control to these doctors. That's why I teemed with old thoughts of power and derring-do. I felt at ease when I was charting my own course. When others did it for me, I filled up with *dis*-ease.

By bedtime Sunday I was at peace about Monday's meeting. I would tell my cabinet exactly what they needed to know and as concisely as possible.

As it turned out, that was the right recourse. I waited until our normal business was completed and then delivered my news in a voice as perfunctory as though I were reporting the weather. Briefly, I referred to "routine repair surgery" in my colon to correct a condition that had apparently been present for some time. As I spoke around the conference table I looked each member in the eye, watching Dan and Bob and Jake and Marilyn and Pud react to my words in a dead silence, seeing Dan from the corner of my eye reach for his coffee mug and Bob for his pipe, noting that color flooded Jake's face while color drained from Marilyn's, watching the usual Monday smirks dissolve from Pud's face. I did not use the word *cancer*, nor the word *tumor* (remembering Jackie), nor did I give anyone any cause for undue alarm.

"The doctor will simply fix the problem and stitch me back up. Done. Finished. I'll be good as new." I smiled. "I'll be in the hospital a few days and then back at my house, where we can meet as needed after my return."

"What hospital?" asked Marilyn, as I knew she would.

"Jackie has the details and will notify you should you need to be in touch. Meanwhile, no flowers, no cards. Thanks all the same"—Marilyn was shaking her head, probably at my austerity—"but just think of me as going to a conference in Boston for a few days. We'll be back to normal in no time. I will have family with me, and I will be in excellent hands." *Alex,* they were probably thinking. *Lucky lady. She has her own personal surgeon to see her through this.*

"Meanwhile"—I smiled again as I reached for the lists from my Sunday workathon—"meanwhile, I have jotted down some thoughts for each of you related to your current priorities. We can discuss these more in detail when we have our next individual sessions. After surgery, of course." I scooted the sheets across the table.

"I'll be in my office until four this afternoon if anything is pressing that needs my attention." The room had grown suddenly quiet. I looked around. Everyone was studying their lists.

"One more thing." I cleared my throat and waited until everyone looked up. "What I have shared with you is a private matter. I am expecting each of you to keep this within our circle —that is, among ourselves as a cabinet. Obviously I prefer that members of the campus or community not discuss this. The nature of this surgery is personal, and each of you knows me to be a private person." Jake shifted in his seat, Bob tapped his pipe, and Marilyn stared into space.

"Should word, however, leak out that I've been hospitalized, or should anyone ask you about my state of health, tell them merely what I have told you: that I have had some elective repair surgery and expect to be back at my duties in a couple of weeks. In other words, there is no need for anxiety, and I'm counting on you to squelch any rumors to the contrary. I will, of course, contact Judge Hall—Carrington—as a matter of courtesy, and John Sigmon as chair of the faculty senate. Any questions?"

Dan, bless his heart, spoke for the group in wishing me safe surgery and speedy recovery. The others chimed in. I relaxed, relieved that this hurdle was over. But when I returned to my desk and reflected on the meeting, I wondered why on earth I had sounded so severe at the end. "The nature of this surgery is very personal." Indeed, indeed. *What a prude am I*, I thought in mild disgust. Why hadn't I softened the whole experience for all of us with a bit of edgy humor? I had thrown a huge surprise on them, was disappearing on them *tomorrow,* and would be out of circulation for at least a week. I could have handled it much better. I could have poked fun at myself and my anatomy. I could have told a couple of Alex's favorite medical jokes. After all, I had heard him tell scores of entertaining stories about the behaviors of the human body. "You're so bawdy about the body," I used to tease him.

And some of these stories, I reflected, remembering, had really been pretty funny.

Chapter 35
SURGERY

The events surrounding my surgery are blurred in my memory, melting into each other like Carolina's blue-gray mountains that fade by layers into a muted distance. I do recall phoning Carrington to report I had scheduled some "repair surgery" and would be out a few days. He probably assumed I would be at Piedmont Memorial, because he asked few questions. It would go against protocol to inquire regarding the nature of the surgery; Southern men did not ask that of women. But he grunted a couple of appropriate sentences, wishing me well and asking if he needed to be "prompted on anything forthcoming."

"Not at all, Carrington. Everything was covered at our last board meeting." I hung up and crossed "Carrington" off my to-do list.

I also recall that Paul kept up a light banter in the car the following afternoon. I laughed at his silliness and felt something curiously akin to excitement, more as though we were en route to the Charlotte Coliseum for a Hornets game rather than to the hospital for surgery. I remember that the anesthesiologist questioned me closely about medications and lifestyle habits as though he were peering into my body before the actual incision. He surprised me by referring to me as a "small woman"; I considered myself unusually tall among my gender. But he was referring to my small-boned, slight build. Alex was right: I *had* become scrawny.

I remember Emily bouncing into my hospital room bearing a bouquet of mixed spring flowers from her Florida yard and reporting that the attendant on her USAir flight had asked if she had been in a wedding. I recall being wheeled to surgery very early the next morning and encountering Emily and Paul together in the hallway. Paul kidded me about my floppy plastic cap that stuck out at weird angles like the headdress of a flying nun. "Great bonnet," he said solemnly, but his eyes twinkled.

I had been surprised when Paul told me he would spend Tuesday night in a Charlotte motel. "It's the only way to give you a send-off to surgery," he'd said when I protested. I felt better when he reminded me about his Wednesday-evening law class. He would simply hang around the hospital Wednesday prior to the class and save himself an extra trip.

"June deserves the Good Wife Award for accepting such weird hours," I told him. He looked at me oddly when I spoke, but I meant what I said. June's patience seemed to know no bounds—or so I hoped.

Now I gave him a thumbs-up from my gurney. Paul and I were getting to be old hands at this scene. Ten days ago he had been cheering me on to a colonoscopy.

As for the surgery itself, I recall nothing, and of the recovery, very little. A nurse held a porcelain pan as I battled deep waves of retching, and Emily pressed a glass heaped with ice chips to my lips. Scissor-like jabs bit deeply into my abdomen the first time I stood up. Emily pushed me in a wheelchair to a sunny sitting room with large plate-glass windows—a pleasant retreat with softly clacking paddles on a ceiling fan and gargantuan green plants in every corner.

Friday afternoon I deemed myself strong enough to call Jackie, whose mile-a-minute voice covered the major news of the week. She mentioned that Susan Atterbury had called twice, both times "with deep concern," so I telephoned Susan Saturday and endured a not-so-mild scolding. "Kat, why on earth didn't you tell me?" she demanded. She sounded sincerely hurt, and I realized with surprise that Bob's pledge of silence at the cabinet meeting had included his wife. I made a mental note to raise Susan on my priority list of confidantes. Her weepy confessional about Jake had forged a special bond extending well beyond that snowy January day.

Although I was racking up a sizable phone bill, I also called Alex, at long last. It was Saturday morning, and my wall-mounted television screen was showing sports fishing in the azure waters near Eleuthra. When he did not answer, I left a brief message. He returned the call Sunday night to my home phone, but when I talked to Lennie early Monday, she had not yet noticed the flickering red light on my answering machine. Alex left another message Monday night. I found both when I returned from the hospital Tuesday.

That night, Alex and I finally made voice contact—nearly two weeks after my colonoscopy and nearly a week since my diagnosis of cancer.

We had not spoken by phone since I had thanked him for the Valentine flowers. Long ago we had accepted long periods of silence as reflections of our high-stress careers.

Now he listened while I chatted cheerfully from my bedroom phone, slightly drunk on pain pills and plumped up by pillows that Lennie had fussily propped around me. What surprised me most was not what he said but, rather, what he did *not* ask. He did not, like Susan, reprimand me for not calling sooner. More than anything, he seemed stunned by my story—colonoscopy, biopsy, surgery—and given to long periods of silence. He asked for Wayne Witherspoon's phone number, as I knew he would, as well as George Hoffmann's. *Here we go*, I thought, as I dictated the information.

But Alex did drop a comment, almost as if to himself, that jolted me. "Of course, there's a small chance that the cancer could have penetrated the muscle walls," he murmured after I had waxed eloquent over my quick surgery. I had never heard a particular statistic in this regard. Neither of my doctors had mentioned the possibility of the cancer returning—only the positive parameters of recovery. I realized I had been hearing the universal language of medicine: promote health and life at all costs and sublimate disease and death.

On the other hand, each member of the medical team *had* referred to risk in some way or another. I thought back through those individual conversations with both doctors and nurses. Of course there was risk. Of course some microscopic cancer cells could have escaped the surgeon's knife. I was a realist, in spite of my upbeat, positive outlook on life. I did not consider myself a Pollyanna, although in my younger years I admittedly had set some highly idealistic professional goals.

I brushed off my concerns and did not pursue his comment, nor did Alex. He promised to come to Hurley as soon as he could break from his schedule, and he asked what he could do to help. For Alex, that meant sending flowers. I figured I could expect an FTD bouquet to appear within the hour.

Regardless, in the weeks following surgery, I frequently felt close to euphoria. After all, the surgery had been successful and my recovery had been fast. I held a full cabinet meeting in my living room less than two weeks after my operation, feeling Marilyn's eyes scrutinize every movement, even while I was ensconced like an empress upon my blue-and-rose flame-stitched wing chair. I made selective public appearances soon afterward.

Much of the campus community was aware that I had experienced some sort of surgery. I received a number of get-well cards, many of which were humorous. The College of Arts and Sciences sent a mammoth pop-out card signed by faculty who added encouraging notations like "Mind the doctor" and "Hope to see your cheerful smile soon." Mary Smiley, Dean Sigmon's secretary in the business school and our eldest female employee, sent a religious card dusted with purple sparkles and bearing such a dour and solemn message that, in spite of my appreciation for her infinite concern, I hooted with laughter. Carrington called on me, having phoned in advance, of course, but he droned through such a drivel-laden conversation that I was convinced he merely wanted to check my state of health with his own eyes.

Overall, however, I did not sense an undercurrent of gossip, and I was grateful for the privacy that had been afforded me in Charlotte. At his suggestion, Paul had checked me into Hillcrest under an assumed name. The hospital, of course, knew who I really was, but not the general public. I was relieved; I did not want the overly curious of Hurley to call all the area hospitals until they found me. As my routine returned to normalcy, I felt my secret safe. Not once during this period had the word "cancer" surfaced.

When I was completely honest with myself, however, I admitted that my euphoric high stemmed well beyond optimism regarding my health. My happiness was personal, and it was centered directly on my friendship with Paul. To call it a "friendship," of course, sounds awkward today, considering all that transpired soon afterward, but in those early weeks of March I was still reluctant to acknowledge that I was falling in love. My professional restraints at the time—my deepest core values that permitted neither personal nor professional transgressions—enabled me to think of ours as a special bond growing deeper through my illness.

Perhaps it was the early hint of springtime that made me focus on my true feelings: the pulsing of green shoots that grew sturdy in my garden and the turgid tips that swelled pink and purple on the branches of the saucer magnolia. Perhaps it was the intoxicating scent of the early March hyacinths that lined my driveway and spilled their perfume from waxy prongs. Perhaps it was my subconscious need to shed the husk of winter and absorb the long gold light of spring for myself, clamoring for renewed life as a breathing, palpable woman.

Whatever the reason, I found myself one morning dressing with unusual care for the March Board of Governors meeting in Asheville. When I heard Paul's voice in the kitchen and Lennie's usual gale of laughter, I fluttered with teenage anticipation. "Steady, steady," I said to myself as I carefully descended the spiral staircase like a prom girl. But when I entered the kitchen, Lennie's head was buried in the refrigerator, so Paul alone saw my flushed cheeks and shining eyes and had a full second to beam me a huge smile of his own. From the moment he tucked me into the front seat of my car and I waved goodbye to Lennie, I felt myself buoyed by external strength destined to carry me through the day. This trip was my first major outing since the surgery. It was especially important for me politically to prove my ability to rebound after illness.

Because the distance was relatively short—little more than two hours to Asheville—I felt ready for the challenge. During the lengthy board meeting, I voiced strong opinions, feeling the heady approval that comes from delivering the well-spoken word and noting tangible nods from colleagues. Afterward, returning to meet Paul at the car, I felt heady with power.

Paul seemed to sense my elevated mood, because on our return trip he turned on my car radio. He selected buttons at random, searching, I supposed, for music. He punched through several stations until I recognized the familiar voice of a Charlotte announcer.

"That's good," I said. "Stop right there. They're doing Broadway musicals this week."

"Since when do you have time to listen to the radio?"

"I was married to a radio guy, remember? Besides, I like background noise around the house."

Paul turned up the dial just as the orchestra began the strains of a familiar tune from *South Pacific*.

"I love this song!" I said happily, settling back to listen. "It's so sad." The mellifluous bass voice of Ezio Pinza filled the car:

> One dream in my heart,
> One love to be livin' for,
> One love to be livin' for
> This nearly was mine.

We listened in silence as the brokenhearted plantation owner, Emile, sang of loss after the American nurse, Nellie, rejected him.

> Close to my heart she came
> Only to fly away,
> Only to fly as day flies from moonlight.

I sighed with the pathos of the words. Suddenly, as Emile moved gracefully into the final chorus, Paul shocked me by joining the singing. He boomed the lyrics with confidence and bravado, gesticulating with one arm like an opera singer:

> Now, now I'm alone,
> Still a-dreamin' of paradise,
> Still sayin' that paradise
> Once nearly was mine!

"Paul!" I clicked off the radio. "You can sing! You never told me you can sing!"

"You never asked."

"But that was—incredible!"

"Thank you, ma'am. I grew up with singing. All of us Staffords could sing."

"I thought your brother had the musical talent. Jeremy."

"He has the most," Paul said agreeably. "I took whatever was left."

I stared hard out the window. The car had started its descent down the steep grade at Black Mountain, and Paul put both hands on the wheel as he slipped into the far-left lane contiguous to the concrete barrier. An overhead highway sign blinked warnings to speeding cars, and markers along the shoulder announced safety ramps for brakeless runaway trucks. We drove in silence as the car repeatedly swung hard to the left, then to the right.

"Have you ever performed solo?"

"Just in high school. *West Side Story.*"

"And you played . . . ?"

"Tony." And Paul burst into song again. "Mah-riii-a. I just met a girl named Mah-riii-a."

"Goodness!" I shook my head, marveling at the strength of his beautiful bass-baritone. "I had no idea."

"Did I leave something out of my application? Was I supposed to report my singing history for the job of assistant police chief?"

"Seriously. You have talent. I can't believe no one has picked up on this before. Do you sing in your church choir?"

"Church?" Paul dismissed the thought with a laugh, slipping back into the right-hand lane at the foot of the mountain. "Marcy and Blair go to North Grove Methodist with their friends. And June works on Sundays. The closest I have been to church in the past twenty years was my wedding day."

"You're joshing me." I suddenly realized that Paul and I had never discussed religion. But before I could pursue that thought, Paul changed the subject.

"How are you doing on time? I'm thinking that if our daylight holds, we might be able to see a waterfall that's just off the highway. Most folks don't know about it—it's not on most maps. It's nothing like Linville Falls, but it's on the way, and I think you'll like it."

"Can we see it from the car? I hardly have on my hiking boots." I glanced with concern at my sturdy black pumps.

"It's about fifteen minutes off the interstate by car, then a brief walk along a marked path. Your shoes are okay. How are you feeling? Are you game?"

"I'm game," I smiled. My evening at Wickfield had been cleared because of the trip. "How did you find this tucked-away waterfall?"

"Eagle Scout project. Had to identify all the waterfalls in western North Carolina and mark them on a map. And visit as many as I could, and take pictures. The photos all looked the same in the end—blurry and grainy, terrible quality." Yes. I remembered well those cumbersome Brownie box cameras of the fifties.

In a few minutes we exited the interstate. The road climbed for several miles before Paul slowed for a right turn onto a narrow rural road. "Are you taking me back to that hidden lake?" I asked suddenly. The territory had begun to look familiar.

"Nope. That's an hour away. Yep, here it is." He pulled into a narrow clearing. Ours was the only car, although the parking space was large enough for seven or eight vehicles. A green trash can marked the head of a trail that appeared to lead into the woods. Paul turned off the ignition and turned to look at me in the abrupt silence.

"Ready, Prez?" He grinned.

"Ready." I reached for the car handle.

Outside, I pulled the collar of my outer jacket up around my neck. The day was fading fast as the sun's rays filtered through the trees' lower branches. Paul turned and reached for my hand. I took it willingly and followed him onto the trail. It was decently marked, with gray wooden stakes lining a flat path of scuffed leaves and pine needles. The woods grew silent. Then, just as I adjusted to the shadows and hush of the forest, I heard the distant splash of the falls. We emerged into another clearing and beheld a cascade of white waters that jounced their way over black granite boulders into a gurgling pool at the base.

The scene was lovely. We were completely alone in this newfound splendor. We stood in silence, craning our necks as we peered through tree branches in search of the slope where the waters began their spill. I shivered a bit at the enormity of the scene. Waterfalls did that to me, almost threatened me—even relatively small plunges like this one that splashed and whooshed.

Paul pulled me close with his arm and tightened his hold around my shoulder. "What do you think?" he asked. "Worth the drive?"

"Amazing," I nearly whispered. *Paul is amazing*, I thought to myself. I slid my arm around his waist and huddled in the curve of his grip.

Which one of us turned first for the kiss, I don't recall—only that we stood there for several minutes in the presence of those stark tumbling waters, lulled by their whir and cadence and pulled together as close as our coats allowed. We touched eyes and cheeks and ears with our hands before seeking the warmth of our mouths. In the end, we embraced silently for what seemed like an eternity, my hands locked behind his neck and my face pressed so close to his that I felt the prickles of his beard scrape my skin.

We said little in the car as Paul led us over the interstate back to Hurley. We held hands tightly, letting them rest on the seat between us, and once I peppered his palm with a multitude of tiny kisses.

"Dear Paul," I finally said, after we had sat, motionless, in my darkening driveway. "We both know the need to keep this professional. But, oh my.

This is getting hard. Very hard. You are becoming so very special to me."
I leaned my head against the back of the car seat.

"And you to me," he said. He cleared his throat, as if thinking. "Let's keep
it simple. And merely enjoy the time we spend together. What do you think?"

"Good plan," I said, closing my eyes. In spite of their wise simplicity, I
found myself almost disappointed at the subtle constraints we were laying
out. I longed for so much more. My body, my hands, my mouth were all
aching for more. I felt surges of feelings I had never experienced with either
Tim or Alex. But I also knew absolutely, as Paul had made clear, that "more"
would not work. Not for me. Not for him. Not for his marriage. Not for
my career.

"Good night," I said, swallowing hard. "No, don't walk me in. I'm fine.
It was a good day, Paul. All of it." I released his hand before reaching to
open my door.

Chapter 36
HUMBLE PIE

Thus, by stepping across a threshold, Paul and I began a new kind relationship, one that has colored my life since. From that point on, Paul was uppermost in my mind each morning as I awoke. While still in the dream stupor of early consciousness, I would lie in bed, sheet curled up around my face, and envision the way he could lift me in the swell of a single glance. I saw his eyes crinkle on the verge of laughter; I heard every nuance of his voice. At night I embraced bedtime, the one hour I could put away my day and fall into reverie.

I scolded myself for such indulgence, reminding myself that I was known for making prudent decisions and that I was *fifty*, for heaven's sakes, not fifteen. My other self argued that fantasy was better than participation and that since I was not actually "involved" with Paul, I was in no danger. I believed it all. Somehow these stolen daydreams steadied me, even without Paul's physical presence.

While the dreams by day steadied me, sleep by night did not. Paul drifted into my dreamscapes, sometimes with confusing outcomes. One night, soon after Lennie and I had planned the annual Easter buffet for our international students, I dreamed I tried to start my car beside a busy highway, only to realize my hands were slimy from handling a slippery turkey carcass. When I stepped out of my car to wash them, I watched in dismay as the car rolled away. As I chased it, it rolled faster, weaving across the highway. Other travelers reached out to help as I ran faster and faster, calling out frantically. Finally a nice man jumped into my car and guided it up a narrow hill to a resting place. I huffed, out of breath, as I approached it. When I looked up to thank the man, he had disappeared. That's when I realized he had driven my car into the Hillcrest Hospital parking lot.

Such troubled dreams might have succeeded in separating me from Paul had not springtime arrived. A Carolina spring does not gently eke forth—it shouts as it unfolds, one phase of color after another. Now it burst into our lives with a glory known only in the South. It trumpeted yellow fronds of forsythia, white clouds of pear blossoms, delicate pinks of weeping cherries, and raspberry hues of redbuds. It rolled out brilliant mounds of jeweled azaleas. The monkey-faced dogwood blossoms made me smile, as did the fragrant skies. Our campus paradise drew photographers—and, as might be expected, lovers.

The young lovers, of course, caught my attention. Through my casement windows cranked open to the breezes, I heard their drifting laughter. I watched couples stroll beneath the oaks beyond the house, arms draped around shoulders. Sometimes I watched discreetly from the privacy of my drapes, spying as I had years ago with Marianna and Sarah on the Arden campus. Then, it had been a game. Now, forty years later, I felt the rise of their yearnings. I was one of them.

These stirrings made me profoundly restless. Throughout the next week I found myself pacing halls and walking the campus with new energy. I missed Paul. He seemed to be keeping his distance as much as I. My eyes searched for him everywhere but found him only when his patrol car rolled through my sphere of sight.

We could have kept up this charade weeks longer, Paul and I, but it was Alex, ironically, who brought us back together. The following Saturday, Alex called. This was not a surprise in itself, for we had been trying for weeks to find a weekend for him to visit. From his first words, however, he did not sound like himself.

"Hello," I answered from the sun porch phone.

"Katherine?" His voice seemed inappropriately high pitched.

"Alex?" I waited.

"How are you, Alex?" More silence.

"The roses were lovely, you know. They lasted forever. Lennie has the last ones in a small vase in the hallway." Yes, he had overwhelmed me with roses after my surgery, a repeat of the Valentine forest of blooms. In fact, they had been from the same florist.

Alex spoke at last. "How are you feeling?"

So I gave him a quick report, mostly medical. He mumbled back a few words.

"I can hardly hear you, Alex. Where are you?"

His words finally came, tumbling in fits and starts. They were shocking and surreal, sometimes halting, sometimes rushed. He was getting married. Next weekend. He was so sorry. He hadn't meant for it to turn out like this. It had happened in Hawaii.

"I wanted you all along, Kat, we were good together, it's all because of her damn religion. She won't even consider an abortion, even though she's a nurse. Just tear up the tickets Kat I was going to propose on the ship I planned it for the full moon I wanted us to marry next summer after you found a successor this is so unfair." As the rambling intensified, my eyes held fast on the window. The grass outside grew white, then gray, finally waving like a field of ashen grain.

It makes no sense, I thought, listening numbly to Alex's incongruous story. *He cheated. He lied about Christmas. He got a nurse pregnant. He got a nurse pregnant. He's going to marry her. But people don't get married any more just because they're pregnant! It's 1990, for heaven's sakes, not like the late fifties when all those nice girls in Arden suddenly had to get married.* There had been a whole string of them, all at once, like Nancy Leary, whose father had owned the fancy new Volkswagen dealership. I could see Nancy clearly, rosy-cheeked and pixie-faced, with dancing eyes and curly bangs. Even Oscar Leary's new money couldn't keep the town gossips from tainting his daughter's name.

I said nothing while Alex's words churned on—something about Connie, and spring break starting next weekend when she could send her kids afterward to stay with their dad, and a nice wedding because she hadn't had one on the first round. *Dear God, Alex is insane. Can't you see the trap, Alex— you who are supposed to be so almighty smart. You're both medical people, for heaven's sakes. Just fix it! I don't care if she is Catholic, damn it. Damn you both!*

But when he finally stopped and waited for my judgment, I sat in silence. There was much to be said, yet there was nothing to say. Absolutely nothing. I could scream and flail and call him a lying bastard. Even if I were to say, "I gave you precious moments of my life! I trusted you with my body and my heart! I brought you to the picnic and showed you off!" it would all be too late—much too late.

I suddenly didn't want Alex anymore.

So I pulled myself together and told him in my politest hollow voice that I wished him and Connie every single *possible* happiness in the world, and I hung up. I didn't pick up the receiver when the phone rang seconds later. I climbed the staircase to my peach-colored bathroom, turned on the shower, and wailed under the faucet. I let the jet stream flow onto my face so that tears and redeeming water were all the same. I soaped myself from scalp to toenails and rinsed the stink of humiliation off of myself. And when every bubblet of suds had been sucked down the drain and my skin felt sleek and silky, I soaped myself again.

Then I walked. I zipped up the jacket to my navy jogging suit, tied the laces on my Reeboks, and covered my face with big sunglasses. I set out down my driveway, feeling the zap of the late-March breeze on my damp hair, and I breathed deeply. *You can handle this, Kat.* I marched past my usual entry into Wellstone, past the fountain and benches, past the Sweetheart Tree, past Warnes Dorm with its rocking chairs and famous dogwoods. I turned the corner and passed the stately lawn of the Arts and Humanities building, striding beyond the imperious Lineberger School of Business with its stunning Corinthian columns, even past the colorful totem pole of directional signs for visitors.

Finally I stopped. I sank onto an empty bench in front of the brick chemistry building, waving back to students strolling by and congratulating myself that at least I could *feel*. I could touch the wind and smell the fragrant trees. My body was whole, not cracked and broken, and it was an extraordinary Saturday afternoon in North Carolina.

That's when I spotted Paul's patrol car. It sat in a no-parking zone in front of his building a short block away. Why was he working on a Saturday? Was he buried at his desk writing a law-school paper? Usually student officers maintained the police office on weekends.

It didn't matter why he was there. I headed in the direction of his car, entered the building through its arched stone doorway, and asked the startled student on duty whether Officer Stafford were in. He jumped up and gestured toward a closed door. I knocked, heard Paul's familiar voice respond, and pushed my way in. Paul was seated at his desk in front of a tape recorder, microphone in hand.

"Dictating?" I asked brightly, turning slightly to shut the door. "That's what Alex complains about the most—the paperwork with his job."

Paul stood quickly, scattering papers. "Sit," he said, gesturing to an overstuffed brown chair. I restrained a smile. He made me sound like a trained dog.

"It's beautiful outside." I took off my sunglasses and settled into the chair. It looked like a relic from somebody's attic, but the plumpness of the pillows seemed inviting. "You really should complain to your boss. What a taskmaster, making you work so hard on a lovely spring day."

"My boss is an ogre," he shot back, "but a mighty pretty one. Only you do look a bit rough around the edges, Prez."

So he had noticed my plastered curls and faded eyes and shattered face.

I ignored the comment, speaking of nonsensical things that did not matter and chuckling a bit too hard at my own cleverness. Paul kept his eyes glued to my face and waited.

"Oh, yes, one more piece of news." Finally. My voice wobbled an instant, and I looked beyond Paul to a framed certificate on the wall, away from those penetrating eyes.

"I heard from Alex. He's getting married next week. Sweet lady named Connie, a nurse with two kids, white dress and country club, all the trimmings. Seems she got pregnant in Hawaii at a medical conference. He probably registered her as his wife. They do it all the time at these kinds of affairs, no big deal to anyone unless they get caught. Which they did. And they're both medical and know how to fix it but she's *Catholic*, see, and even in this modern year of 1990 insists on keeping the baby and getting married. Since that's the right thing to do. And Alex agrees. Since that's the right thing to do."

I stopped. There. I had laid out my humble pie, every degrading piece of it, and now I could lift my eyes and look at Paul. His expression had not changed.

Then the unexpected happened—only, knowing Paul as I did, I should have seen it coming. He did not lecture me. He did not pierce me to the core with a pitying look. Instead, he threw back his head and began to laugh. The laugh became a shout and then a rip-rousing guttural roar that shook both his chair and his desk. Since it was impossible not to react to his convulsions, I, too, began to laugh. And then we were howling, and I was hanging onto his desk, laughing and crying at the same time. The student officer doubtless wondered at our commotion, but I did not care. I wrapped my arms around my rib cage and held it, gasping, before fumbling in my jacket for a wadded-up tissue.

"So you finally caught on." Paul grinned while I unceremoniously blew my nose. "I wondered how long you would take."

"How did you know? You never did like Alex, did you?" The Kleenex sailed into a trash can in a perfect arc.

"Little things. Guy things. We read each other. He didn't like me, either, for whatever it's worth."

That was probably true, I realized, sitting there and remembering. What was it with men? Did they sniff each other like alpha dogs to decide who was limp and who was competitive?

I found it didn't matter either way. I suddenly felt myself relaxing, snuggling into the corner of the rumpled old chair and tucking one foot under the other leg. Paul pulled two frosted Cokes from a miniature refrigerator, and we popped the tabs and took deep gulps from the hissing aluminum cans. And looked at each other. And smiled a lot. That was probably one of the better half hours of my life.

When I stood to go, Paul came around from behind his desk and enveloped me in a massive hug. "I know a perfect little lake that's surrounded by springtime right now. I've been wanting to check it out." We both knew the site, of course.

But I couldn't do it—not today, not tomorrow. "Rain check," I whispered back, holding on to him tightly. He kissed me on the forehead.

I was deep in thought as I walked back to the Chancellor's House. Once again Paul had gifted me with the healing powers of laughter. Somehow, over time, I would laugh again and distance myself from the burn of this betrayal. Right now, however, I felt anger. I pictured Alex looking down upon Connie's pillow, lowering his head toward her as he had hovered over me those hundreds of times in our past. What was this Connie's appeal to Alex? A younger face? Larger breasts? A helpless laugh?

Even more haunting was how Alex might have separated—or blended—his times with the two of us. Had he ever boarded a plane for Charlotte within hours after leaving her bed? The very thought made me want to retch.

Between us, Alex and I had created an intimate history, and in short order those memories were being slammed into a file folder in my heart marked Archives. There was no way to resurrect our old relationship; Alex had disrespected me too much. The damage had been done. Alex could weasel out of this marriage if he really wanted to. Even so, I myself would lose, especially with a woman and baby on his resume.

A baby. I shook my head, trying to imagine Alex cradling an infant. The image of fatherhood did not fit him. Or did it? That was a new thought. *Maybe that's the kind of life he really wants,* I argued to myself. Alex had been married before, once upon a time, so long ago that he rarely mentioned it. The woman had seemed to be no more than a trifling shadow in his past, and there had been no children.

Maybe he's happy with Connie but feels guilty about me, I suddenly thought. *Maybe he actually wants to be a father and knows I would not give him that future.* It was an interesting rationale, almost comforting. It mitigated my embarrassment a bit.

Yes, I realized, arming myself with moral indignation and settling next to the sun porch phone to dial Marianna, *with* Alex I would eventually have lost. Without him, I had the freedom to move ahead.

"What a mess," Marianna said after hearing the ludicrous story. I pictured her straddling the red stool at her kitchen phone, worry etched across her face. "What a sorry, sorry mess. You've been preserved, Kat! Thank the heavens above that you're cutting off cleanly!"

Marianna's words, which were meant to comfort, left me unsettled. I had not been totally honest with her, I realized as I hung up, thinking of my two stolen kisses with Paul. Nor had I myself been entirely faithful to Alex. Perhaps the cloth from which we were fashioned bore the same tweed.

Rain check. I marveled at how easily those words had slipped out, with neither fanfare nor hesitation. So much for my high-browed righteousness over Susan and Jake! Somehow an escape into the woods with Paul no longer seemed so reckless.

In fact, at this dismal moment it felt almost like the right thing to do.

Chapter 37
IN LOVE AND LIGHT

In my English literature classes of long ago, I'd loved teaching the literary device of irony.

"It was ironic," I would tell my students, "that Emily Dickinson, whose prolific poems remained unpublished during her lifetime, died without knowing that someday her poetry would be words of inspiration at college commencements. It was ironic that a devastated Romeo stabbed himself just moments before Juliet awoke from her death-like trance. It's ironic when a heroic soldier performs high-risk feats at war and is killed by a drunken driver two weeks after returning home." My students got the idea.

So I found it ironic when Susan—she of the painful affair with Jake—was the one who warned me about campus chitchat connecting me with Paul. It was the worst possible kind of gossip: meddling talk that began with a frivolous whisper and raised eyebrows. It eventually led, I gathered, to a unified watch for "Paul sightings"—at least among a core group of gossipmongers.

"What do you mean, we were 'sighted' at Backstreets?" I demanded indignantly when Susan had approached me cautiously one Saturday afternoon. It was mid-April, the day before Easter Sunday. Susan had dropped by to return vases from a donors' reception, so I'd invited her to join me for iced tea on the deck.

"It was probably nothing, but I wanted you to know what I heard." Susan fidgeted with her sunglasses while we watched a brilliant male cardinal strut on my deck railing.

"For heaven's sakes, the man is on the Wickfield staff," I huffed. "I eat out with faculty and staff all the time."

"I know, and that's what I told Betty. But you know how Betty is. She reads something into everything. It's just that—"

"So, what did Betty Boyd say this time?" I projected as much annoyance as I could muster.

"Well, she said you both looked—well, cozy."

"Cozy? *Cozy?*" I hooted. "Maybe that's because the waitress gave us a crowded corner booth at the back, and that was because it was the best one available. I hadn't called for reservations. We just showed up. Do you think we would have paraded through the entire restaurant if we were there to be 'cozy'?" I took another sip of tea—a long one. "Paul Stafford is entertaining. He makes me laugh. He makes everyone laugh."

A gargantuan bumblebee nosed its way into a wicker basket of *Coreopsis*.

"So, what else did Betty say?"

"Actually, Patty Horton said something, too."

"*What?* Oh, for heaven's sakes, Susan. And what did the honorable Mrs. Horton have to say?" Patty Horton kept her eye on everyone's business but her own. Someone had actually warned me about her soon after I'd moved to Hurley.

"Well, she said she saw your car pass by one afternoon, and she was certain it was your car but that a man was driving it, and that as well as she could determine, it looked like Paul Stafford. And that someone was sitting in the passenger seat who was about your height. And that the car was headed out of town the back way, down Gumtree Road past the mill village."

"That's a lot of maybes."

"Well, you should know people are talking." I sensed, without directing my eyes at her, that Susan was looking at me sideways.

So I proceeded to tell Susan about my agreement with Carrington and watched her face take on a look of astonishment. "It's just for long trips, like to board meetings, but yes, you may occasionally see Paul driving my car here and there." I didn't elaborate, nor did she pursue the Patty Horton sighting, in which instance, of course, Paul and I had been headed in the opposite direction of a major highway. We rattled the ice cubes in our tumblers and sat in a dubious silence, each absorbed in our own thoughts.

"I think people should know." Susan broke our silence with a conviction in her voice that surprised me.

"Know what?" I held my breath. For a half-second I thought she had figured out my complete history with Paul.

"That Paul drives you places."

"Why on earth?"

"To protect you. To silence the Bettys and the Pattys. To let you do your job without distractions regarding—well, ethics. Gossip can be very diverting."

I wondered for another half-second if the Bettys and Pattys had ever observed Susan with Jake.

"Well, it's not a secret, exactly. I was embarrassed when Carrington sprang this ridiculous plan on me, and it seemed better to go with the flow at the time than add fuel for the town busybodies. I'm sure some had me screwing that doctor who gave me a ride for gas."

"Katherine! I've never heard you talk like that!"

I stopped abruptly, fearing my cynicism might betray Paul and me. "Sorry. Carrington unhinges me, that's all. Every time I think I have him corralled, he gets my goat somehow. Just thinking about that man—"

Susan gave an ominous chuckle. "Yes, hard to believe he developed an entire career making decisions about people's lives. Glad we never met up in the courtroom."

I gathered our glasses and led us to the kitchen. As Susan drove away, I felt the chill of danger. Even though I could joke about the lack of credibility among a few indiscreet women, it troubled me that they were judging Paul and me. I was a zealot for privacy, and any kind of gossip, mild or severe, caught my attention. Even more, I felt guilty about using Carrington to hide my indiscretions from Susan. "Be careful, Kat!" I whispered to myself in the mirror, tugging down my bangs that had crept up in the outdoor humidity.

But Paul had a way of popping up frequently these days, and, in fact, his was the surprise voice on the phone an hour later.

"What are you doing tomorrow morning?" he asked.

"Church," I answered promptly. "Easter sunrise service," I added, in case he missed the point.

Paul seemed to mull that over. "How would you like to see a special sunrise? Something really spectacular."

My first instinct was to respond that nothing was more spectacular than an Easter sunrise service. It was my favorite event of the church year, the time when the pall of Lent was tucked away and replaced with a flood of brightness. I loved the thrill of singing "Christ is risen! Alleluia!" in a church jammed with joyful worshipers. And I reveled in the perfumed scent of Easter lilies.

Still, Paul's suggestion piqued my interest, even more so when he explained what he had in mind. He had recently climbed into the copper dome that sat atop the Marcus Building—an older, renovated building that would soon house the new School of the Arts. "The Mark," as the students dubbed it, was famous not only for the dome but also for its circular rotunda that doubled as an art gallery. The interior columned walls shot sixty feet upward to a spectacular ceiling centered by a round mosaic skylight. This hall was one of my favorite venues, a place I would sometimes visit alone when I needed solitude. I would sink onto a marble bench—one covered with tufted upholstery—and let my eyes wing upward to the beautiful stained-glass window. Its colors were brilliant from the natural light that poured through the dome. Gazing at the mosaic was like looking through the eyepiece of a kaleidoscope. The inlaid patterns of cut glass gleamed in purple and gold and red.

I briefly recalled the earlier police report that had taken Paul up into the dome. The curator had reported what he thought were vandals who, according to the report, turned out to be two students secreted in the parapet surrounding the mosaic. In scanning the report I had thought briefly of Susan and Jake's fourth-floor retreat that snowy day in January. In similar fashion, the embarrassed students had heard Paul climbing toward their lovers' lair.

Now that Paul was familiar with those iron staircases, he was eager to scale the walls once more—this time to watch the sun rise. "Jonathan did it once on New Year's morning, when the trees were bare and the campus was empty. He could see all the way to the interstate on the south and Sourwood Mountain on the north."

"Does Jonathan know you want to climb tomorrow?" Jonathan was curator of the art gallery.

"Yep. He encouraged it, in fact. Said the light is spectacular when it first hits the copper."

"What about me?"

"Well, now, let's see. Do you need permission from someone? The chancellor, maybe?"

"Okay, wise guy," I retorted. "I'll go to your sunrise. Just get me down in time for the eleven o'clock processional at Grace."

"Wear slacks and rubber-soled shoes, and bring a warm jacket. And sunglasses. And Kat, we'll take it as slowly as you wish. There are steps—lots—and they get more twisted the higher we go. Sure you're up for this?"

At my recent post-surgery checkup, Wayne Witherspoon had cleared me for normal activity. Climbing steps seemed normal enough. "I'm good to go," I replied. "The doctors want me to stay physically active."

Very early the next morning I walked the few short blocks through the darkened campus to meet Paul. The dome loomed through the shadows, and I followed a sliver of light to the side door he had described. He greeted me with a thermos of hot coffee and poured steaming brew into the stainless steel cap he had just drunk from. He handed it to me with both hands—a communal cup. The gesture was surprisingly intimate.

Beyond that, Paul had only a flashlight clipped to his belt. "No ropes?" I asked, hoping I didn't sound nervous. "What if one of us falls?" From his earlier description, I knew we would end up on a narrow ledge that circled the inside of the dome nearly twenty feet above the mosaic floor. Another ledge circled the outside of the dome's base, providing a platform for columns that reached up to hold a small cupola and finial.

"We're just climbing steps, Prez, not swinging through the dome. Although that might be fun. Me Tarzan, you Jane." He flashed his famous grin.

I followed him down the hall to a large storage closet. It contained yet another door in its rear, one that opened onto a tucked-away stairwell that led us upward. Our direction turned after ten or twelve steps, placing us on a tiny landing, smaller than the one in my childhood home that held a bench and window. This stairwell turned five more times, lit by the beam from Paul's beacon. We stirred up dust as we climbed into the upper reaches of the three-story building.

"Let's rest," I pleaded as we arrived at the third landing. It appeared to be a small, musty room, like an attic. I was breathing hard. Paul's arm instantly circled my shoulders.

"The circular stairway is next, but the railing helps." I winced inwardly at the thought of yet another flight, but Paul smiled into my eyes. Once more I felt the power this man had on me through the mere act of holding a gaze.

"Let's go." I nudged him on with my knee.

As it turned out, I had good reason to hesitate. The steep steps of the spiral stairway turned tightly like a coil. The backs of my upper thighs strained with each placement of my feet. My wound pinched briefly, and I slipped my free hand below my rib cage and pressed hard. My eyes stayed fastened on Paul's feet as we wound our way straight up through the flickering light. I felt like Nancy Drew exploring the turret of an ancient mansion. Or was it a castle? I was beginning to doubt my sanity in agreeing to come.

Then Paul came to an abrupt stop, and in our cramped space my head nearly rammed into his lower back. The steps had evidently run out. Paul's flashlight played on the ceiling just above his head, and his right hand explored its surface. He gave a hard push, and an iron square—a trapdoor—gave way with a slow whine. Then it fell forward with a clang.

"Almost there," Paul huffed in a muffled tone. I saw his feet grapple for iron rungs on the wall in front. Suddenly he was scrambling up by way of three hand bars and heaving himself into the new space. I watched in dismay as his feet disappeared above me.

"Last round, Prez." Paul's head reappeared, and he reached down with his right arm to encourage me. "It's no different from the jungle gym you climbed as a child. Atta girl." He watched in approval as my hands and feet connected with the iron rungs. I actually grunted as I thrust myself upward, poking myself headfirst through the trapdoor. Paul pulled me through by the shoulders. I lay momentarily on the narrow inner ledge of the dome, gasping for breath, with my cheek against the wooden planking and my rump in the air. It was hardly a Kodak moment.

But once we gained our footing, we commanded a clear sense of the height we had ascended. We were forced to stoop because of the slanting roof, yet I felt my excitement rising. We were at the base of the dome, where eye-shaped windows, or oculi, were beginning to admit the pale purple dawn. A few footsteps toward that light would place us in open air on the outer rim. Far below us lay the silent sea of the mosaic, whose glass tiles were emerging as splotches of dark and light.

"We'll get a better view of the landscape if we sit outside," Paul said. "On the other hand, the light striking inside the copper is said to be nothing short of explosive. And we wouldn't want to miss an explosion, now, would we, Prez?"

This time I beat him to the grin.

In the end, Paul and I held our sun feast both outside and inside the building. First, we sidestepped like crabs a few feet around the east side of the precarious outer balcony, standing upright and hugging the dome with outstretched arms as we inched along the ledge. Paul led the way, calling out encouragement and telling me to look at the dome panels in front of me and to feel with my feet. Since we were hemmed in only by a wooden handrail and widely spaced balusters, I dared not look down. Eventually Paul called a halt to our creeping and pulled me down onto the narrow rampart. We snuggled against a column, Paul's arms wrapped tightly around my waist as though we were at a drive-in movie. The light emerged slowly and began to splash across the skyline. In a very short time—no more than ten minutes—our view evolved from deep blue to pale blue, from pink to saffron. My heightened adrenalin made me almost giddy, and I pretended to strain as though to see the Atlantic Ocean two hundred miles in the distance. The playfulness of the moment produced a flashback to pirate games with my young sisters in Arden's Norbert Hall tower.

"Hark! What is that black spot on the ocean ahead?" I would thunder, pointing to a tree a hundred yards out.

"Help! Help! It's pirates!" Marianna would scream, pretending to run, only to be stopped by Sarah, who would jump from her hiding place with a scarf slanted diagonally across her face.

I could have nestled in that perfect lair forever, watching the sunrise embrace the sleeping city and feeling Paul's breath on my neck. But the early rays were spreading, and Paul was eager that we position ourselves inside to witness the sunburst yet to come. We sidestepped back to the opening that led inside, and Paul caught my arm as I stretched across the awkward gap. Once back on the dome's inner ledge, we were again forced to stoop. Our feet were balancing on rough-sawn lumber, the boards butting against each other like a construction gangway. Paul pointed to the dome's western arc as the best place to seat ourselves, and although protected somewhat by a metal rail, we crept our way there gingerly. The boards creaked as though in pain, and it struck me that human feet had rarely found themselves on this uneven planking.

"Try stretching out sideways," Paul suggested, and that's how we ended up—our backs together like bookends and our legs sprawled straight out in front rather than dangling over the rim. A hush fell upon us as the growing light began to swell through the walls. My heart was pounding so hard that I was sure its reverberations would press through my spine into Paul's.

Then came the sunburst. I have revisited this memory a hundred times since that morning, and each image brings pure elation. Just as Jonathan had predicted, the sun's rays hit the outside copper panels and exploded into the dome. Instantly we were bathed in a cascade of shimmering light that literally moved, pulsing rapidly as though tiny raindrops of gold were pelting the air. Blinded in spite of my sunglasses, I squeezed my eyes shut against the intensity, peeking through squinted eyelids to capture the sight. The dazzle was enthralling, and for an instant I imagined I heard music resounding above me, below me, and on all sides—thousands of choir voices caroling in glorious paeans of praise.

"Angels," I thought happily, hugging my arms tightly across my chest. "Angels and sun drops! A multitude of the heavenly host! This is what heaven must be like!"

Then the effulgence subsided just enough so that I could lower my sunglasses and open my eyes. My gaze took in fully the exquisite gilded light that continued to swim about us. I thought instantly of Emily Dickinson's leopards leaping to the sky in a sunrise "blazing in gold." Emily, with her instincts for the unique in nature, would have loved this.

I sat transfixed in the radiance, inhaling the spangled air and hearing echoes of the magnificent choir music in my head. That's when I felt rivulets of warm wetness streaming down my face. I suddenly realized that the majesty of the golden deluge had so overwhelmed me that I was weeping in its splendor.

Chapter 38
JUNE

The glow of the dome stayed with me for weeks. My sun feast had been extraordinary, even more exceptional because it had coincided with Easter sunrise. Like that winter day at the lake, Paul had unexpectedly handed me a gift, a vision rarely experienced by human eyes. At first it seemed enough that Paul and I had shared the magic of the sunburst. The fact that I thought I had heard an angel choir as well—and oh, those voices rang lyrical and sweet!—was somehow too precious to reveal. Both were high-sensory experiences, the kind granted to very few. It was as though the telling would diminish the glory of those brief moments. I was not willing to release that private joy.

Spring semester ended with its usual flurry and fanfare. To my supreme satisfaction, commencement went beautifully. In late March, when I had been nearly frantic to find a speaker, Bob Atterbury had suggested the father of a graduating senior, a celebrated business executive who had funneled much of his wealth into a summer camp for inner-city students. The man accepted my invitation readily. His speech was short and punchy, the kind that students would remember that they'd liked even if they didn't remember what it had said.

When the cabinet gathered later in May, I called for a review of summer vacation schedules. An unpopular mandate in each of their contracts was to take vacations "at a time complementary to the good of the institution"—old language from an earlier administration intended to prevent an entire cabinet from departing campus at the same time. Pud, who would soon be managing a summer of sports camps on campus, had just returned from a trek on the Appalachian Trail and was sporting a dapper new beard. Dan would be departing soon for a London conference of medievalists and then touring Greek islands with Mimi. Bob and Susan were going to drive their boys to a July Scout jamboree in the Rocky Mountains. Marilyn reminded everyone that she preferred to travel in early September, "when the coffers are full and the budget is singing."

Jake, I noticed, avoided the subject of vacations by exulting over the latest fall enrollment figures—higher than anticipated in spite of our new policy of more selective SAT scores. "Most schools need three years to complete this curve, and we're pushing last year's figures," he boasted. His braggadocio made me wonder if he thought I might reward his good recruiting by keeping him on board. I doodled myself a note that his time at Wickfield was up—new job or no new job. I had coddled him long enough.

As for me, I rarely took what others called a real vacation; the now-cancelled cruise with Alex would have been my first in years. Fortunately, I had discussed that trip with no one except Jackie. But I did share my plans now for a Fourth of July trip to see Marianna. She would be hosting a neighborhood cookout and, in view of my breakup with Alex, wanted me to meet a neighbor whose wife had died from a sudden stroke. Under Marianna's direction the holiday would become a festive event: bunting that draped from the eaves, twinkling lights in the front-yard trees, spareribs on the grill. Although I had no interest in the grieving widower, I had told her I would come.

Jake surprised me that afternoon when I called him to my office. He was a step ahead of me, handing me his resignation in a sealed envelope. He had accepted a new job—executive director of student life at a private college in Tennessee, he said—but as he sat on my couch and described the new campus, I quickly read beyond his stellar adjectives. This job was clearly a step down from his current slot at Wickfield. He had not asked me for a personal recommendation, and I daresay its omission had diluted his search.

On the positive side, at least for me, I could soon hold cabinet meetings without facing the cuckolded Bob at the same table with Jake. I moved quickly to start the search for Jake's replacement. Claire called her Tennessee counterpart to plan a joint announcement of Jake's new position. I dictated the requisite quote for Claire's version of the press release—one that referred merely to our gratitude for Jake's "years of excellent service."

"Don't you think 'years of excellent service' sounds a bit sterile?" Claire asked innocently in my office when discussing the release. "After all, Jake has been at Wickfield for nearly ten years. Should we warm up the quote a bit?"

"My quote will suffice as is," I replied tersely.

Claire hesitated only a second. "Fine, then. I have your quote, and I'll release this as soon as Jake's school is ready." She picked up her notebook and quietly exited.

There followed a steady stream in and out of my office, in spite of the early yawn of summer. Dan showed up to introduce newly hired faculty. Claire brought numerous drafts of the annual report. My mail from Chapel Hill flowed unabated with university policies for review.

Perhaps most irrepressible was the excitement bubbling up from the technology staff in Wellstone's basement catacombs. One afternoon Kevin Merriweather pulled me into his office to demonstrate the newfangled electronic mail, the same "mail" we'd discussed at the January Board of Governors' meeting. The system would soon be ready for Wickfield use. My head swam with Kevin's technical jargon, much of it confusing, but I do remember that he taught me how to send my first e-mail message. I sat at his computer and addressed a brief note to myself by using the strange new wording he gave me: Kembright@wickfield.edu. Then, as he carefully instructed me, I placed the cursor on the Send button and clicked it.

"All done. Now go find your message on your computer," he said, grinning. I raced up the steps to my office as though the words might disappear if I didn't hurry. But the note had safely arrived on my computer screen. It was waiting for me.

I called Kevin on the phone as soon as I read it. "It's here!" I exclaimed. "It really works! But can't you find me an e-mail name more appealing than Kembright? I sound like a brand of furniture polish."

By the time June showed up on my desk calendar, I was surprised at how quickly my fall schedule was filling. Freshman convocation, the highlight of the first full week of August classes, was a huge priority for me—the event at which I delivered my most visible speech of the year. The convocation was attended by the entire student community. Attendance was mandatory for faculty, a condition of their contracts. They would be robed in full regalia and would line up in two columns to applaud incoming freshman students. Since I trailed the faculty as the last in the processional, I was always the first robed figure the freshmen faced as they approached the faculty columns. I loved seeing their surprise as they recognized me with my beaming welcome. I considered this an initiation rite of the highest level, and I worked hard to make it powerful.

This year's convocation would be especially significant for me. After all, I had surmounted cancer surgery and the breakup with Alex, and I felt those kinds of life challenges to be as critical for our students as the skills required of a career. At times like this I congratulated myself once more on my humanities background and those analytical-thinking skills acquired as a fluent reader and writer. There was much to tell these freshmen about core values and ethical decisions. I knew I would stew over my speech all summer, writing and editing multiple times in my head before committing words to paper.

I missed Paul sorely during this time. As soon as the local schools had cleared for the summer and his law exams were over, he and June and their teenagers had headed for two weeks at Myrtle Beach. That's why it was a surprise to hear his voice on the phone a couple of days before the family was due home.

"Got time for a drive this weekend?" he asked. He was calling me at my office. By now I knew his *modus operandi*: the unexpected phone call, the simple invitation, the slight cajoling in his voice. All I could eke from him was that he would meet me Saturday at the Chancellor's House. At one o'clock.

"Dress casually," he added.

But there was nothing casual about seeing him again. I hugged him hard in the kitchen, loving the feel of his arms around my waist. I complimented his mahogany tan and asked why he had returned early.

"I needed to get back," he said. That was all. I didn't press the point.

He didn't say where we were going, but I noticed his pickup. "Another waterfall?" I teased as we climbed in. "A mountain to climb? Rapids to ride? Will I be sore tomorrow?" I pulled on my sunglasses—not that I expected to encounter Betty Boyd or Patty Horton on our drive out of town.

"No climbing," he promised. "No winding steps. This is just a drive."

Paul seemed preoccupied as we drove, so I entered my own silent reverie as the miles sped along. I soon recognized the signs to Paul's secret lake— the two-lane paved road north, the turnoff to the bland asphalt stripe that began to climb, the slowing of the truck as Paul searched for the rutted trail.

Thick green underbrush now lined the path that had once been ice-packed snow. Queen Anne's lace made a lavish white carpet in spite of the blotted sun. Paul lowered our windows as we passed the No Trespassing sign; it hung crookedly now from a rustier nail. We bumped our way through the pine-fragrant forest, emerging at last in the clearing beside the lake.

The lake, which had shimmered with fiery-white crystals in January, was today an elegant lady plumped up in gleaming satins. I fell in love instantly with her emerald-green sheen. We walked to the shoreline of wet weeds and rocks.

"Where's Jay?" I asked suddenly. A Pawleys Island rope hammock was hanging between two trees. It had not been there in January.

"He's been here several times this spring. This is my first visit. Smells good, doesn't it?" Apparently Jay, the owner, was nowhere nearby.

"Did you bring your fishing gear?"

"It's in the truck, but we won't have time. I just wanted to see the place again."

Paul remained pensive, and it suddenly occurred to me that this "drive," as he called it, was more about Paul than me. Which was quite all right. This was, after all, Paul's asylum. I thought about asking if he brought his family here and then thought better of it. Family did not seem to be a good subject today.

"Do you have a favorite hike?" I asked. "If so, go check things out. I'm thinking that hammock looks too good to pass up."

That's how I ended up taking a spectacular nap, lured onto those handwoven hemp ropes by the ruffling lake breeze while Paul's head disappeared around the curve of the shoreline. When my eyes opened later, he was standing beside the hammock, gazing down on me. It took several seconds to awaken fully, and I surmised he had been watching me for some time.

"What time is it?" I asked, trying to sit upright in the sloping bed. It tilted crazily to the left, and I slid my feet to the level ground.

"Time to go," he said. But he was smiling as he spoke, and he handed me a bouquet of fuzzy Joe-Pye weed and purple ironweed, and something yellow that looked like goldenrod but wasn't.

"Oh, Paul. You know how I love flowers." I buried my nose in the yellow blossoms, then gasped and held my breath as I awaited an imminent sneeze.

"They probably won't last, but they're pretty. Like you." Paul continued to gaze and smile, but his usual banter was missing today. I ripped out three vigorous sneezes but continued to hold the culprit flowers as I walked to the water's edge. The toe of my sneaker sent ripples around the jutting rocks. I hated to leave.

Paul did not kiss me that day at the lake. Except for that kitchen hug and a moment when he helped me over slippery rocks, he didn't even touch me. Yet as much as I longed for that brush of hands or light touch of lips, I felt peace simply being with him. I asked for no more. Paul's mere presence in my life brought enormous joy.

I recently asked Paul when he knew without a doubt that he loved me, and he replied, "At the lake. In June." His response explained the blazing love that had poured from his eyes as I looked up from the hammock that day. His was such a simple reply, yet it captured the essence of our bond. In spite of layers of complexity, our love has continued and is simple indeed. We simply *know* it. We don't need friends or psychologists to explain our kind of love. We feel it to our bones and accept it in silence.

Chapter 39
FOURTH OF JULY

The pain struck suddenly. At first it was an annoying flutter in the upper abdomen, the kind one chalks up to mild indigestion—or to "Paul-itis," as I called those secret butterflies that sometimes flittered. But then, one morning in late June, Lennie watched in surprise as I poured a mug of hot coffee down the kitchen drain.

"Too acid," I explained to her raised eyebrows. "I have a nagging pain."

"Call Dr. Hoffmann," she retorted promptly.

"Maalox ought to do it." I placed my rinsed cup in the dishwasher.

Lennie whirled on me like a tiger. "Miz Katherine, you call that doctor today. Maalox, my biscuits! No telling what it be, after all that surgery and everything! Could be them stitches pulled out."

"No, this is a different place. Higher up. My stitches are down here," I said, pressing my fingers against my lower abdomen.

"Don't matter. I say, better safe than sorry. Call that doctor today."

"I will if it will keep you from badgering me," I shot back. Lennie's bossiness made me angry. Sometimes she was simply too officious—much too overbearing for my mood today. I knew she would remind me again as I left for my office, and she did.

The nurse scheduled me for the next day. "Dr. Hoffmann will be happy to see you, Dr. Embright," she said smoothly, as though a hole with my name on it had magically appeared in his schedule. I knew better. As with my appointment in March, someone was being bumped in order to work me in so quickly. George was normally booked weeks in advance.

His eyes were all business when he strode into my examination room the next day. The exam was brief. And George himself was surprisingly taciturn.

"Does this hurt?" he asked, his fingers prodding me with the measure of one whose professional eyes can see beneath the skin and bore through layers of tissue.

"Yes," I said, wincing.

"How long have you been feeling the pain?"

"A few days."

There was yet more silence, as if George Hoffmann were contemplating his next step.

"When is your next appointment with Wayne Witherspoon?"

"It's coming up. Mid-July, I think."

"All right. Here's what we're going to do. We'll take X-rays of that painful abdomen, and Gwen will draw blood for another CBC panel. I'll send the results to Dr. Witherspoon so he can explain them during your follow-up exam."

"Sounds easy enough," I said agreeably.

"But ..." My head turned in his direction as he continued. "He may want to move up your appointment, since today's exam is advancing some of the procedures. So when his office calls you, be ready to follow up in Charlotte immediately. Got it?"

"How soon will you get results? I'm going to Virginia this weekend."

"I'll order these stat." He paused as he watched me reach for my purse and car keys. "But be prepared to respond promptly. Holiday or no holiday. Your health is your first priority, Katherine."

A jolt of uneasiness hit me with those words. Normally I would say something like, "Do you sense a problem?" For whatever reason, those words would not come this time. I simply nodded and gathered my things.

My physical discomfort continued that evening and pursued me relentlessly the next day. Fortunately, the campus was hunkering down for the Fourth of July weekend. Traditionally, early July was one of the slowest times on the school calendar—and for the city of Hurley. Years ago, when Hurley's culture had been intrinsically molded by its manufacturing industry, all the local mills—textile, hosiery, furniture—shut down completely during Fourth of July week. The entire city, it seemed, headed east to the beach or west to the mountains.

"Goodness, things are dead around here," observed Jackie early that afternoon. It was Thursday, and the phone had scarcely rung all morning.

Like me, Jackie was slated to be out of the office both Friday and Monday—one of the few times both of us would be away from campus at the same time.

"What did you work out with Carrington?" Jackie had been trying to schedule a meeting with him for a couple of weeks.

"July 13. It's a Friday, which seemed to suit him. He and his wife will be at the beach next week."

Friday the thirteenth? Still, I nodded with some relief. Carrington was one headache I didn't need at the moment.

As it turned out, the phone did ring for me yet that afternoon. My heart dropped when I recognized Wayne Witherspoon's nurse on the other end. The message was simple: Dr. Witherspoon had the results of this week's tests and wanted to see me in his office for one additional test. A CAT scan. Tomorrow.

"Not before Tuesday," I replied with a condescending, artificial sweetness. "I'll be out of town until then." In truth, I felt nothing short of sheer terror.

"I understand, Dr. Embright, but Dr. Witherspoon said tomorrow. May I put you down for 10:00 a.m.?"

So there it was, just like that. My entire body went numb as I stared into space and heard my voice relenting. Ten o'clock it would be. I hung up the phone and promptly dialed Paul's number. I dared not give myself time to think or analyze or wonder. I needed to stay focused, to make clear decisions, to stay calm.

"I'll drive you," he said promptly on hearing my news. He didn't comment on the suddenness of the medical appointment, and he offered neither condolences nor encouragement. He ignored my protests when I insisted I drive myself. Until now, I had forgotten he had planned to play in a softball tournament this weekend—some father-son league he and Blair enjoyed together. Now I reminded him.

"I'll catch up in the tournament if we win. Don't worry about it." His voice was so firm that I acquiesced on the spot. Frankly, I was vastly relieved. Paul would be the perfect companion.

There is much I could say about the next twenty-four hours. Some details are etched into my memory, while others are indistinct. Suffice it to say that on a gentle June day, when blue skies reigned over Charlotte, when American families packed their cars for vacation getaways and my own sister hung a flag from her wraparound porch in Richmond, an oncologist faced me across his desk. I looked back at him like a cowering cat who smells the breath of a panting dog.

He told me my cancer had returned.

My reaction was not as it had been in March, however, when I'd acquiesced to Wayne Witherspoon's need for hasty surgery. This time I tangled with him, clawing in disbelief.

"There's no way!" I shouted. "You took it out! You got rid of it! You said it was a clean fix!" I sat forward on the edge of my seat, desperate to convince him that he had mixed up my tests with those of another patient, that I was healing well, that this new pain was a mere annoyance and not even close to the place he had cut earlier.

But, like a seasoned tennis player knowing how to lob the ball, he returned my arguments with precision. Microscopic cancer cells had likely been in the bloodstream, he said, "even before the March surgery." The risk of a recurrence "has always existed," he told me. In this case—and here he seemed to pause a split second—in this case, the cancer had surfaced in my liver.

"The CAT scan shows metastatic involvement in the liver. We can see multiple masses—nodules—throughout. That's the new sensation you're experiencing," he said. His eyes probed mine kindly. "The distension of the liver capsule is causing pain."

Liver. I was stupefied. The word was so staggering that shock waves surged. Having nursed both a father and a sister through sieges of cancer, I understood exactly what that meant.

Dr. Witherspoon, who doubtless had anticipated this moment, offered me a bottle of water and asked if I had a "colleague" in the waiting room. He knew I had arrived with Paul; his nurse had met him when we'd checked in. Now Paul was summoned to join us. I didn't dare look at him when he entered the room and took a silent seat next to me. I felt his massive presence and, staring straight ahead, merely held out a hand. Paul enfolded it in both of his.

The conversation continued, this time between the two men. The doctor explained the situation to Paul, who responded in brief utterances. My mind was spinning so fast it seemed to gasp for oxygen. I longed to dash to the restroom, to hover over a toilet bowl, to heave until this horror purged itself from my system. I struggled to maintain control and tried to focus on the words. Suddenly Dr. Witherspoon was waiting for my response—only I had not heard the question.

"Two years," I croaked, raspy. I stopped and cleared my throat. "I need two years." That's all I said. I needed a minimum of two years at Wickfield to mold my ideas into reality, to bring my dreams to fruition, to fulfill my mission. *Two years, God. Please, please. Then you can have me. I won't ask anything beyond this.*

But Dr. Witherspoon was talking again. I tried to concentrate. "There are also enlarged lymph nodes throughout the abdomen. This all changes the prognosis significantly." He offered me a smile of absolute compassion. "I wish I could promise you two more years, Katherine, but in truth I can't even promise one year. The one piece of good news is that chemotherapy and radiation are long-proven treatments and can lengthen and extend the quality of your life significantly. And research is constant. Those of us in medicine live each day with the conviction that tomorrow may bring a discovery of some new miracle drug or therapy. We never give up hope."

Paul intervened at this point, asking precise questions in a professional, clipped voice. *He already sounds like a lawyer,* I thought dimly. But his voice, like mine, was scratchy and raw. And he was rushing his words, stopping and starting again. *God, help Paul.*

"I recommend chemo by intravenous infusion," Dr. Witherspoon answered. "It's simple, it's painless, and she can be treated in Hurley. She'll sit in a comfortable lounge chair for two hours while hooked up to the medication through a port under the skin. She can read, write, do all her regular work. She'll do this once a week for six weeks. Then we'll do more tests." He smiled again, clearly pleased. "And we can start you next week." He reached for a pad and scribbled a note to himself.

That's when I finally found my true voice. "No chemo." My words were low-pitched and measured. "Absolutely no chemo. I'll have no part of it."

Paul whirled on me instantly. "Kat!"

"I mean it. There's no way I'm going through an ordeal that will sap my energy, destroy my creativity, and deprive me of normal functioning, at least temporarily. If you could tell me it would save my life, I might consider it. But you can't tell me that. All you can say is that chemo might prolong my life a bit. But in many ways, a longer life will only be longer agony."

"Katherine, please hear me on this. These cancer cells are aggressive. They move very fast, and we must do the same. Chemo is a systemic treatment that goes after the cancer throughout your entire body. As your physician, I am telling you it is your only hope. Without chemo, you will—"

"I will die an inglorious death, right?" The harsh and taunting voice did not sound like mine. "I've seen it firsthand. If I'm going to die anyway, why force me to walk over hot coals first?"

"Kat, please think about this. You don't have to decide today. Let's take some time and think through our options together."

I hesitated. Paul, as usual, made sense.

"How much time do I have?" I eyeballed the doctor. "Best shot?"

"A year, at the outside. But if you let the disease take its course without letting medical science help you—and we would throw our best your way, Katherine, even the latest experimental drugs—your demise could be very rapid. Maybe a slow regression at first but a fast decline at the end."

A year. I will die within a year. Courage, God, please. Help me through this.

"That's my point, exactly. Chemo would give me a few months at best." He still hadn't answered my question. "What are you saying? Six weeks? Three months? Six months? Will I see Christmas?"

He looked at me evenly. "You probably have a couple of months ahead that will appear relatively normal, at least to others. But you'll need a great deal of rest, Katherine, not your usual schedule. And you'll need pain medication. Lots of it. This won't be easy. You'll need the full support of your staff."

"No. No one must know. I can't stand the idea of everyone feeling sorry for me and trying to find kind ways to say goodbye." I was angry now, furious, and my sarcasm broke in a half-sob. I had fought tears to this point and knew that once they started, my grief would flow unabated.

"Kat. Please. Let's get away and think about all of this. This is way too much to comprehend right now." Paul's voice was pleading.

"One more thing." Dr. Witherspoon hesitated, grasping for words. "I almost hesitate to mention this, because the medical community is somewhat divided on the findings, but indications are that sometimes people survive against all odds if they have a strong religious faith. The more they place their hope in God, the more optimistic and positive their attitude seems to be—or, at the very least, the braver and easier their struggle."

I nodded. This information was not news to me. I believed that Emily's struggle with cancer had been diminished significantly by her faith. But then, Emily's cancer had not invaded her liver. The doctor's words, although meant to encourage, depressed me even more.

Dr. Witherspoon dashed off two prescriptions and came around from behind his desk to hand them over. His checkered gray sports jacket and open-collared shirt seemed too casual for office attire, but today was, after all, the start of a holiday weekend. For a moment I thought he was going to hug me, and I mentally recoiled. I was still very angry with him.

"You're welcome to stay here in my office as long as you like. I have one more patient to examine before I leave for the weekend. Can I get you anything?"

Paul stood and shook his hand while I sat mute. As soon as the door closed behind us, I was out of my chair and into Paul's arms, weeping without restraint.

A minute later the door opened again, as though the doctor had forgotten something. It closed quickly, but not before I caught a glimpse of the gray checkered jacket. I realized vaguely that Wayne Witherspoon had seen much more than one professional "colleague" comforting another. He had seen an intertwined man and woman swaying in pure wretchedness—her fists pounding into his shoulders, his hands caressing her dark hair.

Chapter 40
THE SEASON OF LENT

Silence engulfed us after we left. While we waited on the prescriptions at a nearby pharmacy, I wandered through the store, pretending to flip through magazines and sort through rows of sun lotion. In truth, I saw and heard nothing. When we reached the parking lot, Paul tried to handle me like porcelain when he opened the car door—or so I thought—and I rebelled.

"I'm not an invalid," I snapped. Then, appalled because my words had surely wounded this man for whom I cared so deeply, I leaned my head against the neck rest and closed my eyes. Maybe, just maybe, I could sleep off this horror and awaken to a safe, familiar world.

We were halfway back to Hurley before Paul finally spoke.

"I have an idea," he began tentatively, speaking as though he knew I were awake. My sniffling, of course, made that clear. "I know a place in the mountains where we can go to sort this out. You're on holiday. You have no one to explain to. I'll take you home to pack. Then I'll grab a few things at the house and explain to June that you've been called out of town. Which is the truth. That's where you need to be at the moment: away from Hurley, away from Wickfield, away from your doctors."

I sorted his words through my fogginess. He was absolutely right about the timing. I had promised Marianna I would stay a couple of days beyond her party. In fact, I was not expected back at Wickfield until late the next week. After a quick call to Marianna, I could slip out of sight for a few days, undetected, and figure out how to deal with this bombshell in my life. Marianna would be disappointed but would take my cancellation in stride.

I dared not think of her reaction were she to know the truth.

"What place in the mountains? What mountains?"

"It's rental property owned jointly by Jeremy and me. Only it's empty right now because we're getting ready to enlarge it. There are lumber piles in the back, but it's quiet and totally private, Kat. You can sleep or walk or scream or do whatever you need to do."

"Will you stay with me?" It sounded as though he were going to drop me off in the wilderness and disappear. Not that isolation was anything new. Today, even God seemed to have disappeared. After my steady months of praying to become cancer-free, God had answered those prayers with today's devastation. God, more than anyone, had deserted me.

Paul looked sideways to see if I were serious. "Are you kidding? I'm not letting you out of my sight, lady." He turned on his blinker to pass a slow-moving van—one of those fifty-three-foot monsters that transports several households at once—and reached for my hand. "You can have the downstairs bedroom and bath. I'll take the upstairs. We'll pick up groceries in town. You're in shock, Kat. This is the perfect retreat for you. Pack shorts and jeans and a couple of sweaters and forget everything else."

"What about the baseball tournament?"

"I'll make it up to him. Blair's a good kid. Don't worry about it."

"And June?"

"June won't like me missing the tournament, but she knows that my job goes where you go."

I was far too overwhelmed to worry beyond this point. I numbly agreed to the plan without even asking the location of our mystery destination. In truth, I couldn't care less whether we were going to the mountains, the beach, or outer space. My world had just been shot to hell. We might as well be going to hell. In fact, it seemed we had already arrived.

I have only hazy memories of packing, although I do recall trying to stuff my favorite cotton robe in with my clothes and then choosing a larger suitcase. I also remember grabbing my new meds and a journal and a couple of books. One was the devotional I kept by my bedside; the other was a dog-eared copy of the condensed poems of Emily Dickinson. I scribbled instructions to Lennie, who was due back next Thursday, although I knew we couldn't possibly be gone that long. Today was Friday.

Once in Paul's truck I dozed, feeling the effects of a Benadryl I had taken at the house to calm my weeping. As had been the case with the drive after my colonoscopy, I awakened to flashes of cars and pastures and verdant green hillsides. I had no idea where we were, only that we were headed west. At one point I glimpsed a billboard for the Biltmore House and felt the rise of elevation. After Asheville, we entered a twisting stretch of interstate that hugged steep mountainsides and appeared to be chiseled straight out of Earth's core. We passed through a tunnel. Tight S curves swung us from one looming mound of forest to another.

Paul and I spoke little during this trip. My mind began to sharpen as I emerged from my sleepy stupor. To keep my mind off the cancer, I focused on people close to me. Alex came to mind immediately. Had I erred in not telling him sooner about my illness? One of the top-ranked surgeons in the Midwest had been an intimate part of my life, yet in small ways I had pushed him away. Then I remembered that what's-her-name was already pregnant at the time I had discovered my cancer. Would my news have made any difference? Would Alex have stood by me and let the pregnancy take its course? Perhaps they could have married after my death.

My death. The words were new and ghastly, and I quickly shut down that course of thinking. *You're too darn analytical*, I chided myself. My season with Alex was past history. I tried to concentrate on passing landscapes. I closed my eyes and watched a kaleidoscope of bursting images change color. I alternately dozed and jerked awake.

As afternoon fell into evening, we both lowered our visors against the sun. Shadows slanted across our laps. Paul finally exited the highway, turned onto a two-lane hardtop, and pointed the car toward a nearby gas station and a clump of wood-frame stores. He pulled up in front of the one that bore a real estate sign.

"Key," he explained briefly. "These folks maintain our property."

I watched from the front seat as he shared small talk with the man inside. He returned with an oversized apple-shaped key ring, and we swung back onto the hardtop and headed a short distance to a cheerful red brick building with the familiar McDonald's arch. When I said I wasn't hungry, Paul ignored me and headed for the drive-thru window, ordering enough chicken sandwiches and salads and decaffeinated coffee to last us both into the next day.

Tossing the food sacks into the back seat, Paul paused to grin at me. "Fifteen more minutes, Prez. Can you hang on? The best is just ahead." I attempted a smile back. This dear man was doing so much for me. His generous spirit amazed me. It was selfless—something I had not seen in either Tim or Alex.

Back on the hardtop, Paul drove a short distance before he made a hard left onto a lane of white gravel. The road inclined sharply and crackled noisily under the tires. Although there was still adequate daylight, Paul turned on the headlights as we climbed.

"Our driveway is hard to see once it starts to get dark. I missed it once," he commented. We were surrounded by somber, thick woodlands on each side of the road; the setting sun flickered lazily through tree tops. Our rigorous pathway continued to climb and twist into what seemed like blind curves, but Paul navigated carefully, watching for any sign of approaching cars as his truck plowed on.

"You're definitely a mountain man," I remarked as my eyes drank in the dense setting. "Haven't we made this trip a couple of times before?"

"It does look familiar, but wait until you see the view from the porch. It will take your breath away—guaranteed."

Take your breath away. Such a phrase would have meant nothing a week ago, but this evening it caught my attention. I found myself actually holding my breath as though to store up every possible molecule of oxygen.

Finally we came to a T intersection with a covey of small real-estate signs. Paul turned onto a wider road bearing some semblance of civilization. On the right there appeared a series of mountain cabins that backed up to the forested ridge behind. To the left lay a perfect valley. Clusters of mountains rolled one atop another, layering into a blur of blues and grays and purples.

Paul had been right: The setting did indeed take my breath away. "You've never mentioned this," I marveled. "Don't you want to spend every chance you get up here?" I was captivated. The scenery was, quite simply, exquisite.

"We try to keep it rented year-round, and when it is available, Jeremy's family gets first dibs. They're only an hour away." He had slowed down considerably as we bumped along the narrow road. "It's great country. Country like this can either keep a good man good or restore the worst of men into something decent. Okay, here we are."

We turned into a short paved driveway. In front of us rose a rustic chalet on stilts, its A-frame roof pointing toward the sky and its high front porch half-hidden by towering trees. I stepped down from the truck into the coolness of the gathering twilight. The mountain breeze bathed my taut face and fanned my hair. I felt an instant kinship with this beautiful land.

"Welcome to my humble abode."

"It's perfect, Paul."

He eyed the steep approach to the porch. "Think you can make this?"

"If I can't, you've got a load to carry." I surprised myself with the small joke. A few hours earlier I had felt so dismal that I could not imagine future levity in my life.

My lighter mood seemed to help Paul, who grabbed the food sacks and walked me up the long parade of wooden steps. The view captured my attention as soon as we reached the porch. I watched soft colors weave in the valley below while Paul fiddled with the big key ring and stepped inside to turn on lights. He held the door open, and I walked into a spacious pine-paneled living room. A blue plaid sleeper sofa and two cushioned matching chairs were grouped in front of a wood-burning fireplace. A tall pine cabinet held a large television set and a video cassette player. One wall was covered with an assortment of colorful jigsaw puzzles, matted and framed. A cedar table with two long matching benches centered the room. A kitchen loomed beyond.

I liked it. It was clean and attractive and seemed to ease the gnawing ache within me. Paul led me into what he called the "queen's room"—a reference to the queen-sized bed, although he pretended to present me with a room fit for royalty. I peeked into my bathroom: wildflower wallpaper and updated cabinets. So far, so good.

But what impressed me most was the dramatic spiral log staircase that twisted sharply as it led up to a loft. The banisters had been sculpted by a chain-saw artist with tiny images of local wildlife. Paul eyed the steps dubiously when I announced I wanted to tour upstairs, but I plunged ahead of him, pulling myself upward with the handrail. The loft served as a den of sorts, with a weathered bookcase covering the back wall and a red vinyl lounge chair for reading. The master bedroom, which featured a high window directly over the head of the log bed, extended to the left. Another bathroom hovered to the right. The house could easily sleep six. I loved its roominess. More important, it was extraordinarily private.

Back downstairs, Paul unwrapped the sandwiches and zapped the coffee in the microwave. "I'm starved," he announced. I pulled out plates and silverware and uncovered a pair of stoneware mugs. Paul moved the food to the cedar table while I ditched the paper wrappings. Inspired, I poked around in a catch-all drawer until I found a utility candle and a package of matches. I pushed the taper into an empty Coke bottle and carried it to the table as if it were a piece of fine crystal. Paul, getting into the spirit, lit the candle, centered it on the table, and turned off the overhead light.

Suddenly, and for that first time that day, Paul and I found ourselves facing one another squarely. Early this morning, after I had fluttered nervously in the kitchen and Paul had arrived for the Charlotte drive, I had not been able to look him in the eyes. What we saw now in this moment of utter intimacy was more painful than either of us could bear.

Paul broke first. Huge tears glistened in his eyes. "God, you're beautiful," he whispered.

I answered by leaning forward, grabbing both his hands in mine, and bowing my head. "Dear God, thank you for all the blessings you bestow upon us. Thank you for bringing us safely to this beautiful place. Thank you for this food and its nourishment. Be with us every minute we stay here, and give us strength to find our way through the days ahead. Amen."

"Amen," repeated Paul, squeezing my hands. I stole a glance at him. His eyes, still damp, were fixated on me. "How did you learn to do that?"

"Do what? Pray? I've been doing it all my life." I picked up a grilled-chicken sandwich, poking a slippery tomato slice back into the bun. "And, believe me, I'll be doing a lot of it this weekend. And in the months ahead."

"But how do you know what to say?"

"The words come to me. Some are learned. Some are habit. Some just pop into my head."

He shook his head in what seemed like amazement. "I've never been a praying man myself." He bit into his chicken.

"I'll teach you." The words surprised me, but they made sense. If there was one area of my life with which I felt comfortable, it was my spiritual side. At the moment, however, it was highly confused. God had failed me today, and God and I would soon have a long conversation about that. But it could wait until tomorrow. Right now I needed food.

So ended our first meal in our hideaway: our heads bent over a lukewarm McDonald's supper while a Home Depot candle in a Coke bottle cast dancing shadows across knotty pine walls. In spite of all that would transpire soon afterward, it remains a lovely memory.

Chapter 41

HEARTBREAK IN
THE MOUNTAINS

That first night in the mountains, sleep eluded me. In spite of the new sedative from Dr. Witherspoon, I awoke soon after midnight and tossed fitfully. My head snapped up from my pillow at intervals to look at the lighted face of the plastic bedside clock. It was a digital clock with two-inch numerals whose tiles dropped every sixty seconds—adding one more minute to my tenuous life and counting one minute closer to its end. The consistent tumbling of those green numbers, silent though they were, tolled like bells in my brain. I eventually sat up and threw off the covers, weeping in an outburst of such sorrow that I feared Paul would hear me. Before he had headed upstairs to bed, he had made me promise to awaken him if I could not sleep. But I could not do that. Paul was as exhausted as I.

I threw on robe and socks and padded into the pale-yellow living room. Paul had left on a single light, the lamp beside the sofa. I slumped onto the blue plaid cushions. I longed rather to step onto the front porch, to catch the night breeze and watch the infinite stars, but I feared the sliding glass door would wake Paul.

Wrapped in my own thoughts, I did not hear Paul emerge from his room. "Want to talk?" he asked from above me; startled, I looked up to see him bending over the balcony. We made an incongruous pair, I with my fuzzy socks and puffy face, he like a lifeguard patrolling the beach. He was wearing white pajama bottoms, and his matching pajama top was unbuttoned and open like a jacket thrown on at the last minute.

I tried for something witty to say. "Nice tan," I ventured, distinctly aware of the muscled chest above me.

"What can I get you?" Paul started down the spiral stairs. Earlier, as I was ready to settle in for the night, he had hovered, laying out pills and water and magazines.

Something in me stirred as he approached, in spite of my drained emotions. Even today's trauma could not sever the spell this man held over me. *Darn*, I thought. His torso was amazing for a fifty-something man. His physical beauty brought me pain. I longed for those solid arms to enfold me.

"Guess I didn't take you for a pajamas kind of guy," I said. He was standing by my side now, barefooted. My voice was flat, not flirtatious.

"What other kind is there?"

I gazed at him thoughtfully. I couldn't very well tell him that Tim had slept naked throughout our marriage or that Alex slept in *ironed* pajamas, no less.

"Think I'll try bed again," I said, yawning. I stood up. "These meds—"

"Come to bed with me, Kat." Paul held out his hand. "Let me hold you, rub your back, comfort you. That's all. Nothing more. Nothing we can't handle. I'm here for you. Let me help you."

When I examined his face in that long moment, I was surprised at the depth of pain there. Yesterday's shock had seared Paul as well. He, too, was in grief. I pulled the chain on the lamp and willingly took his waiting hand.

And so we tried sleep again, this time with Paul's arms holding me so closely in his bed that I could hear his heartbeat through the rise and fall of his chest. This new intimacy was more comforting than arousing. We did not make love, nor did we attempt to explore our new closeness. We pulled our bodies together as easily as though we had spent every night together for the past twenty years.

Then I dreamed. I was drifting through a large city, searching for my parked car, worried that I had lost the key. Eventually I found my car in a parking garage and discovered the key had been in my purse the entire time, along with a note from the person who had given it to me. Pleased, I proceeded toward the exit gate, only to find that I had to drive the car up a large number of steps. As I approached the staircase, the steps instantly melted into each other, creating a wide, smooth ramp. I made it halfway up the ramp before stopping; the slope ahead looked impossibly steep. A man came along and told me to gun my engines—that I would go straight up without any trouble. I did as he instructed. When I got to the top, I flew through the exit. The gatekeeper had stepped out, so I didn't even have to pay. I drove into a pleasant grassy area before continuing on my way.

I awoke. The dream was far too confusing to analyze—not that analysis was necessarily a good idea—but I did glimpse overlaps of fear and passion and guilt. I lay awake in the dark, letting the tears slide out silently and wiping them on the sheet.

Somewhere near dawn, when light was beginning to blur the darkness at the windows, I sensed that Paul was awake. I heard a change in his breathing and felt the alertness of his still body. "It's better this way," I said aloud to the silent ceiling above. My voice was calm and decisive. "It's better to die a natural death and return to God than to die a wretched death while still living. Because I would have to let you go, you know."

I turned toward him and fumbled in the darkness to find his face. My fingertips caressed his forehead, his eyebrows, his eyelids, his nose. Wetness was creeping down his cheeks. His hand caught mine. Together we wiped his tears away.

Then we slept again.

Sleep has amazing restorative powers, and the next day those powers rescued me from Friday's distress. I slept late and awakened to an empty bed. I showered, dressed, and picked at the breakfast laid out on the cedar table. Since Paul was nowhere in sight, I ventured onto the front deck and down the steep steps. In the back lot I found Paul moving a load of stacked boards to a sheltered area under the eaves. His face brightened when I showed up, coffee mug in hand. We took a short hike that morning, exploring not only the Stafford property but the meadows and woods beyond. Our elevation was higher than I had realized.

My mind was clearer today. The pain was manageable, but at times I felt fatigue beyond belief as I faced the heaviness of my new situation. The fatigue reminded me of the term "burden of grief," bringing vividly to mind our family's entrance into the church behind Benny's small casket. Before the beginning of the service that day, we had huddled together in the vestibule, standing as brave and tall as possible amid our now-damaged lives, but when the ushers had thrown open the doors into the church nave and the organist shifted from the prelude into the pomp of the processional hymn, we sisters had felt our shoulders collectively sag and our heads bend akimbo. We had stumbled down the aisle half-blinded by sorrow, moving like robots into our assigned pew as though mammoth weights were fastened to our backs.

At least this time I understood what was happening to me. I had lived through enough family tragedy—or near tragedy, as in Emily's case—to comprehend the levels of sorrow that now enveloped me. Today I was ready to bargain with God. Yesterday I had asked him for two years, but today I could compromise at one. If God would grant me enough time to get my professional affairs in order—and, on the personal level, to see my sisters and their families once more—I just might be able to accept this travesty.

It was while Paul was driving into the nearby town to pick up groceries that I had a long conversation with God. I sat on the deck overlooking a small rivulet of a waterfall that splashed its way down the back hillside and spoke with God in depth. It mattered not whether I shouted or wept or whispered, and I did all three. Whatever my method of meditation, we were deep in dialogue.

My sense of anger and betrayal frequently took over: "You didn't listen to me, God. You heard me when we prayed for Emily's recovery, and you restored her to us, whole. You helped me through the surgery in March and heard my constant prayers for recovery. But now, this. This I can't accept!"

The conversation also drove me to see shortcomings in myself. I found myself asking for forgiveness for things I had *not* done—like the time I had sternly told Mildred Stamey at Grace that I was too busy to bring a dish to the congregation's annual dinner, almost scolding her for having asked. *For heaven's sakes,* I stormed to myself now. *Surely you could have given up one of Lennie's chicken pies to share. What arrogance!* It didn't matter that my cooking skills had diminished since I'd become chancellor. Clearly, I was guilty of the sin of pride. In ways that I didn't quite understand, I sensed that I had abused my role as chancellor, relegating God to second place as though empowered to do so.

But, just to make sure God got the whole picture, I recited an entire litany of good works. I mentioned my regular worship at Grace, my lifelong habit of prayer, the impressive menu of charitable donations that dated back to my first job. The longer my list became, the more outraged I became. I was too young, too busy, too talented, and too caring of other people to be taken from life right now. People needed me. *Wickfield* needed me.

God's timing was all wrong. "Wrong, wrong, wrong!" I wailed into the blue afternoon.

But even as I stormed and pleaded in near-adolescent fury, I knew better. My faith was solid enough to know that good works did not buy one's way into heaven. I also knew that God's plans did not always dovetail with our own. I moved from a deck chair to the chaise longue and stared up at the sky. Floppy clouds were scudding across my view, buoyed by the mountain air currents. Above them was a blaze of azure blue, stretching all the way to heaven.

"You'd better be there when I get there," I muttered under my breath.

I closed my eyes, soaking up the fragrance of the beautiful old forests of spruce and hemlocks. I was as close to God as I could imagine, surrounded by his timelessness in the ancient rocks and stoic hills.

That's where Paul found me when he returned from shopping. He noticed my inert form stretched in the chair and stepped out from the kitchen to check on me.

"What are you doing?" he asked curiously when I turned my head to greet him.

"Looking at God."

"Really?" I heard the hint of a chuckle. "And what is God doing?"

"He's looking back at me."

We unpacked the grocery sacks together, and I was touched by Paul's careful selections—magnificent rich strawberries, wine-colored plums, vine-ripened tomatoes bursting with lycopene and antioxidants. I joked that we needed a week to consume it all. Paul stashed the groceries and said little.

We ate lunch in the middle of the afternoon, and were it not for the dark unknown that loomed over us, we could have been an ordinary couple enjoying a normal Saturday in the mountains. I found it very hard to accept—even to believe—yesterday's news. It had now been over twenty-four hours since our conversation with Wayne Witherspoon—and, as I pointed out to Paul, we were still here. We were still functioning. We had not fallen off the face of the earth with this diagnosis.

We were lingering over bowls of strawberries and Cool Whip during this conversation, both reluctant to move. Paul leaned forward and grabbed both my hands across the table. "Fight this thing, Kat! And surround yourself with people who care about you! Let them help!"

"How did you get to be such an expert on dealing with death?"

"Part of my police training."

We talked on into the afternoon. Paul uncorked a bottle of cabernet sauvignon—a surprise among the groceries—and rustled up fat wine glasses from the cupboard. The alcohol gave me either courage or cowardice, I'm not sure which, but the effect was the same: I continued to resist the idea of chemotherapy, while Paul pleaded his case otherwise.

"What did your Emily say about perseverance? She wouldn't like your attitude, would she?"

"Probably not. She was a marvel. She seldom complained, in spite of her pain."

"Not your sister Emily. The poet."

I had to stop to think for a minute. This was the first time we had confused the Emilys. "She wrote about hope. She described hope as 'the thing with feathers that perches in the soul.'"

"There! See? She meant you should hang on and not give up."

I was less impressed. "Maybe it just meant that Emily Dickinson liked birds."

Paul also urged me to share my diagnosis with key members of my cabinet, but I knew how disastrous that could be. News of such illness would surely cripple my leadership.

In time, the wine inspired sleep, and I pled for a nap.

"Sleep as long as you like. We'll have dinner when you wake up." Paul slipped the cork back into the wine bottle, while I headed for the shower again. I washed my hair and soaped my skin as though the silky lather might wash away the cancer. I swept my wet hair into a turban and encircled another bath towel around my torso before emerging from the steamy bathroom. Sleep had never looked so inviting. I slid under the cool sheets and let the gentle rocking of the ceiling fan lull me away.

The light in the room was dimmer when I later heard a tap on my door, and I wondered whether I had slept into the night. "What time is it?" I called out, and Paul pushed open the door. He stood as a giant black silhouette against the living-room lamplight.

"About eight. Brought your meds. You slept through them. How are you feeling?"

"Better." I sat up, hitching the bedcovers under my arms and running a quick hand through my vaguely damp curls. "Come on in." Paul had pills in hand. He perched on the side of the bed in the semidarkness while I gulped the medicine, holding the sheets in place with my free hand.

"Do they teach nursing in law school?" I asked, setting the glass on the nightstand.

Paul did not answer. He merely reached out and stroked my face, running his hand in a straight line down my forehead and nose and stopping at my lips. I kissed his forefinger and pulled it into my mouth.

Somewhere in my innermost subconscious, I surely had imagined the moments that followed—yet they still surprised me, and I remain breathless to this day remembering the desire that overwhelmed us both. Paul leaned in and pulled me tightly against his chest, kissing me with a passion that was new for us. His mouth crushed me so hard that I felt his teeth. We did not speak. Instead, we repositioned ourselves as swiftly as though we'd rehearsed it a thousand times, me pushing aside the towel and climbing onto his lap so that I could look down from above him, bend his head up, and cup his face in my hands. I kissed his eyelids and his nose and his ears before finding once more his mouth. And when Paul at last pushed me backward onto the sheets, he cradled me like a violinist caressing a priceless Stradivarius. He moved gently and with utmost caution, placing his hand strategically to protect my tender belly from the crush of his body. Beyond our rustlings and the gasps of our breathing, the only sounds were the pale thumps of towels and clothing—and the soft sloughing of that ever-rocking fan.

When I was a young teenager dealing with my earliest conceptions about sex, I, like thousands of other pubescent girls, had fantasized that there would be one shuddering moment when my lover and I would first meet in intimacy— and that I would experience the height of perfect ecstasy. Furthermore, my feeble, fervid mind believed this initial passion would be sustained throughout our lives. Sadly, many of us grow up, get married, and hear the clock strike twelve—only to be jolted back into pumpkin patches amid our dashed dreams.

And yet—and yet—there are also rare times when life gifts us with the unexpected. When that occurs, we mentally gape while stars spangle upon our disbelief.

I believe this fully, because on that secret night in the heart of the Great Smokies, I came together with a man named Paul and found myself lifted into a heightened awareness of life itself. The very pores of my skin seemed to pull me inside myself where I could see me wholly—the true woman I was intended to be—and finally acknowledge my intense need for intimacy.

Before Paul, the men in my life had been mere fillips of what I thought avowed lovers should be. Now I knew a different kind of love. Its intensity was quite apparent, but its power over me was yet to be made clear.

Chapter 42

CONFESSION

Emily Dickinson once wrote that life is "so startling it leaves little time for anything else."

Those words flashed instantly to my mind when I awoke a few hours later. I was indeed *startled* by the turn my life had just taken. I lay with Paul's arms still around me, hearing his raspy snoring, feeling the cool dampness of our combined sweat, remembering every detail of our earlier intimacy. The images nearly made me blush. I had become a wild woman, a frenzied lover with unabated desire. I had pulled Paul to me like a drowning victim, clutching him as if he could will survival into my very being.

Paul, in turn, had been present on every level: my lover, my savior, my preserver from the brink. He had pulled me back to safety. I was no longer a woman lost—or so I had thought in those mewling moments of satiety. As I lay on those sheets, catching my breath and drawing in the fullness of the moment, I felt my cup of euphoria filling to the brim.

Now, however, haunted by middle-night darkness and the full implications of our earlier hours together, my heart froze. I was subdued not only by physical disease but also by thoughts of my first-ever sin of adultery. I had a flash of the embroidered scarlet *A* of Hester Prynne, a literary heroine whose shame in front of those Puritan scaffolds I had dramatized to my English students long ago. I thought of the adulterous woman of Scripture, the one surrounded by an angry crowd to be stoned.

I thought also of my father enduring those last horrific days with cancer: the sorrows of his lifetime that surfaced like tsunamis, the regrets that pursued him in his bed like red demons. Dying is not easy for those who lead troubled lives. In his case, his demise was amplified by physical pain so searing that even morphine did not always redeem.

I was in my early twenties the summer he died—a rising college junior who sat vigilant by his bedside in alternate time slots with my mother and sisters. Perhaps Mother knew the history behind his incoherent utterances, but to us five sisters they seemed the ravings of a good man gone mad. We watched with enormous sorrow as he drifted in and out of psychosis.

To no one's surprise, apparently, but my own, he found rare moments of calmness only when I was the daughter by his side. I whispered and soothed him, stroked his hand and bathed his face, read softly to him even while he shuddered in his sleep. And on those few occasions when he could speak, I ignored the odious breath and body smells of impending death, bending close to his head and listening to his muttered words.

Somewhere in the midst of this trauma, like morning light banishing nighttime fog, a woman with the incongruous name of Elly Hurt came into our lives. She was a private nurse hired by the family, and she managed to belie her name by providing every means possible to mitigate Daddy's pain. She hooked him up to a web of tubes and cords with the skills of a mechanical engineer, religiously meting out morphine and fluids that stretched his flimsy life yet a few more weeks.

These so-distant memories now stabbed me into action, sending me silently out of Paul's arms and into my robe. I dressed like a flickering shadow, tiptoed into the living room, and closed the bedroom door behind me. I curled up on the blue plaid couch and gave way once again to a deluge of tears, snuffling as they coursed down my cheeks and merged with the river from my nose. I looked and felt like a refugee from an earthquake. I hoped with one shuddering sob that Paul would not awaken and find me so distraught, yet I yearned with the next that he discover me and offer comfort.

He found me soon enough. "The solution," he said, hovering over me in my miserable huddle, "is food. I'm going to whip up a midnight breakfast fit for a queen." He wiped my flooded cheeks with his fingers and kissed me once on each side with sweet precision. "We forgot dinner," he whispered into my ear.

"You're right," I whispered back. "We started with dessert."

At that he ruffled my hair, kissed me convincingly on the mouth, and headed for the kitchen. Like me, he had found his clothes in the dark bedroom. *Dear God, I love this man,* I thought as I watched him stride across the room, his rumpled polo shirt creased diagonally across his back. The thought of someday telling him goodbye was overwhelming. I reached for the Kleenex box.

By now we had thoroughly confused day and night. Was it really one o'clock in the morning? While Paul sliced strawberries and peeled strips of bacon from their plastic wrap, I headed to the shower once more. This was my third shower since we had arrived. I wondered vaguely whether my new fascination with flowing water was borne more of my need to cleanse myself from cancer or to rid myself of guilt. Not that it mattered.

I stepped into clean clothes and returned just in time to watch Paul pour a bowl of whipped eggs into the bacon-rich skillet. As he stirred carefully, the mixture bloomed into a mound of yellow fluff.

"Where did you learn to cook?" I asked as the food was vanishing beneath our forks. We were both famished. "Okay, I know. The United States Army."

"Nope. Boy Scouts."

"Scouts! No way. Not like this."

"That's where it started. On our campouts, with open fires and rough skillets. The rest I learned covering for June when she worked weekends."

June. It was the first time her name had been mentioned since we'd left Hurley. In an instant, a pain clutched at me, punching me back into the reality of our tenuous relationship. Paul caught my awkwardness and tried to change the subject, but I could not let the matter go.

"June must be wondering where you are."

Paul frowned as he buttered his toast. "As I've told you before, she never asks. She knows I'm with you on school business. That's enough for her. She's fine, Kat."

I took a long draw on my coffee.

"And," he continued, reaching for the grape jelly, "she's a smart cookie—smart enough to know that whatever took me away so suddenly is important. She might be curious, but she won't ask."

Paul's candor comforted me but little. June still weighed heavily on my mind, an issue to be dealt with somewhere down the road. As was my cancer. Although I was determined to keep my illness a secret, I would soon enough have to decide how to manage it.

"My sisters. Oh, God." I groaned the words as I uttered them.

"What about your sisters?"

"This is going to kill them." I realized the irony of my words as soon they escaped, but I kept going. "After what we went through with Emily, almost losing her and suffering so through that whole experience." I looked into space, remembering. "Not to mention Benny, of course. So long ago. But it still hurts to remember all of that." My throat flamed with the memory.

"Tell me about Benny. He was four, right? Three? How did he die, exactly?"

No one had asked me that question in years. Our family had rarely spoken about Benny's manner of death in the months following, but I'd wept over him for years. I never thought about him without enormous waves of guilt.

"I killed him." The roughness of my words surprised me.

"Oh, come on, Kat, you didn't *kill* him. Surely not. The first time you talked about him, months ago, you called it an accident."

"But I caused it. It could have been prevented. It didn't have to happen." I scooted back my chair and stood up, looking around the room as though inspecting it for eavesdroppers. "You sure you want to hear this?"

Paul nodded, his eyes fixed on me steadily.

"We were on a family picnic." My voice caught, and I stopped for new breath. Paul's eyes did not waver.

Suddenly I started pacing around the dining room, my gaze locked on the distant walls—anywhere but on Paul's. I walked in silence, my hands raised to my temples. The scene was hard to resurrect in detail. I had not visited the depths of this memory in a long, long time.

"Get the ball, Benny!"

I shrieked it the loudest that day in the park. I was laying out plastic silverware as Emily and Jane tossed a red plastic ball in the direction of the picnic table. Benny, giggling as he delved into the game, came running toward me, intent on the ball. I stepped out and intercepted it with my foot, giving it a playful kick that sent it spinning over open grass.

Benny turned and charged after it, drawing cheers from the others as his little legs flew toward the brightly colored sphere.

"Get the ball, Benny!" The family cheered him on, my voice shrilling above the others.

The ball followed an incline and rolled onto pavement, and Benny, hard in pursuit, followed. There was an instant of bewilderment for those watching, then shrieks and screaming brakes. Then came the momentary flash of Benny's body launching into air.

Like a nestling bird on a too-soon flight, the bundle tumbled downward, crumpling into a splay on the hood of the car that had struck him.

"Dear God." Paul's voice cracked. I snatched a paper napkin from the table and dabbed at my nose.

"So, you see, I killed him. I kicked the ball that sent him into the street. And I urged him to run after it! I told him to get the ball! I sent him to his death, Paul!" Paul was on his feet now, and I hurled myself into his arms, sobbing into his shoulder.

"Katherine. Shh. You didn't kill him. It was a freak accident! Have you been holding yourself responsible all these years? Dear God. No wonder you feel other people's pain." Paul kissed the top of my hair and rocked me in his arms. "Did you ever get therapy? A psychologist? School counselor? What about Tim? What did he say when you described it to him?"

"I didn't. I met Tim several years later, in college, but I couldn't talk to him about it much. Not to anyone, actually, outside the family. Our pastor, Karl Krueger, visited us a lot in those weeks after the funeral. But my friends who saw me through that bad time didn't talk about it much, either. Everyone felt terrible. It was incredibly sad. It had been a big deal when Benny was born, since Mother was over forty. I was ten. And he was our boy, finally, after five girls."

Paul continued to rock me in place, his voice soothing. "What about your parents?"

"Daddy took it the hardest. He became reclusive. Bitter, even. When he was diagnosed with cancer later, the town said it would be a blessing when he died and joined Benny."

"Colon cancer?"

"Pancreatic."

"Your mother?"

I pulled away a moment to dab at my nose again. "Mom was a rock. She would patrol the hallways at night, listening to the very walls breathe and seeking out the sources of weeping. When she found us she would climb under our sheets and cry with us and let us talk way into those black hours. She did that night after night until we could sleep." I shuddered. "It was a terrible summer."

Suddenly I was tired of morbidity. I was tired of crying, of sore eyelids, of wretchedness. I swished my feet into motion, standing up to stack plates and gather silverware. Paul joined in. Together we loaded the dishwasher and slicked up the kitchen until it was spotless. "Lennie would be proud," Paul observed as he turned out lights and herded me back to bed.

We slept hard until near daybreak. Then I awoke in a moment of cold dread. I lay in perfect stillness, listening once more to the rhythmic intake and exhaling of Paul's deep breathing, memorizing forever his salty skin scent and the light pressure of his arm across my chest. New memories were swirling inside me, and I feared them—ugly black words unspoken to any living soul yet yearning to be released from the secret chambers of my heart. They had lain there for years, taunting me whenever they appeared like slippery ghosts in my sleep.

I had to tell Paul. I had to tell *someone*. I was, after all, dying, and I dared not carry my arcane madness to the grave.

I spoke into the darkness. "There's more."

Paul stirred. He rolled toward me and sucked in his early morning breath.

"Sleep," he mumbled. "Go back to sleep." He breathed heavily into my ear.

I waited, hearing the click of the falling clock digits.

"I killed him, Paul."

Paul's arm tightened. He lay in silence for what seemed like an interminable stretch before he shifted, pulling his arm from behind my head and repositioning himself on his side of the bed.

"It was an accident, Kat. We talked about it. Remember?" He gave his pillow a punch before settling on his back. "It wasn't your fault. You were not responsible for Benny's death." It was as though I were a young Marcy and Paul my parent, patiently explaining old rules to a small child.

I sighed heavily, a laborious lament that shrouded us both.

"Not just Benny. I killed my *father*, Paul. I killed him. I really and truly and honestly killed him."

Chapter 43
THE PILLOW

When the Japanese bombed Pearl Harbor in 1941, Harold Embright was a high school history teacher and football coach—too old at twenty-nine to be drafted into military service. Making him even safer from active war was the simple fact that he was a married father of three young daughters.

At the same time, however, he was an authority figure for the teenage male population of Arden, Virginia, and in that capacity he bolstered the spirits of those who joined the military out of high school. War descended heavily on small peaceful towns like Arden. As the buildup of ammunition continued into the forties, so did the parade of funerals for local boys who returned in caskets. My father attended every one for those he had taught or coached—and for those Protestant denominations that allowed eulogies, he was often a chosen speaker. He painted images of gridiron heroics that even the stricken families knew were hyperbolic, but the heightened words eased the pain and were accepted with silent gratitude.

However, as the years passed and our family increased to five girls, so did local jokes increase about Daddy. His mannerisms went from peculiar to eccentric. In addition to mocking his insistence on gendered bathrooms in our home, townspeople whispered about his quaint manner of walking: head held high, shoulders squared, arms swinging like a marching drum major.

When our mother, Addie, became pregnant with her sixth child, the town actually took bets on the gender of the new baby. For those who bet on a male, Benjamin Olof Embright's arrival was the social highlight of the year.

Perhaps because the town had welcomed him so eagerly three years before, Benny's sudden death devastated Arden. Mourners jammed the church and collectively wept their way through the funeral. For the sake of both our stupefied family and the stricken pastor himself, it was blessedly short.

In the months that followed, Daddy was rarely seen in public outside of his role as dean of students. He stopped eating with colleagues in the faculty club and ceased going to church. Mother assumed the chauffeuring duties for the family. At the suggestion of Pastor Krueger, she drove Daddy several times to see a Richmond psychiatrist for depression—keeping such visits a secret from anyone outside the family, of course.

The pancreatic cancer diagnosis surprised everyone—most of all, Daddy himself. Although I did not understand the full implications at the time, he considered himself a man of power. To lose control at age fifty-two over his right to govern himself—to watch doctors and nurses and daughters make decisions for him—suffused him with gloom. The chemo treatments merely prolonged his suffering. He deplored the caustic bedsores that burned his skin, the shifting positions to ease bone-on-bone pain, the liquid feces that escaped onto sheets that were changed day and night.

In spite of careful treatment and efficient nursing care, Daddy went from irascible to maniacal. Only I, his middle daughter, could bring some level of comfort as he lay dying.

One day when nurse Elly was eating her lunch downstairs, Daddy called my sister Sarah and me to his bedside. Focusing his wet, filmy eyes on our faces, he lifted his head an inch off his pillow and rasped out a plea to end his torture. "No more," he begged. "Not another day. Not an hour." As his balding head dented his pillow again, his hand grabbed a corner of the cotton case. "Cover my face. Press hard."

Sarah turned away in disgust and horror, but I caressed Daddy's high forehead and murmured calming words. When Elly reentered minutes later, both Sarah and I rose to our feet to leave. Sarah turned away and stepped out first, but I lingered a second longer and, for a brief moment, met Daddy's exhausted gaze.

"He's crazy!" Sarah exploded to me in the quiet hallway.

"Shh," I said, closing the bedroom door carefully. "It's just the pain. It will all be over soon."

A few hours later, Elly left to prepare her dinner, leaving me alone by Daddy's bedside.

"Hi, Daddy," I said quietly, tidying the top sheet and sliding up a chair. The moaning and keening had continued throughout the afternoon, interrupted only by intermittent dozing. Daddy became agitated as I leaned over him.

"Now!" he said urgently. His head thrashed on his pillow as new pain surged.

"Hush, Daddy. She's given you the maximum morphine. Give it time to work."

"Not 'nuff," he gasped. "Help. Pillow. Easy . . . " His hands grabbed mine and guided them to the pillow under his head. I slid the pillow away to humor him, holding his head like an infant's to lower it flat onto the white bottom sheet.

But Daddy was trembling. He reached over to pull the pillow from me, and he placed it over his face. His hands groped for mine and pressed them on top of the pillow, his fingernails clawing into my flesh. His body thrashed and writhed as he tried to smash out any semblance of air between the pillow and his face. The terrible noises he emitted were unlike anything I had heard: gurgling, chirping, tortuous sounds. I froze, aghast, my hands bruising under Daddy's clutching talons.

Suddenly, with a loud bleat that leapt from my lungs, I tore my hands away and threw my body crosswise over the pillow, my chest pressing on top of Daddy's face, my own face buried into the sheets beside him. I held my position a few seconds before pulling myself up. I regained my footing, removed the pillow, and looked into Daddy's face. His eyes were closed, his face still.

It was over.

"Peace, Daddy," I whispered. I shed no tears. I was drained, enervated, numb to any senses physical or otherwise. As though simply straightening the pencils on my desk at school, I slipped the pillow back under my father's head, arranging it exactly as it had been positioned before. I closed his mouth, removed a spot of drool, and snapped his top sheet into tight, efficient lines. I walked calmly downstairs, found Elly munching a ham sandwich at the kitchen table, and stated simply that Daddy was dead.

Elly gasped. "What happened?" she asked. "Did his breathing shift like I described? I was listening for him to—"

"Yes," I said. "Yes, he had trouble breathing at the end. Yes, he made strange sounds."

The two of us entered the silent white room upstairs. Daddy lay in repose, his face already set in the mask of death. Elly checked his pulse, peeled back his eyelids, closed them again with her fingertips, and noted the time of death. Together, we then sought out the rest of the family.

Amid the grieving that followed, I remained composed and unruffled—a surprising reaction for one so close to Daddy. "I'm too exhausted to cry," I explained to Marianna, who was distraught. That response sufficed for all except Sarah. She alone bore down on me in a fierce, relentless, silent glare.

I returned her glare with flat, indifferent eyes.

Chapter 44
NIGHTMARE

Telling the story of Daddy's death exhausted me. I told it to Paul in bed, leaning against my pillows and staring straight ahead as my halting words spilled into space. Beside me, Paul was mute. I could not see his face as I recalled these harrowing details, but I knew he felt my pain. At the end of the story, I reached for his hand.

"I did exactly what Daddy asked of me. I helped let him go, let him fly away, gave him some final peace. But he never really left me, Paul. I can't tell you how many times through all these years I have felt him, heard him, sensed his presence nearby. I know it sounds crazy, Paul. I guess *I* sound crazy. But Daddy's still real. I don't think he ever found that peace he sought."

I stopped as the memory enveloped me. Those eyes! Daddy's tortured eyes haunted me yet. I could still see those pitiful, bleary orbs of film as they pleaded with me in silence.

"Dear . . . God." Paul uttered the words so slowly that they sounded like two separate sentences. His was not the voice I expected. I did not know this voice.

What happened next was so unexpected that I could only sit aghast as though watching a horror scene in a movie. Paul leapt out of bed and hit the floor with a thud. The words ripped out of him again, dark and gargled: "Good God, Kat!" His blue forehead vein bulged into a purple jag. He stalked back and forth like a caged lion, even shaking the hair out of his eyes as though tossing a heavy mane. The scene was surreal. I cowered in my sheets, unsure of what to expect.

What did occur I could not see—only hear. Paul disappeared into the outer living room. Next came an explosive pounding sound on the wall, frantic and loud and terrible. That was followed by the scraping shimmy of a table bench scooting across a wide expanse of floor. There was a dull thud and—finally—silence.

I grabbed my robe and bolted toward the dark living room. At first I could not see Paul. The bench had slammed into the television table and overturned, but, in my first wild glance, that seemed the extent of damage.

Then I saw Paul, slumped forward from a corner of the couch. He was holding his bent head in his hands, shoulders fallen, his elbows on his knees. My heart broke into a million pieces. I had done this to him. My story had driven him to this despair. After all, he had made love to a horrible woman, a woman who had killed her own father. After all the rationalizing I had done through the years—all the times I had tried to convince myself that those actions were no crime at all but a courageous act of mercy—I realized now they were merely lies. Paul's reaction made it all plain. He was, after all, a man of the law.

The new pain that engulfed me now was the harshest I had ever, *ever* experienced. It outweighed the shock of my illness. For Paul to be so disgusted with me, so repelled that he could merely sit there in this ghastly silence, was unthinkable. Yes, it was the unkindest cut of all.

Yet I approached him. I had to. I sidled up beside him on the couch and waited for him to say something. When he didn't, I began.

"Paul, look, I know this is a terrible shock to you, and I know you're angry, and I know I made a monstrous mistake, but—"

"Stop."

I stopped.

"Don't say anything."

I waited.

"We have to go. Now. Pack up."

With that he moved past me and up the carved stairway, leaving me huddled on the couch. It was over. All the glorious gildings—the perfect kinship of souls we had developed over the past months, the happiness that had enthralled me hours earlier, ephemeral though I knew it would be—vanished in that very instant.

In heavy silence, we packed up. We had slept little and we faced a three-hour drive back to Hurley, but as purple dawn appeared over our mountains and tinged the sky from merlot to rose, we stuffed our sheets and towels into the washer and tossed clothes into suitcases. I found Paul's socks in the midst of our twisted sheets and laid them, folded, at the foot of the staircase.

When I finally carried my suitcase into the living room, Paul was in the kitchen, boxing our leftover food. I joined him mutely, packing veggies and fruit into plastic baggies and spraying the refrigerator with Mr. Clean. At least the Stafford family in Hurley would eat well this week.

Although I could move robotically to tidy up, my mind was anything but ordered. Paul carried the bulging trash bags out the front door, bounced them down the steps, and tossed them into the back of his truck. Why was he ferrying them away? Was the mountain garbage service inactive, or was he removing evidence of our visit? These hints of hostility gutted me. I was devastated by what was transpiring.

The ride home was three hours of misery. Paul maintained his eerie silence, and I was too heartbroken to try to break it. He spoke briefly when we stopped for gas, and once he asked me if the air-conditioning was comfortable. "Is this too much for you?" he queried as he fiddled with dials on the dashboard, and I wanted to shout, "Yes! This craziness is too much for me!" But all I did was utter a quiet no. Beyond that, we did not speak.

As the miles melted under the asphalt, I felt my muscles tighten. To distract myself, I concentrated on the rolling colors of the Appalachian ranges around us. Their rounded layers fused into each other, blending their hues in harmony. The closest mound was a vibrant, clean emerald. It morphed into a spruce green and was followed by a Wedgewood blue that swam into pale periwinkle. The fifth layer was a powdery blue so distant that it vanished into the horizon. I scrutinized these like a scientist measuring tubes of jeweled liquids.

The timelessness of these worn-down mountains was not lost on me. They had preceded me by millions of years. Yet even as I acknowledged their authority, a new cynicism emerged from deep within. I hurled mute diatribes at these ancient hills and trees and rivers: mountains that spewed boulders onto highways, trees that toppled into dormitories, rivers that overflowed and carried destruction for miles.

"You, too, will die," I hissed silently to a mountain that loomed close to my window. "Just you wait! You won't live forever."

The highway soon entered a narrow valley where the mountains ahead formed a perfect V—a spectacular décolletage that splayed sideways into lovely mounds. The road began to follow the bends of a winding river, one that crawled at least a hundred feet below us. It was buried by thick foliage and was much too low for us to see, but the curvature of the road mimicked the river's journey through a deep and tortuous canyon. Sometimes the road curved deeply, making almost a circle before passing off to the next mountain in the chain. "Swing to the left. Now swing to the right. Dosey-do," I chanted to myself. The rhythm of the swaying car made me drowsy.

Somewhere between the gorge and the outskirts of Asheville, I dozed off. When I awoke I recognized the beginnings of our steep climb up Black Mountain. Last time we had driven this stretch, Paul had surprised me with his stunning musical talent. I toyed with the idea of searching again for my classical music station—anything to break this ghastly solitude. But I couldn't do it. In truth, I had no desire to revive our playful haunts. I had no reason to joke, or flirt, or even laugh. My throat flamed with this pain of despair, and I wondered for one dismal moment if I would ever laugh again. The words of that beautiful aria from *South Pacific* filtered through my memory: "Now, now I'm alone, / Still dreaming of paradise, / Still saying that paradise / Once nearly was mine!" Their poignancy today left me frozen in my seat, dry-eyed and stony. I could not wait to get back home.

Back at the house, Paul confused me yet again. He insisted on carrying my suitcase upstairs, and he brought in the carton of leftover food and set it on the kitchen counter.

"This is for you and your family," I protested, embarrassed.

"You're the one who needs it," he said, pulling baggies out of the box and heading for my refrigerator. He loaded up my drawers and shelves before turning to me. For the first time since we'd left the mountain cabin, he looked at me directly.

"Take your meds, Kat. Get some sleep. It's Sunday. No one will bother you." We faced each other through a very long silence, each full of our thoughts. For an instant I thought he was about to caress my face.

"I'll check on you tomorrow."

And with that he turned and disappeared out the kitchen door. I stood motionless as his engine revved and his truck moved down the driveway.

Chapter 45

QUIVERING ON
THE SHORE

I had been ordered by Paul to sleep, and so I did.

I tugged the silk tassels of my roll shades, crawled under my sheets at 8:30 in the morning, and proceeded to sleep as though sedated by surgery. Perhaps the lure was the cool percale of Lennie's tightly fitted sheets. Perhaps it was the eerie silence of the deserted campus, or the cocoon of my spacious bed. Whatever the reason, I slept a deep and dreamless sleep and stirred only when cicadas whirred in the pale of evening. I lay in the stillness, listening to twittering birds in the garden below and the sound of passing cars. As the pain of memory flooded my being, I marveled that life could continue in such ordered fashion while my private world was crushed.

I spent that evening in the privacy of my yard. There was something both soothing and empowering about the outdoors, something clean about the closeness of nature that spoke to my troubled spirit. I walked the entire yard, poking my finger into canna lily cups to pluck out an errant beetle, toeing the purple-splotched trillium, rubbing a waxy white blossom that hung like a corsage from a low magnolia branch. Later I sat on my deck with a plate of nibbles from Paul's leftovers and listened to the stutter of early firecrackers from the distant soccer field. The last time a holiday had brought me such a respite had been Labor Day, the evening after my hitchhiking adventure in the Virginia mountains. What was the name of that doctor who'd rescued me? Archer. Gregory Archer. A general surgeon. I sipped from my wine glass and wondered whether I should seek a second opinion.

In spite of my better intentions, I thought about Paul. I missed him terribly. My whole body ached as shards of memory lodged in my brain. I missed the smell of his breath and the timbre of his deep laugh. I missed the security he provided—the feeling that eased my terror and nudged me from one hour of my life into the next.

I moved from the deck to my kitchen for a wine refill, wiggling out the cork from the huge open bottle. It was left over from an earlier alumni reception at the house; when full it held a liter and a half of red wine and required both hands to lift and pour. A headache was forming at my temples, not unusual with inexpensive wine, so I gulped down two Advil before moving into the sun room with Alex Hailey's *Evening News*. Since I had napped all day, I also had *Megatrends* on hand—certain to induce sleep if needed.

I should not have worried about sleep. The vapors of wine lulled me instantly, and I dozed off on the couch, classical music from WDAV still lilting in the background. But when my body jerked and I opened my eyes, I was wide awake and charged with energy. I moved through the downstairs, collecting half-empty coffee mugs from obscure corners of various rooms. "Lawsy, Miz Katherine, you do like that caffeine," Lennie had declared during my first month in the Chancellor's House. "After you dead and gone, I reckon I still be finding them behind the couch and under the bed." My scattered mugs became a running joke. I had collected an army of them from my travels. "Wrap yourself in tranquility and elegance," read the one I now emptied into the sink. It came from a bed-and-breakfast in western Massachusetts that Alex and I had visited long ago. The land had been deeded to the owner's ancestors by George Washington.

"No telling what Georgie-boy did on this very spot of earth," Alex had joked that first vacation night as we hoisted ourselves from little stools into our high four-poster bed. He said it with just enough hint of naughtiness to implicate himself. That was so like Alex—either irreverent about life or much too serious. But I wondered again about Alex when I considered the option of second opinions. How ironic—how haunting—that one of Chicago's top surgeons was now so distant.

Now the tears started again, hot and fierce. Everything tangible became a source of scorn—even my refrigerator notes. I scanned the priority phone numbers that were printed neatly on a pink sheet and anchored by a purple magnet. The list first named my personal doctors, starting with George Hoffmann. Next came Dr. Joseph, my dentist, who smelled like Dentyne and performed amazing root canals in spite of pudgy fingers.

There was my manicurist, Janice, a faithful friend who had confided last week that her teenage daughter was pregnant. And there were others: J.P., my chain-smoking financial advisor; the church office at Grace Episcopal; Carrington's unlisted home number.

Carrington. Dear God, how that man jabbed my life! And how he would cage me if he knew of my illness! The tears continued to flow wildly. I pounded my fist on the dining room table, sank onto a brocade-covered chair, and once more flailed out at God. "No!" I wailed into the empty room. "No, no, no!"

Suddenly, like a charging cougar, I sprang from the chair, snapping into a person I did not know. I smashed the piano keys into wretched cacophony. I ran into adjoining rooms and pounded the walls, then circled back to the sun room. "No!" I yelled each time. "No! No! No!" I snatched my empty wine glass and hurled it against the television, watching it crack open into jagged pieces and splash purple dots across the screen. I grabbed the pillows from the couch and spun them like erratic Frisbees across the room. I kicked over a basket of magazines and watched them sail across the carpet: *Better Homes and Gardens, Self, Episcopal Glad Tidings,* an Estee Lauder flyer for Private Collection perfume, the Wickfield University alumni magazine, the Hollins College alumni magazine, the Arden College alumni magazine.

"Idiot alumni stuff," I wept, shoving the magazines into a pile with my foot. "Nothing but new babies and obituaries." Babies and obituaries spelled sex and death, the rulers of our lives. I sobbed uncontrollably.

But tears did not relieve my trauma. I lowered my head under the kitchen faucet to cool my swollen eyes. I swallowed ice chips to ease my burning throat and buoyed myself with new wine.

Then I stalked my house. Like a raving ghost, I visited every room, touched every piece of furniture, and surveyed all that was mine. In my bedroom closet were brand-new clothes for my cruise with Alex, still bearing price tags. Lying flat in a guest-room dresser were old family photos, including the one on top showing Grandma Larson unsmiling yet luminous at age twelve.

I dug further through shallow boxes, searching for a favorite of Benny as a baby, and, when I found it, studied it at length by lamplight. How we'd loved that glorious smile that had lifted his chin and crinkled his nose and eyes! For months after Benny's death this photo had stood on our living-room grand piano with other family photos—until it disappeared one day. We figured soon enough that Daddy had taken it. Mother found it by accident as she was gathering the kitchen trash. The glass frame was slippery from carrot peels, but she washed it off and stashed the photo safely in a bedroom drawer. I claimed it after her death.

In the dining room, my tears continued when I saw the gleaming silver service displayed on a side buffet. It was a much-revered gift from the alumni association and belonged to Wickfield, as did the large silver trays that Lennie kept carefully polished. But the beautiful set reminded me of the vast array of wedding silver I had received years ago from relatives and friends. The pattern was Chantilly by Gorham. I knew its graceful curves and floral curlicues from memory. Since moving into the Chancellor's House I had scarcely looked at my private collection, stored in the bottom of the dining-room hutch. I dreaded seeing it now. It was doubtless green with tarnish.

Yet in my current crazed and grieving state of mind, I suddenly felt compelled to find it. If it was tarnished, I had to polish it! I could not let blemished silver be uncovered after my death.

I lowered myself awkwardly, then, onto the floor and tugged open the heavy bottom drawer of the hutch. There it was, right on top—the flat cardboard carton that held my silver serving pieces. I pulled it out, patting down the curled paper label marked SILVER. SPECIAL. I had printed those letters years ago with the swell of a bride, anticipating candlelight dinners when I would preside over my Austrian lace tablecloth and serve my guests with grace.

But as I lifted the box onto the floor beside me, I was dismayed to see ragged corners and a gaping hole along the side. And as I opened the flaps, I sensed evidence of tampering. The newspaper stuffing appeared shredded, and black flecks, like chunky coffee grounds, speckled the folds. Someone had been into my silver! It couldn't be Lennie, I thought, poking through the crushed wrap and pawing through the layers. She had no reason to get into my personal things. Besides, it would be completely out of character for her.

Frowning, I furrowed my way to the bottom of the carton. And there I found what I had been seeking: a dark-purple felt cloth with long pockets to hold forks and knives and spoons. When opened, it extended nearly two feet in length. When full of silver pieces and closed, it was a bulky bundle fastened with a slender gray tie.

But tonight the roll was not tightly wound. It was loosely bound, probably by me in my haste to close it last time. I flicked away the intruding black specks and unrolled the heavy bundle to its full width.

And then my hand jerked back. Lying inside as though peacefully asleep was a small gray mouse. It did not move. It was obviously dead, but it did not appear offensive. Its shiny fur was smooth. I reached out gingerly to touch it.

Then suddenly, without warning, I wept again. My tears flowed for an ordinary gray mouse that had lost its way and died alone in a dining-room hutch. How he had slithered into that dark corner and chosen his soft deathbed was not clear. What I did wonder, however, was how long he had ventured inside that tomb and whether he intentionally sought out those purple felt folds.

I picked him up and held his still form, stroking his back.

By now my thoughts were overflowing. I wrapped the mouse in a paper towel and placed it into a plastic bag. I tied the handles, set the bag inside my kitchen garbage can, and washed my hands. I then made my way to the computer corner near the pantry. I sat staring into space, picturing that mouse exactly as I had first seen it. Like fingers on a Ouija board, mine began to move over the computer keys. I typed out a poem in free verse, spilling my feelings about that mouse onto the screen in one simple draft.

"I found a mouse today inside my baseboard hutch," I began, "quite dead but not in pain, just prone within a rubbing cloth of felt." I continued for a few more lines. I read it all through twice without changing a word—quite unusual considering my compulsion toward revision. I considered a title; words came quickly. I hit Print, waited through the noisy cranking of the machine, carried the final page into the sun room, and settled down to read:

The Mouse Who Shared My Sorrow

I found a mouse today
inside my baseboard hutch,
quite dead but not in pain, just
prone within a rubbing cloth
of felt.

He did not mean to die, I mused, and
ran my finger down his shiny spine.
I rubbed the chewed-out cardboard box
and shone a flashlight
through the flaky holes.
What I wonder now as I add him to the trash and
dip my rag into the tarnish paste,
scouring the green-gray sterling until my knuckles bruise
(a perfect task for my weeping heart),
is whether his casket
brought him
peace.

Peace. I set the page down and closed my eyes. That was what my madness yearned for—a release from agony, a tiny leaven of hope.

But the purge of words did not salve my soul. Peace eluded me yet. The fear of death now consumed me, wracking me with outrageous images. I had in my life committed enormous errors of judgment. I had led my beloved brother into dangers that took his life. I had succumbed to my father's maniacal ravings and crushed his final moments with a pillow. I had committed adultery with a man who was not only married but an employee of my university. I was considered smart and clever and prudent and respectable, but in reality I had broken every moral code I pretended to champion. I was a fraud. I was despicable. I was unworthy of love and trust.

Even worse, I was dying. I was but months, maybe even weeks, away from an eternity in hell. My tormented mind conjured up the blackest, most heinous images of eternal suffering and pain. So dark were my thoughts in that hour of wretchedness that even suicide failed to inspire me. I pictured cool grass and damp earth, thinking their lure might release me. They only left me cold.

Instead of me descending into hell, hell had prowled in search of me. I was already there.

Chapter 46
BY DAWN'S
EARLY LIGHT

In what was left of sleep that night, I dreamed of home.

I lay twisted in my favorite chair on the sun porch, slumped like a laundry bag of limp clothes, and I dreamed of Arden. It was not a nightmare, nothing borne of earlier thoughts of despair. It was sad, almost sweet, and the young girl who was me in the dream wept a little. She swept past familiar houses on Ingleside Drive toward our family church at the bottom of the hill, arms outspread, bouncing gracefully as though lifted by a silent wind. When I awoke in the gray of dawn, stiff and dry-mouthed, my pillowcase was damp.

That dream led to my decision to go to Arden. My plan was suddenly clear. Today—Monday, July 4, 1990—I would drive to the Shenandoah Valley of my childhood. I would meander in and out of my memories of Arden, the ones I knew in heart and mind. I would drive by our gabled Victorian house as I had done at Christmas. I would walk the campus of Arden College where I had played as a girl and now served as a trustee. I would visit my parents' gravesites in the cemetery atop Pinnacle Drive. In short, I would return to my roots to seek peace from my prison of guilt.

My reason was simple: in truth, in spite of my rantings and flailing at God, I still clung to a tiny core of hope. Pastor Krueger would have called it faith. It was the conviction that God was nearby, in spite of this seeming isolation.

Karl Krueger had schooled me well in the catechetical classes of my youth. Ours had been a fidgety all-girl class who met on Saturday mornings throughout seventh and eighth grades. Our thoughts in those days focused on boys and movie stars and new clothes, in that order of priority, yet Pastor Krueger somehow managed to connect our rambling minds to Protestant theology. He led us systematically through the Ten Commandments, Scripture, the creeds, and church doctrine. By the time we were confirmed on a Pentecost Sunday, radiant in white robes and red carnations and our first-ever high heels with nylons, we were convinced that God's grace was an open and free promise to all—saints and sinners alike. It was a gift we would cling to for life. All we needed to do was accept it.

I was also aware that Karl Krueger had returned to Arden in recent years—retired, to be sure, yet teaching religion part time at the college. I had seen him occasionally on my trustee trips. Convinced now that I needed a confidant—someone other than Paul—I decided to seek him out. Karl had grieved with us over Benny's death and prayed by his side when Daddy was dying. He had married Tim and me in what folks said was the prettiest wedding of the summer of '62. He was like family. Maybe, just maybe, he could pull me from this nightmare.

It was a good plan, I decided, stepping into a sleeveless navy shirtwaist after showering. I normally would have dressed casually for a holiday, but today I felt like a woman preparing for church. I dabbed witch hazel on my red eyelids and Vaseline on my swollen mouth and packed lightly for one overnight. I could return tomorrow or Wednesday and scarcely be missed. I vowed to face the rest of the week, and all the weeks thereafter, with courage and self-discipline.

In that moment I heard the sound of a truck pulling into the driveway. I knew even before peering from my upstairs window that Paul was here. No one else would show up at the Chancellor's House on a holiday at this early hour. In spite of Paul's parting words early yesterday, I had not expected to see him today. Nor did I want to. He had humiliated me with his anger and silence, and in my present fragility I could bear no further censure.

Besides, I knew I looked grotesque.

Sullenly, I answered Paul's knock at the kitchen door. As it turned out, words were not needed. My blotched, distorted face told all. I lifted my chin in defiance and glowered. Paul stared back in disbelief as if I had been sucker-punched in a fight.

"Kat." He spoke it as a whisper. He reached out with one hand and caressed my left cheek with his thumb. He brushed a lock of hair from my bangs.

"Dear God, Kat. You should have called me." He stood there in my kitchen where we had faced each other many times before, stroking my hair lightly as though fearful of further damage. I met his eyes head-on.

"Why? You wouldn't talk to me, remember? Would you have called the authorities? Will you now? Will you have me arrested?" My mocking voice spat out the words. "You were so angry with me you scarcely spoke a word. Am I that loathsome? Come on, admit it, Paul, you made love to a murderess! Tell *that* to your law-school class!"

I could not believe my vitriolic tone. Was this really me, hurling hurtful epithets at my Paul? I sank into a chair at the breakfast table and covered my face with my hands.

"Dear God, Kat. Is that what you think?" Paul scraped out a chair beside me, leaned forward, and grabbed my hands away from my face. "Did you really think I condemned you? Kat, I am so sorry." Again, he reached out to my cheek with his thumb.

"You were upset. You kicked things. You gave me the silent treatment."

"It's not you I'm upset with! Don't you see?"

I did not see.

"It's your *father*, Kat. Katherine, hear me on this! You have revered that man all your life. In spite of his idiosyncrasies and craziness when you were young, you idolized him. Even now, after all he did to you and your family, you refuse to see him for the—the—selfish lout he was!"

Paul was agitated now, pleading with me. I was more confused than ever. Selfish? Lout? *Daddy?*

"He loved us, Paul. He adored us! We were his girls! We were his life!"

"Katherine." Paul said my name as a statement, a command. I tried to concentrate on what he was saying.

"Five girls? And a wife? All using one bathroom while he hoarded the other? You were assigned to that bathroom. Ordered. Mandated. Think about it. Everything in life centered on him. He was the master, the Supreme Justice, the ruthless controller of your home in every way. And probably with his staff. Not to mention the students."

"Not really, Paul," I began, remembering how he'd singled me out in so many little ways. Then I stopped. Singled me out? Again I concentrated on Paul's words.

"And what he asked you to do in the end was unconscionable. When you told me that story about the pillow, I lost it, Kat. I was so angry at him—" His face grew red at the memory.

"I thought you were angry at *me*. Your silence in the car was unbearable. He was desperate, Paul. He was crazy with pain! He couldn't help asking me to help."

"Of course he could help it!" Paul thundered back. "He knew exactly what he was doing! He manipulated you, Kat! He had favored you for years and used your loyalty to get his way with the others. He knew he could count on you at the end. And in the process he sentenced you to years of guilt and fear. All those years of suffering ..." His voice trailed off, and I remained frozen, my thoughts whirling.

"I thought my story appalled you."

"It's a tragic story, Kat. It's not pretty. We can spend time wishing it had not happened, but it did. Your father went berserk. He created frenzy. You were an unwilling partner. He was at the point of death when this happened, and he subsequently died. There's no way to determine how he died or in what precise moment. I don't know exactly, nor do you. His death was legally closed long ago, Kat. Let it rest. Forgive yourself for the part you played, and move on."

But can God forgive me? I thought to myself.

"I'm truly sorry I confused you, Katherine. I was thinking too hard, I guess—envisioning what you had been through all this time." Paul leaned forward and kissed the backs of my hands, then sighed heavily and dropped them. He slumped back in his chair and studied my face, realizing for the first time, I think, exactly how ghastly had been my past day and night.

So Daddy—my hero since childhood, the one I had loyally defended when my sisters did not—had betrayed me all along. While I had seen him as a lovable and doting father who turned crazy with pain, others had seen him as selfish and conniving. He had controlled me to the point where I believed my final act was dutiful. Loving, even.

I felt physically ill as I churned with these discoveries. Little things that had bothered me in the past began to fit now: the way Mother kept peace in the family by accepting Daddy's demands, the way my sisters often quarreled with him, the way certain townspeople loathed the man. What amazed me most was that I, an educator, had seen neither his bad behaviors nor my passive responses for what they were. Daddy had been a *benevolent dictator*. I knew the term well. I had even been to professional conferences where the description was widely discussed as a leadership style to avoid. Stories were rampant about universities that had lost momentum and faculties who'd lost morale because their presidents were bent by unbridled arrogance in the name of "benevolence." How could I have been so blind? How could I analyze an abhorrent behavior on a professional level but be blind to it in my personal life?

"Paul, I'm going home."

"Home?" Paul's face drained white. "What do you mean?"

"I'm going home to Arden."

"You're *resigning*?" Paul's voice held a note of terror.

"No. Just for today. I'll probably be back tomorrow." I reached out and laid my hand on his. The simple touch steadied me instantly.

"Why? Why Arden?"

"I hope to talk to someone there. Someone who knew my family, knows my history."

"Tim?"

"No, no, not Tim. Tim lives in Atlanta, remember?" I paused, choosing my words. Paul had not grown up in the church as I had.

"He's a retired professor at Arden. For years he was minister of the church where I grew up. And I want to see old landmarks. And my parents' graves." I didn't mention that I hoped to see my own burial plot, to confess my dark deeds to Karl, to seek forgiveness for all I had done that was displeasing to God. I couldn't talk about these things with Paul. Not yet. My emotions were much too raw.

"I'll drive you."

"No. I need to go alone. While I still can." I dropped his hand. "Thanks, but think of this as a pilgrimage. I need to figure out how to mesh my illness with my job. If what Wayne Witherspoon told us is correct, I must make the most of each day. I have a responsibility to many people, Paul. There are students and faculty and trustees. And personal friends. There's the media to deal with. I don't know how sick I'm going to become, nor how fast. For now, at least, I don't want any of them to know the depths of this illness. I will need every ounce of strength to fight it and do my job. I can't waste time traveling to new doctors or reading up on colon cancer or weeping with friends. If this were early cancer, then yes, but apparently we're well beyond that stage. It's important to keep this all a secret for now. I'm adamant about that, Paul, and I'm trusting you to keep your silence."

"Of course." Paul's eyes misted.

There was more to talk about, now that I understood Paul's earlier anger. In truth, however, I scarcely knew where to begin.

"Paul," I said hesitantly. "About—well, about June—" I stopped.

"Let's not go there," he interrupted. "Concentrate now on your trip to Arden. Stay focused. We'll talk about the other when you get back."

The "other." We both knew what that meant. But Paul was right. Right now I had to sort through my older guilts. My newer ones would have to wait.

I slipped onto his lap. I pulled his head to my chest and buried my face in his hair. As usual, we held that embrace a long time without moving.

Chapter 47
TO ARDEN

Energized by my reconciliation with Paul, I loaded my car and turned its nose toward Arden. I sped up the interstate toward Virginia with no thought for caution. Had my mind been calmer, I might have remembered my Labor Day debacle with an empty gas tank and proceeded with prudence. Today, however, I left caution to the winds, my wheels racing as fast as my thoughts.

"Don't panic!" I whispered to myself at the outset of the trip. For someone who had received a virtual death sentence three days earlier, this was nearly impossible to do. My head ached horribly, from left eyebrow to right frontal lobe. I fought for reason. After two explosive and draining nights, I found a new sense of control behind the wheel.

To keep focused, I centered on my family. They would be devastated by my illness. I pictured their desperate conversations, a dozen phone calls at the onset. "Not Kat," Emily would sob to Jane. "I was supposed to be first, remember?" Jane would call Marianna from the West Coast and despair that her advanced pregnancy made it hard to travel, and Marianna would call Sarah and bewail the fact that Kat was the family's lifeline. It was painfully ironic. Today I was flayed and raw, yet my sisters saw me as an anchor.

The more I thought about my family, the more convinced I became that telling them now was not a good idea. Marianna and Emily, for starters, would be at my side in an instant. Too much family too fast might trigger attention. I must delay telling them as long as possible, I decided. Much would depend on how well I could tolerate the progression of the disease. Some patients were quickly crippled by cancer, while others kept a surprisingly ordinary lifestyle. We had had such a neighbor in Arden years ago—an attractive elderly lady across the street who had quietly died from cancer one day after she'd raked her yard and piled the leaves onto the front curb. Newcomb? Yes, Elsie Newcomb, the widow whose name we'd chuckled over because she'd worn an assortment of lovely combs to sweep back her snow-white hair. On the day she died, I had watched her walk serenely down her driveway to get her morning paper and settle in her porch rocker to read it. She'd died during her afternoon nap. "She was riddled with tumors," her daughter told us after the funeral, describing the pain pills Elsie had taken for months. Our family had had no inkling that she had cancer.

Then there was Tim. I pulled out to pass a poky eighteen-wheeler, wondering briefly why it was hauling cargo on a holiday, and then asked myself why my thoughts were suddenly fixated on Tim. After all, he was no longer family, although he would be if we had shared biological children. It was probably because Paul had brought up his name, I reasoned, angling back into the right-hand lane. A new sadness crushed me as I thought of the lost years with Tim. Our careers had taken off in different directions, and we had both succeeded in our respective fields, but might we still be together had we given marriage a higher priority? And children. I remembered my old arguments against having children and wondered whether having children in the mix today would make my illness easier or harder.

Where will I be at the very end, I anguished, mopping tears so I could see the windshield. Would I die in the daytime? At night? Would it be raining? Who would be caring for me? Lennie? My sisters? A nurse? Certainly not Paul, although he was the one I craved the most.

I wondered about my old friends. Would I ever see them again, or did it really matter? Sometimes when visiting Sarah in Arden I'd chanced upon Sally Gordon, who had married a local businessman and produced a litter of children. My Hollins friends had disappeared through the years, but I'd kept up sporadically with my Carolina sorority sisters. I remembered how we had envisioned ourselves at our fiftieth college reunion, visiting our favorite haunts in Chapel Hill, checking out the Rathskeller and Gimghoul Castle and encircling the Old Well for a class photo. When would that be? 2012? It was hard to imagine such a year, even such a century. But time and lives would continue after I died; *I* simply wouldn't be there to participate.

I sped on.

Tim's face was continuing to haunt me. *He will need to be told*, I thought. I would want to be told if he were ill, and I would want Rosa, his wife, to give me the courtesy of speaking to him in private before his death. Actually, there was much I would like to say to him, but not within the context of my pending death. I remembered when we'd celebrated his early promotion to weekend anchor when he was scarcely thirty. Like excited children at Christmas, we'd splurged by reserving a weekend package deal at a luxury resort hotel. I'd had my first-ever facial in a candlelit room that smelled like oranges, and Tim had played golf in a foursome that included someone famous at the time from the PGA tour. Afterward, we'd sat at a wrought-iron table on one of the hotel's countless balconies and eaten smoked cheese on heart-shaped Melba toast. Our cold white wine had been as smooth as spun glass.

But our rising prosperity had not equated with a happier marriage. What Tim wanted—those silky print shirts of the seventies that men wore as if they were fashion models, the blown-dry hair with sideburns, the sporty BMW—had clashed coldly with my contemplative world of academia. Our arguments increased, and my discontent grew.

"I never did like your husband," my good friend Sandra told me soon after Tim and I had divorced. Sandy and I had been Kappa Deltas at Carolina and had rediscovered each other as neighbors after we had married.

"Why ever not?" I asked, astounded. Everyone liked Tim. He had enjoyed enormous popularity early in his career, and after those initial ratings had soared, he'd managed to compete evenly with rival newsmen from other channels.

Sandy looked down. "It's a strange story," she said, laughing nervously.

"That's okay," I said calmly. "Let's hear it." I had no idea where this conversation was going.

"Well, Ray and I were eating out one night at Hallston's Grille, and we saw Tim there. He came in, alone, about seven, obviously after he had finished the evening news."

I nodded. Nothing unusual here. The national news followed local news at 6:30, so the evening anchor team was free to leave for dinner—and yes, Tim often ventured into downtown restaurants alone. We lived too far away for him to go home for dinner, at least on a regular basis, since he needed to prepare again for the eleven o'clock news.

"The waiter seated him on that tiered level in a prominent seat near the railing. Ray and I were on the floor, not far away. Ray's back was to Tim, but Tim and I were in direct eye contact. I waved once he had settled in, but he never waved back or even seemed to acknowledge us."

That part did seem strange. Tim and I had socialized numerous times with Sandy and Ray.

"At least, not until he had ordered. Then he seemed to relax, and I caught him smiling at me. So I nodded and smiled back." Sandy squirmed.

"Go on."

"Well, then I looked down and kept eating, and when I looked back up at Tim, he was still smiling. Only—it seemed now to be more than smiling. He was actually sort of—*twinkling*."

"Twinkling?"

"You know—winking and nodding, then looking away."

"That doesn't sound like Tim."

"I thought the same thing, but there he was, looking straight at me and sort of preening. There was no doubt that he was coming on to me, Kat. It was distracting, to say the least."

"Did you tell Ray? Did he whirl around and catch him at it?"

"No. The whole thing rattled me, and I didn't say anything. I started ignoring Tim, but he still kept smiling at me, even after his food came."

"Did you and Ray stop and speak as you left?"

"No, because Tim ate fast and left ahead of us. And no, he didn't detour over to our table. He just left, sort of in a hurry."

I let out my breath with a rush, not aware until then that I had been holding it in.

"So," I said in summary, "while we were married, my husband flirted brazenly with one of my best friends." The story stabbed me, even though Tim and I were divorced by the time I heard it. Fidelity had never been a question mark between us. *Not all divorces are caused by affairs!* I sometimes wanted to scream to anyone who was listening.

"I can't blame you for being offended," I added. "Did you ever confront him?"

"Well, here's the best part. Ray and I got up to leave, and Ray came around to help with my jacket, which was on the back of my seat. So now I was turned in the same direction Tim had been facing. And lining the entire back wall behind me were mirror tiles. Mirrors, Kat! The whole wall was one gigantic mirror! Tim had not been smiling at me at all! He probably didn't even recognize me because he was too busy smiling at himself! And practicing camera poses, from what I could tell. Isn't that a hoot!"

I burst out laughing, and Sandy smiled in relief.

"Some women have to worry about other women," I said wryly. "But not me. Me, I had a husband who was in love with himself."

How different my life might have been had I met Paul before Tim. I held that thought for a moment as the asphalt under my wheels began to point up a steep grade. There was something seductive in imagining a hungry, eager Katherine with a twenty-something Paul Stafford. And yet—well, I was wise enough to dismiss such musings. Paul and I might have had little cerebral attraction at twenty-two and twenty-four. I did not have time to fantasize about the what-ifs.

My thoughts strayed to Susan and Jake, and I was startled at my compassion for both. Was their affair as passionate as mine? Did they weep together when Susan let Jake go? I really should call Susan, I thought suddenly. I had not talked to her since Jake and Alma Earle had left Hurley in mid-June.

When I spotted the exit for Pinckney ahead, I realized I had been driving hard without a break. I needed coffee and space to stretch my legs. "Dr. Gregory Archer, Surgeon. 1201 Vine Avenue," I chanted aloud as I steered off the highway. I remembered once again the words from that business card, words that had stuck like flypaper through these months. I pulled into the same gas station where Dr. Archer and I had picked up gas for my impotent car months ago. I turned on the pump and listened to the throb of the flowing gasoline as it poured into my tank. I briefly pictured my body hooked to a machine that pumped high octane into my veins. For one daunting moment I wondered if I had erred in refusing chemo. Would it knock out the pinging in my body's engine?

"Second opinions don't hurt," I thought as I waited for the receipt to slide from its slot. Dr. Archer could check my records, look at test results, consult with my doctors—even offer a new opinion. I had liked him that day ten months ago and trusted him quickly. He had stuck by me through every minute of my little crisis, filling my tank with that smelly metal can and waving me goodbye when I pulled back into traffic. We had connected well. He was yet another I must contact soon.

"Katherine, you are not going to die," I vowed to myself as I returned now to the highway with a cardboard cup of steaming brew. The fresh coffee boosted my spirits, and I actually laughed aloud as I sailed past the now-infamous weed patch where my Ford and I had huddled on Labor Day.

My mood lifted even more when I finally drove down the big hill from the Arden exit into my old hometown. The streets were bright with the holiday. The annual parade had apparently just ended, because families were jaywalking across Main Street, headed to their cars with flag-bearing tots in tow. I crept behind a long float decked out in patriotic streamers. As a ten-year-old, I had ridden on top of a cherry-red fire truck in this same parade, waving at the crowds like a homecoming queen. I was the elementary school winner of a city-wide essay contest about fire prevention. The grand prize—mine alone—was the fire truck ride on the Fourth of July.

Finally I broke out of line at the corner where St. John's stood and made a hard right, charging up the steep incline of Ingleside Drive. I passed my old house with scarcely a glance and pushed on for several blocks, winding through residential streets of increasingly lovely homes whose rooftops stretched upward from their forested lots. At the highest peak in all of Arden, I reached my destination: Arden Memorial Gardens. The familiar lettering, now faded, arched between two aging wrought-iron pillars that marked the cemetery's entrance.

I steered my car onto the narrow paved road of the grounds, passing a long column of Leyland cypress trees and a mammoth hedge of *Ligustrum* before curving around a small pond with a spewing fountain. A right turn, then a quick left, and I was there. The Embright family plot unfurled before me like a cherished heirloom quilt. I stepped from the car, absorbing the splendid spread of silent headstones, and walked through cushioned grass toward the familiar maple tree ahead. Below lay Grandpa and Grandma Larson, side by side as in life, flanked by a single stone with words they had written together while still alive. Next were the mounds of my father, Harold Ralph Embright, and my mother, Adelaide Larson Embright. Between them lay Benny, whose simple engraving read *Benjamin Olof Embright, 1950–1953. He pierced our hearts like a shooting star.*

I turned to the smooth shawl of grass next to Mother. It lay as silent as a garden plot begging for seeds. This space was my own burial plot, purchased years ago following my divorce from Tim. It had cost a thousand dollars, a significant sum for me at the time, and I had been told that if I made different burial plans in the future, the money would not be refunded and the plot would remain empty. I had viewed this spot many times with little emotion, but today the grass seemed to quiver under the high July sun.

I stared fiercely at our family stones for several moments before taking in the larger scene around me. The hillside dropped sharply on the north side, rolling below to a pasture occupied by a herd of grazing Black Angus. In the distance was the interstate on which I had just driven, now dotted with toy cars. Beyond, the horizon filled with pillowed blue mountains that hedged the Shenandoah Valley.

Home. This very spot would be my earthly home much too soon. I looked above to the clouds dotting the afternoon sky and tried to picture heaven. "God, I'm not ready to leave this beautiful earth," I whispered to the breeze fanning the hilltop. "I can't possibly leave Paul, whom I dearly love, even though he's not mine to love. Besides, you might not want me the way I'm feeling now. I'm much too angry."

Another car drove slowly into view, its windows rolled down and a Sousa march playing on the radio. My words suddenly faltered.

"Help me, Lord, to get ready."

With that, I returned to my car and drove away. I did not look back.

Chapter 48

FORGIVEN

When I first spotted her, Eva Krueger was standing in her front yard, peering up into the branches of a dogwood tree. The squat brick house behind her was plain, functional, and utterly inviting. I lowered my window as I pulled up to the curb and turned off the ignition. Eva glanced at me curiously as I emerged.

"Hello!" I called out. She apparently did not recognize me, although I had seen her in Arden only months before. I pulled off my sunglasses.

"Katherine!" Her astonishment made me smile. "Whatever brings you here today!"

"You, of course," I said warmly, walking up the grassy lawn and knocking her straw hat askew with my bear hug. "How are you, dear lady? And what's in the tree?"

"A male cardinal, singing his head off. There, do you hear him? He's been singing nonstop for twenty minutes."

I did indeed hear him: *Purdy-purdy-purdy, what-cheer, what-cheer, cheer-cheer-cheer.* His whistle was clear, and his vibrant scarlet plumage splashed through the low green branches.

"He certainly sounds happy."

"It's a song of joy to his mate," she said. "Do come in! I was just about to take some lemonade to Karl out back. He'll be absolutely delighted to see you."

"I can't stay," I said hastily. "I just drove in off the highway. Passing through." I paused a second longer to listen to the cardinal's sweet carol, turning my head toward the tree before following Eva. *What-cheer, what-cheer, cheer-cheer-cheer …*

An hour later, my plans had changed significantly. I was not only joining the Kruegers for hamburgers on the backyard grill but also for breakfast the next morning. My small suitcase had been carried into the house and parked next to the headboard of their Duncan Phyfe guest bed. As usual, the Kruegers did not ask many questions. When they realized I was traveling alone with a suitcase in my trunk, they extended the invitation without a blink of the eye.

I was surprised at how comfortable I felt with these two elderly people who had known me for—how long? Forty years, at least. I settled into the back porch chaise longue with the cold lemonade and wished I could stay there, without moving, for the next hundred. I watched Karl as he sat in his weathered rocking chair, the sun glinting through the screen onto his shiny bald head. His hiked-up Bermuda shorts exposed bony knees and long white socks. He seemed almost tiny now, having grown more stooped each year while Eva became stouter and wider-hipped. Karl made the usual small talk while Eva busied herself with strawberries in the kitchen. As he waxed poetic over his Beefeater tomatoes and Arden's improved SAT scores, I listened politely, wondering how much to tell him. I desperately needed him to hear me without judging—to sympathize, embrace, advise me, love me.

When there was a pause, I plunged. "I'm sick, Karl."

My voice cracked. I did not look at Karl—only at the skids of his rocking chair, which came to a dead halt before starting again, slowly.

My words followed quickly then: the diagnosis, the timeline, my refusal of chemo, my need for secrecy. When Karl finally spoke, his voice was full of tenderness beyond imagination.

"This is hard, Katherine. This hurts me greatly. You are a very courageous woman." He spoke all the right words—platitudes, mainly, the kind the skeptics would call trite but which he surely thought would comfort me.

They didn't.

"Don't make me a saint, Karl." My warning sounded almost angry. "You don't know what all I've done." He raised his eyebrows. And I tumbled on, grieving once more over my role in Benny's accident, which he remembered well, and then the huge issue of Daddy's death. My voice was flat, almost cold, when I described the pillow scene—a reaction that surprised me. I had shown emotion when describing it to Paul.

Karl was silent for several minutes after I ended my jarring stories. When he finally spoke, he looked far out into the yard past the shapely catalpa tree.

"Your father's death—that's a pretty heavy load, Katherine. And you've been carrying it alone all these years?" He looked at me now. He sat with his thumbs on his chin, his hands folded under as if in prayer. But from this point forward, his eyes never left mine.

"Completely. And I'm terrified, Karl. I thought I was doing the right thing for Daddy, but now I'm totally confused. Did I help him but damn myself? He was probably hours from death, and I could have walked away and shut the door, but I could not have lived with myself if I had left him in pain one more minute. Oh, Karl, his eyes!" I visibly shrank from the terror of the memory.

"Do you remember back when your Grandma Larson died? You had the same mop of curls then that you have now." Karl's face softened. "Your mother wanted me to talk to you girls about death, and I told you that your grandmother was gone but that God was bigger than death. And that he promised the day would come when we would all be together again."

"I remember." Karl had been an enormous influence on my young life, a sterling symbol in his long-sleeved white surplice and embroidered stoles that changed colors with the church seasons. Did I dare tell him about Paul? Did I dare *not*? I feared his disapproval immensely. If he censured me, I might just walk out of the house on the spot and drive back to Hurley.

"But—I am no longer a child."

"Oh?" He was still watching me, waiting.

I pressed the cold glass against my cheek. "But, well, the story gets even more complex, Karl." There. I could not back out now. I laughed roughly, too loudly. Then the tears began to stream, and I let them course, tasting their saltiness as they pooled around my mouth. I was about to bare my innermost soul to this dear man. I would somehow stumble through a confession of all that seemed to doom me and try not to watch his face when he perceived the depths of my sins.

But I had underestimated Karl Krueger. "There's a man?" he asked.

Just like that. *How could he possibly know?* I nodded, miserable.

"Tell me about him."

I smiled through the tears. This part would be easy. I began with the empty gas tank last September and how Paul had broken down my hostility during our first road trip. How we were drawn together the night of the hurricane. The first surgery. My breakup with Alex. The medical forays to

Charlotte. Paul's kindness. His wisdom. His strength. His sense of humor. I laughed as I talked. I leaned into my story, talking with my hands. Without a doubt, joy suffused my face.

"He's been good to me. He's been good *for* me."

"Is your pain, then, that he is married?"

There! He said it. He said it all, and his face was still kind.

"Yes."

Now I was watching *him*. He scratched his nose. And he told a brief story about how guilt-ridden he had become, years ago, when a parishioner had committed suicide. "It happened on my watch," he said, "and I missed the signs completely."

He's nervous, I thought, disappointed. *He's digressing.*

"But that didn't make you responsible, Karl."

"Exactly. But I shouldered that guilt for years until I was able to forgive myself."

Now I could see where this was going.

"But in my case, I share the responsibility—for Daddy's death, for my behavior choice with Paul."

He nodded. "The wife, then—is she aware of your relationship with Paul?"

"Oh, God, no. And she never will be. I will literally take that secret to my grave." *I sound like Susan*, I suddenly thought in surprise. She had said something similar when discussing her secret life with Jake.

Karl whistled softly through pursed his lips and made a steeple with his index fingers—the same gesture Daddy had taught us girls when we were little: "Here is the church, and here is the steeple; open the doors, and see all the people." When he opened his interlocked palms, he would wiggle his "people" and make us giggle. Now the image deepened my sadness.

"You're in love with Paul?"

The back screen door banged. I pondered that question as I gazed out into the Krueger's fenced-in yard, watching Eva as she carried an aluminum pan to a corner compost pile while their ginger-coated retriever frisked about her feet. Paul and I had not confessed love to each other. We had danced around our relationship for six months, watching and fantasizing and daring each other in tiny steps. I had never denied him anything. In fact, although I had prided myself on keeping him at bay, I had probably encouraged him in countless little ways.

Then I had a vision of me entangled amid the sheets with him, drenched and shiny-skinned and sated. The simple memory made my heart hammer. I had never felt such glorious exhilaration with Alex, not even in the early flush of our relationship. With Tim I had experienced the usual joys of first-time love, but with Paul I had risen to the ecstasy of poets. Our closeness was born of things well beyond the physical. I trusted him. Explicitly. I cared for him with a depth that astonished me.

"Yes," I said firmly. "I love him very much."

Karl said nothing. We sat in silence, watching Eva return to the back stoop with her empty pan, squinting against the midafternoon sun.

"So what do you plan to do next?"

"I thought you would tell *me*. I need some relief from this nightmare."

Karl cleared his throat. "Well, let's set your illness aside for the moment."

I nodded.

"Your so-called 'nightmare' is about your fears. All self-imposed, by the way, which means you can overrule them. Benny's accident, for example. Can you accept that it was indeed an accident, a freak one, a tragic one, a terrible loss to your family, but *not* intentionally caused by you?"

I drew in a deep breath and let it slide out slowly. "Yes, I think so."

"Good. Let it go, Katherine. Forgive yourself completely. Let it rest."

I nodded again. We sat in silence for several moments, watching the retriever chase a gray squirrel up the catalpa tree.

"Now. About your father's death. The coroner ruled death by natural causes, right?"

"Right."

"What you described sounds more like a suicide attempt driven by his unbearable pain. He manipulated you into helping him. In 1960 the idea of assisted suicide was rarely discussed—unlike today, of course. I assume you've kept up with the growing awareness of euthanasia and all the controversy surrounding it."

"Yes."

"At the same time, Katherine, I am not at all convinced that you were responsible for your father's death. Your father was highly agitated. He tussled with you over the pillow in an extreme state of distress. It's very possible his heart simply gave out in those moments, especially considering his state of frailty."

"But I pushed down on the pillow for a few seconds, Karl. That was intentional."

"Katherine, you did not enter that bedroom with the intention of ending your father's life. You were clearly coerced. I'm sorry you've felt it necessary to keep this a secret for so long. Still, your story will be kept in strictest confidence by me. The clergy-penitent privilege is long-standing. Even if I didn't hold clergy confidentiality, there would be no point in resurrecting a case that has been closed for thirty-some years, especially considering your illness. You've made private confession to God of your remorse, your confusion, through the years?"

"Thousands of times."

"Well, then. He has heard you each time and loved you each time. Can you believe me when I say he has forgiven you thousands of times in return? Let this one go, too, Katherine."

I closed my eyes and leaned back against the cushioned chaise longue, feeling relief squeeze from me like water from a sponge. When I opened my eyes a minute later, Karl was raising his index finger toward the kitchen door. I knew Eva was hovering outside, knowing better than to interrupt but seeking a sense of how much longer we would be talking. *She's a trouper*, I thought drowsily to myself. *A good wife. A perfect wife.* I suddenly blanched. That was how Paul described June. June was a perfect wife, too. *June, Paul.* I braced myself.

"Your friend Paul: Is he a man of faith?"

"No, not really. His wife and the two children are lovely, polite, smart, but I gather there's no strong religious affiliation. No reason, other than family routine and schedules, I guess. The children sometimes attend a local church with friends, not their parents. Paul has mentioned he is not a praying man."

Karl nodded. "But you are a praying woman."

"Absolutely. And even more so since I met Paul and began to sense our attraction."

"So. Would you say, then, that your friendship with Paul has helped deepen your relationship with God?"

The words stunned me. Of course. *Of course!* I had been so wrapped in my guilt over Paul—self-imposed guilt, as Karl called it—that I had failed to see how God fit into the picture. Suddenly it was clear: God, in his infinite wisdom, had intervened in my life, and Paul's, and connected our lives at this crucial time. Even this spontaneous hour of confession was part of the intervention. I had not planned my visit to the Krueger home until this morning. Like God's grace, it had come to me, freely.

Part of me wanted to shout, "Yes, yes, a thousand times yes! Paul is part of my journey of faith!" Instead, I listened as in a trance to Karl's quiet reflections. He reminded me that there is no coincidence with God, that his wisdom and timing are impeccable. "It seems clear that Paul is meant to be part of your life right now, and you a part of his," he said. I let those words soak in while the soothing voice flowed on.

Then he uttered a sentence that leapt out at me: "Of course, his wife and children are a major commitment to him, so you and Paul will need to define clearly to each other the specific roles that are right for you—or not—from this point forward."

I read him perfectly. That second night in the mountains had brought us bliss, but I had shared a part of Paul that belonged exclusively to June. I remembered words I had uttered in the depth of our sleepless first night— that even if I were not dying, our relationship would eventually have to end, and that the schism would surely hurt like death.

But—and this was the new wisdom emerging now from Karl—because I *was* dying, Paul and I had the unique ability to move beyond our one night of passion toward a different kind of togetherness: a coupling of even greater depth and dimension as we confronted my mortality.

I wish I could tell you my hour of confession ended with some sort of dramatic flair, but nothing was farther from the truth. There was no heraldic moment when I knelt with humbled head and felt Karl's touch, or heard him intone, "Rise, Katherine, your sins are forgiven." In fact, he didn't even use the word *sin*. He used, instead, the word *love*, speaking several times of God's overwhelming tenderness for both Paul and me. At one point he reminded me there is no marriage in heaven like that known on earth.

"The joys of heaven far exceed what we dare dream about," he said. "In heaven we are reunited with all believers, all on an equal basis and far beyond the divisions that cause human jealousies and miseries." Karl gazed far out into the backyard as he spoke, his eyes seeming to focus on a distant point. "Eva and I both believe this with all our hearts, and because we do, neither of us has any fear of death."

There's room for all of us in heaven, I thought in some wonder: Paul and June and me. It was not really a new discovery—simply a new perspective.

"Katherine," Karl said, shifting the subject, "I'm not sure I agree with your distrust of chemotherapy. I will pray for God's healing touch to bring you to full recovery, but if he directs you in a different course, I will pray for you to accept his will with grace. Either way, we know he will embrace you fully and walk with you through every bend of the road."

Karl had used a worn-out metaphor—"through every bend of the road." I might have rendered a C grade to an English student for such triteness. Still, his words brought a semblance of comfort. In recent months, Paul and I had literally driven many bends of the road.

"Life will become difficult in the months ahead. This disease may progress aggressively. I've seen it happen too many times. Eventually you may want to give up your secrecy and let family and friends grieve with you. You will feel great relief when you can remove your mask, no matter how much comfort you think this façade will bring you. And you will be closest to God when you allow him to lead the way."

I squirmed. This man could truly see into my heart. He was telling the superorganized Katherine Embright to let go of the gavel and hand it over to God. The Katherine who loved to lead and control would need to become an obedient servant. Accepting that role might well become my hardest hurdle.

"One more thing, Katherine. You own a great deal of power, even in dying. You can show the rest of us how to die with grace. Your illness will make you look at others with new eyes of compassion and may lead you to little acts of kindness—not grand acts that crash and burn but small words and gestures that will resonate long after you are gone. You'll see. Just stay focused on your faith. Your illness will challenge it over and over again. When you are at your lowest with pain and fatigue, you may want to fight God, curse him, and despair until the thought of death is almost welcome. I urge you to continue to believe in God's grander plan for you, even when it's beyond your current comprehension. This will be hard, but Eva and I will be praying for you daily to trust in God and remain strong."

Before I left early the next morning, overcome with final words from Karl and tight hugs from a teary Eva, Karl gave me yet another gift: an offer to conduct my funeral at the Embright family church in Arden. With my burial plot only minutes away from St. John's where I had been raised, it all made perfect sense. I had shuddered earlier at the image of a funeral, but now I envisioned a triumphant service of hope. Wickfield could give me a memorial service, one which colleagues and legislators—even political enemies—could attend. But a worship service in Arden— my childhood home, the place where my cycle of life began—would make my circle whole. I accepted on the spot.

"Remember, life is but a foretaste of the feast to come," Karl reminded me.

As I pulled away, sunshine was flooding the yard, and every bird in the neighborhood seemed to be welcoming the new day. I lowered my window to wave goodbye and heard, rising through these anthems, the clear love song of yesterday's cardinal. *What cheer,* he sang. *Cheer, cheer, cheer, cheer . . .*

I turned my car toward Wickfield. I could not wait to see Paul again, and I knew exactly what I needed to tell him.

Chapter 48
A NEW LIGHT

"What do you mean, we can't?"

Paul turned sharply on the sofa in my living room to face me in disbelief. I had not called him to meet me at my house. He had simply shown up soon after I had opened the garage to tuck in the Victoria, a bit dusty after her morning ride from Virginia.

Now he was scowling with the square-jawed face I had come to love. I reached for his hands and folded them in mine.

"Let's be sensible about this, Paul. Do we really think we're going to sneak away to make love during every available break? Is that my future—stolen moments unto death? Are we to be like those students you caught in the rafters of the dome?" I almost mentioned Susan and Jake in their fourth-floor den but caught myself in the nick of time. Theirs was one more secret I would carry to my grave.

Paul merely looked down at our pressed hands.

"This is about so much more than a ticking clock, Paul. This is about decisions, the hardest kind. Of all the choices I've had to make since coming to Wickfield, this one wracks my heart the most. But I need every ounce of strength to fight this disease, to think clearly, to manage my job. I don't need the stress of broken rules. It's enough just trying to keep my balance when I'm doing everything right." I dropped Paul's hands and stood up.

"But the most important part is that I've been given a new vision of where I'm going. In whatever time remains for me, I want to be the very best chancellor and colleague and sister and aunt and friend that I can be. I want that time to count. I'm creating my legacy, Paul. I'm making history for Wickfield, institutional memory, and I want my record unblemished.

I can't risk mistakes. I can't risk unnecessary gossip. The gossips will have a field day once my health starts to decline. I refuse to give them more."

"I want to hold you, Kat. Touch you. Kiss you." Paul's words were almost a whisper. They ached with pain.

"You don't think I want that, too?" My voice crackled. "Paul, all I have to do is close my eyes and—"

I couldn't finish. Memories of that last night in the mountains were just a heartbeat away—the way Paul had touched me just so, or cupped my neck so I could catch my breath, or cradled me in infinite tenderness. I had never before felt so cherished.

I continued. "Beyond my legacy, this is also a moral choice, Paul. I can't bear the thought of hurting June or the children. How much longer before she asks more questions? You feel the same way, Paul, I know you do. They mean the world to you."

I was pacing as I talked, striding back and forth between the couch and piano. I slumped suddenly onto the piano bench and began toying with the keys, pressing out C major chords, then racing my fingers up and down the scale one octave. I did the same thing in the key of C-sharp, D, D-sharp, and E. When I got to the F, my hands moved into the gloom of minor chords.

Paul slid in beside me on the bench. "This is about that minister you saw, right? What did he say to you? You're different, Kat." He lowered his forehead to my shoulder, and my right hand instantly left the keyboard.

"Paul, listen to me." My voice was breathy, my mouth and hand close to his ear. "That minister made everything crystal clear for me. He didn't judge me. He didn't judge you. He merely accepted us and our story and embraced us both. He reminded me that heaven is mine merely for the asking and believing. And I want heaven, Paul. I want it more than anything, so that's my new focus. And I want heaven for you, too. I want to welcome you when you arrive. Karl helped me see for certain what can lie ahead for all of us. The promise of heaven is a sure thing—not like our uncertainties each day on earth."

"But isn't that what your forgiveness is all about? You sin, then get forgiven, then sin again, then get forgiven again?"

"It's not that simple."

"Why not?" Paul was not making this easy.

"Because heaven comes as a gift—a free one. All we have to do is believe in it and accept it. And I'll reject that gift if I willfully break God's rules. My love for God is so strong that I absolutely want to please him. Obey him. Follow his plan for order.

"But let me be clear, Paul. I'm not being frightened into good behavior. I'm choosing it intentionally because I want to. In spite of what some hell-and-brimstone guys on TV say, no one is ever terrified into heaven. We are all loved into heaven." I was thinking in particular of one late-night evangelist who was known for his oversized toupee and waxed-tip mustache as much as for his fearsome themes of guilt. His television presentation seemed the antithesis of the love and forgiveness of my faith.

We sat there in silence. Paul seemed desolate beyond words.

"Paul, remember Easter morning when we climbed into the dome?" It was a rhetorical question; of course he remembered it. "I didn't tell you at the time, but when that bright light exploded around us, I felt I was at the very gates of heaven. It wasn't a dream, Paul! I actually heard choir voices around me. They were real! They lasted only for a few seconds, but they were as certain as these piano notes. And they were so beautiful I didn't want them to stop."

Paul's shoulders stiffened. He moved back and looked straight at me. "You heard them, too?"

"Too? *Too?*" I stared. "What do you mean? Paul! What did you hear?"

"I heard singing. It was clear as a bell, very real, very—big. It was as though someone had opened a door into a cathedral just as I passed it and hundreds of voices were bursting out. It came and went quickly, but it was right there, all around us. When you didn't say anything, I figured I was simply reacting to the light."

I was truly stupefied. If Paul and I both heard celestial music at the same time, God had surely been speaking to us during that Easter sunburst.

"That's exactly what I heard! No, it was more—a miracle, Paul! These things don't just happen!" God was clearly revealing himself. I was almost mute with the wonder of it.

But Paul had questions. "What does it mean? Is this good for us?"

"It means that God is intervening in our lives. It means he sees our struggle. It means he loves us. Beyond that, we'll simply have to wait. And listen some more."

Paul stood abruptly. He crossed the room to the window facing Grove Boulevard and, pulling the sheers aside, watched the traffic flow at the edge of the wide front lawn. A motorcycle rattled past. A horn blared. He watched for a couple of minutes, although to me it seemed an eternity. I desperately needed him to envision the forthcoming months, to understand my difficult choice, to make this choice his own as well. I needed his support. I needed him as a teammate. *Please, God, help Paul to see.*

When he turned back to me, tears hung from his eyelashes, and he made no effort to hide them. He silently pulled me from the piano bench and pressed me against him. My arms went around his neck; my cheek adhered to his.

"I can still hold you like this, can't I?"

"You'd better," I said through my own choked tears. "I'm counting on you to help me all the way through."

"Do you have any idea how much I love you, Kat? I can still love you, can't I?"

"You'd better, because I plan on loving you to the very end."

There it was—our first mutual confession of love. We clung together in silence. The grandfather clock in the foyer chose that moment to whir into its ditty of Westminster chimes. We stood fused throughout the somber bonging as the clock clambered all the way to noon.

Finally I stirred. "I *need* you, Paul. Now. More than ever. There will be major decisions to make, some very soon, and right now you're the only one I can trust. I'll tell Lennie soon, and Jackie. We'll need them both on the team. Don't tell June, of course, but do make your peace with her. This must be hugely confusing to her. She deserves better."

"Understood." He kissed me then, a tender kiss on each cheek and another one on my forehead. "Yes, Prez. I'm here for you for as long as it takes." He grinned at me, the old teasing smile that swallowed my eyes and my heart.

And suddenly, having reached this new peace with Paul, I felt quite all right—almost, indeed, like my old self.

Chapter 50

WANING SUMMER

Like the gradual flowering of crepe myrtle in summertime Carolina, my soul then began to steady.

For starters, my mind began to clear. In spite of the appalling ultimatum from my doctors, I began to think of the illness more as a distant threat rather than an impending disaster. The timeline was hazy. The pain, so far, was more nuisance than restraint. Even so, the air of crisis was strong enough to force a plan of action for the months ahead. The administrator in me wrote out a list of goals and strategies.

The trip to Arden had triggered this change. Even as I clarified my plans for Wickfield, I experienced a willful surge in my faith. Those hours with Karl Krueger had relieved me of years of guilt. They had restored my belief in the power of forgiveness and created a roadmap for my soul. My vivid nighttime dreams reminded me constantly of this restoration of faith. In one dream I tried on new makeup with a group of women, using too much dark mascara that spilled over onto my face and made me look grotesque. The others laughed, saying I looked like a clown, but a man who was observing showed me how to use a concealer like a white-out pen. It blotted away the mistakes so that I was able to start over.

Even more significantly, I was reaching an amazing new high in my relationship with Paul. We had broken through the net of sexual tension that had distracted us for months, finding a peculiar kind of relief in the flood of freedom that followed. And even though our coupling in the mountains had plunged me into guilt soon afterward, we had reconciled with a precious new intimacy that morning in my living room. This unique bend in our journey was hard to define, but its spirituality far superseded any sporadic bursts of lovemaking we might otherwise have chosen.

My life, or what remained of it, was settling down. The anguish of the diagnosis began to dull. Replacing it was a sharp new concentration, a focus that lent clarity to my thinking as if with the simple turn of a camera lens. I began awakening each morning with a sense of urgency that helped me strategize every moment of my day and scrutinize every word I would utter. I dressed quickly, with purpose and precision. I sat with my planner at my bedroom desk and thought through every upcoming event.

I even planned when and what I would eat, paying extraordinary attention to nutritious foods.

"Blueberries," I said to Lennie when she returned from vacation. "They're in season right now. See if Food Lion has those buy-one-get-one-free specials."

"Already on my list, Miz Katherine," she replied mildly. She was writing on a note pad, making out the Friday grocery list.

"And strawberries, too, and raspberries from Michigan. They were in yesterday's ad."

"Law, Miz Katherine, you planning a party? Can't one person eat all them berries."

"Great for snacks. And get some fresh greens, like spinach. Or collard greens."

"Collards? Miz Katherine, you don't never eat them collards. I tried to fix 'em for you one time, with ham and onions, and you turned up your pretty nose. You on a diet?" She looked at me suspiciously. "How 'bout that pain in you belly from last week? It back?"

I hadn't told her my news yet. I was still wondering how to tell her and how much, knowing full well that if I glossed over the facts, Lennie would soon enough figure out the truth.

"Dr. Hoffmann is watching what I eat. The pain is better, thank you."

I changed the subject, and we dropped the matter for the time being. I would soon have a similar conversation with Jackie, which I dreaded. For now, Jackie was helping me get ready for next week's meeting with Carrington. I planned, first and foremost, to review upcoming events.

"We'll start with a preview of the freshmen convocation," I said later that morning, while Jackie tried to scribble as fast as I snapped out my thoughts. "He's to sit on the stage. Make sure his robe and hood are ready."

"They were cleaned before the May commencement."

"Just check. And we'll review the Board of Trustees calendar for the entire year and the Board of Governors' meetings I'll attend. Make copies of CVs of all the new faculty, and attach copies of their photos. That final candidate for Jake's position is coming in next week—that woman from Florida, Elaine Somebody. We'll simply tell Carrington that the search is nearing an end and we hope to make an announcement soon."

"Sinclair," said Jackie. "Elaine Sinclair. What about the School of the Arts?"

"Yes, Carrington will need an update on the unveiling, but we don't have a date yet. Probably early April, but it's critical we settle that promptly. Need to talk to Dan first about the dean search, and to Bob, since he's working on a naming gift. Oh, and Claire. Schedule us a meeting for early next week, since she's on top of the most updated campus calendar. What about Alumni? Have they sent us their dates yet?"

"I think they're waiting on one last chapter to report in. Raleigh. No, it's Greensboro. And Marla's still on vacation."

"Oh yes, volunteers." Dismay clouded my voice. "We can't control them but can't live without them. Marla needs to tie up those meetings. Add a note to that effect to my discussion list for Bob."

"Got it. And I'll make Carrington a copy of the last Board of Governors' minutes. And the latest media clips from PR."

Jackie's office skills were legendary—a comforting thought as I anticipated the impact of my illness over the next few months. She had devised a filing system that superseded anything I had worked with before. She could pull a document as soon as I started describing it, and she had the memory of an elephant. I wished she had been by my side in the earliest years of my career. With Jackie, I might have progressed up my career ladder even faster.

On the morning of Carrington's appointment, I mentally practiced my responses to his possible health inquiries. As a matter of delicacy, Southern gentlemen avoided direct questions about a woman's health, but as board chair, Carrington did have the right to an update on my post-surgery condition. I would somehow have to deflect him without telling an outright lie. I was as ready as possible, I decided as I steeled myself for our meeting. The fact that it was Friday, July 13, did not lessen my discomfiture.

When I saw Carrington, however, concerns for myself vanished. I inwardly gasped when his tall shadow merged into my threshold. He had lost so much weight in two months that the skin on his face fell in fleshy dollops. His visage was gray, like sooty snow. His slumped shoulders suggested an inward weight, in spite of the obvious loss of pounds.

Concerned, I framed my questions carefully at the outset. "How have you been, Carrington?" I asked, taking my usual chair as he lowered himself stiffly onto the loveseat.

"I've had better days," he mumbled in his gravelly voice, crossing his knees, then uncrossing them, then stretching out his legs as though seeking a comfortable spot to park his feet. It occurred to me that he didn't want this meeting any more than I did.

So that's the way we began, with me asking cautious questions about *his* health—not too pointedly at first, just enough to encourage him to speak with some candor. No, he hadn't seen a doctor. He hated doctors, because he knew more about his own body than those young punks with their too-shiny stethoscopes. Yes, Edith was concerned that he had lost a few pounds, but her doctors dealt with female problems. He snorted. He felt fine, thank you, but he had probably overdone a few chores around the yard. He pulled out a rear-pocket handkerchief, coughed rather dramatically, and settled into silence.

As we proceeded into my agenda, he flipped through those documents so carefully prepared by Jackie and Claire, stabbing his finger on a paragraph here and there as though to keep his place. He said he hated to see Jake go—"a fine young man." He asked if the new School of the Arts would teach organ as well as piano, a question that seemed totally out of character for him. "It all depends on funding and hiring," I replied smoothly. "We definitely want superior faculty. Many of the private schools have enticed the best in the arts. We'll need to compete well."

He asked a few other questions, all quite perfunctory, and then, with an alacrity that caught me by surprise, slid forward on his seat and rose to his feet.

"I must go, Katherine." He looked at me sharply. "You doing well? You look a bit peaked. Around the mouth."

Peaked? Around the mouth? What in the world did that mean? Was Carrington making his usual undercuts, or was cancer starting to reflect in my face?

"I feel fine, Carrington. It's been nearly four months since my surgery. Time has a way of healing."

"How's your car?" Carrington asked the question suddenly as he turned toward the door, like someone saying "By the way, how's your daughter? I haven't seen her for a while." I froze.

"Handling well. Very well." I swallowed.

"Well, I never did like those Crown Victorias, or any kind of Ford, for that matter. State of North Carolina should have gone with General Motors. Big mistake."

"Well, I'm sure GM was disappointed when they lost that bid, but as you know, it's all about money and politics in Raleigh." Carrington was well known for his love of Cadillacs, which he traded for new every couple of years. I suspected he owned a sizable amount of General Motors stock.

Jackie's eyes opened wide when I opened the door into her outer office and emerged with Carrington. Including our discussion about his health, his visit had lasted scarcely twenty minutes. I nudged him toward the hallway, chatting inanely about nothing important. I didn't need any more questions about cars.

That night I inspected my face carefully for telltale signs of illness. Nothing appeared different to my eye. My curls still bounced, my skin glowed pink enough, my stance remained erect. My skirts were feeling looser in the waistband, but since I didn't own a bathroom scale—my weight rarely fluctuated—I would use next week's appointment with Wayne Witherspoon to track the inevitable weight loss. I poked at the skin around my mouth. How could my mouth looked "peaked"? Had my recent tears left tracks, like an airplane's trail of vapor? I finally decided Carrington was throwing daggers in his usual inimitable style.

Early the next Friday, I slipped away for a few overdue days with Marianna. Contrary to my usual routine, I told no one where I was going—not Lennie, not Jackie, not even Paul. I simply told Dan to "man the ship" until I returned to my desk Tuesday. I wanted to grant myself the gift of freedom—the sun on my face through my window, the breeze in the trees along the mountain interstates. I wanted to see flags flutter from high poles, to hear babies squeal, to watch eager shoppers throng the malls—all without a tether to my office. I wanted to feel life at my fingertips before the constraints of duty and disease bore down. I longed for Marianna's companionship, and I wanted to feel her sisterly embrace before she knew of my illness. Her sharp eyes would detect my earliest signs of distress. I had to go now.

"You look different," Marianna said casually Saturday morning over breakfast. It was too hot to sit on her deck, so she had set our places on the glass-topped table in her morning room. My hand paused on my coffee mug.

"It's been quite a year," I said agreeably, taking a sip. I did not look at her.

"Actually, I wasn't thinking of your job stress. It's a more personal change, somehow. Peaceful." She smiled as she reached for the strawberry jam. "If I didn't know any better, I'd say you were in love."

In love? The comment stunned me. Had Paul somehow etched his name across my face?

"Yes, you do know better," I said, maybe a bit too sharply. I hoped she would drop the matter. Marianna was the one who had queried me at Christmas about my "Viking."

"How are things working out with that guy who was assigned to drive you?" she had asked while we unloaded the dishwasher late one night. "The one you called a Viking."

My mind had raced, vaguely recalling a casual phone conversation after that first ride to Queens College.

"I said lumberjack, not Viking. Broad shoulders. He's okay. Not boring." And I had changed the subject.

But I thought about her comment long after I hugged her in her driveway Monday morning, holding her as long as I dared before escaping behind my sunglasses and forcing a cheerful goodbye. I probably did look different. After all, I had been through a huge emotional purge. In the course of only three weeks, years of pent-up debris had rolled out of my heart and bathed themselves in the catharsis of my tears. I felt whole. Complete. Free. Forgiven.

And I'm sure Paul—and God—had everything to do with my perfect metamorphosis.

Chapter 51
GRACE

Resignation. Perhaps that was the "peace" Marianna had seen in my face. I was resigned to dying. The thought of death no longer made me shudder. I was intrigued by that bald fact and stared it in the face, trying as was my habit to analyze what it meant. When my car crossed the state line, I scarcely saw the "Welcome to North Carolina" sign. I was too busy figuring out a simple truth of life: so many choices in our lives are ruled by our fears. We fear constantly for our jobs, our families, our safety, our finances. When impending death looms up, those fears often lose their power and are replaced by the fear of physical pain and loss.

In my case, however, the fear of death had been replaced by my conviction of the gift of God's grace. Peace indeed. Apparently, according to Marianna, it showed. Now I fully understood what people meant by *faith*.

My thoughts turned to the incoming freshman class. Somehow my convocation speech needed to inspire them to rise above life's fears. It would be challenging to capture that idea within the current wave of academia's new "political correctness." Sensitivity was important, yes, but it should not be so stringent as to block channels of communication. As the vanguard of a state-funded university, I had been well versed on the rising new sensitivity toward all forms of diversity, from race and religion to sexual orientation. "Political correctness" would not let me share my personal story of faith on stage, but perhaps I *could* help students find their own path. It would take clear thinking, courage, and time. I had about a month to stew over my ideas, and I needed to get them on paper before pain and medication clouded my efforts. Time was my enemy.

Suddenly I felt the need to talk to Jackie. It was nearly eleven. Wickfield, which I had happily left behind on Friday, now crowded my thoughts. I spotted a phone booth the instant I pulled into a gas station, and I quickly placed a call to Jackie's desk. Unless she had taken one of her rare breaks, I knew she would pick up. And she did, instantly, and in a breathy voice. "Chancellor Embright's office."

"Hi, Jackie, it's Katherine. Just checking in. I'm—

"Katherine! Where are you?"

"I was just about to say I'm on 85 at a Shell gas station near Henderson. I'll be in tomorrow, unless I'm needed this afternoon. Why? What's going on?"

"Katherine! We've been frantic! No one knew where you were! How far is Henderson?" Her voice ended in a kind of wail.

"Okay, Jackie, what's happened?" My calmness surprised me. Fire? Sniper? Whatever it was, I could handle it.

"It's Carrington. He died during the night Thursday. It was lung cancer, only no one knew. His daughter called us Friday about noon, but you had already left. I've tried to reach you every day. We've called everyone, looking for you. How soon can you get here?"

Carrington! My heart turned over. I heard his voice: *You doing all right, Katherine? You look a little peaked around the mouth.* My hand gripped the receiver.

"When's the funeral?"

"Today! Now! At two this afternoon at Grace! Can you make it? Dan has rounded up the cabinet, and everyone is to sit behind the family. And the board has been called in, too, as many as can make it. The church will be packed!"

My head spun. *Today?* Dear God, how could this be? The one time I had severed myself from the office, this had to happen! A wave of anger took over. I wanted to rail at Carrington as though he had intentionally chosen to die just as I was taking a desperately needed break. Even in death he bedeviled me. I actually found myself glancing up at the clouds, half-expecting to see him leering out of the fluffy whiteness and laughing in fiendish delight.

Darn. Darn! I simply had to make that funeral. My own state of health was no longer an issue. It was politically imperative for me to be in that pew with my cabinet when the pallbearers carried the coffin down the aisle.

Jackie interrupted my thoughts.

"Paul Stafford has an important message for you. He's been hounding me to death trying to find you. He thought you might be with your sister in Virginia, but we didn't know her married name." I scowled to myself at that. Didn't Human Resources have a list of all my family phone numbers? But Jackie was still talking.

"Paul thinks he can get you a highway patrol escort if he knows your exact location, so I must call him immediately. He assumes you're in the Victoria. Right?"

"Yes. And Paul has the license tag." Paul! Once again, Paul was being sent to my rescue. My spirits rose immediately. I needed to get some gas and start flying down the highway. Now!

"I'm on the north side of Henderson at a Shell station, and I'm headed southwest on 85. But Jackie, I'm well over three hours away, maybe 200 miles, and it's nearly eleven. I don't know if I can make it. It will be close, even with an escort." My mind was spewing thoughts, making a mental to-do list. Gas. Bathroom. Clothes.

That's when I glanced down at my travel outfit. I was wearing casual black summer slacks with tiny white checkers. I had on sandals. No stockings, of course. And a short-sleeved orange linen jacket, brightly cheerful. Again, thoughts tumbled fast.

"Tell Paul to go by the house and ask Lennie for my black summer jacket with the big white buttons and those low-heeled black shoes I wear to work. And to bring them to the church and wait for me at the front door so I can make a fast change."

"Got it. He said something like that himself. And to not worry about parking. Pull up to the front of the circle. He'll be watching and will take over your car."

Atta boy, Paul, I thought as I slammed down the phone and rushed my car to the nearest pump. After a quick dash to the ladies' room, I was headed back to the highway. I had Marianna's snacks and bottled water to keep me company. Beyond that, the only idea in my head was to make that funeral on time.

But no help appeared as I plummeted down the rather desolate stretch toward Durham. Traffic was light. I drove as fast as I dared, thinking at one point that it might be smart to speed enough to attract a patrolman, then deciding such a move would merely delay me. I wondered what Paul was going through at the moment. How would I be recognized along the road? How would I be intercepted? My foot stayed steady on the pedal and my eyes stayed peeled on the road ahead, but for miles I saw only a sizzling concrete arrow and clones of green pine forests.

As I neared the busy outskirts of Durham, my senses went on alert. Traffic increased. I passed a patrolman headed east, intent on another mission. I passed signs to Duke University and the turnoff to UNC-Chapel Hill. Paul and I had been here only months before. *Please, God, show Paul how to get the help I need.*

Then, ahead on the far side of a long downhill curve, I spotted a state trooper, his black sedan sitting alone on the side. I flicked my lights and snapped my head toward him as I sailed past, hoping to catch his eye but seeing only his enormous wide hat. But he pulled into traffic immediately, and I quickly slowed to fifty-five. As he pulled in close behind me, he turned on his blue lights. I fished around in my purse for my wallet even as I braked and angled my car onto the easement; he would need my ID. He was at my window in seconds.

"Katherine Embright, Wickfield University." I held out my license.

The officer tipped his huge Stetson and flashed his badge in return. "Officer Jim Holston, Chancellor. I hear you need an escort."

"Yes. How fast can we go?"

"About eighty at first. Maybe eighty-five. I don't want to take you too fast. This is a highly congested highway. Much depends on how well traffic moves over. Stay behind me. I'll try to clear the passing lane. After Greensboro, another trooper will take you rest of the way. Don't pull over when I do. Just slow down, and he'll pull ahead of you. Do you have gas?"

"Nearly full."

"Good. Don't let anyone get between us."

"Ready." I gave him a thumbs-up.

He tipped his hat again as he moved away, and I watched in my mirror as he buckled up, spoke into his radio, and pulled onto the pavement.

And away we went. My palms were sweating so badly at first I had to wipe them on my slacks every few miles. But cars peeled away gracefully as the blue lights bore upon them. I wondered what other drivers thought as they saw me, a lone woman, clenched to the steering wheel in close pursuit. Shouldn't it be the other way around?

But I dared not look at a single face. I kept my eyes on the brim of that hat, gliding with the trooper in and out of traffic. We passed the famous outlet malls of Burlington and barreled on toward Greensboro, once hitting ninety before intervening with the city's numerous merging lanes. Death Valley—that's what they called this area where different interstates branched off for Charlotte and Winston-Salem. I held my breath as we bullied our way through.

Another patrol car soon appeared on the roadside ahead. I braked cautiously as Officer Holston signaled with his blinkers and began to pull over. The new sedan pulled ahead of me. There were more blue lights, and the race was on again. I dared not look at my watch. For the next hour I merely held on, prayed, and tried to breathe.

When we finally approached Hurley, I wondered whether this new officer would sail on past my exit or escort me directly into town. For the hundredth time I wished I had had a phone installed in my car. Paul and I had discussed it when he first began driving with me, but we had somehow dropped the idea soon afterward. Hopefully Paul was on the radio with the officer right now, directing him to the downtown exit that would take us straight to the church.

Yes, he found the exit! The next few minutes were a blur: the steep exit ramp, the skeletal crossbar at the railroad tracks, the left turn at the downtown square, the lovely Episcopal church with its circular brick driveway and perfect green landscaping. I spotted a long black hearse and a horde of cars. I strained for a glimpse of Paul.

Then something seemed to go wrong. The trooper turned suddenly to the right and pulled to the side of the church. He was supposed to take me to the front door, and Paul was supposed to meet me there with my shoes and jacket. I crawled after the sedan and had to brake hard when the trooper suddenly turned into a tight space that seemed carved out for him.

The next moments were surreal. Paul, like a paratrooper fallen from the sky, tapped sharply at my window. I lowered it and heard him say, "They're holding for you. Lennie has your clothes. Come on. Now! No, leave the keys so I can move your car," and dear Lennie was *right there* beside the car helping me into the black jacket and holding out the pumps for my bare feet to step into. She also handed me a different handbag, the dressy single-handled black one that I often carried to church. I had completely forgotten about a purse. "Kleenex and mints," she said in a low voice, tapping the purse. "Go on, now, go! They waitin' for you."

The trooper, a tall black man in gray uniform, had emerged from his car and was waiting, grinning broadly as though he had just passed the checkered flag at the Indy 500. Like the other officer, he tipped his Stetson. On impulse he held out his arm, and I took it as he escorted me to the front door. I removed my sunglasses as I stepped inside the cool vestibule. The space was crowded with the casket and several men in black suits and white dress shirts. I recognized the familiar faces of several Hurley civic leaders, including Mayor Barnhardt. Standing against the wall were others whom I assumed to be members of the Hall family. These included several small children who seemed much too young to be grandchildren. Did Carrington have great-grandchildren? I should know, but I actually had no idea. I spotted Edith Hall, who was staring at me intently as though to catch my eye, and I sidled quickly to her side. We embraced silently.

Then an usher signaled that he would take me down the aisle, and I entered the familiar nave, now hushed. A shadowy mass of dark suits and dresses filled the pews. As I proceeded down the carpeted aisle, I heard rustling and the whispered hiss of "chancellor." Ahead was the splendid white marble altar and gleaming brass cross. To my extreme relief, I also spotted the friendly balding patch on the back of Dan Jones's head, and my spirits rose instantly. Dan turned and smiled hugely as I stopped at his pew; he scooted over while I accepted the usher's printed program. I slipped into the waiting space and saw Bob Atterbury's arm reach across Dan; I squeezed Bob's offered hand. Beyond Bob sat Marilyn, whose girth took up the width of two seats. Her hand flounced across Bob's lap but landed ingloriously on Dan's thigh. I reached over and touched it lightly, noting at the same time that Pud had his nose buried in the bulletin and that Claire was waving discreetly from her end of the pew. I suddenly missed Jake. I took a deep breath and settled in.

Only then did I dare glance at my watch. The time was 2:06.

Chapter 52
CARRINGTON'S CELEBRATION

I am Resurrection and I am Life, says the Lord.
Whoever has faith in me shall have life,
even though he die.
And everyone who has life,
and has committed himself to me in faith,
shall not die for ever.

The voice in the back of the church was distinct as it began, but it grew even clearer as the priest who was reading the words continued down the aisle. The funeral procession crept forward slowly: the tall cross raised high by a solemn-faced teenager, the church officials in black cassock and white surplice. Behind the mahogany casket and pallbearers came the large family of mourners. I loved the beauty of all liturgical church services, including funerals. The piped music, the stained glass, the candles—all filled me with a reverence that was hard to find outside church walls. They quieted me. They cleared my mind.

Now, however, as I caught my breath from the highway chase and responded to the solemnity around me, I found my reactions curious. I stood and sat and knelt on cue, but my mind seemed to have departed my frame and climbed into the church's vaulted rafters. I felt myself starring in one of those out-of-body movie-type scenes when someone who has just died slowly rises above the set to watch those reacting to his death.

In effect, I sensed that I was participating in my own funeral.

The worship was a celebration of Carrington's life, and, like an Easter service, embraced the Resurrection. I thought back to Easter in mid-April. After that spectacular sunburst in the blazing copper dome, I had attended services at Grace, singing "Jesus Christ is risen today" with gusto as the choir marched in. I remembered the sweet infusion of scented white lilies that had lined the carved railing leading to the altar. Other than that, nothing tangible about the service stuck in my memory. What I remembered most about mid-April was falling in love with Paul.

Now, however, I heard all the words. The *Book of Common Prayer* led us through the liturgy. Carrington's remains lay before us in the closed casket, overlaid with a white linen pall and positioned on a funeral bier in front of the altar steps. The family, who took up the three rows immediately in front of us, sat motionless. Even the children were subdued. Knowing Carrington's love for intimidation, I wondered what kind of family man he had been, what lasting impressions he had created as patriarch of this large brood. The bulletin named key family members and relationships; the list was long. And yes, great-grandchildren were included.

"Father of all, we pray to you for your servant Carrington," intoned the voice, "and for all those whom we love but see no longer. Grant to them eternal rest. Let light perpetual shine upon them. May Carrington's soul and the souls of all the departed, through the mercy of God, rest in peace. Amen."

As I closed my eyes there in the twilight of the sanctuary, feeling the ancient rhythms of the familiar words, a profound sadness enveloped me. Days ago Carrington had been alive with flesh and breath and dreams. Today, he was gone—as I would be as well, soon enough. My own frail mortality taunted me. One of the younger family members seated in front of me—a teenager about the age of our Wickfield freshmen—brushed a hand under his nose. I slipped a Kleenex from my purse and dabbed my own nose, mentally chiding myself for displaying such emotions in public. I reminded myself that Carrington had made my life miserable, that he had heckled me even before my inauguration, and that I was at this moment surrounded by Hurley's most esteemed citizens, who expected me to respond with the dignity of my office. There was no room today for sentiment. Everyone knew what a difficult and even *outrageous* man Carrington had been. His contentious courtroom behavior had become the stuff of Hurley lore, woven into stories to entertain for years.

And there I sat, my old foe quite dead and no longer a thorn in my side, yet conjuring up tears for myself that threatened to spill over. I stiffened. I could not, would not, succumb to self-pity! I would not betray this secret sadness within me! For the next few minutes I tried every trick I knew to keep my composure. I glanced up at the ceiling and froze my gaze. I held my breath and released it slowly. I counted backward from a thousand by threes. I considered slipping one of Lennie's mints from my purse but then dismissed the idea. The crackling wrappers would be as noticeable as tears.

Finally, I simply concentrated on the homily. The words now flowing from the pulpit were ticking off the chronology of Carrington's community services, including his longtime devotion to Wickfield. There were personal family stories tinged with humor. At one point quiet laughter rippled through the nave, but I remained stony-faced, fixated on keeping my composure.

Then, like a good cook dipping deep into the kettle to scoop the richness of the stew, the minister began to reveal a different side of Carrington—a hugely generous Carrington quite unknown to the general public. He described the time Carrington showed up with a secondhand Chevy for a Grace family facing bankruptcy—and insisted on remaining anonymous. He told how Carrington had once sat on the couch in the minister's office asking what amount was still needed for the new parish hall and then writing a generous check so that the congregation made their campaign deadline. There were more checks: Hugo relief in Hurley, Hugo relief in South Carolina, new mattresses for the Boy Scout camp at Lake Hurley, kitchen appliances for the domestic-abuse shelter, a generous donation to Grace's organ fund "because Carrington loved organ music so." Bit by bit the minister described a Carrington most of us had never dreamed existed.

Especially me. I had been so busy waging war with the man that I'd never considered him capable of making peace.

"You look a bit peaked around the mouth, Katherine." These words hung as clearly in my memory as though Carrington were standing by my side. Could it be that Carrington, in his state of ailing health, had sensed my own illness? Did he catch something in my countenance that others could not see? Do dying spirits, like ghosts-to-be, reveal themselves to each other?

The possibility made me catch my breath. I stared hard at that casket, my eyes boring through the frame in a futile effort to coax a response from the grave.

I might have made it through the service without visible tears had it not been for the music near the end. I've never quite understood the overwhelming power of music—only that it has the capacity with the slightest turn of a chord to evoke emotions as tender as a kiss. So it was with the funeral choir. Shortly before the pallbearers gathered to lift the casket for departure, the choristers stood one last time in their burgundy robes, raised their black music folders, and delivered a rendition of the "Nunc Dimittis" so exquisite that it left me stupefied. I was familiar with the story behind the famous canticle—the exuberant words of old Simeon, a devout Jew, who, upon seeing the infant Jesus in Jerusalem, declared himself now ready to depart from earth.

"Lord, now lettest thou thy servant depart in peace," caroled the sopranos. Somberly, altos and tenors and basses twice echoed "depart in peace."

The combined chords wove in and out in perfect harmony, rendering a sweetness that ripped my heart. I bit my lip hard to hold its quiver and closed my eyes, picturing the joyous tears of the aged priest as Mary the mother handed him the babe in the temple. I imagined Simeon gazing into the tiny face, the one whose life he recognized as bringing hope to the entire world. "For mine eyes have seen thy salvation," sang the choir, their voices swelling, "which thou has set before the face of all people." Then their words soared: "A light to lighten the gentiles, / And to be the glory of thy people Israel!"

A light for those who did not yet believe, and a promise for those did!

I was struck by Simeon's peace with death, now that he had seen the Savior. Now—but only now—could he depart in peace. Those final words were repeated three more times like a silent benediction rising above the congregation. For several seconds the church was as quiet as death itself.

Then came a rustle as the congregation rose, and Carrington's family began to shuffle from their pews toward a side aisle. Since this allowed them to exit without facing the congregation, I instantly knew what I would do. I slipped on my sunglasses, picked up my purse, and as the mourners in front of me began to move, I eased my way into the family line. I did not alert Dan. I was too intent on escaping the scrutiny of curious eyes behind me. I spoke to no one and did not join the family's procession to the reception hall. I merely headed for the nearest side exit and stepped out into the glaring sunlight of the parking lot, which was filled with cars but devoid of people. I knew without being told that Paul had been watching from the back of the church and would find me, and he did—very quickly, in fact. I scarcely had time to adjust my face before the big Victoria rounded the corner of the church and pulled to my side. I moved to the passenger door and slid in next to Paul.

"Home?" he asked. I nodded. My throat ached, and my eyes felt like oculi burning in my skull, but Paul was here and I was safe again. We rode in silence until we parked beside the rhododendron and moved into the empty sanctuary of Lennie's Cloroxed kitchen.

It was there, in the vacuum of the room that held so much of our secret history, that I found myself once more in Paul's arms: weeping and weeping as though my heart would utterly break.

Chapter 53
AUGUST PAIN

"You okay, Kat?"

Dan sounded concerned as he spoke the words; he was walking me back to my office following our cabinet meeting the next Monday morning. Exactly a week had passed since Carrington's funeral, days in which I was bereaved of peace. I tried not to think about that service. Yet in moments when Carrington was not on my mind, a brief image from the service would scud across my vision, and I would turn away to hide the look that apparently consumed my face.

The cabinet, I sensed, were confused by my sadness. Everyone knew that Carrington and I had feuded. "The swag-bellied old goat!" I had sometimes sniffed in exasperation during private conversations with Dan and Bob. Perhaps they thought me guilt-ridden for such lapses of professional demeanor. In today's cabinet meeting I had carefully thanked each member for attending the funeral, my voice cracking a bit in the effort. Bob and Pud had quickly flicked their eyes away, studying the day's agenda with great intensity. Marilyn had wide-eyed me with her usual curiosity. Dan had looked concerned. It was going to be hard to fool this group.

"I'm fine, Dan," I now replied, trying to look cheerful as he held my office door for me. We settled in my office and dug into a list of pressing issues, including the hiring of the dean for the new School of the Arts. As usual, I felt better as we worked. Multitasking was my panacea, the one escape where I could immerse myself into a concentrated state of mind that shrouded me from outside distractions.

I wasn't really fine, however. Wayne Witherspoon reminded me of that on a visit soon after, watching me wince as he pressed down on the top of my abdomen. He didn't have to tell me the tumor was growing; my increasing pain had already convinced me, as did my growing weakness. Throughout July I had felt the distensions of tumor and tissue well up beyond the strength of my pain pills—enough so that I found myself sometimes holding my lower left side with my right hand. When he said he was ordering a new CAT scan, I felt it to be futile; it would merely confirm what we both already knew.

"How much time?" I demanded in his office after the exam. Paul, who had driven me to this Charlotte appointment, was outside in the waiting room, probably pacing like an expectant father whose wife was about to give birth.

When he averted his eyes and looked down, I knew. Like many empathetic physicians who personally feel their patients' pain, Wayne Witherspoon was treading this ground very carefully.

"Well, as we discussed last month, the cancer has invaded the liver." Yes. I already knew that. I waited.

"Katherine, I fully respect your decision to refuse chemotherapy, but I want you to reconsider. You are at a stage where chemo can help us stabilize your cancer. For example, we can—"

"Can you keep me from dying?"

"We can prolong your life."

"You can prolong my suffering."

"We can delay your death."

"The chemo will kill me before the cancer does."

"Let's take that chance."

"No. Don't ask me again."

We sat in silence for a few seconds, the surgeon and the chancellor. We were respectful with our disparate views but alone in our thoughts.

I spoke first. "I need to know I have at least a little time."

"Yes?"

"There's so much yet to do. I'm about to hire a new vice president and a new dean. We're just months from launching the new School of the Arts, one of my pet projects. But even more immediate is a major speech I'm to give in three weeks to the incoming freshman class. I need to know I'll be able to deliver it. Without faltering. There's so much I want to say, more than ever now that . . . " I trailed off.

But I was encouraged when I walked out of the office. In addition to a prescription for stronger pain medicine, I had excellent advice from the nurse on how to restructure my time. In the face of advancing pain, she said, I should break duties down into easy steps. Hers were very simple words that I already knew, but it helped to hear them from another. Focus on priorities. Prepare thoroughly for major moments. Work from home as much as possible. Show up only when an appearance really counted. Cut out unnecessary trips. Cut out unnecessary meetings. Delegate. Rest. Take naps.

The advice would be impossible to keep, of course, but hearing it was a start. I remembered rendering a similar list to Tim, long ago. His star had been starting to rise professionally at the time, and his television fans had demanded chunks of his energy. Now it was my turn to heed the wise words.

As for the freshman convocation speech, it challenged me on several levels. This was to be a welcoming speech, my first conversation with the freshman class beyond the banal chitchat of the opening reception in my home. It needed to excite them toward excellence, inspire them toward creativity, and awaken them to awareness of life far beyond their self-absorbed worlds. I wanted to seize these eighteen-year-olds, shake them up, and whack their rear ends a bit. Few speakers from my own college days were more than a blur. There was one exception: an extraordinary visiting poet at Hollins whose readings of lyrical imagery had enflamed my passion for Emily Dickinson.

Inspired by this memory, I returned one evening to the poems of my beloved Emily. I buried myself in my home study, pulling from bookshelves my favorite critiques of Dickinson poetry and stacking them on the floor around my reading chair. I browsed through a multitude of pages, many marked with penciled notes from my graduate-school days. My notations were so faded that I sometimes strained to catch their faint shadows. What astonished me after an hour of reading was the pertinence of these long-forgotten lines to my current life.

"That it will never come again is what makes life so sweet." I looked up, my throat stricken in amazement. Oh, the moments that would never come to me again!

"Dying is a wild night and a new road." Again, the words fit my life. There had been that chaotic night when Paul and I had hurled ourselves into Hugo's tumult, a symbolic death of our old lives. There was the "new road," both literal and figurative, that Paul and I had been traveling together to bring us to this juncture. How dare this Emily, a nineteenth-century recluse and ruminator, pinpoint my future so precisely!

I turned more pages.

Then I found a line that might work for the speech: "We never know how high we are till we are called to rise; and then, if we are true to plan, our statures touch the skies." I liked it. "Called to rise" spoke of possibilities beyond classroom and campus. The imagery was strong. The message was clear.

Even so, I wrestled more. The "called to rise" quote lacked the tenderness I was seeking—the idea to be aware of others and extend compassion beyond self. I thought of the bureaucracy that crowded my academic world, the competition for tenure and full professorships, the clawing to reach the top. I thought about my fast rise to senior leadership and wondered how many people I had jarred in the climb. Academia could be a cruel world, even evil. I needed to steer my students to thoughts of the human condition, to moral responsibility, to an extension of their future lives beyond the traps of self-absorption. That was, after all, academia's more noble side: concern for one's fellow man, the need to improve life, the quest for change.

I read on.

And then I found it—or, rather, Emily found me. It was as though she had silently entered the dimness of my study to stand within the glow of the lampshade, her frock a simple white, her hair in a bun, lips parted in a slight smile, and hands extended.

"Take these," the Emily-ghost said, offering me words from long ago. They were perfect words. They even hinted of my pending death. I read them and gasped, seeing again Professor Grinstead in our Bingham Hall classroom holding the heavy American literature textbook in one paw of a hand, hearing his ponderous voice delivering these very lines from memory while gazing out the window at Carolina's forested quad. I read them again, and I wept.

> If I can stop one heart from breaking, I shall not live in vain;
> If I can ease one life the aching,
> Or cool one pain,
> Or help one fainting robin
> Unto its nest again,
> I shall not live in vain.

There it was—the germ of my speech, my North Star. I would introduce my freshmen to the "belle of Amherst" and through her spare but lyrical language nudge them to appreciate life's simplest truths.

My decision exhilarated me. This poem would shape my speech, which in its finality would reflect both the professional and personal sides of Katherine Embright.

The title of my speech? I laughed out loud in sheer delight as I printed it in decisive block letters: ONE FAINTING ROBIN.

Chapter 54
GETTING READY

As my convocation speech began to take shape, I found myself turning to pressing matters concerning my health. It was becoming obvious to me that I could no longer keep my illness secret from Lennie and Jackie. These two women worked with me more closely than any others on my staff. They knew my daily routines, my habits, and my temperament. In supporting my needs, they accomplished as much for me personally and professionally as my entire cabinet put together. And they were loyal to me—unfailingly. "I would trust either of them with my life," I had once told Alex in my early months as chancellor.

In truth, I had come close to telling Lennie about my illness in late July, but the words burned like one of those new "horse pills" that lodged in my throat. Finally, one morning in early August, Lennie brought the subject up herself. From her apron pocket she fished out two empty vials from prescription pills and placed them in front of my coffee cup.

"Miz Katherine, what a them things? They was in you bathroom trash can."

For a flashing second I felt a rising fury—anger that anyone would dare to go through my trash and confront me with something personal. Then I thought of the rationale behind it. After all, Lennie was doing what she felt was right. Her personal definition of "housekeeper" included keeper of the chancellor in the kindest ways possible.

"They yours?"

My sense of humor rescued me. One vial had contained Lortab, a pain-reliever containing the narcotic hydrocodone along with the analgesic acetaminophen. The other was for Phenergan, which controlled nausea.

"Guilty as charged. What's the fine, officer?"

Lennie's eyes narrowed as she studied me.

"You sick again, Miz Katherine?"

My eyes dropped, but only for a second. I had to handle this just right. "Well, that's what they tell me, Lennie." I looked firmly into her soft brown eyes. "Only—this time it's going to be hard to fix."

"How hard?"

My face fell, and she knew.

"Who know?"

"No one, Lennie, no one. Just the doctors and their people. And you mustn't tell anyone, Lennie. I'm keeping this a secret. Promise me, now."

"Mistah Paul know?"

"Paul? Oh yes, of course, Paul knows. He drives me to the hospital, but he's the only other one. My sisters don't know."

"Miz Susan?"

"No, Lennie, I'm telling you, no one knows. No one on the cabinet knows, although I plan to tell Jackie, probably today. Please hear me on this. This is a personal health issue. It's important to keep this private, to keep the gossip down, to keep everyone from sitting around and speculating. I can't bear the idea of people playing guessing games about my body. There's a new tumor, Lennie, and we can't tell exactly how fast it's growing. But it's pooching out, and sometimes it throbs so hard I think I'm going to burst." I took the Kleenex she offered and blew into it. "Everyone will find out in time, of course."

Lennie sat perfectly still at the table, brown hands folded, head bowed as though saying grace. A gentle tremor shook her slight frame. In less than a minute she had gone from a scolding mother hen to a frightened chick. She had become Emily Dickinson's fainting robin, needing help "unto its nest again."

"Lennie, I know how scary this sounds. I'm scared, too. I'm scared of this crazy new pain, and I know it's going to get worse. Sure, I can fight it with these crazy pills, but one of these mornings, maybe even in a few weeks, who knows, I'm going to take these darn things and find they don't touch my pain. When that happens, I don't know what we'll do. Maybe Doctor Witherspoon will hook me up to tubes and whistles and pump morphine into me so I can just get through the hours. That's no way to live, and I certainly can't lead Wickfield like that. These pills make me so sleepy I can't function at my normal capacity, and we can only imagine what heavier drugs will do. So that's scary."

Lennie reached for the coffee pot.

"And I'm scared of people, Lennie. Not scared *of* them. Scared of losing them. Of separation. Of making them sad, too. That's one reason I can't tell my sisters just yet. Or my Wickfield people. I'm too busy grieving for myself right now. I can't take on their grief, too."

I mopped my hands over my face. There was much more I needed to say.

"But there's one area where I'm not scared, Lennie. I'm counting on heaven. It's one glorious place, and I'm headed there with a smile on my face. I know I don't deserve it, but it's been promised, and I accept it as a gift, so I'm convinced I'll get there. And I fully expect to see you there, too, my dear lady." I watched as she refilled my coffee mug with an expert turn of the wrist. With Lennie, everything about serving food was an art.

"Oh, you will. I believe that, too, Miz Katherine." Lennie's tears were fading, and she faced me now with a calmness that filled the room. "You soul is anchored in a good place, and so is mine. That heavenly light be shining on you so bright it point me the way to you. I find you again. Don't you worry 'bout that."

"And you, Lennie, you will always have a spot here at Wickfield. Don't you worry about your future after I'm gone."

Gone. It was the first time I had used a word of such finality. Lennie teared up again, but I sensed my words brought her some relief. I meant what I told her. I would leave written instructions for Dan on how to take care of Lennie, along with a check large enough to amplify her monthly pay stub for years to come.

Those written instructions to my cabinet members were important; I had been working on them bit by bit, but the effort drained me emotionally. Now, I showed them to Lennie. I led her onto the sun porch, to the mirrored antique secretary that stood in the corner—the one Grandpa Larson had given my grandmother on their first wedding anniversary. The hinged cover was down, holding my checkbook and a stack of bills that I had started paying the night before—that is, until pain had overtaken me and sent me to bed.

I raised the cover carefully and tugged at the drawer underneath. Inside was a stack of letterhead envelopes, each addressed by my hand to a specific member of my cabinet. There was also one for Elaine Sinclair, the new vice president who had just been hired, and for Claire, and for Chief

Sutton—even one for Lennie herself. And because of my close friendship with Susan Atterbury, I was including a special one for her.

"I'm working on these at night, Lennie, a few at a time. When the time is right, you are to hand-deliver these *immediately* to Dan Jones and have him distribute them to their rightful owners. The contents are confidential. Tell him that. They are not to be delivered or opened under any circumstances until after I am gone." In addition, of course, was the matter of the binder I was preparing for Paul—the story of our journey as it was continuing to unfold. It was taking a great deal of my time these days. I would tell Lennie about that later.

Lennie stared in silence at the envelopes. The import of her future role seemed to awe her.

"This is supremely important, Lennie, and I'm counting on you to handle this promptly and efficiently, in your usual style. Of all people in my private circle, other than Paul, I am counting on you the most."

At that, Lennie buried her face in her apron. I have never seen a woman weep so hard yet maintain her dignity as I saw that day with dear Lennie.

That left me with the job of telling Jackie, and like Lennie, she inadvertently helped bring about the dreaded conversation. That same afternoon after sharing my news with Lennie, I mentioned to Jackie a small task to be done— nothing major, just some special filing supplies that we needed to order. In response, she pointedly reminded me they had been ordered a week ago and that we had discussed it. Detecting an edge to her voice, I asked her into my office, gesturing for her to sit at the round work table. I carefully shut the door between our offices before joining her at the table.

"Thank you for reminding me," I said, folding my arms on the glass top and leaning toward her. "I appreciate your sharp attention to details, because I will doubtless have many more forgetful times in the future, and I will need you to smooth my way through them. Even cover for me, if need be."

Jackie sat impassively, and I continued. "The doctors have found a new growth in my abdomen. We don't know a lot about its future course, but the doctors want me to rest as much as possible. And they've put me on some heavy-duty pain pills to take intermittently, as needed, but they make me loopy—you know, cloud my thinking a bit, make me sleepy, make me forgetful."

"Will you have surgery again?" Jackie had scarcely taken a breath since I began speaking.

"We'll have to see. Right now, we're hoping these pills keep me comfortable."
You're hedging, Kat, hissed a voice in my head. *Give her more.*

"Your job will be to keep me on task. I'll work from home if I get overtired, and you may need to work with me at the house. Like before." Jackie nodded.

"But beyond that, you will become my gatekeeper in ways you've never had to be before. Lennie knows, and Paul Stafford, who drives me to a specialist in Charlotte. But other than those two, and now you, no one knows about this little nuisance, not even my family. And that's the way it must remain, Jackie, at least for now. In time, if this illness creates new problems, I'll certainly give the cabinet a heads-up, as well as any others who might need to know. But I want to do it on *my* timeline, not theirs, and that's where I'm counting on you, Jackie. Hear me on this! I know my cabinet, and in spite of their superb talents, they could plague you to death with sly little questions. Academics hate the threat of change, you know. The corporate world criticizes us for that."

Jackie rolled her eyes dramatically and pretended to groan. "Oh, yes, and we both know who will be first in line to my door." She was clearly referring to Marilyn, and I was grateful she chose to lift the mood by attempting a joke. But we both knew she didn't fool me, nor did I fool her. I was convinced she saw through my veneer. Although I had not spelled out specifics, Jackie comprehended exactly what I needed her to know.

With those two conversations behind me, I next pursued the completion of those personal letters to the cabinet. They became a major project for my summer evening hours, and I worked feverishly on them for the next two weeks. It was good to have something so pressing to keep me on task. My summer calendar stayed fairly clear of campus events in the evenings. I watched little nighttime television, with the exception of indulgences with *thirtysomething* on Tuesday nights, but traditionally I became a voracious reader during my summers. Last summer, in fact, I had raced through a half-dozen book titles, some quite entertaining, even decadent. A couple were questionable enough that I had intentionally shelved them each night rather than leave them out for Lennie to eye. There was no need to endure one of her scoldings.

This summer, there was no time for books. Now, name by name, I wrote letters to the people on my list, typing as long as my strength permitted.

My letter to Dan was long and probably too visionary, rich with details I had not yet shared about the School of the Arts. My most fervent hope was that he would continue my high aspirations for Wickfield.

Bob's letter included a description of a monetary gift I was leaving to create a formal arboretum and aviary in the wooded space behind Wellstone—one to be designed by the biology and zoology departments and managed hands-on by their students. The acreage was considered prime real estate for campus expansion and was high on Bob's list for a new science building. My idea would carve a niche from that space for a living laboratory to study both flora and fauna, creating at the same time a sculptured garden for the enjoyment of Hurley residents.

For Pud, besides the usual rah-rah about Wickfield's sports, I encouraged an increase in the number of women's sports programs, starting with swimming and volleyball. We already boasted a top-flight softball team, conference champs two years in succession, but Pud was so focused on men's football and basketball that creative ideas seemed to sail over his head. My suggestions, at least, were a seed.

For Marilyn, I acknowledged the "huge job" she was doing for Wickfield, smiling a bit as I chose those words. Wickfield had become her life, and, in spite of all that was annoying, her proven performance had earned her distinction. Privately, I wondered how long her health would hold out.

To Sam Sutton I composed a standard thank-you letter, acknowledging the outstanding work of Officer Paul Stafford in accommodating me during my illness. I kept it simple and professional. I dared not say more.

For Elaine Sinclair, our new hire to take Jake's position, I wrote a simple welcome to Wickfield. Since she was not present yet on campus, her letter was a bit tricky. I didn't know exactly how long we would work together, if at all. Time is everything, I thought dully as I typed—a friend to the healthy but a threat to the infirmed. I told Elaine that Wickfield's students were "terrific" young people and that I envied the opportunity awaiting her.

For Claire, I spent considerable thought before typing. I considered her one of the best hires of my tenure. She was smart, energetic, and superb at social skills. Even so, she was also vulnerable, partly because she was single and attractive and thus capable of being snatched by future job or marriage offers. I decided to name her to the cabinet immediately and have her report directly to me rather than to Bob. I would nurture her for as long as my health held.

To Claire's letter I also offered specifics for how to handle the death of a college president. I imagined her reading my letter immediately after the news of my death hit campus. Besides the media, she would need to call Governor Mendenhall's office in Raleigh and Charlie Pettigrew's staff in Chapel Hill. Regarding her future, I encouraged her to keep her roots firmly with Wickfield. My tears flowed freely as I wrote. I saw much of my younger self in Claire.

I had not yet written Lennie's letter; it would be short. It would contain paperwork for a college fund I had established for young Robert, a seed to grow sizably over the next dozen years. I would tell Lennie to imagine Robert as a teacher or dentist or engineer but to let him serve with great integrity and "soul" wherever life led him. Lennie would know what I meant.

As for Susan, I would write hers at the very end. It would begin "Forgive me, dear Susan," and it would end with my vision of her twenty years from now, the distinguished wife of President Robert F. Atterbury. I could easily picture Bob as a future college president or the CEO of a corporation. And I readily visualized a sixty-something Susan—blonde hair lightened to ash to hide the gray, crow's feet crinkling her eyes, slight grooves etching her mouth, yet somehow ageless—and always beautiful.

As for Paul, the record of this year together—our "spiritual journey," as I was beginning to see it—was taking shape, even now, under fingers that sped over my computer keys with a fury. In truth, I had been writing for nearly a year, keeping a very private diary since the beginning of my friendship with Paul. Now I marveled at my prowess as an editor, tying together old words and new ones as they bloomed in my memory. It was an easy story to record, one that rained down upon my computer screen with an urgency fueled by my diagnosis. I printed out new pages each night with care, adding holes with my three-hole puncher and inserting the sheets into the binder.

"Give this binder to Paul after you give the letters to Dan," I will tell Lennie soon. Paul will know what to do with it.

Chapter 55
ONE FAINTING ROBIN

Apparently, I was on Susan's mind as well—or so it seemed when she dropped by to see me, unannounced, a few days later. Actually, it was the very day before freshman convocation.

Her arrival in Jackie's office caught me off guard. At the time, Claire and I were poring over a copy of the newly printed convocation program. I loved everything about it—the thick creamy paper with deckle edges, the elegant design, the colorful description of academic regalia. The document represented the best of Wickfield. Claire had shepherded it from drawing board to printing press, using management skills well beyond her writing expertise. Claire, we had discovered, was also good at organizing special events. In fact, Bob had asked her to help spearhead the convocation.

"About your speech title—it's unusual wording," Claire said, commenting on "One Fainting Robin." As always when Claire was embedded in a project, her eyes sparkled. "It will pique everyone's curiosity."

"The title comes from Emily Dickinson," I began—which was when Jackie knocked and stuck her head in.

"Susan Atterbury is here," she said. "She says she'll wait."

Susan rarely stopped by my office. My first thought was that she had figured out my illness. I blanched for a second, unprepared to battle her questions. But Claire quickly scooped her paperwork into an accordion file folder and stood to leave. Susan was, after all, the wife of Claire's immediate boss.

"Here's the order of march," she said briskly, handing me a diagram. "Nothing new, I'm told. Faculty will line both sides of the brick walk to the entrance. Seniors will line both sides of the outside sidewalk along the street. Freshmen will proceed through both double lines and down the aisles into their reserved section at the front. Faculty will sit front left. Platform party will enter the stage from the right."

"And parents and upperclassmen will sit wherever they can," I sighed, studying the drawing. If there were to be a public-relations issue, it would come from parking or seating problems with parents.

Claire greeted Susan warmly as they passed in Jackie's office, but Susan brushed past absently. That was unusual for Susan, who was known for her graciousness. She flung herself onto my upholstered couch in tragic silence, looking for all the world like someone awaiting a jury's verdict. I slipped onto my flowered chair across from the couch.

"Susan, what on earth?"

"It's Jake."

"No! What happened?"

"He's back."

"Back?" How could Jake be back? I had fired him.

"In town. Their house sold, finally. He's back for the closing. Just Jake."

"I see." Somehow I had lost track of the fact that Jake's house was still on the market. And did the seller have to be physically on hand to close? Wasn't that what attorneys were for?

"Have you seen him?"

"No, but he's called from the Charlotte airport. He wants to see me this afternoon." Susan threw up her hands.

"How do you feel about that?"

"How do I *feel*? Good God, Kat, what do you think? Part of me longs to see him, and part of me hopes he gets hit by a truck on his way here."

"I see."

"No, you don't have any idea, Kat. You and Alex were different. Neither of you were married." Tears welled in her voice. "I loved this man once. Part of me still does. I'm committed to Bob and my marriage, but darn, Kat, you don't just dump a tubful of feelings down the drain like dishwater."

"No, you don't." The irony of Susan's words were not lost on me. I knew exactly how she felt.

"What are you saying?" Susan glanced at me sideways.

I stood up and walked to the big window. For a brief moment I recalled the day I'd discovered Susan and Jake on the fourth floor. I had watched the flakes fall that day from this very spot, and my heart then had seemed as heavy as the wet snow. Today the campus was verdant with summer foliage. Life went on.

"I think you should see him, Susan. People will tell you old lovers can't be friends, but you and Jake can prove that wrong." I turned and met her eyes. "Meet him at Hardee's for a cup of coffee. Let him see you as you are now—strong without him, solid with Bob, moving on. Give him permission to be happy for you. Ask about his new job and Alma Earle and wish him well. Give him a goodbye hug in the parking lot. Just make sure it's a public spot to confirm your innocence. And a merely friendly hug."

"Should I tell Bob?"

"Sure. Stop by his office and tell him Jake's in town and that he suggested you meet for coffee. Ask Bob if he can join you. We both know Bob. He'll turn it down but will ask you to tell Jake hello."

"How did you get so smart, Kat?"

"Hey, you're talking to a PhD in English."

"Seriously. You're so smart about people." She paused, choosing her words carefully. "Is that what you would do if Alex showed up? Meet him for coffee?"

Susan was the one Wickfield person who knew the whole dismal Alex saga. I had told her in confidence one day when she had stopped by the house. She had been horrified—terribly hurt for me. This was the first time she had mentioned his name since then.

"Maybe. But I would buy an extra cup, very hot, to toss on him at the end."

I grinned when Susan burst out of laughing. "Just kidding. Alex is a decent man who met my needs at the right time. It's too bad he didn't have the character to meet my larger expectations. What time is the house closing tomorrow? If Jake's available, maybe he could attend the convocation. You, too. Bob will be on the stage with the cabinet."

"Great idea." Susan picked up her purse and slipped the strap onto her shoulder. "Don't know what I'd do without you, Kat. What any of us would do. We all love you dearly, you know." She hugged me tightly, her silky hair brushing my face, and I breathed hints of honey and almond.

The next morning, standing outdoors as the procession was forming, I spotted Susan's yellow jacket as she slipped through the huge double doors of the auditorium. Jake, wearing a dark sport coat and tan slacks, was with her. "Be careful, you two," I whispered to myself, although I had complete faith in Susan. For a moment I felt a pang. I missed Paul. He was working parking detail for the convocation, and he had an early evening law class in Charlotte. I wouldn't be seeing him today.

Then the robed faculty moved forward between the lines of wildly cheering seniors, followed by the wary freshmen who had suddenly appeared two by two from the other direction. I studied their faces as they approached the seniors, who continued clapping specifically for them. Some freshmen seemed startled by the applause; others blushed. I wondered if the freshman women knew how closely they were being scrutinized by the senior men. Scouting was traditional at this event.

The seniors folded in behind the freshmen, and the cabinet and platform party followed. I brought up the rear. As the organ music greeted us inside the dim foyer—Elgar's stirring coronation march that hammered my heart—I swallowed one final prayer. Throughout the week, as I washed down pain pills and refined my wording, I had prayed intermittently for strength to make it through the speech.

Even Lennie had picked up on my duress. "What time you speech today?" she had asked this morning at breakfast. Peering through her spectacles at the fine print on the Tylenol bottle, she'd carefully read the dosage aloud. My plan was to overload on strong nonprescription pain medicine so that my delivery would not be marred by narcotics.

"Ten o'clock. Why don't you walk over and watch the procession gather. Those colorful hoods make quite a spectacle."

"No, not that part. You speech."

"Why?"

"'Cause I be on the floor praying for you when you get up to talk. Just tell me the time."

I was astounded at Lennie's faith. It was innocent, purer than mine. "About 10:30," I told her. "But pray before and after, too. I'll take all the help I can get."

Even as I marched down the aisle past shadowy faces, my head erect and eyes straight ahead, I felt the familiar pinch of pain. It increased minute by minute, building in momentum and spreading throughout my abdomen, pulsating in that peculiar quiver that sometimes forced me to stand or walk. I sat in my stage chair and endured it while the student body president told a joke, while the college choir performed their requisite two anthems, and while Dan made his somewhat stuffy remarks about the "distinctive aspirations" of academic success. Finally, at that very moment when I thought I could no longer tolerate the throb, it was time to make my way to the lectern.

And then—a miracle! When I looked down upon those expectant faces, raising the microphone just a tad toward my chin, I quickly suppressed the pain. These freshmen were the children I had never birthed. They were Wickfield's alumni-in-the-womb, America's future parents. I would hold them in my hand for the next few minutes, and I knew I must own them in the end.

So I began to weave my words. My comments were perfunctory at the outset: the welcome, my early history as a freshman English professor, my longtime affection for novices to college life. I described the traditional activities that would enrich their college years. I reminded them that their high-school commencement speakers had uttered grand commands for high achievement. To extend that thought, I quoted Emily Dickinson about "rising up" so that "our statures touch the skies."

Then I shifted gears. I compared the freshmen to toddlers whose growth spurts would leapfrog within the next twelve months. I noted that the prefrontal lobes of their brains—those yet-developing parts that governed critical thinking and consequences—would mature in quick spurts. Without such progress, I warned, fear and discouragement could sideline them.

"This morning, I see you in the tenderness of youth. Each of you wants fiercely to be an adult, but you have not yet walked that rite of passage. You have not yet wept with homesickness, or slumped in agony over a too-low grade, or grieved in heartbreak from a lover's quarrel. You have not yet been ripped with pain upon discovering your social conscience. You have not yet been devoured by the first-time betrayal of a friend. These are only a few of the universal experiences that engulf all college students. As bewildering and frightening as they may sound, be assured that experiencing them will build character, define integrity, and create true maturity.

"Although I say you are not adults quite yet," I said, "some of you may think otherwise. Some of you will confuse your new freedom with maturity. Be careful. Psychologists tell us that true maturity has not set in by age eighteen or even nineteen. College freshmen walk a treacherous path, and some are surprised when they trip and fall. I can still hear the remorse in the voice of a freshman I taught years ago, a promising young student who, over his Thanksgiving break, had to tell his parents that I had caught him plagiarizing an essay written by someone else.

"'What did your parents say when you told them?' I asked him the following week. He looked down at the tips of his shoes. 'My mother cried,' he said."

The auditorium was silent.

"I urge you to tread this freshman quagmire with cautious steps, guided by earlier lessons from your parents and teachers and coaches. Remember that although they are no longer at your immediate side, their voices are seared within you. Those of you who succeed this year will hear those voices sing in your memory. You will think twice before making a decision, and if you are ever in doubt about the wisdom of a certain choice, you will reject it. Next year and the next, those decisions will be easier. Somewhere during this monumental growth spurt—also known as your "college career"—you will become a truly critical thinker. These college years will grant you amazing discoveries: the joy of words, the magic of numbers, the wonders of the microscope, the drama of history. These discoveries will astonish you and excite you, nurture hidden talents, create future careers, develop lifelong wonderment. When that miracle takes place, you will advance from eager but immature to eager and wise. And that transformation will make all the difference in the measure of success you offer the world.

"I assume many of you are familiar with last year's blockbuster movie *Dead Poet's Society.*" A small ripple went through the audience; the coming-of-age story had resonated with all ages. "You'll recall John Keating telling his new students to listen to the voices of the dead alumni whose framed photos lined the school's walls. '*Carpe,*' those ghosts would breathe. '*Carpe diem. Seize the day.*' Keating challenged his young charges to do something extraordinary with their lives. I challenge you to do the same—to read and think unceasingly, to form personal opinions, to initiate change when injustice seems to prevail.

"At Wickfield, you will find many professors like John Keating—teachers who care about your minds, who challenge you to take intellectual risks, who inspire you to become true critical thinkers. They take pride in Wickfield's liberal arts foundation and in the values established a century ago by our early founders. If you respond with the same energy your professors expend in the classroom, your four years at Wickfield will be rich indeed.

"But there is one additional step I want you to take as Wickfield students. To 'seize the day' involves passion, yes, but that passion is meaningful only if you stretch beyond your sometimes messy, self-centered lives to show concern for the well-being of others. To do that you must reach beyond the boundaries of youthful self-absorption. You must avoid the temptation to 'seize the day' merely to compete, to score, to win, to achieve only for yourself. In other words, you must 'seize the day' with *com*-passion as well."

I glanced at my watch. I was exactly on schedule. "To illustrate my point, I'd like to ask members of the freshman class to please rise." Pain was penetrating my concentration. As the mystified students shifted out of their seats, I slipped my hand into the heavy folds of my academic robe and pressed my hand against my abdomen.

"Over the next sixty seconds, I want each of you to introduce yourself to four people: the person to your right, the person to your left, the person seated in front of you, and the one directly behind you. Include your name and hometown and look directly into each person's eyes as you speak. That's all you have to do. To illustrate, I will introduce myself to members of the platform party." And with that, I left the lectern, took a few steps over to Nick James, the student body president, and extended my hand. The cabinet, without coaching, instantly rose and sprang into action. Dan and Bob shook hands and slapped backs, smiling broadly. Marilyn pulled Pud into a spontaneous embrace, pressing him exuberantly against her chest. Behind me I heard laughter as four hundred freshmen chattered away.

Back at the lectern, watching the students settle back into their thudding seats, I felt the urgent need for stronger medications. My tasseled hat was heavy on my head. Beneath the robe, my clothing was damp.

"Four new names," I continued, picking up my pace. "Remember them. The lives of these four classmates will synchronize with your own during the next four years. As you can see, your college success will be dependent in part on others around you. In similar fashion, you will find it impossible to succeed in the work force without showing compassion for your colleagues. Learn the secret to that future success now. Look at those around you, every day. Look *into* them. Read their eyes. Listen to the heartbeat of their lives. Be aware. Be sensitive. Learn to care about people, even if they don't look like you or they think differently from you."

I was gripping the edge of the lectern now, shifting my weight from one leg to the other as I flipped to the final page. Pain arced throughout my body. My eyes swept over the typed sheet. I quickly cut the next two paragraphs and dropped to the end.

"I'd like to close this morning with words again from Emily Dickinson. When I studied her poetry as a college student, I learned to love her gentle language and vivid images. I leave you now with one of her loveliest. Since Emily numbered her poems rather than giving them titles, I call this simply "the fainting robin" poem. I hope its message will remain with you long after we part—that it will haunt you the way perfume clings to skin, the way starlight lingers in the sky, the way music weaves its chording in your head."

I cleared my throat and took a deep breath from my diaphragm. Just a few more moments! Slowly, I began to read:

> If I can stop one heart from breaking,
> I shall not live in vain;
> If I can ease one life the aching,
> Or cool one pain
> Or help one fainting robin
> Unto its nest again,
> I shall not live in vain.

"My prayer for each of you is that your years at Wickfield will not be lived in vain—that you will rise up with all the intelligence and energy God has given you, that you make morally courageous decisions, and that you become not simply critical thinkers with convictions but *humane* thinkers. May your choices lead you to help countless 'fainting robins' and enrich your own lives in the process.

"May God bless each one of you *mightily* in the months ahead and bring us together again soon, richer and wiser."

The auditorium rocked with thunder as I returned to my seat. The faculty rose to their feet, and the freshmen followed suit. Stunned, I sat briefly, then stood again to acknowledge the loud ovation. Mercifully, in that moment the organ burst forth with the recessional march, and I turned to lead the platform party off the stage.

Chapter 56
THE FOURTH FLOOR

The fire began that same afternoon in Wellstone's stockade room—a room popular with campus visitors since it contained, somewhat like a museum, a colorful piece of century-old history.

I shuddered the first time I heard how convicts had borne the brunt of Wellstone's construction—how they'd actually hewed their own basement dungeon and surrounded the concrete pit with rocks and mortar. Even more dire were the stocks, still intact: timbers laid horizontally between upright beams, with cut-out holes for shackled hands or collared necks. It disturbed me to think of the punishments meted out by prison guards, not to mention the humiliation heaped on such victims by fellow prisoners. It sounded medieval. Paul reminded me once, when I commented about the degradation, that strict law and order were high priorities among early state institutions. At the same time, life had been rough in the South in the late nineteenth-century; class and racial divisions ran deep. I had no doubt that misery was rampant among the prisoners—abysmal living conditions, raw and broken bodies, empty lives void of hope.

Partly in respect for those who'd suffered while constructing Wellstone—and yes, perhaps in part because of my secret obsession with ghosts—I tightened the rules for visitors to our infamous basement prison. In one of the earliest policy changes of my administration, I charged that the room be kept securely locked when not in use and viewed by the public only through formal tours led by designated staff. I added a rule forbidding cameras except for such purposes as historical research.

Yet another rule: absolutely no smoking.

That morning, even as the freshmen were marching to their convocation, Sam Sutton had entered the stockade room with a passkey to show it to a group of friends—law enforcement officials, he said later, although Paul was convinced they were weekend cronies who hunted deer together. Sam did not clear his visit with the business office, which oversaw buildings and grounds; he merely led his entourage through the furniture-clogged storeroom that housed the narrow stairwell leading down to the stocks. Jackie later saw their heads pass by her office as they left the building.

I knew nothing about Sam Sutton's dungeon escapade at the time. I had headed to my house immediately after the convocation, carrying my cap and gown for relief from the heat and downing my pain medications as soon as I entered the kitchen. Earlier I had cleared my calendar until two o'clock, but it was nearly 2:30 when Lennie awoke me from the fog of deep sleep. I felt the desperate need to get to my office. I gulped down a Lortab before I left the house. Surely my long nap would ward off new drowsiness.

At the office, Jackie suggested we review the mail first, since it had piled up all week. We sorted through the most critical; Jackie was excellent at composing quick responses for my signature. Then I attacked the pink mountain of phone slips. Many were votes of confidence from the faculty about the convocation.

"Emily rocks!" exclaimed Ruth Ingram, English Department chair.

Jerry King, head of Social Sciences for umpteen years, said, "Best semester start I can remember!"

Marilyn had left her own handwritten note: "Are you okay? From behind, you seemed to be swaying at the lectern."

"When was Jake here?" I asked Jackie, reading her handwriting on yet another pink slip. The note merely said, "Jake Mooney stopped by to see you."

"Right after the convocation. He wanted just a minute with you—was headed to the closing on his house. Said he'd try to come back later."

I called Susan next, making sure Jackie had closed the door securely. "How did things go with Jake?" I asked.

"We had a wonderful talk, Kat. All he wanted was to apologize to me." Susan's voice was close to breaking. "For putting my marriage in jeopardy. So I apologized back."

"Interesting. I missed him earlier. He stopped by after the convocation."

"Yes, to apologize to you, too. He's changed, Kat. He's different."

"For the better? Did he say why?" The Jake Mooney I knew would require nothing less than heart surgery to suddenly become a "better" man.

"I can't explain it." Susan seemed to be struggling for words—which was unusual for her. "He seems kinder. More thoughtful. He's lost a lot, you know. The new job is nothing like what he had here."

I knew about loss. I knew despair, the feeling that everything I had ever loved was being snatched away with the force of a whipping wind. Perhaps Jake had hit bottom when his glory days at Wickfield ended. And, of course, there was the matter of Susan. To lose something as rare as Susan would be disastrous for any man.

Yes, I thought, hanging up and reflecting on Susan's words, Jake's fall from professional grace had doubtless forced him to find a different "grace"—the redemptive kind.

So I apologized back.

Suddenly, the clutter on my desk seemed meaningless. I needed seclusion, a quiet place to sort things churning in my mind. After Susan hung up, I walked past Jackie, who was on the phone, and turned as though going to Dan's office. Instead, I headed past his door to the grand foyer and began climbing the wide central staircase to the second floor. My feet were slow but steady on the burgundy carpeting as I cautiously ascended the wide, curving steps. Although I heard distant chatter and slamming doors, I encountered no one on the second-floor landing, nor on the third. I was exhausted by now, breathing heavily, but I grabbed the banister for support and began to pull myself, one cautious step at a time, up the treacherous cupped stairs to the secluded fourth floor.

As I knew I would, I found an instant sanctuary amid the statues. The thick smell of dust engulfed me, and the marble figures were cool to my touch. The door to the observatory creaked open when I pushed it, and I slipped into the shadows of the dimly lit room. The air was stifling. I moved to crack open a window—the same one where Susan had stood immobilized that snowy day with Jake.

Without warning, I found myself engulfed in tears. I fell onto the ancient couch, ignoring the crust of powder on the upholstered pillows, and sobbed as though my world had just ended. I wept because I was relieved the speech was over. I wept because I didn't want it to be over. I wept for the love Susan and Jake had felt and lost. I wept for my sisters and their families, whom I missed terribly. I wept for Jane's two-week-old baby, a niece named Adelaide whom I would never see. I wept for today's freshmen, who had no idea how many of their dreams would be dashed. I wept for my body, which was failing rapidly. I wept for my looks, which were beginning to desert me, and I wept for Wickfield, which was about to lose its leader.

But most of all, I wept for Paul, and I wept for me, and I wept for the love we had found but could not keep. I wept for Katherine Embright, the bright-eyed teenager who'd believed faithfully in perfect love, and for Katherine Embright, the fifty-year-old who'd found ultimate love much too late. I wept for June Stafford, whom I had betrayed. I wept for summer, which was ending, and for autumn leaves just ahead, and for the sweet smell of Christmas spruce.

I fell asleep in the midst of my bereavement and slept hard, deeply, as though making a trial descent into the slumber of death. I heard nothing of the chaos on the floors beneath me: the pandemonium when a fireball raced up the basement steps after smoldering for hours in the stockade room, devouring old desks and chairs in the storeroom before bursting up the stairwell into the grand foyer. I did not hear the fire alarm below me, that raucous horn whose shattering wail made conversation impossible. I did not see the rush to flee Wellstone, nor the gathering on the lawn of hundreds of faculty, staff, students, and townspeople as flames shot out of first-floor windows and smoke seeped from the second floor. I did not hear the whining fire trucks, nor the loud drone of the water pumps, nor the sirens from what must have been every emergency vehicle in Cutler County. I did not see members of my cabinet huddling together on the grass, an hysterical Jackie in their midst asking who had seen me last—even sending Pud racing to the Chancellor's House to ask a frightened Lennie if I were there.

In truth, the most dramatic event of my chancellorship was taking place directly below me, and I was missing it all.

In the end, it was the smoke that woke me up, choking me as it invaded the fourth floor and crawled beneath the observatory door. When I saw the sickly yellow film, I thought for one curtained moment that I had died, that I had gone to hell and was doomed forever. Then that guttural instinct to live drove me, hacking, to the door. I left it open as I fled into a gray-green wall of smoke, gasping frantically for breath. It was a nearly fatal error, the fire chief told me later, since the window I had opened could have fanned flames into a fourth-floor inferno.

But even as I staggered down the hall toward the staircase, stumbling heavily against the ghostly statues, I felt less terrified than I might have felt were I not ill with cancer. I was, after all, a dying woman. There was something poetic, almost Jane Eyre-esque, about a recluse dying in fettered chambers. That romantic thought came to me later as I was recuperating at home, and my purple-prose imagery made me laugh a bit. In that last desperate dash, however, my thoughts were on heaven. "Save me," I gasped aloud as I slumped onto the steps, and I wasn't referring to surviving the fire.

The two firemen who found me on the staircase clamped an oxygen mask over my face. They carried me, limp and unconscious, down the remainder of those dangerous cupped steps to the third floor, where they hustled me to the south end of the building and away from the worst of the fire. They emerged with me onto the back lawn, out of sight of the crowds, and I gained consciousness just in time to see the whirling red lights of an ambulance summoned to the rear of the building. I pulled the oxygen mask off my face. The sticky air felt heavenly.

"How did you find me?" I asked as I was being placed onto a gurney.

"Someone suggested we look on the fourth floor, even though we knew it was closed off. We had searched the rest of the building thoroughly."

"Who?" I asked, still confused.

"Some guy who said he used to work for you. And a woman who was with him. Said you went up there alone sometimes. It was a close call, Dr. Embright, but looks like you're going to be just fine. Thanks to them."

The fireman looked me in the eyes as the attendant closed the ambulance doors.

"Guess you owe them both a big vote of thanks."

Chapter 57
THE ONES WHO COUNT

During the short ride to the hospital, the EMTs slapped me with that mask again, and I gulped long, steady drafts of oxygen. My eyes burned and my throat flamed, but my mind was amazingly clear. I knew what lay ahead in the emergency room: a team of medical experts who would swarm over me, undressing me, poking me, listening to my lungs, examining me for signs of smoke damage. In their overall scrutiny, it would not take them long to find the protruding tumor. In an emergency setting I would be outside my usual cocoon of medical protection. I didn't trust the setup; there would be too many players beyond doctors and nurses, too many openings for leaked information. I needed a plan to ensure my privacy.

The answer came to me as soon as the ambulance pulled up to the emergency entrance: I would pitch a little fit to throw everyone off. I would insist that I felt fine and that I would be examined only by my own physician, George Hoffmann. Although I risked making a fool of myself, perhaps being labeled a diva, I really didn't care. I had pledged to carry this hidden illness to my grave, and I was darned if today's drama would unravel my careful secret. As for my personal state of health, I was not worried. If my lungs were burned, it really didn't matter whether they were treated tonight or not. They would be failing me soon enough. I would arrange for someone on my staff to pick me up at the hospital, and I would recuperate in the comfort of my own bed.

My plan worked. The lead physician, a young fellow with a closely cropped red beard and clear-rimmed glasses, began to bear down with his stethoscope as soon as we were in our curtained cubicle. I let him go only so far before I began to protest, thrashing on the table a bit, struggling to sit halfway up in indignation and loudly invoking the name of Dr.

Hoffmann. The nurse threw me a beady glare and tossed out some medical terms that sounded as though she might sedate me. That's when I switched gears, explaining as pleasantly as possible with my raspy vocal chords that I merely wanted my personal physician on hand before we proceeded. I summoned the voice I often engaged when negotiating with my cabinet—the I'm-open-to-your-suggestions-but-expect-you-to-follow-my-lead voice. It had served me well on Monday mornings around the conference table, and now it bought me a little time in the emergency room. A frazzled George Hoffmann showed up in short order, his tie crooked.

"Katherine, Katherine, what have we here?" he asked as he crowded into my tiny examining area. "Terrible about Wellstone." He seemed to be buying a little time himself. It occurred to me he didn't know how much the initial exam had exposed and exactly how much he could say.

"Was anyone hurt?" I asked. It was the first moment I could focus on the school's tragedy. According to my two firemen, at least a third of the building had been affected by flames, smoke, or water. The chancellor's suite, apparently, had been spared.

"No loss of life, no injuries, I hear. Everyone got out, which is amazing, since the fire moved fast. Grove Boulevard is a mess in front of the campus."

"Well, there's nothing wrong with me that a good night's sleep at home can't fix. I'm a little croupy, that's all. Why don't I see you tomorrow at your office?"

George nodded to the ER physician and the nurse, who glided away silently. I lay still this time, trusting the feel of his healing hands. He did not rush. He pulled my eyelids up and down, checked my ears, peered up into my nostrils and down into my throat. Then he began the quiet process of listening to my chest, moving the stethoscope here and there, asking me to breathe deeply. He moved to my back, thumping his hands along my spinal column and listening closely. Then he settled me on my back and looked me in the eye.

"How's our unwelcome visitor?" He perched the stethoscope around his neck, his hand on the sheet over my abdomen. "Wayne Witherspoon said you saw him last week."

"It hurts," I said simply. He lowered the sheet a bit. His probing fingers found the spot, and I yelped a bit as he pressed down.

"What are you taking?"

"Lortab, twice a day, and a stronger yellow pill at night."

"How's that working for you?"

"Not that well. I overdrugged myself this afternoon. That's why I didn't hear the fire alarm."

He pulled the sheet back up and patted my arm. "Nine o'clock tomorrow, my office. I'll see you first thing after rounds."

"Aye, aye, sir," I said, trying to lighten the mood. He sounded somber.

"The good news is that I see only mild soot inhalation, and your lungs, which could have been severely burned, sound clear enough. You are a very lucky lady; your injuries are mild. The nurse will give you something to help your breathing overnight. No wine, no alcohol. Call immediately if you have problems."

He left, and I got dressed. The beady-eyed nurse reappeared with a breathing apparatus, along with some convoluted instructions on how to use it, which I basically ignored. There were also purple pills in a cardboard sample packet. Her manner was terse, suggesting she was miffed that George had given me preferential treatment. She also brought word that a Dan Smith was waiting outside for a private word with me.

Dan? If I had not been so weak from my ordeal, I would have hugged him when he and Mimi stepped inside my cubicle.

"Dan! Mimi! Thank goodness! How bad is the damage?"

"Katherine! How are you? You scared us to death!"

"I'm going to be fine. Can you drive me home? My earlier ride seems to have disappeared on me."

"Really? You mean they're letting you go home tonight?"

"Your voice sounds terrible. Can't you spend the night just for observation?"

"I'm just hoarse. I'll see George again in the morning. How did the fire start?"

"We're waiting on the fire marshal's report. Lots of possibilities."

My mind sorted out Dan's words quickly. If the fire had been caused by faulty wiring or stored chemicals, the fallout could be costly in terms of negative publicity. Wellstone was on the National Register of Historic Places.

"Who's handling the media?"

"Bob and Claire, and they're overwhelmed. We were live on the six o'clock news. Claire's waiting for a statement on your condition—even better, a quote from you if you're well enough to talk about the fire."

"No quote from me. You be the spokesman. Make sure the story is the fire, not me. The statement is that I was treated briefly at Piedmont Memorial for mild smoke inhalation and released. Prognosis is excellent. Period."

"I'll call Claire from the nurses' station." Dan turned to Mimi. "Bring the car around to the ER circle. The media won't recognize you."

"What? The media is here? At the hospital?"

"Hopefully not. When we couldn't find you, Claire simply told them at first that you weren't 'here,' so they took that to mean you were out of town. Later, word somehow leaked out that you had been found in the smoke."

Good girl, Claire, I thought, as I waited for an attendant to push my wheelchair to Dan's car. Dan hadn't mentioned the fourth floor, and I fervently hoped that little factoid would not become public. I was pleased that the staff knew to downplay anything negative about my state of health. I had trained them well this spring.

It was dusk when at last we drove through the streets of Hurley to the Chancellor's House. We slowed to a crawl on Grove Boulevard in front of Wellstone, where two fire trucks remained on the grounds. Long stretches of yellow tape wrapped around the front sidewalk; a small crowd was still gathered on the grass. Dan wheeled into the side street beside the house and made the big loop that brought us up the back driveway. I spotted Lennie's aging Buick in its usual spot and felt a pang of guilt, wondering who was caring for Robert while she stayed late. Another car was barely visible in the dimness of the driveway, and for one wild moment I thought it might be Paul's. But no, he was still in class in Charlotte.

"Looks like Bob is here," said Dan, referring to the shadowy Volvo sedan, "and Claire may stop by to update you from her end. She spoke briefly to the cameras when we were live. There was also a clip of the convocation. Marilyn said to tell you she is worried to kingdom come about you—think that was her exact wording—but that Mama wasn't feeling well, so she couldn't stay."

I managed to laugh at Dan's perfect mimicry. My throat still hurt, but I was feeling better by the minute.

Inside the kitchen, my spirits lifted even more. Lennie hugged me at the door as though I were Rip Van Winkle twenty years later. Her kitchen was surprisingly messy, with sandwich materials and assorted blocks of cheese spread out on the main counter. Apparently the staff had made their way to my house when word spread that I had been "found." After all, what better place than Lennie's kitchen to wait for word from the hospital? Besides, Wellstone was now closed off. Most members of the cabinet had lost access to their offices.

I heard distant chatter at the front of the house, and Dan and Mimi led me down the hallway into my living room. It was equally messy with sandwich plates and wine glasses. Sprawled around as though conferring in an underground White House were the rest of the cabinet, who had not heard us come in. When I appeared, ashen-faced from my ordeal and leaning heavily on Dan, a cheer erupted. Susan shot out of her seat and across the room to embrace me. Bob and Claire were busy in the corner with phones and pad and pen, but both managed to look up and wave. Jackie's tight hug was silent, and I knew I had some explaining to do; Jackie hated so to lose track of me. My escape to the fourth floor had clearly traumatized her. But although there were stories to be shared, no one asked questions. Everyone simply appeared relieved.

My mind by now was numb, in spite of decisions that needed to be made immediately. As if he could read my mind, Dan took charge.

"Susan, why don't you take Katherine upstairs to her room. The rest of us should leave her to rest and get our own rest, too, because tomorrow will be a huge day. We'll meet at eight sharp and start sorting through an 'after-fire action plan' to present to Katherine. When she's fully recovered, that is, which we hope will be very soon." Dan turned to me, and I returned a weary smile. My body hurt all over. My head seemed about to explode.

Upstairs, Susan tucked me into my bed as tenderly as though I were her daughter. She looked tired, and I realized hers had been as emotional a day as mine. Apparently she had walked Jake back to my office in the afternoon when he'd tried a second time to see me. Together, they had been part of the mass exodus when the fire alarm had blared.

"Which one of you told the fire chief to search the fourth floor?" I asked at one point.

"Jake," she said simply as she plumped my pillows and straightened my bedcovers.

I didn't respond. There was much to think about. My mind could handle only so many details.

"I'm so glad you're seeing George Hoffmann again tomorrow," Susan added, changing the subject. "Are you sure you'll be all right tonight?"

"Good as gold. Thanks for everything, Susan. You've been my rock today." I sank back on the pillows, exhausted. "No, leave the door open. Lennie will be coming up to check on me."

I listened to Susan's footsteps on the staircase and heard departing voices as she and Bob said their goodbyes. For a moment I thought another man's voice seemed to join the group before I heard a car drive away. I waited. I heard more voices and then slow footsteps on the stairs.

"Mistah Paul's here," Lennie said in my doorway, her hands clasped in front of her. "He wanna come upstairs. What you want me to say?"

Yes, it was Paul! My heart gave that now-familiar lurch.

"Oh, that's fine, Lennie." I yawned, giving a little stretch. "Send him up. Maybe there's a report by now on how the fire started."

Lennie's slight frame seemed to grow in size as Paul hurried up the steps and paused at the open door. Her high sense of morality made her a mighty mite. There was no way she would be comfortable letting Paul into my room unless she stood on hand to chaperone. She nodded to him, and he entered my room almost on tiptoe. I was grateful that Paul's back was to Lennie as he stood by my bedside so that his hulking outline obscured my face. The width of his shoulders was just enough so that she could not see the love blazing up from my eyes, nor the tenderness pouring down from his.

That's what I thought, at least. I was aware that Lennie's shadow left the doorway a minute later, and I instinctively listened for her footsteps down the stairs. I did not hear them, nor did Paul, for we were both listening, saying little in those first moments. Paul pulled my desk chair over to my bedside and sat down.

Then I saw Lennie's slim brown arm as it reached for the doorknob and pulled the door firmly. Together, we heard the soft sound of her steps as she descended the stairs.

Chapter 58
THE ONES WE
LOVE THE MOST

In hindsight, I'm convinced the next hour of our lives was one of the richest. Perhaps I say that because it was all so recent, and I find myself cherishing every second of what little time remains. What made it memorable was the way Paul and I couldn't talk fast enough, our words spilling over each other, our thoughts tumbling and even stumbling in our need to share every detail of our day. He winced as I described my pain at the lectern and my near stupor on that fourth-floor couch, but he laughed at my emergency room subterfuge. He was a wonderful listener.

Paul's story had its own share of drama. A fellow student had heard the live report while driving to class, and he'd mentioned it just before the class began. Paul searched out a pay phone in his building to call June for details. Then he drove "like hell"—his words—back to campus, where onlookers were still huddled on the front lawn in the growing darkness. He had no trouble locating Sam Sutton, who was talking to the fire marshal in front of Wellstone. Sam appeared relieved when Paul showed up. He turned to him in some disbelief.

"Paul, the fire marshal here thinks the fire started in the stockade room," Sam had told him. "I find that mighty hard to believe. I was in that very room with a group of visitors at ten o'clock this morning, and I could plainly see that everything was in order. It sure the hell beats me."

"Cigarettes!" I exclaimed upon hearing this. "Of course!"

"It well could be," Paul agreed. "Ole Sam looked mighty uncomfortable."

"I bet! Like he needed a stiff drink."

"Like he needed a strong alibi. We'll see what the fire detectives come up with. Regardless, I should have been here, Kat." He shook his head in chagrin, utterly disappointed that he had been off campus when the fire broke out. "Keeping the campus safe—keeping *you* safe—is what I'm here for. I blew it. I would have found you in minutes, Kat, if I had heard Jackie was looking for you."

I almost laughed at his dejected face. "There's no need to berate yourself. Some things can't be controlled. You were working toward that degree, working toward a better future for you and your family. And you aren't responsible for saving me, Paul. I was in God's hands today. I'm listening hard to him, and I gather he's not finished with me yet."

I didn't want Paul to leave. I ached for him to crawl under those sheets and hold me the rest of the night—to share the "compassion" I described in my speech, to pepper away the day's trauma with his kisses, to shield me from the looming fears ahead. That scenario, of course, was out of the question. The evening had grown late. Lennie was waiting downstairs for instructions, and June was waiting at home for Paul. All was as it should be.

Just the same, I loved the way Paul took a minute to make me comfortable. He leaned over me in those final seconds before he left my room, nuzzling me with infinite care, brushing his lips lightly over my eyes, my cheeks, my mouth.

"Good night, sweet lady," he whispered. His restraint was perfect.

"Good night, sweet Paul," I whispered, kissing him back. Our love was brave as it hung over my bed.

In the week that followed the fire, I saw with nothing less than wonder the tangible presence of God. I no longer waited for him to appear, or speak, or nudge me. I merely turned around and he was there. It quickly became apparent to me that the fire was God-sent—quite literally.

As a result, we had a couple of interesting conversations, God and I.

"God," I whispered under my breath early that next week, "did you orchestrate this fire to help conceal my illness? If so, thank you for letting me rest here at home without making excuses to others. I don't have to endure those noisy construction crews. I don't have to smell that stinky charred wood or track sawdust into my office. I don't have to battle those plastic hallway drapes the staff is complaining about." I paused a moment midway through my prayer. Marilyn said those plastic sheets rattled like cheap shower curtains.

In short, I retreated to the sanctuary of my own home to "rest" from my trauma. That, of course, is what the public believed, thanks to a carefully worded press release from Claire. The day after the fire, the *Charlotte Observer*'s coverage of the fire included a brief side story headlined "Wickfield chancellor rescued from fire." I responded a bit cynically when I spotted those words in large letters on page one. A more accurate headline would have said "Dying chancellor nearly dies in Wickfield fire."

As follow-up, Claire's release simply said that Chancellor Katherine Embright was "resting comfortably at her home" after being overcome with smoke and was grateful for the numerous public inquiries about her well-being. The fourth floor was never mentioned in any public format. In fact, my staff, for whatever curious reason, never pursued my whereabouts on that day. Not even Jackie.

The larger truth is that George Hoffmann, after examining my growing tumor the morning after the fire, had ordered me directly to bed. "Katherine, you're a very sick lady," he'd growled, "and I frankly don't see where you have the stamina to keep going. I must have had a moment of insanity last night when I let you go home." He almost snapped at me when I protested, and for a long moment I nursed hurt feelings, wondering why he seemed so cross. Then I understood. We said little to each other during the remainder of the exam. Sometimes words are best left unsaid.

Lennie sprang into action once I was house-bound, shifting my sleep quarters to the downstairs bedroom at the back of the house. She moved my personal grooming items into the quaint purple bathroom, tucked well away from traffic in the main hallway. I felt a bit like Beth in *Little Women*, the ailing sister whose illness earned her the "pleasantest room" in the March home during her final months.

I saw another sign of God's timing with the emergence of Dan's new leadership. "God, about Dan," I began in another prayer. "Thank you for giving him the opportunity to grow into my job while I am still here. Please help him to think clearly under pressure, to develop new priority skills, to move forward with this transition even though he cannot yet see its destination."

I felt better after this prayer. At my insistence, Dan became the man of the hour, the go-to person sought by those involved with Wellstone's recovery. The faculty and deans, most of whom knew their roles blindfolded, rose up as well. Maybe Emily Dickinson's words in my speech had made an impact: in that week following the fire, the entire staff rallied as though their "statures touched the skies." Dan relished his new responsibilities, and the fall semester kicked into gear. I watched silently with enormous relief. Wickfield was in good hands.

I also felt God's protection well beyond His presence on those smoky staircase steps. By working at home, I was able to control my work pace more efficiently than had I been in my Wellstone office. The sun porch became my new "office." Jackie visited me daily with paperwork. Dan and Bob and Claire dropped by frequently. Claire, in fact, brought me the news that the campus alliance of gay students was planning an imminent march along the Grove Boulevard side of campus.

"They'll have placards asking for equal rights, but it's nothing to be alarmed about," she reassured me, as though fearing I would be dismayed. A national gay rights movement was building momentum, but this would be the first time Wickfield would see an actual demonstration.

But I was not dismayed. "They have every right to march," I reminded her. "They want a voice, and they deserve to be heard. Who's your contact?"

"A student from Raleigh. Alexander Wilson."

I was not familiar with the name. "Give the group every courtesy," I said. "Have they alerted the press?"

"Knowing Zander, I'm sure they have. He'll cover every detail for publicity."

Zander? That name, now, did indeed seem familiar. Zander . . . . I concentrated, trying to focus, exasperated that my medicines fogged my mind too much to remember dim details.

To keep my brain as sharp as possible, I began using my telephone relentlessly, even when infused with pain. I spoke to Charlie Pettigrew in Chapel Hill, to various state legislators in Raleigh, and to Wickfield trustees. With the legislators I soothed, argued, negotiated, and cajoled, calling up old debts and reviving faded promises. Like late summer's gasp of fullness and glory, I fought for Wickfield's future with every iota of energy left in me.

No doubt I became in those few days the drama queen of the telephone lines, the voice that made secretaries raise eyebrows to their bosses and mouth, "It's her." There were probably jokes flying hither and yon, like "I wonder what she's smoking now," or suggestions that smoke inhalation might be better than a spider bite for super-human powers. Lennie despaired when I waved away her teapot and lunch trays, but I really didn't care. The throbbing in my lower side was like the ticking of a time bomb. I had much yet to do.

As for this fast failing of my body, I was nothing short of astonished. I wanted to yell at George Hoffmann and Wayne Witherspoon, to tell them they had tricked me, lied to me, promised me more time! I felt their sadness, saw how even when assuming their most professional demeanors they betrayed their personal grief.

"Not yet," I sobbed to God late one night on my deck, my tears mixing with the early September rainfall. "Please, just a few more months!" It was a steady rain, not a furious late-summer thunderstorm, yet the darkness was so dense I could scarcely see where the rose beds began. The beast that had stalked me for two months was closing in, circling me with the hundred claws and lava breath of a mythological monster. Night was my enemy. This was the time when pain prevented sleep, when I sweated into my sheets and groaned aloud in agony. I knew my face would soon be turning gray, my eyes hollow with dark circles. On this particular night, my cotton robe and socks puddle-thick with rain water, I pleaded to the falling heavens for more time. Yet even as I prayed, I realized that "more" in this case probably meant suffering beyond belief. In my moments of deepest despair, I wondered whether I should be praying for immediate death.

Later that same night, as I wrestled with my bedcovers to get comfortable, I made the decision to call Tim. This was not a strange decision, considering that I was beginning to see my life as a novel whose pages were speeding toward the end. I wanted to back up the pages to the Tim chapters, to grab a glimpse of those youthful days when we'd been carelessly happy, heady on wine and life. I could not remember the last time we had spoken, although I was certain the encounter had been pleasant. Tim and Rosa sent an annual Christmas card, their names imprinted at the bottom with gold lettering: *Mr. and Mrs. Timothy M. Bernay.* Tim and I had never sent ostentatious cards when we'd been married. I was pleased that Tim always scribbled a personal line of greeting, perhaps to relieve the austerity of the card's design.

I left a message on Tim's office phone early the next morning, my eyes bleary from lack of sleep. I was certain he would call back, although I assumed it would be later in the day. The evening anchors were not required to report to the station until 2:00 p.m.

I was wrong. Tim called back before lunch, his voice like a jolt of caffeine. "Hi, Lady Katie," he boomed with his magnificent vocals. At least he didn't call me "Kitty Kat." That was a term of endearment he had sometimes used when he was, well, being endearing.

It's strange what happens when your mortality is threatened and once-familiar sounds confront your space. What I thought would be a call to cheer me up was suddenly a trigger to my innermost emotions, and I struggled to keep my voice composed. If Tim noticed, he didn't say anything, at least not at first. We made the usual small talk about family and old friends, and he quickly had me laughing at his quips. Tim was a professional, no doubt about it, and not just because he was known to vast audiences. He was blessed with a gift of gab that could slide him through any situation.

"So how have you been?" he finally asked, and I plunged forward with a story about my March surgery and subsequent recovery. He seemed to be listening carefully, as if still able to read my emotions between the lines.

"And how is Kat today?" he asked, and this time his voice range had lowered. It was that silky radio voice, the one I had fallen in love with as a college girl long before I met "Timber Nay" in person. Those golden tones had hoisted him high in radio ratings before he hit stardom in television.

He knows, I thought in near panic, realizing that Tim, indeed, knew me extremely well.

"I'm hanging in there," I said, suddenly wishing I hadn't called.

He said nothing back, and then we were in the middle of one of those awkward silences when neither party knows whose turn it is to move the chess piece.

"Listen, Tim, I was thinking," I said, babbling a bit to fill the space, "about something that happened a long time ago." I stopped and tried to laugh, but the laugh sounded like gargling. "Do you remember that time we were supposed to go to the beach for the Fourth, just a long weekend? I was working on some paper, and we didn't have much time, and when we showed up at the motel at Ocean Drive, the lady said she didn't have a reservation for us, and I got mad and said I knew I had mailed it in because I remembered writing North Carolina by accident, so stupid, and striking it out and writing South, and she said she was very sorry but they were completely full, and so we ended up in some godforsaken place at Windy Hill, far back from the water, where the kitchen reeked with spices and we figured the previous renters had sprinkled crab boil mix to get rid of roaches."

Tim was completely silent. I took a breath and continued.

"Well, I promised you I knew I had mailed it, and you said you believed me, but when we got back, I found the letter tucked in the back of a kitchen drawer where I had stuffed it while looking for a stamp. I had never mailed it. I tore it up and threw it away because I was embarrassed to show it to you, and every Fourth after that I made some insulting remark about that nitwit woman at Ocean Drive." Again I stopped for breath. And waited.

"Yes," Tim finally said, in a voice that didn't sound like Tim at all.

"Anyway," I said, my voice growing stronger, "I just wanted you to know. Not that I actually lied to you, I guess, but I wasn't really honest, either. I just wanted to, you know, clear the air."

Tim went through another long pause. I studied the pattern in the bedroom rug, the border where the fleur de lis changed into little circle flowers every couple of inches. *Please say something,* I implored. *Anything.*

"Kat," he finally said, his voice still strange, "is that the only time you lied to me while we were married?"

I considered his question carefully. "Yes, I'm pretty sure. Why?"

"You were faithful to me, weren't you?"

"Yes, absolutely. You know that. And you were faithful to me. Right?"

"Right." We had had this conversation years before, shortly before we divorced.

"Well, if that's the worst you could come up with, I think your future place in heaven is pretty secure." And then we both laughed, a long and healing laugh, except that a few silent tears were mixed in with mine.

"Why did we get divorced in the first place, Kitty Kat?"

"I've wondered that myself. If we had both tried harder, we might have made it."

"But then you wouldn't have had your great career. Because you would have been following me to Atlanta."

"Or maybe you wouldn't have had yours, Mr. Big Shot. Because you would have been following *me.*" He had the grace to laugh again.

"Tim, you've been faithful to Rosa, too, haven't you?" I could have slapped my mouth the moment those impetuous words escaped. His current marriage was not my concern. His response surprised me even more: complete silence.

"Well, anyway, it's not too late to make things right, you know, to turn things around, to at least be remorseful to God."

"Thanks."

"So, when are you coming to the Carolinas? The mountains will be lovely in a few weeks." I was grabbing madly for words—anything to get past the growing sadness in Tim's voice.

"Well, when are you coming to Atlanta? Any more conferences?" I had called him once from a meeting at the downtown Atlanta Sheraton, shortly after Carrington had offered me the Wickfield chancellorship. Tim had been elated for me, as I had known he would be. For some reason it had seemed crucial at the time to tell him myself.

"I'll let you know."

"And call me if, you know, anything changes."

"Of course. You, too."

There was another long pause, as painful as the first.

"Love you, Kat."

"Love you, too," I sobbed, not caring that he heard. I wept for several minutes after hanging up, my head buried nose-first in my pillow. I was grateful I was in my bedroom where Lennie couldn't hear me. I was beginning a mental list of things to tell my sisters. Soon.

"Marianna," I would say, "one of the first things when you are notifying people will be to call Tim. Urge him to come to the funeral, because I really want him there. Rosa, too.

"And be sure you have them sit with the family."

PART II

DEATH

Katherine's account of her conversation with Tim was the last she actually wrote. As I read through the typed pages in her binder—given to me by Lennie the day after her death—I thought it fitting that her written memoir closed with thoughts of her former husband.

When she entered Hillcrest Hospital the next day, her ability to type ceased. But a hospital room did not end her story. Katherine continued to convey her thoughts, revealing them in short bursts as I visited her bedside those final days. In the time we had alone, she sometimes talked nonstop, fueled either by her medications or by a desperate drive to share all that was so suddenly transpiring. Occasionally her words were mere whispers. Sometimes I recorded them on my handheld tape recorder, holding the mike close to her mouth. She asked to keep it by her side whenever I left and later said that speaking into it helped her deal with bouts of pain. Other times I merely typed into the night, recording her thoughts from memory. Since I was an observer to much that occurred during her hospitalization, I was able to fill in her brief narratives with what I knew to be her voice. She seemed pleased when I told her I was doing this, because she wanted our story to be accurate. Katherine, if anyone, understood the power of words.

These pages, thus, represent Katherine Embright's final thoughts and words as transcribed from her recordings (and my reportings) between Thursday, September 6, 1990, and Tuesday, September 11, 1990.

Following her story is my personal observation of events that transpired immediately after her death.

—Paul O. Stafford
September 30, 1990

Chapter 59
SISTERS

Thursday, September 6, 1990

Marianna is here. She drove in late last night and arrived while I was sleeping. Lennie put her in the blue bedroom, the one that faces the side campus where the students wander through. Tim, it seems, called Emily in alarm after we had talked. Emily in turn called Marianna, who called me.

"Kat, what's going on? Are you sick again?"

"It hurts like crazy," was all I had to say, and Marianna packed a bag. I knew this would happen.

Actually, I'm glad to have her here. She smells like Wind Song bath powder. Her cheerful voice is like sunshine, although she's clearly annoyed I didn't call about the fire. The Wellstone fire had little coverage outside the state. She doesn't know yet the extent of my illness. Unless she's guessed.

Wayne Witherspoon is admitting me this afternoon to Hillcrest for IVs and morphine and whatever else he'll dream up. This is just for a few days. Evidently I'm dehydrated. He wants to send an ambulance for me, right now, but I've negotiated for borrowed time. I'm going to meet with the cabinet at noon. In my living room. I just got off the phone with Dan, who readily agreed to call everyone. I tried to be casual enough when I suggested it: just an informal gathering over lunch to assess progress after the fire. I also mentioned, rather as an aside, that I "had agreed" to be hospitalized for a few days "for exhaustion" and that I would prefer he not tell the others on the cabinet until after the meeting—"just so that doesn't become the focus of the meeting," I explained. He's very supportive. He thinks it's all a "good idea" and commented on how exhausted I seemed this week. I promised him Lennie would fix ham sandwiches and her famous brownies. She needs something to do today other than worry about me.

Paul will drive me to the hospital after the meeting. I insisted on that, and Sam Sutton, who has finally confessed that "someone" among his visitors last Friday "may" have lit a cigarette, is making no waves.

Frankly, I think I'm just exhausted from all those phone calls, and I admit I haven't eaten much this week. A few days in the hospital, pumped up with IVs and bed rest, should do me a world of good—assuming I can stand all those beeps and whistles.

Marilyn keeps staring at me, as though I've suddenly sprouted a purple beard. She's nearly rude, the way she keeps turning toward me with long gazes. She took over the roomy Queen Anne wing chair as soon as she came through the front door. She is working quite a balancing act, holding her Royal Doulton plate on her knees and turning to look at me. She took two brownies.

Dan is doing a superb job of leading the conversation. Everyone has some little story about the Wellstone restoration. The construction noises annoy everyone. Bob says the whining saws remind him of Hugo and make him nervous. Marilyn hates the drills, says they sound like woodpeckers grinding away on her barn. Claire says no, that the entire campus sounds like the whir of ten thousand cicadas. Yes, Claire is here, too, now that she's on the cabinet, and Marla from Alumni and Kevin from Technology are visiting. Dan added them just for today—good choices. Pud can't make it because of a lunch with the coaches.

Dan asks for a report on my telephone calls but jokes first that I talked this week with everyone except the pope. Everyone laughs and looks at me. I have chosen to sit on the straight-legged Duncan Phyfe chair near the hallway in case I need to sprint to the bathroom. I joke back. I share conversations from memory, without notes. I mention that I expressed special concerns about new discoveries in technology that are erupting every day and that I hope higher education can join with private business for the benefit of "everybody." I remind them that the new e-mail seems to be higher education's exclusive domain right now—that Mayor Barnhardt hadn't even heard of it. I thank everyone for all they do for Wickfield, especially for "rising up" after the fire. My voice tires. I am exhausted. I tell them I hope to be back on the job soon.

When the group is leaving, Bob takes me aside and says Susan is eager to talk to me as soon as I'm feeling better. I send her my love and promise to call in a few days. And I absolutely mean it! When I return from the hospital, I will break my silence and tell the cabinet and close friends about this illness. It's time. Having Marianna around reminds me of the importance of involving loved ones. Perhaps I should have done this already. It will be good to have Susan hovering around, even if hugely sad for us both.

Yes, my mind is made up. I will share my news in a few days. And Susan will be the first one I tell.

Paul shows up as soon as the lunch group leaves and places my overnight bag into the trunk with infinite care. I introduce Marianna, who stayed upstairs and out of sight during the meeting. "I've heard a lot about you," she says to Paul and smiles, her eyes almost flirting. I glare. Marianna has *not* heard a lot about Paul. No one has, and I need Paul to know I have not betrayed him to anyone. Lennie catches my warning look and turns away.

Marianna says she will follow us shortly, as soon as Jane returns her call from California. Lennie follows Paul and me into the driveway and chews on her lower lip. I remind her that I'll be back soon. "Better than new," I tell her, although we both know I'm stretching a bit on that point. She hugs me so tightly that her nails dig into my neck. I smell lemon balm on her hands. She's removed her apron, and I'm surprised to see she's wearing her best dress, the navy one she usually saves for Sunday, and her sturdy low-heeled Sunday shoes rather than her soft-soled tie shoes. Come to think of it, she wore them yesterday, too.

Paul holds the door while I slide into the front seat and buckle up. He then circles around and heads the car out, nose first. I lower my car window and stick my arm out, waving cheerfully from the front seat. Lennie waves back, standing alone in the driveway. I smile broadly and keep waving. She's still waving when we make the turn onto Grove Boulevard.

Now we're driving south on the four-lane highway toward the interstate into Charlotte. We've worn down the asphalt on this stretch with our numerous trips, and here we come again. It was this same Thursday exactly a year ago when Paul and I made our first trip together, down this very highway toward Charlotte. I start to mention that, then hold the thought. I comment instead on the wedges of roadside lilies, the red poppies in the median, the slopes of yellow *Coreopsis*. No state in America beautifies with wildflowers like North Carolina. Paul says little, and I notice he's driving too fast. He's gripping the steering wheel tightly, like a NASCAR driver. "We're not going to the Charlotte Speedway," I tell him gently. He slows down and reaches for my hand. It feels good. I feel that surge that grips me every time. It's not fiery anymore. It's something better.

I hate hospitals. Even when I visited Alex at his Chicago hospital and heard his name blared on the intercom, I was not impressed. Doctors are highly trained, and most are highly competent, but they're not superheroes. Little things depress me, like the antiseptic smells and squishy shoes. I wish they could get the darn lighting regulated. It's either too dim, like a church nave on a weekday, or too bright, like my sun porch in the morning. The elevators, where gurneys line up for transportation, are unsettling—down for surgery, up for recovery, back down to the basement for the morgue.

Paul releases me and my bag at the ER with reluctance, trying to help me into a waiting wheelchair but being rebuffed, politely, by an attendant in green scrubs. He leaves to park but promises to find me shortly. Since I'm a direct admit, I can circumvent the emergency room. The orderly rolls me into an elevator and pushes the button for fifth floor. He wheels me a few feet and then turns down a hallway marked ONCOLOGY in large black letters. A young nurse takes over when we arrive at Room 540. I can remember that number; I was born in 1940.

The shades in my room are drawn against the afternoon sun, and everything is yellowed by the fluorescent overhead light. The nurse pulls back the bedcovers and tells me to undress and change into the gown she lays out. She seems nervous. "It ties in back," she says, as though I didn't know. I protest and tell her I brought my own gown and robe. "Good!" she smiles, as though there's no problem. "After the doctor examines you, I'll help you change into it." I tell her I can manage just fine by myself, thank you. She's scarcely older than our Wickfield nursing students.

Mine is a private room, typical hospital fare. A table on rollers sits next to the bed, with an extended arm that fits over it. It holds the usual glasses and pitcher and a kidney-shaped pan for patients who throw up. I hope I'm not one of them, at least not on this visit. There are two guest chairs covered in bland gray vinyl, plus a bedside stand with a phone, a clock, and a TV remote control. High on the wall in front of me is a television set. At least I'll be able to watch *The Today Show*.

I roll myself gingerly under the sheets and lie back on the pillow. It's thin, not plump like mine at home, but it still feels good. I sink at once into drowsiness. A young man knocks and enters, wheeling a cart with an IV bag. Others, all wearing green or blue scrubs and those ugly shoes, follow with more contraptions. I gather from their conversation that one is called an O2 "sat" machine; it's a gray box with beeps and readouts. Someone puts a butterfly clamp on my finger, and the numbers on the machine start dancing. I try to breathe normally without sounding so breathy.

Dr. Witherspoon shows up, and everyone evaporates. He helps me sit up while he listens to my chest and back. He seems to take forever; I want to lie down again. He lowers me back onto the pillow, lowers the top sheet, and pulls up my gown to expose my stomach area. He presses me all over, starting under my breasts and proceeding to poke every major organ. He asks me what hurts and doesn't hurt. It all seems futile, since everything he touches is painful. He pulls the sheet down a bit more, exposing me so much that I swallow hard, and presses the distended part. I groan. He listens again with his stethoscope. I ask him what all the black and gray and silver machines are for—there's quite a collection by now—and he says I'm being monitored for heart rate, blood pressure, and oxygen. Also state of consciousness. That last one surprises me. "We'll make you as comfortable as possible, Katherine," he says. He is a kind man. I know I'm in good hands.

He bumps into Marianna and Paul as he leaves me, and I see the three of them huddling outside my door. Marianna appears to be bombarding him with questions, while Paul stands silent, listening. I long for a nap, but they enter my room together. Paul is carrying a magnificent vase of long-stemmed red rosebuds that he obviously purchased from the florist's cooler near the lobby. They're expensive, the kind Alex used to send; I've priced them before. I reach out for the vase gingerly and grasp it like a rare piece of art. I rub my nose slowly across the ruby bud closest to me. Paul smiles so tenderly that I blush.

Marianna fusses around the room, taking the vase and positioning it on the stand so I can see it easily. She turns the fuller buds to face me. She pours a glass of ice water and waits while I take a couple of sips. She leaves to check on "something" down the hall.

Paul and I look at each other. It seems like two weeks since I met with the cabinet, not two hours. I feel like saying, "What just happened?" Instead I say, "You don't have to stay." Paul grins as though I said something quite funny. He pulls a chair next to my bed and takes my hand. "I'm staying until they kick me out," he says.

A technician enters, sticks my left arm with a needle, and draws blood. Someone hooks me up to the IV drip, tethering it to my left arm with a catheter and tape. A nurse follows and fiddles with it. Every time she moves my hand, the needle riding the top of my hand bites a bit.

The nurse tells me she's administering morphine into the drip. Morphine at last! I close my eyes and doze off.

Marianna comes in again, waking me up and smiling from ear to ear, and Paul drops my hand and stands. A woman enters behind her, also smiling. It's Emily! All the way from Atlanta! I grin, happy as heck to see her, and she bends over my bed and kisses my cheek. But I'm concerned, because she'll have to make at least two trips, right? Atlanta is close, only a few hours by car, but still, I hate to think of the girls making trips back and forth. This is one of the reasons I withheld my news until now.

Paul stands in the background, watching the sisters interact. Emily turns and introduces herself, and I hear her say something like "thank you for all you've done for Katherine." *Yes, thank you, God, for Paul. Thank you for bringing him into my life at this juncture to teach me about love, to comfort me, to cherish me.* The prayer is silent, but I watch these three dear human beings who are here for me and find myself unable to make conversation.

Emily mentions she has driven straight through from Atlanta and hasn't eaten since breakfast. She and Marianna leave together for the hospital dining room. Paul and I resume our quiet vigil. He assures me that he was able to re-register me under the same pseudonym we used last time. He reminds me that the hospital management knows exactly who I am. *Thank you, God, again. For Paul and all the ways he knows to care for me. I could never have done this by myself.*

Wickfield seems far away. I drift back into sleep, Paul's hand on top of mine. I awaken in a drowsy stupor and hear the others chatting around my bed. A new nurse, a heavy-set pregnant woman, checks my vital signs.

My pain has eased a little.

Chapter 60
HOURGLASS

Friday, September 7, 1990

I feel better. Even with last night's interruptions. The morphine works. It has taken the edge off the pain that has gripped my gut.

My shades are drawn, yet I'm confident the morning sky is clear. The sun rays are strong on my windowsill. I wonder what's happening at school right now. It's still early. The new cross-country team is probably running laps down the Grove Boulevard sidewalk, all the way into town. Claire's morning newspapers should be on the Wellstone steps, delivered to their secret spot behind the potted ficus tree so early joggers won't steal them. Fridays are always busy. I must call Jackie first thing. She surely knows by now that I'm in the hospital. And Dan! I wonder if he's in the office yet. It's nearly seven. Maybe. He's usually an early bird.

I like watching TV in bed. That cute Katie Couric—how does she manage to look so perky every day at the break of dawn? She's from Indianapolis. Paula Abernethy, who taught communications at Keck College, was from Indianapolis. She had met Katie a couple of times around Indy before she went national. Said she was lovely. No, I think the lovely lady was Jane Pauley, come to think of it. She was from Indianapolis, not Katie. Tim meets all of these celebrities at national gatherings. I like this remote control for TV and the way they mount these sets high on the wall. Maybe Maintenance can mount my bedroom set before I get home. I'll be spending more time in bed. I need to call Lennie.

A nurse enters, brisk and cheerful, and helps me shuffle a few feet to the bathroom. I'm still wearing yesterday's hospital gown. We trail the IV cart with us. It's a tight squeeze in such a small space, and she slips out and closes the door. When I shuffle back, she helps me settle under the sheets. The aroma of coffee is strong in the hall, and today it smells appealing. Dan seems glad to hear from me—relieved, I think. He says he called Piedmont in Hurley to check on my condition but was told I wasn't there. "I'm in Charlotte," I tell him, "because all my records are here. And they know me here. It's just easier." He doesn't question it, doesn't ask which hospital, and if he starts calling around, he'll never find me. "I'll call you later," I say when hanging up. "No, I don't want visitors. I need rest. Remember, you're in charge." I try to flatter him a bit—not that his confidence needs shoring. Dan is the right man at the right time. Jackie sounds guarded when I call at 8:30, which suggests she has other people in her office. Probably half the secretarial staff in Wellstone is clustered around her desk, assuming the word has spread that I'm in the hospital. It probably has. Even if Dan told the cabinet to stay mum, the news will slip out.

"I'll call you back," she says, but she obviously doesn't have a number. "No, I'll call you," I say.

We hang up without a real conversation, which ordinarily would have bugged me. This morning, however, there is much to focus on here. Like eating. My eating seems to be very important to the nurses, but I'm not hungry. A woman enters with a pink cafeteria tray. I pick through some of the scrambled eggs, and the nurse beams and says "Wonderful!" All I want to do is lie still in one position. Marianna and Emily show up, eager to help, but there's not much they can do. I doze off. When I awaken I am suddenly nauseated, horribly sick to my stomach. I can't find the little tray in time and vomit into my sheets. Two women show up to change my linens and do it quickly, even with me rolled over to one side of the bed. They float out a clean bottom sheet and together give it sharp whack. They tug the four corners onto the mattress and give expert jerks to the top sheet when they tuck it at the foot. They work professionally and say little. My head hurts. I want to sleep. Paul may come by late this afternoon. His law class starts at six, and I have told him he mustn't miss another one. I also told him to stay home Saturday, to spend time with June and the kids. "Maybe Sunday," he said before he left last night. Marianna is spraying the room with Lysol. I seem to be getting sicker by the hour, not better.

I am tired this evening. Paul shows up before class. He knocks and enters. I show him my morphine pump and tell him the meds are making me sick. He senses my fatigue and stays only a few minutes. He mentions a surprise for when he returns Sunday, and he smiles when he says it. Marianna turns on the evening news, but it's all about war—Iraqi soldiers fighting in Kuwait, a political execution in Liberia. I hate it all.

So much death, I think drowsily as I feel myself melting into sleep. So many are dying. Dying. I feel my mind dropping into the dark abyss of slumber. I am a child again in Arden, snuggled in the old Victorian bed I shared with Sarah, the crafty sandman watching over us nearby. *Sarah. Sandman. Sander. Zander—*

Suddenly my eyes flutter open, and my mind jerks into alertness. Zander! Zander Wilson. Alexander Wilson from Raleigh. As clear as daylight, I now remember exactly how I know the name of this student heading the gay rights demonstration.

Zander had been identified in September as one of the three closest friends of David Weise.

Saturday, September 8, 1990

It's late Saturday night. Marianna and Emily have returned to their motel room. Nothing stands out except that I've been miserable all day. I woke up during the night with a fever. I got the shakes, and I threw up again. And again. Today has been more of the same. My trips to the bathroom take longer. I'm almost too weak to drag this darn cart along, but I can't bear the idea of a bedpan. I need a good night with full sleep, to rally, to get stronger. Paul is coming tomorrow. I must be strong enough to talk to him.

It's obvious that many now know where I am. Jackie has probably contacted Chapel Hill, just to keep Charlie in the loop. She's so professional, that Jackie. She'll make it clear that I'm exhausted from the fire and need rest. *Thank you, God, for surrounding me with exceptional staff, and guide them during my illness. Help them to make clear decisions in my absence. Help me to sleep soundly tonight, with minimal pain. Help me to get stronger fast. Keep Paul safe tomorrow. Help me with Paul tomorrow. Help him with me. Amen.*

PREZ: A STORY OF LOVE

Sunday, September 9, 1990

It's Sunday, and my sisters flit about my room, watering Paul's roses and straightening my covers. Marianna has picked up a pink can of room freshener at Eckerd's. It's called Spring Bouquet; its scent is more floral than the medicinal Lysol. The skies outside are gray, ready to open with rain. About ten I start to doze off, and Marianna says she and Emily are going downstairs. I awaken to low voices and someone crying. When I focus, I see Sarah! She's dabbing at red, swollen eyes. I'm surprised to see her—glad, of course, but surprised. There's no need for the entire family to come, not yet. Jane is busy with the new baby. Still, it's wonderful to have three sisters here at the same time. Usually it's Christmas when we're all together.

About three o'clock Paul breezes in, holding an umbrella and grinning from ear to ear. My sisters light up. Sarah gets introduced, and Paul pretends to be overwhelmed with "four beautiful Embright women" at once.

"There's one more," they chorus together, and everyone laughs. "Jane is our baby sister, but she's just had her own baby—baby number five," Sarah explains. Paul already knows this but acts impressed. I love watching him interact.

Paul brings more flowers—this time from Wickfield! They all collected in Jackie's office on Friday, and Paul slipped into Wellstone to load them into his car. One is an arrangement of white lilies and pink roses with a card reading, "When the Kat's away, the mice will play, so hurry back before we get in trouble!" It's signed, "Love from your cabinet." The handwriting is unfamiliar, so I picture Jackie dictating the note to the florist and making sure *Kat* is properly spelled. There's also a stunning pot of peach-colored mums, elegantly wrapped in foil and ribbon. It's from Dean John Sigmon and the business-school faculty. They can afford the expense. Still, I am touched, not cynical. My roots are with the arts and humanities, but business professors are among my strongest supporters.

The women make excuses to go downstairs "for a while," and Paul takes his usual seat to my right. "I've known them forever," he says after they leave. "They're exactly as you described them."

Paul looks wonderful. He's wearing that same yellow polo shirt he wore to the faculty picnic last fall. As it did then, his chest hair peeks out a bit at the throat; I notice flickers of silver. I'm hoping he'll talk so I won't have to. I'm exhausted, but I'm happy to be alone with Paul.

"There's something I want you to do for me," Paul says. He pulls up a chair next to the bed and leans over to take my hand.

"What?" I ask, smiling. He's probably teasing me. Dear Paul. He's trying so hard, even though he's hurting hugely.

"Teach me how to pray." He looks straight at me when he says these words, and I see he is definitely not teasing.

"Of course." I swallow hard. For a moment I can't look at him.

"It's easy, really. First you say thank you. Then you ask for help. That's really all there is to it."

"Show me."

"Come here," I whisper, and he leans his head in toward mine. I lift one hand to his face.

"Close your eyes."

I close mine, too, and I pause a moment. *Lord, tell me what to say.*

But simple words come readily to my lips. God has been teaching me a long time.

"Thank you, dear Lord, for all the blessings you have given me," I begin. Paul is motionless, head bowed.

"Thank you for my family who loves me, for doctors who heal, for nurses who care." I peek through half-lidded eyes. Paul's eyes are still shut.

"Thank you for Wickfield in my life and for all it has come to mean to me." *More words, Lord,* I plead.

"Thank you for Paul in my life. Thank you for letting him teach me how to love again." My voice breaks, and I stop for a moment.

"Help Paul. Help him every day. Help him in his work at Wickfield. Help him with law school. Help June and Marcy and Blair." A muffled sob escapes, but I can't tell whether it comes from me or from Paul.

"Help him to remember how to pray. Help him to pray every day. Guide him throughout the rest of his life. Show him how to live his life well. Teach him. Hear him. Love him."

I open my eyes and see that Paul's eyes are open, too, but filled with tears. He's looking straight at me. I look back, unblinking.

"And remind him every day, dear Lord, how much I love him. Help him to remember. Amen."

I must have dozed off for a few minutes, because, when I awaken, Paul is talking softly, close to my face. I watch his lips move and remember how I loved kissing them. As ill as I am, I can still see that Paul is a sensual man, a beautiful human being in body and heart and soul. He mentions how great the front quad looked when he drove by it, how the students were lying on blankets with their books. He tells me that Dan inquired about our hospital trip—but not too much—but that Marilyn insisted that since she and I "are such good friends," she needed to know exactly where I was and precisely the nature of my illness. I scrunch my eyes to picture the conversation. "I'll tell the cabinet when I go back," I say. "Very soon. I should be strong enough in a couple of days. I'll probably work from home."

Paul says nothing. He pulls my hand to his mouth and kisses it. I see with alarm that his eyes are teary again, that he's trying to speak and that his mouth is trembling.

"You've no idea what an impact you've had on my life," he tells me. "You have changed everything. I'm a different person, Kat." He stops and searches for words. "I'm a *better* person. Wiser. Kinder." He stops again, his face contorted. He waits to regain control.

"My life has direction now. Law school makes perfect sense. It was the right choice. Before you, life was just drifting along." His mouth moves closer to my ear; his hand strokes my face.

"And I will love you forever, Kat. I will never, ever forget you. You must believe that."

I lie motionless, my eyes closed. Is this a goodbye speech? No way! I can't bear this!

"Did you hear me, Kat? I will love you forever."

I open my eyes. I'm beyond tears. So this is death, and I'm not ready. From somewhere deep within my well of pain I sense that our final farewell, if this be it, must be peaceful, not weepy. Paul must remember me smiling. I look at him directly and try to smile.

"Beautiful Paul." My words are a whisper. My lips feel thick as if numbed by the dentist. I try again.

"Stay, Paul. Be with me at the end."

He tries to laugh a little. "It's not today, Prez," he says, kissing me on the cheek.

"Sing to me."

"Sing?"

"Sing me to heaven."

"Okay," he finally says. "Actually, I've memorized the words to your favorite hymn. I already knew the tune."

He takes a minute before starting, and I keep squeezing his hand, afraid I will doze off too soon. His beautiful baritone opens up, its richness wrapping itself around me like a prayer shawl.

> Beautiful Savior, King of Creation,
> Son of God and Son of man,
> Truly I love you, truly I serve you,
> Light of my soul, my joy, my crown.

When I wake up, Marianna is wiping my face with a cold cloth, and Emily and Sarah are seated in the chairs, watching. My fever has returned.

And Paul is gone.

Chapter 61
MONDAY NIGHT

Monday, September 10, 1990

It's Monday, I think. The shades are drawn, and the lights are on. Day and night seem the same.

Paul comes back. Marianna hugs him, and Emily jumps up and offers him the chair by the bed. He sits down and takes my hand.

Dr. Witherspoon comes in, and Emily and Sarah slip out the door. Paul moves to the window. Dr. Witherspoon takes the chair and settles in. He's wearing a dark suit and a tie with red stripes. He looks nice and smells like Aramis, as though he shaved at home again after supper. I'm both weary and wary. I look into his face reluctantly, not sure what to expect. He almost apologizes for the rapid weakness I've experienced since being admitted. To hear him speak, one would think it was his fault that the cancer has advanced so fast.

"When can I go home?" I ask when he sits down next to my bed. I think I know the answer before I ask, but I ask anyway.

He takes a ballpoint pen out of his inner pocket and toys with the clicker. "We're going to keep you here a while longer, Katherine. You're very weak." This all seems hard for him.

"I'm not going home, am I?" I attempt a smile, but tears seep out anyway. Lennie's trusting face looms, her eyes on my car as Paul pulls out of the driveway. Marianna presses a Kleenex to her mouth. Paul remains at the window.

"Your heart is failing. Actually, all your systems are starting to shut down—not just your heart but your kidneys and liver and GI tract. You will grow much weaker tonight and tomorrow, and at some point you may slip into unconsciousness. The staff and I will do everything we can to make your last day, your last hours, comfortable. Your family can be by your side."

The room is silent except for the steady breathing of the bedside machines.

"So soon?" My voice is a whisper.

"None of us were expecting this, including George Hoffmann. The cancer has been very aggressive—exceedingly. We all knew this day was coming, of course. Just not quite so … just not … now."

He's grieving, I think in surprise. My death is almost here—that fearsome moment that taunts us from birth. It's almost here.

"The end—what will it …?" I try to regain my voice, to sound normal, to lessen the sadness of the others in the room. I fail. My voice wobbles and falls down.

"Your breathing will change and become raspy." He stops and clears his throat. "Similar to a dry rattle. You will probably be unconscious when this occurs. We will continue the oxygen and IVs and pain medicine. Sometimes patients have moments of lucidity near the very end, as though the body gathers up every remaining ounce of energy and bursts forth all at once."

"Will I die tonight?"

"No. You're not there yet."

"Tomorrow?"

He stands up. "Let's see what your numbers are in the morning." He bends over and rests the back of his hand on my forehead. The little motion is almost maternal. My mother used that same gesture when checking her children for a fever.

"You have a beautiful family, Katherine, both in this room and at Wickfield."

"Yes. Yes, I do, don't I?"

Chapter 62
ASTRONAUT

Tuesday, September 11, 1990

We're standing in a spaceship, excited. Liftoff will come any minute. My sisters are here, and Paul, and Dan and Bob and Lennie. The rocket booster blasts us into space, and we soar mightily toward the heavens. We laugh in sheer exhilaration.

Then the rocket booster falls away, and I'm alone, flying through the inky blackness of the universe. I'm no longer in the spaceship, but I feel no fear. I'm riding the stars like an acrobat, diving and looping and somersaulting in great joy. The stars surround me, close and brilliant, blazing like giant sunbursts. My hair is long and lustrous, streaming in wavy ringlets like the tail of a comet.

My speed increases, and I find myself swimming through space, moving my arms forcefully like a breaststroke champion. I aim myself toward a pinpoint of light in the distance. I feel intense happiness as I approach the light, which looms larger and beckons more brightly with each swoop of my arms. This fiery ball quickly fills my entire sphere of vision, nearly blinding me. And just ahead, through the light, I see figures jumping up and down as if in a state of great excitement. They all look alike, shimmering shapes that move gracefully, yet I'm able to identify each one instantly: Mother, Daddy, Benny, Grandmother and Grandfather Embright, Grandma and Grandpa Larson.

Off to the side, one more figure moves into view. I concentrate to see clearly. It's Carrington.

I am soaring now, a true astronaut who sails the stars. The figures join hands and form a large circle, and I flip myself downward into a dive, my fingers pointed toward the circle. As I approach it, I flip again, aiming for the middle and landing feet-first with my toes precisely in the center. The group closes in, embracing me, and together we dance around and around in pure ecstasy. The faster we go, the more energy we create. We dance and dance and dance, heat increasing all around us, until the light spills over like liquid gold and explodes. It billows around us into a brilliantly colored cloud that shimmers in all the hues of the rainbow.

I know without a doubt that we are in the presence of God.

Chapter 63
COMMENCEMENT

Tuesday, September 11, 1990

"Jesus!"

I sit upright, trembling, my eyes searching the room's dim light. A man sits alone on the edge of my bed.

"Yes, Kat, yes. He's right here," he tells me.

Why does the man sound so far away? He's next to me. I feel strong arms holding me close.

"Remember the light, Kat? It's coming. It nearly blinded us that day, remember? And the choir music? It's back, Kat! It's all around us! Listen!"

I listen. I hear it. I hear those same glorious voices Paul and I heard that morning in the dome. God is here. I feel warmth. I feel the deepest joy I have ever known. There is no greater gift.

Paul lays me back against the pillows. I reach out, searching for him. His hand finds mine. My heart reaches out, searching for Him.

I close my eyes. I'm ready. I wait for the light.

PART III
LIFE AFTER DEATH

Epilogue

The Tuesday night Katherine died, I was at her side. I almost did not make it. I had to interview students whose cars had been vandalized behind Richardson Hall, and it was nearly six when I sprinted out of Hurley toward Charlotte. All the way, I prayed—something I've learned to do recently for the first time in my life. I pleaded with God to spare Katherine's life a few more hours. I also thanked Him for the joy she had brought me.

When I entered her room, it appeared she had slipped into unconsciousness. She was lying on one side with a pillow at her back, facing the windows. Her breathing was labored. Marianna hoped she would simply slip away in her sleep. I yearned for a remission, for moments of lucidity. I don't know what the sisters thought of our relationship, for our love was very apparent in spite of my gold wedding band.

But Katherine and I understood.

Around nine I asked the women if I could watch Katherine alone, promising to send for them in the cafeteria if anything changed. They readily agreed; the day's vigil had been long. In truth, I wanted to speak to Kat aloud. I reasoned that if she could hear me, I might be able to soothe her through any moments of distress.

As soon as we were alone, I pulled my chair close to her bed, close enough for me to touch her hair. She appeared peaceful, a true-to-life sleeping beauty on her bedroom bier. At the same time, I wondered what was bouncing inside that brain of hers, what she could see or hear. I praised her courage in waging this battle while fighting so hard for Wickfield. I sang to her, whatever came to mind: Elvis, Johnny Mathis, Billy Joel. I added a lullaby I once sang to my children.

In time I simply held her hand, my eyes closed. I may have dozed slightly, but I'm absolutely convinced the music that soon drifted to my ears was not a dream. It was real. Kat held perfectly still as I moved onto the top of the bed and pulled her thin shoulders into my arms. What I heard was majestic choir music, the same music we heard when we'd watched the sun rise. It swirled like an invisible mist, swelling and cascading softly. I saw no one, but it seemed apparent that Katherine and I were not alone. I watched her intently, wondering if she could hear the music in her sleep.

And in a flash so fast that I gasped aloud, Katherine was suddenly awake, pushing herself out of my embrace into a half-sitting position with her elbow, looking out into the dimness with urgency. In spite of the fact that it was nine o'clock at night and a mere single lamp was burning, I could see her as clearly as though moonbeams lit the room.

"Jesus!" she called out.

I held her head against my chest, speaking into her ear as I assured her He was right beside us. "Listen!" I said urgently. "It's the music! It's our music, Kat!"

I pulled away slightly to look at her face, which was transfixed and full of concentration. Her body was taut. I'm convinced she heard both my voice and the music. I rocked her another minute as the music swam and faded. Then I laid her back on her side and pulled the sheet once more around her waist. Her left hand flailed in midair, looking for mine. I grabbed it and held it tightly—listening, straining, scarcely breathing. When her hand went limp, I tucked her arm under the sheet.

At the precise moment of Katherine's death, I had a wild desire to see exactly what her mind's eye could see. Perhaps I needed to confirm eternity. Perhaps I simply could not let her go. Regardless of the reason, I now positioned myself on the edge of the bed and lay sideways, facing her. I pulled her as close as propriety allowed in a desperate attempt to share her first vision of heaven. I could not see it, but I do know that in one brief second her pain seemed to fly out of her body as if on wings—and that she knew I was beside her.

When the three sisters tiptoed in a short time later, they saw a strange sight: me holding Katherine on top of the sheets, my forehead pressed tightly against hers, a newspaper protecting the sheets from my shoes. I stood up and faced them, disheveled with tears and totally unashamed. We gathered together in one huge embrace—three women who loved their sister beyond words and a man who would love her forever.

There was brief confusion the next morning at Wickfield. The sisters and I crossed signals, so to speak. I assumed the family would notify the university, but, immersed in their deep grief, the sisters assumed I would. As a result, it was after nine when the first inkling of Katherine's death reached Wellstone. Strangely, it came in the form of a long-distance phone call to Claire. The public relations director at Arden College called to request "a recent photo of Chancellor Embright, since she was a trustee here." Perhaps intuition sharpened Claire's tongue, because she snapped back, "What do you mean, 'was'? She's still your trustee." There was complete silence on the other end, and Claire heard the woman cover the receiver with her hand and whisper to someone, "Dear God. They don't know yet at Wickfield!"

Claire told me later that she burst into Dan's office and interrupted a meeting; that Dan saw her face and excused himself; that she pulled him by the hand into the hallway and whispered that, according to Arden College officials, Katherine had died the night before. Dan dismissed his meeting and called Lennie, who told him to call Hillcrest Hospital. The receptionist at Hillcrest confirmed Katherine's death at 9:30 p.m. Tuesday.

Dan ordered the deans into an emergency meeting, not revealing the reason until they were all assembled in the Oval Office twenty minutes later. Claire, meanwhile, raced to deliver the news to Bob and Pud and Marilyn.

As the story spread through campus, disbelief descended. Classes came to a halt. Faculty disappeared behind closed doors. Students gathered in silence as the flag in front of Wellstone was lowered to half-mast. Claire called the *Hurley Herald* and asked the editor if he could delay the afternoon printing. "There better be a damned good reason," he growled, and Claire burst into tears. "Our chancellor is dead," she wept. The editor ordered two reporters and a photographer to campus and told the press room to hold. The *Charlotte Observer* carried a front-page story Thursday, and all three Charlotte television stations sent crews to Hurley.

I'm told a splendid moment occurred during Dan's meeting with the cabinet and deans; Claire described it to me later. As everyone sat in shock, trying to absorb the enormity of the news Dan had just delivered, Lana knocked on the door and announced the arrival of Lennie. The room fell silent as this tiny brown woman entered the Oval Office, her face crumpled in grief but her back erect. She walked the length of the room to the head of the table and handed Dan a packet of letters.

"Miz Katherine said to get these to you straight away," she said simply. For a brief moment it sounded as though Kat were alive and well at the Chancellor's House, that this drama was one hideously bad dream—but as Dan distributed the hand-addressed letters, it became clear that Kat had embraced our lives not only as she lived but also as she died.

The auditorium was packed for the memorial service that Friday. Sam assigned me to coordinate with Governor Mendenhall's staff and our own security, a job that allowed me to observe the mourners as they arrived and were seated. The Embright sisters and their young families filled the first two rows. This included a woman I assumed to be Jane, who shepherded four children while her husband carried a pink-bundled newborn in his arms. The cabinet and their spouses sat behind them, along with Lennie and Jackie. Bob Atterbury kept his arm around Susan, who seemed to shrink in her seat and burrow into the curve of his shoulder. Governor Mendenhall and President Pettigrew sat on the stage with fellow chancellors and the board of trustees. The remaining thousand seats were packed with faculty, students, staff, alumni, business leaders, legislators— and loyal townspeople.

I have never seen the Wickfield auditorium so full. Entire families came. Mine was one. When I crawled into my bed the night of Katherine's death—it was nearly one o'clock—June turned her back on me. I stared at the ceiling a few minutes, sensing her frozen form, and spoke simple words into the darkness: "Katherine Embright died tonight." June bolted up and cried out in protest, then wept openly. I pulled her close and explained as much as I could, at least the part I was free to tell. At last she understood my preoccupation of the past two months.

"I loved that woman," she sobbed into my chest.

"So did I," I replied.

It was June's idea to take Marcy and Blair out of school for the memorial service. I was a proud husband and father watching June scour for three aisle seats halfway down the left side. Katherine would have been touched.

All in all, it was a splendid service, one that Katherine would have approved.

But the one she would have loved the most was the funeral service at the church in Arden. Since so many wanted to attend from Wickfield, Jackie organized a caravan of cars to follow the hearse to Virginia. I volunteered to drive Jackie and Lennie and anyone else who needed a ride. At the last minute, as our entourage gathered in the parking lot behind Wellstone, I fell into conversation with the hearse driver, George. As soon as he learned of my Security role, he suggested I ride in the front seat with him. Susan Atterbury overheard the conversation and immediately offered to take Lennie and Jackie in her car.

That's how Katherine and I managed to have one last ride together.

Our procession circled around the entire outer perimeter of the campus, where students and faculty lined the curbs. Then it turned east down Grove Boulevard and through downtown Hurley. Soon we blended into interstate traffic and proceeded toward Virginia, our headlights gleaming for two hours in a queue in spite of the morning sunlight. We were a sad processional as we drove through those mountains toward Arden.

Half an hour outside of Arden, our group pulled off at an exit with a Bob Evans restaurant. Everyone took time to freshen up and brace ourselves before the service. When we arrived at the church, we discovered that Katherine's sisters had reserved pews for us behind the Embright family. They insisted at the last minute that the "Wickfield people"—that was our entourage—follow the coffin into the church behind the family. And that's how Katherine and I managed to have one last walk together.

For a mountain boy who used to go fishing on Sunday mornings, the church service was like nothing I had ever seen. The church's arched ceiling, the stained-glass windows that told stories, the marble altar centered with a large gold cross—all were amazing. The words were printed in the funeral bulletin, so it was easy enough to know when to stand and when to sit. The minister was Katherine's childhood pastor, Karl Krueger, the one who had helped her make sense of her life when she'd learned her cancer was terminal. He referred to Katherine's "prodigious skills, eloquent diction, and genuine concern for others." I confess I had to look up "prodigious" later and felt that the word had perfectly captured Katherine's enormous talent. When he concluded his sermon, I sensed that Karl had seen into Katherine's heart as completely as I had.

Overall, the service was sad. At one point the choir sang "Beautiful Savior," the same hymn I had sung to Kat days earlier, but the harmony was so precise that I had to close my eyes. Susan and Mimi and Claire and Jackie and Lennie sniffled throughout, and I confess I whipped out my handkerchief a couple of times. We didn't have to kneel—although that would have been fine with me—until near the end. That's when the choir sang a blessing that was nothing but the word "Amen" over and over— seven times in all. It was fascinating to hear how the repetition of one word could be so hauntingly musical.

As I said before, Kat would have loved every minute.

I don't remember much about the burial—just that George and I led a procession of cars up some winding back streets to a peaceful hillside cemetery. I remember a tent, and people grouping together, and the casket as it sat beside the fresh grave. I recall that I stood perfectly still while Kat's nephews and nieces tossed rose petals as the metal box was being lowered. Claire slipped her arm into mine as we watched, and she was trembling.

After the burial, our Wickfield group went to the home of Katherine's sister, Sarah, where women from the church were serving lunch. There was a lot of love in that house, so thick it was almost tangible. In spite of our melancholy, everyone was able to relax a bit. I actually saw Susan laughing during a conversation, as if briefly relieved of her deep grief.

Claire came over to me at one point to ask how I was doing. She's a perceptive young lady, because I was missing Kat hugely at that moment and doubtless wore the bleakness on my face.

"Who is *that*?" she suddenly hissed, grabbing my arm. "Over there by the window. He's a dead ringer for President Bush! Look, Paul! Is Barbara here, too?" She laughed at her silly joke, and I followed her gaze to the gentleman, who was in deep conversation with Emily and her husband. I stared in surprise, because he truly did look a lot like George Bush. He was attractive, quite tall, and very slender. His dark-blond hair was turning gray at the temples.

A little later I bumped into this man at the dessert table. He glanced up at me the same moment I spotted him. We studied each other like fraternity brothers who shared some distant past. "Paul Stafford," I said, extending my arm. We shook hands, still sizing each other up.

"Tim Bernay," he said in a deeply resonant voice.

As our group prepared to make our departure—after the hugs and tears from the sisters and the promises to stay in touch—I turned toward the hearse, ready to make the return trip with George.

"Paul, wait!" called a voice, and I turned to see Marianna hurrying toward me with a magnificent pot of white lilies.

"Take these and enjoy them for yourself," she said, thrusting them toward me. "They just arrived from some Pennsylvania cousins. They smell heavenly, and Katherine loved fragrant flowers so. They're rather exotic, don't you think? I think they might be rare."

"Like Katherine," I said, smiling as I accepted them.

"Like Katherine," she smiled back, her eyes shining. She leaned forward on tiptoes and kissed me on the cheek.

George and I were the last of the Wickfield group to leave Arden that day. I said little during the ride through the mountains, letting George chatter on about his twin grandsons in Florida and inhaling the deep perfume of the lilies in my lap. I was acutely aware of the long barren space behind our seats. I missed Katherine with an aching that I still feel today. I kept thinking of her sleeping on that hilltop, although my new faith assured me she was not alone.

When we cleared a hill with a long curve ahead, I knew we were fast approaching the location where Katherine had run out of gas that long-ago day. I had a sudden inspiration.

"Pull over, George, just ahead. I'll show you. There it is, that little clearing with the yellow grass." And as soon as the hearse came to a halt, I opened that heavy door and bounded out, holding the fragile lily pot like a football in the crook of my arm. I surveyed the weedy setting, noting the rise to a ridge and the sudden plunge into a ravine filled with trees.

Inspired again, I returned to George. "Any chance you've got a shovel in your trunk?" I almost hesitated to ask. It seemed an irreverent question to pose to the driver of a hearse.

"Your lucky day," George said.

So, in memory of a rare and beautiful lady, I planted those rare and beautiful lilies along that mountain highway. I dug a wide hole into the ridge in front of the ravine. I removed the plant from its floral foil and slipped the dirt ball into place with my hands, tucking the trailing roots deep into their new refuge. With luck they might survive, I thought as I brushed the loose dirt from my hands. Then I remembered the dregs of my Bob Evans coffee in the hearse and went back for the Styrofoam cup, ignoring George's curious look.

"Katherine loved coffee," I whispered to the lilies as I poured the cold brown liquid around the dark soil. "Grow, pretty flowers! Grow!"

Back in the hearse, I glanced sideways at George, who shook his head in wonderment as he revved up the limo's big engines.

"What was *that* all about?" he asked.

"Never mind," I smiled, fishing for my seat belt and settling back into the seat. "Long story."

BECAUSE I COULD NOT STOP FOR DEATH

Because I could not stop for Death,
He kindly stopped for me;
The carriage held but just ourselves
And Immortality.

We slowly drove, he knew no haste,
And I had put away
My labor, and my leisure too,
For his civility.

We passed the school where children played,
Their lessons scarcely done;
We passed the fields of gazing grain,
We passed the setting sun.

We paused before a house that seemed
A swelling of the ground;
The roof was scarcely visible,
The cornice but a mound.

Since then 'tis centuries; but each
Feels shorter than the day
I first surmised the horses' heads
Were toward eternity.

—Emily Dickinson (1830–1886)
Manuscript c. 1862

A Final Word

September 30, 2013

I buried my wife, June, today. For forty-seven years she accepted me unconditionally, loving me with her magnificent heart in spite of my untold transgressions. And I loved her back, watching her mature as a wife and mother while our children grew into young adults. The website for the funeral home has collected loving messages from relatives and friends. Many have come from our close circle of friends, others from old friends at a distance. One I especially treasure came yesterday from Susan Atterbury, whose husband, Bob, recently retired after nine years as chancellor of Wickfield University.

Susan wrote: "Bob joins me in expressing our sorrow upon June's death. We will miss her beautiful spirit and many gifts. She was blessed to have had you at her side throughout her brave fight. Her death reminds me of our beloved Katherine, who was so fortunate to have known you under similar circumstances. Our hearts go out to you and Marcy and Blair and the grandchildren. Come see us the next time your travels bring you from Asheville to Hurley. The welcome mat is always out. Fondly, Susan."

It's the memory of Katherine Embright—an extraordinary woman of wisdom and inspiration—that leads me to write these words tonight. In my security deposit box is the story of our memorable year together at Wickfield—a year she accurately called our "spiritual journey," since it led me to my faith and gave her new clarity about forgiveness and joy.

The binder that holds Katherine's typed notes—the ones she wrote in secret during that final year of her life—has resided in my bank vault since the year she died. My plan now is to retrieve it after all this time, despite the fact that this story reveals personal failings on my part. I want to share it with my daughter, Marcy, now that her mother has passed on.

It's important to me that Marcy know more about Katherine Embright, this remarkable woman whose funeral Marcy attended in 1990. In particular, I want Marcy to know not only about Katherine and her unique relationship with me but about the steady affection Katherine held for Marcy's mother.

Marcy's marriage is undergoing some sort of distress, but whether the confusion stems from her husband's side, or Marcy's, or both, I'm not sure. Perhaps Katherine's intimate voice will give Marcy some special insight. As a wife and mother and professional woman, Marcy will surely benefit from Katherine's bold words. Their candor reveals the personal struggle Katherine experienced as our relationship grew.

My impression upon reading Katherine's story—and I nearly memorized it in those weeks following her death—was that Katherine wrote with a sense of mission. Although she designated the story for me, I'm convinced much of it was meant to be shared. She wanted to shout about her personal faith, to exult in it with all who cared to listen.

Because Katherine shared her spiritual beliefs with me, they subsequently became my own, and in time they spread to my entire family. This faith within the Stafford family has continued to grow through the years. For me, personally, there has been one particularly cherished memory. At each Easter sunrise service throughout these twenty-three years, I have reflected back to my first one—the Easter dawn I experienced inside that sunlit copper dome with Katherine. Like Saul of Tarsus, the young Pharisee of Scripture later called Paul, I first met God in a blinding blaze of light.

The church today was packed for June's funeral. I sat with the family on the front row rather than in my usual place as choir director, but the choir could not have performed with more magnificence. They closed the service with the "Sevenfold Amen," a piece I introduced to the choir years ago and which now serves as the benediction for all of our funerals. Their voices hung over the congregation at the end, lingering like a warm embrace. June would have rejoiced over such beauty.

So would Katherine.

—Paul O. Stafford, JD

Acknowledgments

Although my indebtedness for this book is far reaching, three people should be acknowledged from the outset, with my deepest gratitude.

The late William C. Friday, beloved President Emeritus of the University of North Carolina, gave his personal blessing to the development of this book, including my fictional reconstruction of UNC's renowned sixteen regional campuses and the inventions of Wickfield University and Hurley, North Carolina. He also described for me the operation of UNC's board of governors.

The late Martha Kime Piper, former Winthrop College (now University) president, hired me as her Executive Assistant for College Relations and, with her inimitable grace, taught me many of the finer points of higher-education administration.

Ned Cline—North Carolina author, journalist, and longtime friend—responded patiently and bravely to my sometimes intrusive questions about his experience with colon cancer. He also introduced me to numerous connections to further my research.

The late Dr. Patricia Sullivan, former chancellor of the University of North Carolina at Greensboro, showed me how one can radiate a personal faith even while serving in a public position. Dr. Beverley Pitts, former president of the University of Indianapolis and former acting president of Ball State University, described incidents in her career that placed her under intense media scrutiny. Dr. Lorene Painter, former education professor at Lenoir-Rhyne University, walked me through steps of the grieving process following her husband's death to colon cancer.

My daughter-in-law, Dr. Stephanie Garrison, described hospital procedures and equipment and discussed patient diagnosis and care. My son, Robert Garrison, weathered questions regarding law enforcement.

My early readers included Jane Faust, faithful friend since third grade, who kept nudging my writing at exactly the right time; Eileen Beall, whose insight into my characters kept me tweaking at the computer; sorority sister Suzie Matthews, who wept her way through an early draft; Lenoir-Rhyne's Lorene Painter and Carolyn Huff, who made wise suggestions regarding the narrative framework; and the Reverend Dr. William Menter, who helped me create the character Karl Krueger.

Abigail DeWitt, writer-in-residence at Lenoir-Rhyne during my teaching years there, showed me how to bridge the first-person narration after Katherine's death. Monty Matthews, builder *extraordinaire*, helped me orchestrate the Easter sunrise climb into the copper dome. Rannah Ryan taught me the nursing language of surgery. Dr. John Trainer and Brian Baker described the aftermath of Hurricane Hugo in the piedmont area of North Carolina. Jon Bennett kept my computer running and my manuscript in order. Jennifer Berry, Sarah Wallace, Barbara Herman, and George Kinney gave me the gifts of time and encouragement.

Author Robert James Waller of *The Bridges of Madison County*, whom I interviewed for Indiana University's *Kelley* magazine, lent encouragement far beyond what I imagined or expected.

My colleagues in The Writing Academy, whose friendships and talents I cherish, offered their wisdom and faith, as did fellow members in the Sidney Lanier Book Club.

My family cheerleaders—Ruth and Don Matkins, Elizabeth and Roger Hull, Cathy and Richard Whittecar, Heather and Kevin, Stephanie and Rob—surrounded me with love and patience.

In closing, I celebrate three extraordinary college presidents, all women, whose lives crisscrossed mine while carving out titles of "first woman" in their respective fields. When she was named president of Winthrop College in 1986—a year before she hired me—Martha Piper became the first woman president of a public four-year college in the Carolinas. Frances Bartlett Kinne, former president of Jacksonville University under whom I served as public relations director, was the nation's first woman to become dean of a fine arts college and the first woman to serve as president of a Florida university. Betty Lentz Siegel, who as an education professor taught me child psychology, became the first woman to head a campus within the University of Georgia system. Today she serves as President Emeritus of Kennesaw State University and Endowed Chair of the Siegel Institute of Leadership, Ethics & Character.

Although *Prez: A Story of Love* is fictitious in both characters and plot, I found myself remembering Martha, Fran, and Betty countless times as I created Katherine Embright. Each was a trailblazer in higher education, and each made exceptionally brave leadership decisions. As Katherine came to life, I heard these three voices clearly, and I considered countless examples of their wisdom, intuition, and courage.

The character of Katherine Embright reflects their best.

Bibliography

Alcott, Louisa May. "Playing Pilgrims," in *Little Women*, 3. (New York: Bantam Dell, 1983.)

Dickinson, Emily, *Poems: Three Series, Complete.* (Public Domain: Project Gutenberg, 2004.) N. pag. Web. 12 Mar. 2014.

The Episcopal Church, "The Burial of the Dead: Rite One." *The Online Book of Common Prayer.* (New York: The Church Hymnal Corporation, 1979.) N. pag. Web. 12 Mar. 2014. www.bcponline.org.

Frost, Robert, *Robert Frost: Collected Poems, Prose & Plays.* (Library of America, 1995.) N. pag. *Poetry Foundation.* Web. 12 Mar. 2014. http://www.poetryfoundation.org/poem/171621

Lyte, Henry F. "Praise, My Soul, the King of Heaven." 1834. (Public Domain: Henry J. Gauntlett, 1902.) Web. 12 Mar. 2014. http://library.timelesstruths.org/music/.

Rodgers, Richard, and Oscar Hammerstein II. "This Nearly Was Mine" from *South Pacific,* copyright 1949 by Richard Rodgers (music) and Oscar Hammerstein II (lyrics). (New York: Columbia Records.) Web. 12 Mar. 2014. http://www.stlyrics.com/lyrics.

About the Author

MARGARET GARRISON grew up in Concord, North Carolina, a part of North Carolina's piedmont region that appears in her novel. She spent an exchange year at Japan's International Christian University in Tokyo. She earned an undergraduate degree from Lenoir-Rhyne University and a master of arts degree from the University of North Carolina at Chapel Hill. Her extensive career has included several years in high school and college teaching and in university marketing and communications in North Carolina, South Carolina, Florida, and Indiana. She lives today in North Carolina. This is her first novel.

CPSIA information can be obtained
at www.ICGtesting.com
Printed in the USA
FFOW02n1345010715
14808FF